until i met you

Center Point
Large Print

Also by Tari Faris and available from Center Point Large Print:

You Belong with Me

This Large Print Book carries the Seal of Approval of N.A.V.H.

RESTORING HERITAGE • 2

until i met you

TARI FARIS

CENTER POINT LARGE PRINT
THORNDIKE, MAINE

This Center Point Large Print edition
is published in the year 2021 by arrangement with
Revell, a division of Baker Publishing Group.

The text of this Large Print edition is unabridged.
In other aspects, this book may vary
from the original edition.
Printed in the United States of America
on permanent paper.
Set in 16-point Times New Roman type.

ISBN: 978-1-64358-806-3

The Library of Congress has cataloged this record
under Library of Congress Control Number: 2020948238

To my parents,
Dave and Joyce Thompson.
Thank you for believing
I could be an author
and doing everything in your power
to help me become one.

one

Today was a new start, and this time running back home wasn't an option. Libby Kingsley pulled alongside the curb in front of her brother's house and shoved her car into Park. She reached back and ran her fingers through the thick fur of her yellow lab asleep in back. "We're here, Darcy."

The dog stretched his neck and leaned into the scratch. He was the perfect balance of confidence and calm—two things she needed more of.

Her phone rang, and she pulled it out to check the display. She sighed and answered the call. "Hi, Mom. I'm here safe and sound."

"How are Luke and Hannah?" Her mom's words were casual, but she'd probably been tracking her phone every mile of her drive from their Chicago suburb to Heritage, Michigan.

"I haven't even made it out of the car." Libby leaned over her steering wheel, taking in her brother's restored Victorian. The midday sun highlighted the white siding, black shutters, and large bay window. "But the front of his house looks amazing."

"He's done so much with that place in such a short period." Her mom carried on as if she was ready to talk all day. "Perhaps marriage and a baby on the way gave him that extra push of determination."

Libby scanned what she could see of Heritage. A moving truck was backed up to the house next door, the rear door rolled up and the ramp extended. If someone was moving in, at least she wouldn't be the only new face in town. "Maybe I'll find those in this small town too."

"A husband and a baby?" Her mom's voice wavered. "Don't rush into anything."

A man Jane Austen couldn't have written any better stepped out of the neighboring house and marched to the moving truck. Black hair a little long on top, square jaw, and arms strong enough that he could probably unload the truck single-handedly. Libby swallowed against her suddenly dry throat. The guy's gray T-shirt pulled tight across his wide shoulders as he lifted a box and disappeared into the backyard.

Heritage was looking pretty good.

"Libby?"

The guy reappeared but this time with a large white dog on his heels. Darcy's ears perked up as he watched the other dog nudge the man's leg with a chew toy hanging from its mouth. The man knelt and scratched at the thick white fur, then tossed the chew toy into his backyard. He grabbed another box from the truck as the pup dashed behind the fence again.

Darcy whimpered at the window, and Libby ran a soothing hand over his head. Okay, so the dog was not always the example of calm. But could she blame him?

"Now, Libby." Her mom's voice shook her back to the present. "You remember what happened last time you—"

"No, not a husband." She dismissed the image of the man. No doubt he had a pretty little wife around there somewhere. "I meant I want to find an extra push of determination. Or purpose. Or something adultlike. I think this job will be a good fit for me."

"Did Hannah give you any more details about the library?"

Darcy nosed her shoulder, and she offered him another scratch. "I've worked at enough public libraries to know it'll be pretty straightforward. Besides, it's time I stop hiding from the past. It's time to live again." Her voice rose, bringing silence from the other end. A new job, new address, and new life were just what the doctor—er, therapist—had ordered, even if her mom didn't want to hear it.

Libby rested her forehead against the steering wheel. "Besides, Mom, I want to be near Luke and his new family. I want more than the occasional text or phone call. I want a front-row seat watching his kids grow up. We missed so much with him. I don't want to miss any more."

"Maybe you could talk him into moving back here."

Libby picked at a thread on her skinny jeans and resisted the temptation to pull it. "He's happy here, Mom . . . and I think I could be too."

"You can always come home, Libby." The tenderness in her mother's voice nearly undid her. Her mother was a strong, wise woman, but losing Luke at such a young age had broken something in her—in all of them. Ever since, her mom had a hard time letting her children go. Libby had let her mom rescue her three years ago. She'd gone home to heal and never left.

That was why this *had* to work. Going back was not an option for her. It was time to stand on her own two feet.

She reached for the leash and snapped her fingers. "I've got to go, Mom. I'll call later."

Darcy's caramel-colored snout shoved between the front seats before Libby could get her phone back in her purse. "Whoa, boy."

Heavy paws jammed into her leg as a bundle of fur blurred past her the instant the door popped open. Clearly, he hadn't learned his manners from his namesake—Fitzwilliam Darcy. The finest example of a swoon-worthy hero if there ever was one. Her college roommate always said that Libby's love of literature made her standards for dating too high. But since her last boyfriend had held her at gunpoint and left her a borderline agoraphobic for three years, maybe her standards weren't high enough.

Libby climbed from her car, soaking in the sweet scent of the moist ground and new beginnings. A cool breeze holding on to the tail of a summer storm whipped her long blonde hair around her neck, sending a shiver up her spine. The first week of August in Michigan should be warm—hot even—but Michigan was known for playing dice with the weather no matter the season.

She pressed the lock on her key fob and waited for the comforting click before giving the handle a test tug. Her two bags, pillow, and box of books in the back seat would be safe on the street, right? The town was practically Mayberry, but then again, experience had taught her appearances could be deceiving.

The leash in her hand jerked her toward the town square across the street. Libby recovered her balance and pulled Darcy toward Luke's porch. "Later, boy. I promise."

The brass hippo that Hannah had told her about lay facing her on the sidewalk about halfway between Luke's and the new neighbor's house. It was like he'd shown up to greet her. Maybe he had. What was his name again?

"Libby! Just in time." Luke burst through the door, rattling the hand-painted Welcome sign hanging on the door. His brown curls stuck up at odd angles as if he'd been combing his hands through them over and over. Was his hoodie inside out?

Libby glanced at her watch. "I'm two hours ahead of schedule."

"Right. Sorry, just give me a minute." Her younger brother, normally the example of cool and collected, charged down the stairs and threw a bag in the bed of his red pickup. He circled her light blue sedan and pulled at the door.

"You locked it?" He shot her a grin. "You're in Heritage now, not Chicago."

She clicked the key fob but didn't comment. Leaving the doors locked was a habit she was okay with keeping.

Luke hefted her box of books from the back seat. "I know you want to get your own place, but there isn't a lot to rent right now in Heritage. But we have an idea. We bought the house two doors down to flip, but it needs a lot of work like this one did." With long-legged strides, Luke took the porch steps two at a time. "We thought you could live there while I'm working on it. You'd be close by but still have your own space. And the owner will give you the best rent in town."

A dog barked from the other side of the door, accompanied by a thud.

Luke propped the box on his hip as he opened the door, blocking his shepherd-Lab's escape with his knee. "Easy, Spitz."

12

Inside, Luke dropped the box by the door and reached for Spitz's collar. He invited Libby inside with a wave of his hand, then closed the door behind her.

"Sounds great." She set her bag next to the box. "Should I carry my stuff there now?"

"No, it's not quite ready. But almost."

She detached Darcy's leash just before the two dogs pounced on each other. Pawing, sniffing, circling. Spitz spun and dashed through a large dog door with Darcy at his heels.

"Hey, Luke, do—" She turned to where he'd just been standing, but he'd disappeared. They wouldn't have a dog door without a fence, right?

She hesitated in the entryway, then moved to the window. Both dogs romped in the fenced side yard, happy as could be. Maybe she needed to stop freaking out over every little thing. Beginning with her dog playing outside.

Libby sat on an antique bench in the entryway and slid off her shoes. She placed them next to a square basket filled with shoes and a few chewed tennis balls.

The dark wooden floors, white baseboards, and painted blue-gray walls had been there at Christmas, but something still felt different— warmer. Maybe it was the sweet smell of vanilla and cinnamon that hung in the air. Her stomach growled and she pressed her hand against it.

"Sorry for the poor welcome." Hannah, her

sister-in-law, walked in as she secured her long dark hair in a messy bun on top of her head. Dressed in what appeared to be Luke's old sweatpants rolled up at the ankles, a burgundy oversize sweatshirt, and a pair of polka-dot socks on her feet, she shuffled toward Libby and wrapped her in a hug.

Hannah still had a few months to go, but there was no hiding the fact she was eating for two. Beckoning Libby into the kitchen next to the entryway, she slid into a chair at the table with careful movements and reached for a sheet of paper. "I wrote out some notes for you. Make yourself at home. Hopefully we won't be gone long."

"You're leaving? Is everything okay?" Libby hated how weak her voice sounded. But it was easier to be brave when she wasn't going to be alone in a strange town.

"I'm having a bit of bleeding." A slight waver accompanied her words as Hannah rubbed her hand over her belly.

Libby's chest tightened as a list of worst-case scenarios ran through her mind. "You have three months to go, right? Why didn't Luke call me?"

Hannah placed her hand on her back and shifted positions. "I'm twenty-seven weeks. It started just about an hour ago, and you don't answer your phone while you're driving."

Libby gripped the back of the chair next to her,

reminding herself to breathe. In through the nose, out through the mouth.

Hannah leaned forward and placed a hand on hers. "Don't worry, though. My doctor wanted me to get checked but said it could be a number of things. With any luck, we'll be back tonight. That's what we're praying, anyway."

Right. Praying.

Libby had stopped putting faith in prayer over twenty years ago when Luke never came home.

Hannah pointed to a plate of oatmeal raisin cookies wrapped in cellophane on the table. "I made these for the new neighbors. We haven't seen them, just the truck. Luke says they may just be workers because that house is in bad shape. But I made them cookies anyway. Oh, and Luke put your bike in the shed. Patty, is it?"

"Petunia." Knowing her bike was near released a bit of the ever-present knot in her stomach and shoulders. Luke had brought it up in his truck last week. It had only made sense, but a week without Petunia had been rough. Bike rides were one of the few times she didn't feel weighed down by life. "I know it's weird that I name my bike."

"I think it's awesome. And I'd offer to go for a ride with you"—she patted her rounded belly—"but we'll have to wait a few months."

Luke burst back into the room with another bag, his chest heaving as if he'd been doing sprints, and grabbed his keys from the hook. "Ready?"

Hannah reached for Luke's hand. "How much stuff do you think we need?" She turned back to Libby. "Lib, I know it's a lot to ask, with you being new yourself, but would you mind delivering the cookies while they're fresh? Tell them we'll stop by once this little one settles down a bit. Oh, and Spitz needs to be fed."

"Cookies to the neighbors. Feed Spitz. Make myself at home." Libby forced a confident smile as she made check marks in the air.

Luke reached out and gave her shoulder a gentle squeeze. "We're glad you're here, Libby." He slid an arm around Hannah's waist and guided her toward the front door. "We'll call as soon as we know anything."

His words rolled over in her head a couple of times. Libby blinked away the tears blurring her vision as she offered a final wave. She closed the door and pressed her back against the wooden panel.

Luke was glad she was here. That's what mattered. Life had given her and her brother a second chance, and this time she'd be here for him. And if right now being here for Luke looked like taking care of his dog and greeting his neighbors, then she could do that.

Returning to the kitchen, Libby scooped up the covered plate piled with warm oatmeal raisin cookies and looked out the window toward the moving van. Her hands shook a little, and she drew in a slow, calming breath. One thing she'd learned from her therapist was that avoiding a hard situation now made it twice as hard later.

She straightened her shoulders and rehearsed the words. "Welcome to the neighborhood. Welcome, neighbors. Hey, you, welcome."

It shouldn't be that hard. Friendly people moved to small towns, right?

Libby slipped on her shoes and stepped onto the porch as the Mr. Knightley–incarnate neighbor slid into the cab of the moving truck with a second man. This guy had blond hair and was less literary hero and more military but just as attractive. The first guy started the engine and pulled away before she'd even gotten to the first step. So much for item number one.

She went back inside, turned the dead bolt, and returned the cookies to the table. She added food to Spitz's bowl and then found a bowl for Darcy.

Item number two—check.

Now to make herself at home.

How was she supposed to do that in someone else's house? Crossing the dark wooden floors, Libby circled the living room a few times. Her twin brothers, Logan and Liam, would have claimed the two matching recliners that faced the large flat screen in the corner, but that wasn't her style. She dug her toes into the plush area rug.

A brown microfiber couch by the window

17

caught her eye. Maybe it wasn't the couch as much as the open novel that lay facedown on the arm. Or maybe the discarded white knitted throw that still held the shape of the absent reader. That had potential.

Libby snatched *Persuasion* out of the box Luke had left by the door, sank into the other end of the couch, and pulled the throw over her legs. The knotted muscles at the base of her neck started to unravel. Yes, this would do.

Now all she needed was Darcy. But since he'd run off to play with Spitz the instant his bowl was empty, for now she'd have to be content with Captain Wentworth.

Three pages into chapter 8, her phone buzzed. Pulled from her book coma, Libby stretched and dug her phone out of her purse. It was a text from Hannah.

> Still waiting on tests. We have an
> underground fence. I left a collar for
> Darcy by the back door. Thx again.

Libby sat up straight. Underground fence? She glanced out the window at the wood-plank fence she'd seen earlier. What about that one?

Her eyes darted to Spitz asleep in his bed in the corner and then searched the room. Where was Darcy?

"Darcy?" She tossed the blanket aside and

jumped to her feet, knocking her book on the floor. She ran into the kitchen. "Darcy!"

Nothing.

Flinging the back door open, Libby rushed outside, the early evening air biting her cheeks. She ran around the corner of the house and froze. The wooden fence wasn't Luke and Hannah's. It was the backside of the neighbor's fence.

She cupped her hands around her mouth. "Darcy!"

Still nothing.

She yelled his name louder. Her heart smacked against her rib cage as adrenaline flowed through her veins.

Libby dashed back inside and shoved her feet into her shoes, then sprinted out the front door. Standing in the front yard, she called again. And again.

She ran to the sidewalk, looked down the street, and cocked her head, listening for barking in the distance.

Empty. The street was quiet as far as she could see.

Darcy had wandered off once or twice before, but that had been at home where he was familiar with the neighborhood. He didn't know this place and neither did she. She didn't even know where to begin looking.

What if he . . . What if . . .

Her mom was right. She should've never left

home. And now she was paying the price for thinking she could have a fresh start.

Austin Williams had only two goals this summer—to keep the family landscaping business from going under and to make his dad happy by getting along with his brother, Nate. But right now, both seemed out of reach.

He navigated the long hallway toward his dad's assigned room, taking care not to knock the end table against the wall. A door up ahead opened. Then closed. Then opened. Then closed. When it opened another time, the wheel of a walker made it into view, but that was all. Austin set the end table against the wall and rushed forward. A tiny woman struggled to navigate her walker through the doorway. Austin pushed the door wider and helped guide the walker out.

Her smile creased deep lines in her face and added a twinkle to her eyes. "You're a handsome fellow. Do you work here?"

"Nope. Moving my dad in." He made sure she was stable before he stepped back.

"If he's as handsome as you, I'll have to meet him." She attempted a wink, then moved down the adjacent hallway.

Austin was still smiling when he arrived at his dad's room a minute later. "I think you'll like it here, Dad. I already got you a date."

His dad's vacant expression fixed on the blank

TV as he rubbed the top of his head. His hair had gone fully gray in the past year, but he still had it all. "You forgot to hook it up. I'm going to miss the game."

Austin wedged himself between the console and the wall, connected the cables to his dad's forty-eight-inch flat screen, and tested the power. All seemed to be working, and just in time. He checked his watch. He couldn't wait for Nate any longer. He knew better than to depend on his brother, but he'd foolishly done it again. Now he had to rush to get the truck back or be charged for another day.

"This is the last box. Thanks for leaving me the heaviest one." His childhood buddy Grant walked through the door of the assisted-living suite and set the box by the door to the bedroom.

"Consider it an initiation into the family. Besides, you can't let those old military muscles of yours go soft."

"Since I married Caroline last year, I'm not sure the initiation idea works. And if you want to talk about going soft, I saw you struggling with the grill earlier." Grant brushed his blond hair out of his eyes and turned full circle, taking in the room. As if there was a lot more to take in than the generic white walls, gray Berber carpet, and a kitchenette. "Looks good."

They'd gotten the TV set up and hung his dad's prized, autographed Alan Trammell jersey.

Tomorrow he'd have to locate the photo of his father with the baseball legend to hang next to it.

"I don't like it." His dad shifted his position on the brown leather couch and propped his broken foot on the wooden stool with a thud. At least his dad had gotten to bring his own furniture. He would've hated institutional furniture.

"It'll feel more like home when we get everything unpacked." Austin found the box labeled "Photos" and peeled back the tape. He pulled out an old family photo from ten years ago. Back when his mom was still alive and when he and Nate had been more than brothers— they'd been best friends.

Time heals all wounds.

What a dumb saying.

He set that photo next to an old black-and-white wedding photo of his parents. Austin couldn't imagine a love like that. They'd known some hard times, but they'd lasted. They'd trusted each other with no strings attached. No one loved like that anymore. Everyone had their agenda. That's why life was easier single.

He set a few other framed photos out and then pushed the box aside. "I'll unpack the rest of the boxes tomorrow. It took longer than I expected to unload the truck."

Because he'd planned on it being a three-man job, not a two-man job.

Grant dropped into the well-worn, overstuffed

recliner. "Give it a chance, Uncle Henry. The staff is great, the building is well maintained, and you have a nice view."

Austin glanced at his watch and then out the window of Reflections Care Home. Long summer grass had grown over the edges of the glorified pond. Still, Grant was right—the pine trees and the way the setting sun painted the water orange and yellow on nights like tonight would be calming for his dad.

"I meant the TV. I want it there." His father pointed to the exact place Austin had put it three tries ago.

"You said it had a glare there." Austin's hand tightened on the keys in his pocket, but he kept his voice calm.

"Forget it. I'll move it myself." His father grabbed his cane and hobbled toward the bathroom, his walking cast causing a muffled thud on the dense carpet with every step until he slammed the door.

Grant shot a look at Austin, stood, and jerked his head toward the TV. "I'll help."

"Thanks. Then we have to get going or I'll be late."

Grant detached the row of cords from the TV. "I don't remember your dad being this . . ."

"Grumpy? He's not usually."

"You don't think I confused him by calling him Uncle Henry, do you? I know he's Caroline's uncle, but he always felt like an uncle even before."

"No, he just doesn't want to be here, and I was the one who forced the issue." Austin lifted the TV and waited while Grant slid the console to the other corner.

"Because of his broken foot?"

Austin set the TV back on the console and started attaching the cords. "That didn't help. But when he nearly burned the house down trying to make eggs last month, I had to draw the line. I should've forced the issue two months ago when he decided to go for a walk and got lost. He ended up five miles away, unable to tell anyone where he lived or who he was."

"You aren't worried about that here?" Grant gathered the wires and handed them to Austin.

"This is a specialized unit for Alzheimer's. It feels more independent—like an apartment. But there are alarms if they wander. Plus they'll make sure he eats and gets his daily medications." Austin fitted the first HDMI cord to the satellite box, then inspected the TV for the right input connection. "I can't be there all the time, and he refused to have someone stay with him. Even if he's lucid half the time, he needs someone around the other half, and I can't do that and work."

"How's the business going?" Grant settled back on the recliner.

"We aren't under yet." He connected the last cable and tested the power.

Grant leaned forward, elbows on his knees, and chuckled. "Caroline thinks you should breed Shiro."

"I know." Austin sighed, not relishing the idea of a houseful of puppies, but a litter from his purebred Japanese Akita could bring in over ten thousand dollars. That might be enough to hold off some of his creditors a little longer. The last thing he needed was to get the truck repossessed. "I have to decide soon too. She's in heat."

"If you have any questions, ask Caroline. Did she tell you that she's been researching adding a service-dog breeding program to the ranch? She's taken a couple classes, and we have enough books on dog breeding and service dogs in our house to open a library."

Austin scrolled through the input menu with the remote and cringed. He'd switched two HDMI cables. "I'll keep that in mind."

His dad emerged from the bathroom and walked toward the couch, leaning on his cane with a stronger limp. "When are we eating lunch?"

Grant looked at Austin with a raised eyebrow. "We ate on—"

"Are you hungry, Dad?" Correcting him only caused frustration. Austin had learned that early on in his father's illness. "I bought some of those nutrition shakes you like." He grabbed a bottle promising to taste like a vanilla milkshake from the almost bare fridge and handed it to his dad with a large white pain pill.

"Knock knock." Nate opened the door, holding a white grocery sack. "Canned meat and spray cheese. Housewarming gifts of champions."

"Nate, you saved me from eating this junk." Their dad waved the bottle, then set it on the end table. At least he'd taken the pill.

"I told you he'd make it." Grant glanced at his watch and shrugged. "Sort of made it."

Austin didn't comment. He just stared at the face too much like his own. Nate had the same black hair. Same gray eyes. Same build. Same cowlick on the left side of his forehead. People had confused Nate and Austin for twins a lot growing up, even though there were ten months between them. They still had a similar look. But no one would confuse them these days. Not with the four tattoos Nate had—or was that five now?

Austin returned to the TV, squatted down, and undid the two wrong cords.

Nate set the grocery bag on a small oak table by the door and pulled out the spray cheese and a box of crackers. "I know I said I'd be here two hours ago, but an emergency came up at church and—"

"Not a problem." Their dad cut Nate's words off with a wave as he reached for the food in

Nate's hand. "I know you have important things to do. Austin has lots of time."

Right, because saving the family business their father had run into the ground was no work at all.

Austin checked his watch again before attaching one of the cords. "I've got to drop the truck off before I'm charged for another day." He shot a look at Nate. "Can you still give Grant and me a ride back to Heritage?"

"Sure thing." Nate dropped onto the couch next to their dad and pointed to the spot where the TV had just been. "I would've put the TV by that wall."

"Think so?" Their dad studied the wall. "Maybe you're right."

"You'd better get moving if you're going to get the truck back, Austin." Nate stood, shoved his hands in his pockets, and nodded toward the TV. "I'll meet you at the place after I get the TV moved."

Their dad smiled at Nate like he'd been the one who'd offered to rearrange his entire day to get him settled.

Austin dropped the remaining unattached cord and stood. "Can I talk to you in the hall?"

Nate's back stiffened, but he nodded and followed Austin out.

Austin leaned against the floral wallpaper opposite the door. "What were you thinking showing up with that junk food? Did you read *any* of the material I sent you?"

Nate winced and had the decency to look embarrassed. "I will. It's been a busy week."

"Alzheimer's symptoms are exacerbated by nitrates. Nitrates are in highly processed foods. Canned meat and spray cheese are about as processed as you can get. The article even used both as examples of some of the worst foods."

"I won't buy him any more." Nate picked at the oak chair rail lining the wall. "I'm sorry. I just bought his favorites. I didn't know."

"Of course not." Austin pushed off the wall and paced down the hall a few steps, then back. "You didn't know because you haven't been the one watching Dad slide into this dark disease over the past year or spent your free time researching it. You haven't been trying to pull the family business back from bankruptcy that Dad nearly landed us in because he couldn't seem to remember the commitments he'd made or the bills that were due."

Austin stopped and stared at the paneled ceiling. After drawing a slow breath, he leaned back against the wall and met his brother's gaze. "Listen, Dad wanted to be near you, so I found him a respectable place fifteen minutes from Heritage. I found him a local doctor who specializes in Alzheimer's. I even rented a house in Heritage so I could be within driving distance and finish the town square job that Dad signed a contract for without asking me. All I'm asking you to do is read what I send you."

"You could've lived with me."

Austin snickered. "You think that would've worked well?"

A twentysomething blonde nurse wearing light-blue scrubs pushed a cart past them and offered them a smile, blushing as Nate smiled back. The guy hadn't even given a flirty smile—just something polite. What was it about him and women?

"The board wants me to meet with you about your plans for the town square before the interview with *Reader's Weekly*."

Austin's attention snapped back to Nate. "You?"

Nate rubbed the back of his neck. "As assistant fire chief, I'm also on the town council. And since it's our family business and I volunteered to be your assistant, I became the point man for the project."

"I don't need an assistant." Austin pushed off the wall.

"With Dad in here, you'll need help with a project this big."

"I don't believe this." Austin clenched his molars and took a step toward Nate. "Almost bankrupting us six years ago wasn't enough? Now you decide to come back and finish the job?"

"I'm trying to help you save the business. You're going to hold my past over my head my whole life?"

Austin stiffened. He hated the feeling that he was being the unreasonable one here. But he had been the one busting his tail to get them out of the hole Nate had dug for them. "Choices come with consequences, and some things can't be undone."

Their dad's door popped open as Grant stepped out. His wide military shoulders wedged between them. "I see you two are finally talking. Good progress. But just so you know, we can hear you in here. And your dad is setting up a game of chess to play with Nate."

"Of course he is," Austin mumbled. "The golden child has arrived. Break out the games."

"That's not true." Nate glanced at Grant as if looking for backup.

Grant shrugged, clearly not wanting to take sides. "It's a little true." He ducked back inside the room, shutting the door behind him.

Nate reached for the door handle. "We need to meet before Wednesday. That's the day of the interview. Just let me know when and where."

Austin didn't respond. Following Nate back inside, he reached for his coat. "I've got to get the truck back." He winced at the edge in his voice and the way their father's brow had pinched into a scowl.

He'd promised himself that he wouldn't let Nate get to him today. So much for that. And by the look on their dad's face, he'd let him down too.

Austin forced a smile and clapped a hand on their dad's shoulder. "I'll stop by tomorrow, Dad, and help unload the last of the boxes."

Nate picked up one of the photos from the box. "Why is this here?"

"That's me and Greg." His dad pointed at it with a smile. "We had some great adventures together. You remind me a lot of him, Nate."

The muscle in Nate's jaw twitched as he put the photo back in the box and took a seat next to their dad.

His dad patted Nate's hand. "Tell me about life as a pastor."

Grant pointed at the TV. "I'll move that and come with Nate."

Austin shoved out the door without another word. No doubt Nate believed that Austin had brought the photo on purpose, but he hadn't. He had no idea how it got in the box. He hadn't even seen that photo in years.

Austin pulled up the directions on his phone. The quicker he left, the quicker today's stress would melt away.

On the app, an icon indicated an accident, and a dark red line followed US 31 South. Exactly where he needed to go.

With traffic, he was looking at a forty-five-minute drive. No way he'd get the truck back in thirty minutes.

Terrific.

Numbers ran through his mind of how much this was going to cost him.

He dug the keys out of his front pocket, unlocked the truck, and slid behind the wheel, resisting the urge to slam his fist against the dash. He gripped the steering wheel, his knuckles whitening.

He needed to find another job fast or figure out how he was going to work with Nate. Because history had proven he and his brother were an explosive combination.

Maybe breeding his dog was the better option. He pulled up the number he'd been given for a possible stud appointment and hit Send. After all, a houseful of puppies would be easier than working with his brother.

two

The ride back to Heritage had to have been one of the longest in his life. Austin slid out of Nate's church van and offered a wave over his shoulder to his brother. "Thanks for the ride."

Nate only nodded.

Grant rolled down the passenger-side window. "Caroline and I'll stop by in a bit before we take off."

Austin nodded at Grant and jogged to the door, avoiding the third step of the porch. He'd nearly twisted his knee that morning when the step shifted under him while he carried in the recliner. The steps had definitely moved up on the list of things to fix in this place—the very long list.

Austin wiggled the key in the front door a few times before the rusted dead bolt gave. The previous owner hadn't thought locking the door was necessary. He'd never quite understand small towns. Stepping over a few boxes, Austin dropped his keys on the chipped Formica countertop and whistled for Shiro. Nothing.

His phone rang and he pulled it from his pocket. "Hello?"

"Hello. This is Lisa. You left a message about breeding your dog?"

"Yes. She's a purebred Japanese Akita." He snapped for Shiro but still got no response.

Lisa took his email address for some paperwork she'd need to send him, then rattled off a list of details. If he let her keep the puppy of her choice from the litter, it wouldn't cost him anything up front. This was the perfect arrangement for his cash flow problem.

Digging through what was left behind in an old junk drawer, Austin pulled out a scratch pad and Sharpie and scribbled as much as he could with the partially dried-out marker. After agreeing on a time the next day, he hung up and leaned against the wall.

If this worked out, it might be enough income for him to hire an assistant. Nate was right when he'd said he needed one, but working with his brother, even if it made the most financial sense, was a bad idea for everyone.

Austin pulled a Coke from the fridge and cracked it open. It wouldn't be that bad. Shiro would make a great mom. Where was that dog anyway? Austin walked through the kitchen toward the mudroom and froze. The back door stood open and a dog-sized hole had been punched through the screen. Guess it was time to fix the latch on the back door too.

He sighed and walked out on the back deck. "Shiro."

Shiro ran toward him at full speed from behind

his makeshift greenhouse. He knelt to greet her just as a yellow Lab ran to catch up. A male yellow Lab with an in-heat Shiro.

No. No. No.

Maybe they didn't. Maybe it was fine. Ugh. It wasn't like he could ask.

Austin grabbed the strange dog by the collar and pulled him toward the gate.

"Darcy," a female voice yelled from outside his fence. The dog in his hands perked up at the sound, pulled free of his grasp, and ran toward the voice.

Austin followed him around the corner and nearly collided with a leggy blonde who would make him take a second look on most days. But not when her dog might have cost him ten thousand dollars.

"Don't scare me like that. You can't run off. I need you." She knelt next to the dog and wrapped her arms around his neck. "Thank you. I've been looking for him for more than an hour."

"Maybe you should have looked in the hole he dug from your backyard to mine." Austin pointed to a sizable hole under the fence. His voice came out harsher than he intended, but what woman let her dog run free like that?

"I—I'm sorry." Her head snapped up as her blue eyes rounded. "I did look in your yard first. He must have roamed the neighborhood and circled back."

The doe-eyed look wouldn't work on him. Becky had that particular manipulation perfected, and he refused to fall for it again. "He wouldn't have run off if you'd had him on a leash."

"I thought the yard was fenced." The woman stood, keeping one hand on the dog's collar. She wiped her other hand across her tearstained face and pushed her honey-blonde hair behind her shoulders. She lifted her chin and narrowed her eyes, highlighting a faint trace of freckles across her nose. There weren't enough to make her look youthful. Just enough to deflate his anger a bit.

He blinked and focused on the dog. The last thing he needed in this town was to form some sort of attachment. Especially with someone who didn't seem to have her life together. He shook the thought away and tried to catch up with the rant going on in front of him.

"—and Darcy may have used that hole, but he didn't dig it. Look at his paws. They aren't dirty enough for that."

"Just keep your dog on that side of the hippo, would you?" He pointed at the brass hippo that lay on its belly on the sidewalk. What a strange place to put a statue.

"But the hippo—"

He didn't hang around to hear what she had to say about the odd town decoration. He secured his gate and turned to face his dog. Shiro lay next to the hole with her nose partway in as if waiting for that blasted Darcy to pop through again at any moment.

From this side of the fence the hole was hidden by a patch of tall weeds. He knelt and studied the dirt that had been disguised by the poorly trimmed lawn. The woman was right. The way this dirt was packed, there was no way the hole had been dug today. Which meant he hadn't checked the yard properly this morning, and he was lucky a friendly yellow Lab was the worst of it.

Austin stood, grabbed a few river rocks from the garden, and dropped them in the hole. A mistake like this wasn't like him. Maybe moving his dad into the care home had been harder on him than he'd realized.

He strode back to his house and yanked open the back door. "Shiro, come."

Her white ears lay flat as her head stooped lower.

Austin drew a deep breath and ran his fingers through his hair. This wasn't the dog's fault. None of this was. Not his dad's disease, not Nate, not the job, not Austin's irresponsibility, not even the insufferable beautiful neighbor or her out-of-control dog.

"Shiro." He did his best to make his voice light. "Come on, girl. I'm sorry."

The dog trotted toward him and nuzzled her snout in his leg. Austin knelt and dug his fingers into the thick fur around her neck, bringing a contented groan from her.

"Knock knock." Grant opened the front door with Caroline at his heels.

"Please tell me your rent is ridiculously low, Austin. This place is a little gross. Who is your landlord?" Caroline tucked her red hair behind her shoulder as she scanned the room. She paused in front of the couch but didn't sit.

"The mayor just bought it." Austin pulled a clean sheet from a box and spread it over the couch. "He offered me cheap rent if I do work. Mostly just tearing things out so new cabinets, counters, and floors can be installed."

"What does Becky think of it?" Caroline sat on the edge of the sheet but didn't sink back into the couch.

"We broke up."

Grant and Caroline exchanged a look before Caroline finally spoke. "I'm sorry."

"Yeah, right." Austin spread another sheet over a recliner for himself as Grant settled next to Caroline. "Don't try to pretend that you aren't inwardly throwing a party."

"Are you upset?" Caroline rested against her husband.

"Actually, no. I feel . . . relieved." Austin leaned forward on his knees, then rubbed the back of his neck. "Did you know I tried to break up with her four different times over the past few months but she always talked me out of it? She should have been a lawyer."

"That's called manipulation. One of the many reasons I never liked you with her." Caroline pounded the couch with a fist, sending a bit of dust up. "I think you only started dating her because your dad liked her. But that was all a part of her act too."

"Easy, fighter." Grant rubbed Caroline's back as he let out a chuckle. "They broke up. It's over."

"Are you sure you're over her this time?" Caroline pinned Austin with a glare.

"She said if I came to Heritage not to bother calling again." He held out his hands. "Here I am."

"Where's the ring?"

"I wasn't that lucky."

"But she let you keep Shiro?" Caroline snapped her fingers, and Shiro wandered over and nuzzled her face in Caroline's hand.

"She never had an interest in Shiro after we brought her home. I think it was all a power play to see if she could get me to spend that much money on a dog. Speaking of which, how long until you know if a dog is pregnant?"

"At least twenty days." Caroline ran her fingers through Shiro's thick fur. "Did you decide to breed her?"

"Yes. No. Yes, I decided to breed her. I called

about a stud appointment, but I just found her with another male dog."

Grant broke into a full laugh. "Let me guess. The other dog isn't a purebred Japanese Akita."

"Lab. Do I have to cancel the appointment?"

Caroline struggled to suppress a smile and failed. "I'm sorry. You really should cancel it. If you go, you could have a multiple-sired litter. Then you'd have to go through DNA testing for the pups before you could file for their papers. With no guarantee there would be any purebreds, you could lose money. You should really wait six months until she's in heat again."

Austin dropped his head in his hands and closed his eyes.

Twenty days until he knew if she was pregnant. Six months until he could breed her again. Three months until he'd have to file for bankruptcy.

Looked like hiring an assistant instead of Nate was no longer an option.

Nothing was as bad as it first seemed. This was Libby's new motto for life, but if this was what the town considered a library, there might be exceptions. Stepping farther into the room, she surveyed the tight rows of novels covered in an inch of dust. A yellowed sign with "New Releases" in stenciled marker hung above the shelf.

Libby pulled a book off and sneezed as the dust

plumed in the air. As she flipped it open to the copyright page, her stomach dropped. 1993. The library had been closed for more than twenty-five years. That was why the computer on the desk still had a slot for floppy disks. It probably ran on DOS.

"She needs a bit of dusting, I'd say."

A heavyset man with a wide grin peeking out below a thick mustache stood in the doorway. He brushed what was left of his gray hair to the side and extended his hand. "Mayor Jameson."

She closed the distance to the door and shook his hand. "I'm Libby Kingsley. Hannah told me about you."

"And she told me all about you." He laced his fingers across his belly and eyeballed the room. "It's not much, but I'm sure with your experience it'll be top-notch in no time."

Top-notch? Right now she'd settle for passing health code.

"Did Luke say you had a budget for new books?" One of the fluorescent lights flickered overhead at an irregular rate as it hummed. "Or a new building?"

Okay, so Luke hadn't mentioned a new building, but dropping a few hints wouldn't hurt.

His head bobbed. "Some. Don't worry about that yet. One step at a time. Maybe we should start with an inventory of what we have. Wouldn't want duplicate books."

As long as she ordered titles from this century, she was safe.

Libby forced a smile in place as the man turned back to the door. "Let me know if you need anything. I'm just up the stairs and down the hall."

One big cozy town hall family. Who put the library in the basement of the town hall? Maybe she'd understand if it was centrally located, but this building couldn't even boast that.

Luke had hinted it'd take a lot of work, but she never imagined this. This library didn't need to be reopened. It needed to be resuscitated. She coughed against more dust.

Time for some fresh air.

Libby shut the door behind her and locked it. Not that anyone would want to steal anything. If someone did, at least they could claim insurance.

As soon as she got home, she slipped on some tennis shoes. Michigan summer didn't get better than today, and she wasn't going to miss the opportunity to go exploring with Petunia. And if she ever needed the stress relief that Petunia offered, that was today.

Darcy nudged her leg, and Libby knelt and scratched his ears. She wasn't the only one anxious to enjoy the weather. "I'll take you for a walk this afternoon."

A solid knock echoed through the house.

The only person Libby had met in town

wouldn't be knocking on her door. Mr. Mean Hot Neighbor—as she'd started referring to him—had disappeared into his house when she went out to get the mail. And lucky her, she still had to deliver the cookies. Or what was left of them.

Another knock rattled the front door as she approached with slow steps. They were determined, she'd give them that. Maybe she'd peek out the living room window before opening the door to a stranger.

Libby pulled aside the curtain, only to find a tall platinum blonde with her hands cupped over her face peeking back. Libby screamed. The woman straightened to a height that had to be near six feet, waved, and hurried back to the door, waiting for it to open. As if peeking in a person's windows was perfectly acceptable.

Libby inched open the door. "May I help you?"

The blonde's flawless face lit up. "Libby, right? I'm Olivia."

Olivia's smile held as if that explained it all. Libby searched her mind back to Luke's wedding, but she'd met a lot of people that day.

"I'm Janie's sister and Hannah's friend. I met you briefly at the wedding, but I don't expect you to remember that."

"Right." Libby relaxed her grip on the door and opened it a bit wider.

Olivia must have taken that for an invitation. Stepping past Libby, she walked in and plopped down on the couch, welcoming the two dogs as they nudged closer for her affection. "I'm sorry I wasn't here sooner, but life's been crazy."

Small-town friendliness was as unsettling as it was funny. But there was no doubt Libby liked Olivia. And why not? The girl oozed confidence. What Libby wouldn't give to be able to enter a room like that.

When Libby didn't comment, Olivia jumped in again. "I talked to Hannah a few minutes ago. Looks like they're transferring them to U of M."

Libby dropped into the recliner opposite Olivia. Ann Arbor? Warmth drained from her face. That was more than three hours away.

"You didn't know. I'm sorry. I happened to call right after the doctor was there. And they only told me a few things and then had to hang up because another doctor was walking in. But don't worry, they're great, the baby is great. I'm sure they'll call you when they have more details."

Libby drew a few slow breaths. "Healthy baby is good. Did Luke say where he'd stay?"

"He doesn't want to be far away. He's working on his contractor's license through online classes and said he can do that anywhere. He also said something about looking for a house to buy that only needed minor interior work. It'd give him a place to stay. And he could work on it in the evenings. Hopefully sell it for a small profit in a few months."

"Makes sense." Libby wrapped her hands around her middle. She refused to fall apart in front of a stranger. "He inherited a lot of money from a grandmother he didn't know he had. I know he wanted to start investing in real estate."

"He's so good at that type of stuff."

"So, you've been assigned as my friend until they get back?" Libby released a little laugh. How sad was she that her family felt they needed to arrange friends for her?

Olivia winced. "Not like that. I mean, I'm leaving town myself in a week or two for a job—Lord willing. They were just worried about you."

"Worried?"

"They said they were afraid you'd hightail it out of town if they didn't get back soon." She offered a laugh. "But I told them there was no way. Heritage was lucky to have you, and besides, who wouldn't love this place?"

Pressure built in Libby's chest. No. She blinked hard, but the tears still filled her eyes. A small hiccup escaped as a steady flow of tears ran down her face.

Olivia rushed forward. "Oh, sweetie. Are you okay? Tell me everything."

"I should never have moved here. What made me think I could do this? I wanted to be brave—strong." She stood and paced to the mantel. A wedding photo sat on top next to the word "Home," which had been spelled out in large wooden letters. "But I'm not. I can't make a home here. All I've done is move from my parents' extra room to Luke and Hannah's extra room. I'm still hiding. And I tried to make friends, be neighborly, but he yelled at me."

"Someone yelled at you?"

"Then there's my job."

"The library?"

"That's *not* a library. It's a dust-mite breeding zone or at best a literary graveyard, but not a library. Who puts a library in a stinky basement?"

"Heritage is full of quirks. Some are more likeable. Like Otis. I saw he was here to greet you, but he moved over by the diner this morning." Olivia stood and propped her hands on her hips. "Let's start at the beginning. I told Hannah and Luke I'd make sure you were taken care of, and that's what I'll do. What are you doing right now?"

Libby shrugged. "I was going to go for a ride on Petunia."

"Petunia?"

"Sorry. My bike."

"Perfect. I just ran two miles, but I could stand to burn a little extra energy today. I'll go steal my sister's bike from next door. She's on her honeymoon, she won't care." Olivia checked her watch. "I have to be back in time to go serve at the shelter with the church. You can join me if you want."

"With your church?" Now probably wasn't the time to mention she didn't do church. "Maybe next time."

Within a few minutes, they were cycling north on Henderson at a comfortable pace. About two miles out of town Olivia turned down a dirt path and stopped in front of an old building. She dropped the kickstand. "Hope you don't mind the break, but I figured we needed to talk about some of your problems too. And biking makes that difficult."

"My problems?" What had Luke told Olivia?

"How can I get you to want to stay in Heritage unless we address some of them?" Olivia dropped onto the bottom step of the building. "Let's start with the man who yelled at you."

Oh, those problems. She could talk about those. She followed Olivia to the building but didn't sit. "I think he's Hannah and Luke's new neighbor. Or at least someone there to work on the house. I'd rather never see him again."

"In a town our size, that isn't likely." Olivia leaned back on her elbow. "There aren't too many people I can imagine yelling at you though. Well, there is one. Gray hair, good-looking in a Richard Gere sort of way, and acted like he owned the world?"

"Not gray. Black. More good-looking in a— who's that guy who plays Superman? Not Christopher Reeve, the new guy." Libby climbed the steps and tested the door. Locked.

"Henry Cavill? Well, that rules out Dale Kensington." Olivia sat upright. "You said he was moving into the house next door?"

"Or helping someone move." She peeked in one of the windows, but thick dust obscured her view. "What was this place?"

Olivia looked up. "A one-room schoolhouse. Want to see inside?"

Libby worked the door handle again with no luck. "It's locked."

"Of course it is." Olivia pushed to a stand. She motioned for Libby to follow her. "What did he yell at you about?"

"My dog got in his yard." Libby high-stepped through the tall grass as they circled to the back of the building. She'd have to do a tick check later.

"That's all? Sounds like a grump." Olivia stopped at a door on the back side. She slid a loose board to the left, then reached her hand through. The door popped open with a click. "I'll figure out who this hot guy is and help you take him down a notch."

There were no steps on this side, so Olivia lifted herself up in the doorway, then offered Libby a hand. Libby took it and pulled herself up.

"I didn't say I thought he was hot." The door slammed shut, and she sneezed as dust filled the air.

Olivia brushed off her hands and led them

through a small mudroom to the main room. "You said Henry Cavill. That says it all."

The main area was about fifty feet by twenty feet with three windows on each side. Wooden beams stretched across the ceiling with cobwebs covering the expanse between. The floor appeared solid but the wood weathered and worn. Amazing.

"You seem pretty curious about this Henry Cavill person." Libby squatted down and ran her fingers along the weathered gray boards. "Are you in the market for a boyfriend?"

"I have my own difficult man in my life. I don't need yours." Olivia's voice echoed in the room.

"You have a boyfriend?"

"No. I have a complicated relationship. We volunteer together. Flirt. And just when I think we're about to take a step forward, he takes about five steps back. We've been doing this little dance since we met almost two years ago, and my patience is running out." Olivia jabbed her hands on her hips. "That's why I applied for a job in Phoenix. I can't keep going on like this."

"In Phoenix?"

"Yes, but I'm here to help for now. Let's talk about the library. What does it need most?"

"Calling that place a library is an abuse of the word." Libby ran her finger down the glass pane of the window, leaving a trail behind. "I think it might be dustier in there than it is in here."

"It needs a good cleaning? I can help with that."

"It's more than the dust." Libby brushed off her finger. "No one will want to go there. It's a dungeon. A library should be central in the community. A place people want to be—want to gather. I thought about seeing if any of the empty storefronts along the square were available—"

"Don't bother. There's no way Kensington would give up that space. He has his heart set on strip-malling it as soon as he can get Leah and Caroline to agree to sell their share." Olivia ran her hand over some markings on the wall. "And since Hannah had that section of houses along the square zoned as historic, all of them have been bought up to restore and resell. The only land in the middle of Heritage left is the square, and, well—"

"That's it!"

"What's it?"

Libby scanned the wood for obvious water damage. "I watched a whole program about moving buildings on PBS."

"You want to move a building? To where?"

"To one of the corners of the new square. How perfect would that be?" She crisscrossed the room, feeling for any weak boards.

"They had a fire to clear the old buildings from that square. I'm not sure how they'd feel about dropping a new one in their place."

"But hadn't Hannah originally wanted to keep the Manor?" Libby leaned against the aged chalkboard that still hung on the front wall.

"Yes, but there was beautiful history in the Manor." Olivia checked the time on her watch.

"This schoolhouse has beautiful history too. Imagine it. The library in this old one-room schoolhouse in the square." Libby did a full turn with her arms stretched out.

Olivia paused and studied the room again. "You're a genius. But would they do that?"

"I don't know and I don't know who to ask. If Hannah were here she could—"

"You could take it to the committee." Olivia made her way to the back door and popped it open again.

Speak to a committee? A chill traveled up Libby's spine. "I don't talk to crowds. How about I submit a report?"

"It isn't a crowd. Only about five or six old men—and Nate." Olivia bit her lip, then lowered herself to the ground and held the door for Libby. "A presentation wouldn't be enough. You'd need someone to champion this, and I think I know who to ask."

"You do?" Libby scooted to the edge and jumped down into the grass. A tick check was definitely in order when she got back.

"Yes. Nate. And I happen to be serving at the shelter with him tonight."

"You'll ask him?" Which meant she didn't have to go through the stress of meeting another stranger. And with Olivia's charisma, there's no way this Nate guy would say no. This was almost too good to be true.

"Yes, but it's still a long shot, so don't get your hopes up." Olivia disappeared around the corner of the schoolhouse.

Not get her hopes up? Was she kidding? For the first time since arriving in Heritage, she was starting to believe that moving here wasn't a mistake after all.

Why had he worried about this? Everything was going great. Nate scrubbed the last of the creamed corn residue away from the large stainless serving pan, then handed it to Olivia. "Here you go."

"Thank you." She took it and sprayed it down at the industrial sink. Steam billowed up around her, causing white-blonde ringlets around her face where a few wisps of hair had escaped her bun.

He grabbed the next pan with a stronger grip. Friends. They were only friends.

Serving alongside Olivia exposed a gap in his life that he hadn't even realized was there. Her passion to love people and love these kids filled him with the hope that they could make a difference here.

Who was he kidding? It filled him with hope that a relationship between them could work, but that was false hope.

She set the pan on the counter to dry. "Can you move old buildings?"

He picked up the chili pot and began to scrub. "Me personally?"

"Your family's company. Do they do that?"

"No. They'd contract that out. But we did that for a project before. Whether it can be moved or not depends on the building. How old are you talking?" He grabbed a pad of steel wool and worked on a bit of overcooked chili that had cemented to the bottom.

"The one-room schoolhouse on the corner of Mathews and Chapel."

"Chances are that building doesn't have electricity or plumbing unless it was upgraded later. That move would be a snap, assuming the structure is still sound. I'm pretty sure the town still owns it. So if you plan on stealing it, you probably shouldn't tell me. Since I'm on the town council and all."

She pulled the towel from her shoulder and swatted him with it. "Very funny."

"Where would you move it?" He handed her the pot and pulled the plug in the sink.

"I met Luke's sister. She was hired as the new librarian and wants to make the schoolhouse the new library in . . . the town square." She rinsed the pot, then took the towel from her shoulder again and started drying it.

"In the town square? Does she know we just emptied the town square of old buildings?"

"I was hesitant at first too. But it makes sense." Olivia hung the pot from a hook on a rack. "It'd only take up one corner, and there would still be plenty of space between the library steps and the gazebo. I think if Hannah was here, she'd love the idea."

"Hannah? The one who set the old buildings on fire?" He handed her another pan to put away.

"Hannah who was also crushed when the Manor burned to the ground with the vet houses." A smile tugged at the corners of her mouth as she bit her lip. "What do you say, board member? Is it a possibility?"

When she looked at him like that, it always made him want to throw caution to the wind, pull her into his arms, and tell her he'd make it happen. But that was a big no-no. He grabbed a cloth and set to wiping the counters down. "I don't think a building is a part of the plan."

"I thought you said on your way here that the plans weren't finalized. This is the solution. Could you at least talk to the committee about it?" Olivia turned on the hot water and rinsed both sides of the sink. "Libby is willing to put together a proposal, but can you see if they're at least open to the idea?"

"Moving a building is a big project in itself." Nate looked up, prepared to say no, but the hope in her eyes stopped him. He turned his attention back to the pan in his hands. "I'd need to look into a few things. Make a few calls."

"That would be perfect." Olivia gripped his arm with a little squeal.

Nate stilled as the warm water from her hands dripped down his forearm and disappeared under his sleeve. Why did every part of him have to be so affected by her?

"Nate?" Her voice had lowered, and the vulnerability in it almost broke his resolve.

Nate swallowed hard and backed up. "I'll finish in here. Why don't you see if Mrs. Jones needs any help out there?"

Olivia yanked the towel from her shoulder and dried her hands before marching through the swinging door, her steps more forceful than necessary.

He'd kept Olivia at a safe arm's length for the past year and a half, and everything was working—sort of. He grabbed a towel, dried the counter, and did his best to forget the way her hand had made him feel.

The tattoo boasting "master of my fate" taunted him from his forearm. God may have pulled his life out of the pit he'd dug, but that time had cost him so much, not the least of which was the possibility of a future with Olivia. Nate pounded his fist on the metal cart, sending an echo through the room just as Olivia walked back through the door.

"What did that cart ever do to you?" Her laughter tugged something deep inside he couldn't identify. "Mrs. Jones said we're done out there."

Nate shoved his hand in his pocket and faked a smile, forcing his eyes anywhere but in her direction. "Ready to go?"

"Sure." The hurt in her voice had become too familiar. It was easier when she was mad.

Nate pushed out the back door and marched toward the van boasting Grace Church on the side. The white fifteen-passenger van seemed a little overkill for just the two of them, but it was that or take his motorcycle. Having Olivia's arms wrapped around him wouldn't help his resolve in the least.

Olivia fell into step next to him. "My professor got me a phone interview with the *Phoenix Tribune*."

His step faltered. Phoenix? As in 1,600 miles away? He drew a calming breath and ignored the pressure choking him. "That sounds exciting."

He opened her door and waited, his gaze fixed on the ground at his feet.

She paused in front of him, her pink Converses toe-to-toe with his boots. He was all wrong for her . . . in so many ways.

"You really wouldn't care if I moved across the country?"

Nate took short, even breaths, but her sweet vanilla scent still got in. Teasing him. He just had to keep it together a few more minutes. "I'll . . . I mean, we'll miss you. The church, that is, but I want the best for you. If you think this is it, then I'll wish you the best."

"Look me in the eye and say that again." The words came out just above a whisper.

He lifted his eyes to hers. Must be strong. "Are we going to play junior high games?"

"This isn't a game, Nathan. But I'm tired of feeling like it's one. You treat me like I have the plague most of the time, but then you look at me like—"

"Like your pastor." Nate focused on the trees past her shoulder.

"No. Like you want to kiss me . . ." Her voice hitched and she cleared her throat. "Kiss me as much as I want to kiss you."

Nate's heart thudded in his chest as his eyes found hers again. That was a mistake. With one look she reached in and offered a balm to his wounded heart. What would it feel like to let himself be loved by Olivia?

Her fingers brushed against his side as her eyes closed. She was closer now. But had she moved or had he? He swallowed against a dry throat.

He had to stop this. If he allowed it, he'd

never be able to let her go. He couldn't chance destroying her life too.

Nate took a quick step back. "We should go." He willed his pulse to slow as he walked back to his side of the van. He slid into the driver's seat, set the engine to life, and pushed in the CD sticking out of the player. Who knew what someone had left in there, but it was bound to be better than awkward silence.

Olivia slid into the passenger seat and slammed her door. Hard. She was back to being mad. Mad he could handle.

"You know what, Nathan Williams? I've about had it with you. You're being an idiot."

Nate kept his eyes on the road, sending up a silent thanks that he had an excuse not to look at her.

"Olivia, you know I think you're an amazing . . . asset to the church. Nothing can happen between us. I'm your pastor." Nate drew a deep breath, ignoring the ache in his chest.

"Stop hiding behind the church. You aren't a priest. Pastors marry all the time. Pastors date all the time. *You* asked *me* out, remember? I had a good time, and I thought you did too."

Nate white-knuckled the steering wheel and clenched his jaw. "It's never been my intention to hurt you or send mixed signals."

"Mixed signals?" She huffed and crossed her arms. "Like flirting with me one minute and treating me like I disgust you the next? Or looking at me back there like you care for me and then telling me that if I move to Phoenix the church will miss me? Your signals are more than mixed, buddy, they're . . . I don't know a word that means worse than mixed, but they're that."

"I do care for you, Olivia." His chest tightened as the words came out in a low volume, but as the silence stretched out, he had no doubt she'd heard.

"But not enough." Her voice lowered on the last word.

Stopping at a red light, Nate thrust his left arm toward Olivia. "See this?"

"Your tattoo?" Anger still pinched her face.

"Yes. It says 'master of my fate.' I got this when I was eighteen, and I lived by this motto until I was twenty-two. That's four years. Four long years of many very bad choices."

Olivia sighed. "It's not like your other tattoos and piercing scars say 'choirboy.' I know you have a past, Nate. What does that have to do with me?"

She didn't get it. "Do you remember our date?"

"Our one and only date? Yeah—pretty clearly."

The light turned green and Nate eased through it. "Do you remember our talk right before I dropped you off?"

"No."

"Well, I do." Nate merged onto the highway.

Why couldn't they be home already? "You said you'd never been kissed. You talked about how you'd waited all through high school, all through college, until you found someone you thought you could marry."

"Did you think I was pressuring you to kiss me or, for goodness' sake, marry me? Because that wasn't it at all. I mean, it was our first official date and you were asking me questions. It came up."

"Don't you get it? You waited. For a date, for a kiss, for . . . everything."

"You don't want to be with me because I'm too pure? Now, there's irony for you. I finally find a guy I want, and he won't have me because I waited for him."

No, that wasn't it—not fully anyway. But it was easier to say that than to explain he didn't trust himself not to turn out like his deadbeat uncle— that in ways that mattered he already had turned out like him. It had been the week after their date that he'd found out about Chase. That had been the real game changer. But that wasn't a story he could tell. For now he'd stick to the facts he *could* share.

Nate huffed and changed lanes. "You can't tell me that while you were waiting, you were dreaming of a future husband who was out getting wasted and sleeping with any willing girl. Trust me, there were a lot of willing girls."

Olivia flinched. He hated being so crass, but she had to understand how dark his past was. He wasn't even telling her the worst of it.

"You deserve more than I can give you. So much more." Nate's throat tightened, and he rubbed his hand over his tattoo.

"Don't play the martyr, Nate. It isn't a good look on you."

"I'm not being a martyr. I protect those I . . . care for. And I'm protecting you."

"Don't I get a choice?"

He shrugged. "I'm not going to let you choose less than you deserve. Choices come with consequences, and some things can't be undone." Wasn't that what Austin had been telling him? Right before he'd left the photo for him to find. Talk about a slap in the face.

"You aren't less than I deserve, Nathan." Olivia's voice cracked as she reached out to touch his arm.

The warmth of her hand and the feelings it stirred nearly undid him. He leaned toward the window, letting her hand fall away. "When your perfect guy comes along, you'll be glad you didn't waste your heart on me."

He'd never forget the cruel smile on his uncle's lips when he'd found Nate hungover in the barn. He didn't remember much of the night that preceded it, but it couldn't have been good. His uncle just stood over him and reminded him that they were cut from the same cloth. That Nate wasn't fit for family life. That if he were smart he'd never marry, because he was destined to wreck every life he touched.

Hours later his uncle had walked out on Caroline, Leah, David, and their mom, never looking back.

His uncle's words had loomed over his life like a nightmare prophecy. Nate had fought against the idea for years. But the day he'd met Chase was the day he'd been confronted with the irrefutable evidence that his uncle had been right. It was then that he knew he could never have a future with Olivia—or anyone.

three

The streets were too wet for her much-needed ride on Petunia, so the smell of chocolate and sugar would have to do. Drawing a deep breath, Libby savored the sweet scent as she took a pan of cookies from the oven and set them on top to cool as her phone rang. She dropped the oven mitts on the counter, checked her smartwatch, and tapped her wireless earbud.

"Hey, Mom."

The deep voice of Dustin Lynch was replaced by her mother's tense tone. "Have you talked to Hannah and Luke yet?"

"I talked to them just after they got settled in their room at U of M. Is there news?" Libby turned off the oven and pulled a paper plate from the pantry.

"They did another ultrasound, but because the placenta is attached at the back side of the uterus, the doctors still can't tell how far it's grown into the uterine wall. Since they've gotten the bleeding to stop, they're hopeful." Her mother paused, and Libby checked her watch to see if they'd been disconnected. When her mother spoke again, her voice was rough. "But they have warned them that this situation is dangerous for both mother and child, and a high risk that she will have to have a hysterectomy during the birth."

Libby dropped into a chair at the table. "A hysterectomy? But Luke said he wanted like a dozen kids."

"I know. Just keep praying."

Pray? Her prayers had proven pretty ineffective in the past. She didn't really trust that to change.

"Your mother called again."

Libby stood and claimed a spatula from the drawer. "I don't know what you're talking about. *You* are my mother."

"Angel called. She wants to see you."

"Just because she gave birth to me doesn't give her a right to step in and out of my life at will. If this was a normal adoption, I could choose not to have any contact with her."

"I know. But she *is* my sister, and as much as I hate the choices she's made—minus when she dropped you into my life—I love her." There was another long pause as if her mother was waiting for her to respond. But Libby had nothing else to say. "I refused to give her your number and told her the choice was up to you. If you want to contact her, you can, but . . ."

"But she's a toxic person. Honestly, I can't handle that right now." Libby's voice shook slightly.

"I think that's wise, but I wanted to give you

the choice." Her mom paused, then shifted her tone. "What else are you up to this morning?"

"Making cookies for Luke and Hannah's neighbor. I ate the ones Hannah made. All two dozen in just three days. That has to be a new record for me."

"You're still going to take that man cookies after he was so rude?"

"I'm doing it as a favor to Hannah and Luke." She began moving the cookies to the plate.

"They'd understand if—"

"Avoiding uncomfortable situations is what derailed my life last time."

"No, a man with a gun derailed your life." Her mom's voice was gentle but firm.

She ripped off a piece of cellophane and covered the plate. "But then I chose to hide from . . . everything. I refuse to go down that rabbit hole again. It has to be different this time."

"Just don't let him push you around."

"I won't. Talk to you later, Mom. Love you." She ended the call and scooped up the plate. She eyed Darcy asleep in the corner with Spitz. Normally she'd take Darcy as a buffer. But under the circumstances, she'd leave him home.

Her fingers shook as she slipped on her shoes. Her latest novel called to her from the arm of the couch, and every cell of her body screamed at her to put the cookies down, wrap herself in a blanket, and retreat into the fictional world.

No. She gripped the plate tighter and stood. She'd do the hard thing first, then she'd reward herself. If she hurried, she could be tucked away reading in just five minutes.

Libby opened the door and marched across the driveway before she could change her mind. She took the neighbor's steps two at a time, then gave three solid knocks on his door.

No response.

She took a step back but then forced her feet to stop. Avoidance wasn't an option. She could do hard things.

She eyed the truck in the driveway as a dog barked at her from the front window. He had to be home. She knocked again with a little more force. If he didn't answer, she didn't know if she'd be able to muster the courage to try again.

The door flew open, but the screen door obscured his face. "What?"

She attempted to swallow as all moisture evaporated from her mouth. *Breathe in. Breathe out.* She searched her mind for a thought . . . a word. Oh, why hadn't she practiced this?

Think. He wasn't Colin. He might even be a nice guy . . . deep down.

"Can I help you with something?" His tone had softened, but his words were still rushed. "I really have to go."

She lifted the plate a little higher. "Cookies."

Well, that was brilliant.

The white dog she'd seen the day she arrived pawed at the door, and the guy pushed it behind him. "Lie down, girl."

The dog obeyed, and the man leaned his shoulder against the screen door to open it, holding his body at an odd angle.

His dark hair was a bit messier than last time, and a five o'clock shadow covered his chin, but his blue shirt made his silver eyes pop. He held the door a little wider and winced. "Can you put them in the kitchen?"

Could she put them in the kitchen? He couldn't just take the cookies and end this whole interaction? Not to mention she wasn't about to step into a strange man's house.

When she didn't move, he nodded toward a chair on the porch. "Or just leave them there."

"Leave them on the porch?" Might as well toss them to the squirrels and ants now.

He winced again as he adjusted the grip on his left arm. "Do what you want. I've got to take care of this."

A drop of blood landed on the porch a few inches from her foot.

"You're bleeding?"

"Yup." He angled his arm, trying to get a better look at it.

The back part of his left sleeve was covered in blood. Libby jumped back as another drop hit the porch. "You need to go to the hospital."

"It's just a scratch." His voice faded as he let the screen door smack shut and disappeared deeper into the house.

"A scratch?" She yanked the door open and followed him in as her mind flipped through the first-aid training she'd taken two years ago. RICE was for a sprain. ABC was for assessment. What was the wound acronym?

She grabbed his sleeve and he let out a small cry. "A scratch that has soaked the back of your shirt with blood. Why didn't you take care of it?"

"I was trying to bandage it, but someone kept banging on the door."

"You can't just slap a bandage on it." Libby followed him through a living room area into the kitchen. "You have to care for it. CARE. That's it."

"What's it?"

"CARE. Check. Apply pressure. Raise. Ensure bandage is effective." Libby set the cookies on the counter and eyed the wound. "Check the wound for impaled object. How did you cut it?"

He pointed to a broken jar on the floor. "I tripped back and fell on it. It broke when I landed on it."

Libby knelt next to the broken mason jar and fit the pieces together. There were just three large pieces, and they all seemed to fit like a puzzle. At least he hadn't shattered it. "I think we're okay for C. A—apply pressure. I guess you did that. R—raise it above your heart."

"The bleeding has almost stopped. I think we can just jump to B for bandage." He motioned toward a first-aid kit spilled all over the counter.

"It's E. Ensure bandage is effective."

He lifted one eyebrow in her direction. "How can I ensure it's effective if I haven't bandaged it yet?"

A small giggle escaped Libby. "I guess it's just to make the acronym work."

"I prefer the BEC method."

"What's that?"

"Bandage. Eat cookies." He turned on the hot water and started washing the blood from his hands.

Libby grabbed his sleeve again and inspected the sizable tear. "Take your shirt off."

"What?" His movements paused as his brows shot up.

"I can't bandage it with that sleeve covering it."

He reached for a towel and slowly dried his hands, his eyes never leaving her.

Why was he looking at her so strangely? She ran through the past few minutes in her head. She'd gone into a strange man's house, then demanded he remove his shirt. Okay, so she deserved that look. Her hands began to shake, and she dashed over to the sink, stuck them under the hot water, and added a fair amount of dish soap in hopes he wouldn't notice. "Never mind. The shirt is ruined anyway."

Five minutes ago she hadn't even wanted to cross the driveway. But something about seeing the blood had triggered her emergency action response. As her adrenaline faded, she had to keep focusing on the problem in front of her. It was that or run away screaming. And she was done running.

Libby dried her hands and pulled at the edges of the torn sleeve. He winced as the ripping fabric slowly gave way, but he didn't make a sound. If the muscled arm—which had seen many hours of manual labor—was any indication of how the rest of him was built, then it was better she'd skipped the whole shirt-off thing. No way she'd be able to focus on the wound.

Libby grabbed some gauze, soaked it with warm water, and started wiping away the dried blood. "This may sting a little."

He didn't comment but just stared out the window as she scrubbed the edges of the two-inch gash that ran down the back of his tricep.

"This may need stitches."

"If you don't bandage it, I'll just slap some butterflies on it after you leave."

"I assume you're up-to-date on your tetanus shot, Mr. I'll Doctor Myself." Libby wiped the wound again with clean gauze. At least the bleeding had stopped.

He nodded and ran his free hand over his dog, who had walked over to lick his hand.

"What's your dog's name?"

"Shiro."

"How did you pick that?" Libby pulled off the tabs of the butterfly bandage, then stretched it across the wound.

He didn't even flinch. "She's a Japanese Akita, so I picked a Japanese name."

Libby added a second bandage. "What does Shiro mean?" She pulled the cloth away and inspected it.

"White."

She reached for the third and final butterfly strip but paused as a laugh bubbled up. "White?"

"Yes. She's white." He dug his hand into the dog's thick fur again. "At least I didn't give a boy dog a girl's name."

"Darcy isn't a girl's name. He's the hero of Jane Austen's most famous work."

He glanced at her over his shoulder. "The moody guy?"

"He wasn't moody. He was complicated and deep." She applied the final bandage with less grace.

"Ow."

"Sorry." She ripped open a gauze pad and pressed it to the wound. "Maybe I should've named him something interesting like Tan. You shouldn't knock moody men. You're the king of moody."

"I am not." The laughter in his voice eased some of the tension that she'd held in her shoulders for the past three days.

"I think Darcy and I would both disagree."

"Okay, fine. But only around you—and my brother." The last words came out mumbled.

Libby cut four pieces of medical tape, applying them one at a time to the edge of the gauze. "You don't always yell at neighbors and their dogs?"

"Only when their dog may have fathered a litter of mixed-breed pups."

"What?" Her fingers faltered on the tape.

"Shiro was in heat when I found Darcy in my yard. I had a stud appointment for her the next day."

"Did they . . ."

"I don't know. And we won't know for almost a month. But I had to cancel the stud appointment."

"Sorry. I guess you had a reason to be grumpy. I never got Darcy fixed because I thought I might get a female Lab someday and breed them. I never considered something like this happening."

"I'm sorry I yelled at you." His voice grew softer.

Libby taped the final edge of the gauze down. "And about the hippo . . ."

He spun to face her. "What's up with that thing? Where did it go?"

"I think he's over by the diner right now." She carried the trash from the bandages over and dropped it in the bin. "He moves around the square. That's all I know. You should ask a local for the full story."

"You aren't a local?"

"The day you moved in was my first day in town." She washed and dried her hands again, then leaned her back against the sink, taking in the kitchen for the first time. Half the counter was missing, as well as a section of cupboards. "Was there an accident?"

"I'm gutting the kitchen—and the living room—in exchange for lower rent." He picked up one of the chocolate chip cookies and took a bite. "You made me cookies?"

Warmth crawled up her neck. "No—well, yes, but to replace the ones Hannah made for you. She's your *real* neighbor."

He lifted one eyebrow. "You aren't real?"

"I'm real." She shifted from one foot to the other. "That's just my brother and his wife's house, not mine. Luke and Hannah Taylor are your neighbors, but they had to leave the day I arrived and asked if I could bring the cookies by."

He popped the rest of the cookie in his mouth. "Where are the cookies Hannah made?"

"I . . . ate them."

His chewing stopped. "You ate my cookies?"

"Not all of them." She put the contents of the first-aid box back together. "I gave Darcy a few."

"You fed my cookies to your *dog?*"

"Well, he likes oatmeal raisin. These are chocolate chip, so I didn't offer him any of these."

"Kind of you." He reached for the plate with his good arm and lifted another one. "So you're living with your brother and his wife?"

"For now. Then I'm moving to the house on your other side." She pointed to what she hoped was north.

"Will I get cookies again from you guys when you become my real neighbor? I could get used to this."

"No promises. And it isn't 'you guys.' Just Darcy and me. But don't worry, that yard is fenced. I already checked."

When he didn't comment, Libby added the scissors to the first aid kit and secured the lid. "Make sure you watch that for infection. If it isn't healing, you really should see a doctor."

"I'm good." He locked eyes with her as if he were trying to figure her out.

Good luck with that, buddy. She couldn't even figure herself out.

"If you just moved here, do you know my brother, Nate?"

Libby held out the first aid kit. "The pastor's your brother?"

"So you do know him." His shoulders seemed to tense.

"No, not really. I met him at Luke and Hannah's wedding last year. But we never really had a conversation. Why?"

"No reason. Everyone loves Nate, and I'm

sure you will too. It's just nice to meet someone who doesn't already think my brother walks on water."

"Does he—walk on water?"

"Sometimes I wonder." He set the first aid kit on one of the half-filled boxes. "Thanks again for the help with the arm. That would have been tricky on my own."

"No problem." She followed him back through the house. "Enjoy the cookies."

"I will." He held the front door open for her, then extended his hand. "By the way, the name is Austin."

"Austin? Like Jane Au—"

"No. *In,* not *en.* I am no hero."

Maybe, maybe not. Only time would tell.

"I'm Libby." She took his hand, and the warmth made her want to hold on a touch longer than necessary. It was time to go. Not because she found him threatening but because she found him less threatening by the minute, and that in itself was dangerous. She had a gift for trusting the wrong people, and she couldn't walk that road again.

Leaving Heritage wouldn't be easy, but it *was* necessary.

Olivia grabbed a cloth and wiped down the new dark gray Formica counters at Donny's. It'd take a while to get used to not seeing the scratches and stains that had taken up permanent residence over the years.

When her sister Janie and her husband, Thomas, had bought the place from Lucy and Don last year, they hadn't been able to afford a lot of changes, so they had focused on what showed the most wear—the counters and the red vinyl on the booths. The small changes had made a big difference, and that's what she was counting on for her own life.

Lucy pushed through the swinging door that connected to the kitchen, her gray hair brushing her shoulders as she walked. "That sister of yours better get back from her honeymoon soon. I'm too old for this. There was a reason we retired and sold the business."

"You have more energy than three people combined." Olivia hung the rag she'd been using under the edge of the counter. "But never fear. They're supposed to be back next week."

"Two weeks sounded a lot shorter before I was getting up at five in the morning every day again." Lucy gathered a few mugs left by patrons and added them to the bin under the counter.

Olivia checked her watch. "I need to take my break in five minutes. I have a phone interview."

"Ooh, is this with that big paper in Arizona?" Lucy checked a to-go order and then scooped out a piece of pie from the display and slid it into a box.

"No. I had that interview this morning. Which wasn't much of an interview. They basically said they needed more print time before they would consider me. My professor insisted I have a backup plan, and she knew someone at the *Grand Rapids Gazette*, so she arranged this interview a few weeks ago. I mean, it isn't as far as Phoenix, but getting out of Heritage for a while will be nice." More like getting away from Nate was a necessity. "But my professor said it should be a done deal, so I put my notice on your—I mean Janie's—desk."

Lucy set the pie by the cash register and taped the order slip on top. "We'll miss you, but it's good to see my little birdies fly their nest. I just can't imagine this town without you. And Nate will be missing you for certain."

Olivia paused. How much did Lucy know? She was sure they'd kept their non-relationship out of the town's eye, but Heritage was known for being a fishbowl.

"I mean, you run almost half the programs at that church." Lucy waved at a couple leaving, then wiped the perfectly clean counter again.

Olivia picked up an empty napkin dispenser, carried it to the counter, and started filling it. "Nate did mention that the church would miss me when I left."

"You've already told him?"

"I mentioned I was leaving the other night when we went to the shelter."

"He didn't say anything else?"

"Only that I'm a great asset to the church."

Lucy shook her head and set an empty dispenser in front of Olivia. "He'll come around. Give him time."

"I think he's run out of time." Her phone rang and she didn't recognize the number. She waved it in the air. "Interview. I think I'll go sit on Otis out front for good luck."

"Unless you want to be interrupted, you better choose the back alley." Lucy shooed her out the door.

Olivia exited the back door and leaned against the brick wall facing the back lot. It wasn't pretty, but it was quiet. She drew a deep breath and hit Accept. "Hello, this is Olivia Mathews."

That sounded professional.

"This is Frank Lang. I don't need another reporter right now." The man's words were clipped.

"Huh?" That was less professional. She cleared her throat. "I mean, Dr. Brown said—"

"Dr. Brown is an old friend. She said you needed some ink time, so here is what I can offer you. Freelance. You write something—if I like it, I'll pay you for it and print it."

"And if you don't?" She pressed her head into the wall.

"Then you write something else."

This changed everything. No steady job meant no steady paycheck. So much for the apartment in Grand Rapids. Thomas and Janie would let her keep her job here at the diner, but that would mean remaining in Heritage. Maybe Libby would let her rent one of the rooms in that house.

"Are you interested or not?" Frank Lang's gruff voice echoed over the line.

It wasn't like she had other options, and print time was print time—if he liked her work. "I'll do it. Is there a story you want me to start with?" She kicked at a pebble at her feet. The guy didn't seem easy to please, but perhaps if she started on a story he was looking for, it'd give her a leg up.

"You single?"

She kicked at another pebble but stumbled. "Excuse me?"

"I want a feature on dating. There are all these new ways to date these days. I want you to put a spin on it from a young single person's perspective." His voice muffled as if he was reading a list. "Online, fast dating—"

"Speed dating."

"Exactly." A slight chuckle accompanied his words. "See, you're just the person to do it. Are you single? Because it might be hard to research if you're in a relationship."

Olivia's mind flashed to Nate, their conversation in the van, and the fact that he'd barely acknowledged her at the diner the other day. "I'm single."

"You want to take it?"

She'd been on only one date in her life—with Nate. And that hadn't turned out all that well. She wasn't against dating. She'd just decided long ago that she wouldn't waste her time dating a guy she couldn't see herself marrying. Nate had been the first guy to really catch her attention—then throw it away.

"If you'd rather not—"

"I'll take it."

"Great. Have it on my desk in two weeks." The line went dead.

That was it? Olivia pulled up her contacts and tapped out a text to her sister.

Looks like I'm not leaving Heritage anytime soon.

Olivia's phone rang and Janie's picture flashed on the screen. "You aren't supposed to call me on your honeymoon."

"We're driving to our next B&B. What happened? Did you not get the job?"

"Sort of." Olivia pushed away from the wall and paced to her car. "I somehow just agreed to write an article on modern dating when I've never dated—modern or not."

"You sort of dated Jackson in high school."

"I hate it when people say that. We were only friends."

"He'd have dated you if you'd let him. Half the school thought you were dating."

She did a 180 and paced back to the diner. "Don't remind me. Getting voted cutest couple our senior year was so awkward." Olivia leaned her head against the wall. "I may turn it down."

"You can write anything you set your mind to. Remember when you wrote that article about climbing Mount Everest in high school? Even I was ready to give it a try, and I hate the outdoors."

"I guess you're right." Olivia checked the time. "But it's only freelance, so I need to keep my job here if that's okay."

"I'll talk the boss into it." Janie laughed at something Thomas said but Olivia couldn't hear. Probably for the best.

"See you in a week." Olivia ended the call and slid her phone back in her pocket. She marched right to Janie's desk, picked up the letter offering her two weeks' notice, and tossed it in the trash. It looked like she'd be here indefinitely.

She returned to where she'd left the napkins, but Lucy had finished. Olivia leaned against the counter and pulled out a notepad. Speed dating. Internet dating. Was there YouTube dating? No, that wouldn't work. Would it?

"Ma'am, can I get more coffee?"

Without looking up, Olivia grabbed the pot and

started filling the mugs of all the patrons at the counter.

"Thank you." The familiar baritone snapped her out of her thoughts as she filled the third cup. Her head jerked up. Her favorite pair of smoky gray eyes—her kryptonite—watched her with a hooded expression. She meant to offer a curt nod and turn away, but her feet didn't seem to work anymore. The tension in his face tugged at her heart.

"You okay?" Blast her heart for caring so much.

"Yeah, sure. Family stress, that's all." He dropped his gaze to his mug. "How did your interview at the paper go?" When she didn't answer, he looked up and chuckled. "Lucy mentioned where you were. Is this about the job in Phoenix?"

"No. They want more experience." Was it her imagination, or did Nate's shoulders just relax a bit? "This was a paper in Grand Rapids. He wants me to write an article on dating."

"What?" Nate coughed, spilling a bit of his coffee onto the counter.

She grabbed a cloth and wiped up the spill. "My boss wants a story on modern dating."

"You aren't going to do it, are you? I mean, you haven't even—"

"Dated? Yes, I am aware. But it's never too late to start. It sounds like fun."

"You'll just go out and date random strangers?"

"Maybe. Or maybe guys in town. Although you may not see me as dateable, I doubt that's the sentiment of every man around here."

"Olivia—"

The bell over the door chimed, and in walked Mayor Jameson, Bo Mackers, and Dale Kensington.

"That's my three o'clock." Nate picked up his bag. "We're talking about that idea you had for the schoolhouse in the town square. Wish me luck."

The mayor nodded at Nate, then offered her a full smile. "We'll start with four coffees in the corner booth when you have a second."

Olivia turned around and picked up the coffeepot. When she turned back, Nate had already joined the other three men at the booth. Just a ridiculously high tip next to his abandoned cup.

She gripped the money and resisted the urge to throw it at him. Now she had to do the stupid dating article or admit to Nate that he was right. She had no idea what she was doing when it came to dating.

"It was supposed to be an interview for the magazine." Austin resisted the urge to scratch his face where they'd just powdered it. "Why is there a TV camera?"

Nate shifted in his chair as the makeup lady

turned her attention to him. "It was just an article, but a station from Grand Rapids called the mayor about an interview, and he decided to do them at the same time."

"Perfect." Austin wrinkled his nose and finally scratched at his cheek, causing the makeup lady's purple lips to pinch as she batted his hand away.

Libby stood at the edge of the crowd that had begun to form. Her dark blonde ponytail and yoga pants probably meant she'd just come back from another bike ride. He'd seen her more times than he could count on that ugly purple bike.

After the encounter with her dog, he'd seen her as immature and irresponsible, but the way she'd taken charge of his injury on his arm two days ago changed that. And she'd been funny.

Somehow in those twenty minutes, she'd worked her way under his radar, and he'd found himself thinking way too much of her the past couple of days. What would it be like to spend the whole day with her? Find out what made her laugh—besides his dog's name.

"There has also been another change to the plans." Nate handed him a pack of papers.

"What?" Austin skimmed through the pages, heat spreading across his skin as he read. He slapped the packet on the edge of the chair but lowered his voice. "You can't do this. We already have a contract."

Nate produced another piece of paper. "The

contract spells out that the town may change the plans up until the seventeenth of August. That's still five days away. Besides, this is better for you. You'll make more money."

"But this will take another month at least." Austin rolled the papers in his hand tighter and tighter. A delay in the job meant a delay in payment. His checkbook didn't have room for that.

"It isn't final. The committee just wants you to present a plan to include the schoolhouse."

"I could say no."

"Not the best publicity for the business." Nate leaned toward him. "It isn't like you have other jobs to get to."

Nate was right, and Austin hated that his brother knew it.

"I tried to give you the heads-up last night, but my calls kept going to voicemail."

Austin didn't comment. He'd seen Nate's calls and ignored every one. He hadn't felt like getting into it again last night.

He unrolled the pages and flipped through them, reading as fast as he could.

He paused on the words "Assistant landscaper: Nate Williams" and held the page up to his brother. "What's this?"

"That's why I'm in the interview too." Nate lowered his voice again. "It only makes sense."

"I'll hire my own assistant."

"I'll work for free. And—"

"Austin Williams?" An attractive young brunette approached with her hand outstretched and a cameraman on her heels.

"Yes." Austin stood and shook her hand.

"I'm Sydney St. James from Channel 21 News. It's quite exciting for one of our small towns to win a national contest like this. We'll be following the development through the entire project."

Entire project?

The idea of being in the spotlight made his skin itch, but local news coverage might just be the answer to save Williams and Son Landscaping. It'd do more than the national magazine. After all, they didn't need national business; they needed local business.

He offered a polite smile and shook her hand. "It's nice to meet you. I'm happy to help any way I can."

"Great. We're going to shoot the interview in the gazebo." She led him to one of two high stools that had been set up. "Can you believe this weather? Cool one day and hot and muggy the next. I'm glad today is nice."

Austin nodded, not sure what else to add.

She glanced at her notes, then back at him. "I hear the woman who entered the town in the contest isn't here right now. Is that correct?"

"Hannah Taylor? No, she's not available at

this time." At least that's what he thought he'd heard.

She waved her red nails in the air. "No worries, I'll splice in interviews with her later."

Austin ran a hand down his gray shirt. At least he'd chosen a solid color. That was supposed to be better on camera, right? It was the only solid one he had left now that he'd ruined the blue one.

He covered a smile at the memory of Libby asking him to take off his shirt. Well, not so much the asking as the moment that followed. Her face had gone redder than Austin had even thought possible.

Nate took the stool next to him as a boom with a fuzzy microphone hovered over his head. "You ready for this?"

"As ready as I can be for looking over the plans in thirty seconds," he whispered for Nate alone.

Nate shrugged. "I tried to call."

Sydney's gaze bounced between them. "Wow. You two look a lot alike."

Nate ran his fingers through his hair. "We're brothers."

The lady with the purple lips returned with a scowl and ran a comb through Nate's hair again. "Don't touch it."

Sydney settled on her stool and skimmed through a set of note cards. "Do you do a lot with the business, Nate?"

Nate reached for his hair but stopped when he

glanced at the hair lady again. He slid his hand along his pants leg. "Uh . . ."

"He hasn't done much with the business since high school." No matter how mad he was at his brother, Austin wasn't about to throw him under the bus. After all, he was the pastor here. Who knew how much the town knew of his past.

"You two will look great together on camera. If we get a few shots of you working side by side, this might just get picked up nationally. Our very own local *Property Brothers* meets *Going Yard*. I love it."

What was she babbling about? They weren't going to be working side by side.

Sydney motioned to the cameraman. "Make sure to get that brass hippo in the background. I love it."

What? He shifted in his seat to look over his shoulder. Sure enough, the hippo sat in the middle of the sidewalk, staring at them as if he'd shown up for the interview. This was getting weird.

"And ready in five." The cameraman counted down.

The newswoman shook her hair and offered the camera a million-dollar smile. "Michigan has had its ups and downs with the economy. But even in the worst of times, we Michiganders pull together. It's that pull-together attitude that defines this state, this small town of Heritage, and Williams and Son Landscaping."

She turned toward them as she spoke, and the cameraman shifted his shot to include them. "Nate and Austin are brothers helping each other help this town. Nate, you must have had great faith in your brother to recommend him for this job."

Nate studied Austin before looking at the woman. "My brother is a great man and an amazing landscaper. I'd trust no one more."

"Will you be helping him?"

He sent Austin a quick glance. "As much as he'll let me."

Austin fisted his hand. Nothing like throwing down a challenge in front of the town, not to mention everyone watching.

"Heritage is a great community that prides itself on embracing the future while remembering the past. Tell me about your decision to move the one-room schoolhouse to the square."

How was he supposed to expound on an idea that he'd only heard about ten minutes ago? "Nothing has been finalized. We still have to determine if the move is possible. But it's the newest idea that has been presented."

"Whose idea was it?"

Nate leaned forward. "The new librarian, Libby Kingsley, came up with the idea. As soon as I heard it, I had to take it right to the board."

Libby? She'd said she didn't even know his brother. Then again, maybe she was just telling him what he wanted to hear. Maybe the cookies were just a ploy to soften the road for her precious schoolhouse. Memories of Becky and her manipulative ways flashed through his mind.

Austin scanned the crowd, which was abuzz with the news. Libby stood in the middle, red-faced and wide-eyed.

"Austin, you said the last time you two worked together was in high school. Are you looking forward to working with your brother after all this time?"

And there it was. Be honest and look like a jerk, or play this game Nate started and hope it didn't blow up in his face. But the fact was he needed good publicity or the business was done. And like it or not, everyone was charmed by Nate.

He dropped his arm around his brother's shoulders. "Of course I am. Nothing could please me more. Right, little brother?"

"You two seem to have an idyllic brother relationship. Have you always gotten along this well?" Sydney shoved the microphone toward Nate.

Austin squeezed Nate's shoulder extra tight. If Nate was going to use this interview to force his hand on working together, then he had better be ready to play the part of happy brother.

four

Did Austin expect him to lie? Nate swallowed hard as he took in the crowd. Members from his congregation, his board, even Olivia, stood in the gathered crowd awaiting his reply.

He peeked at Austin out of the corner of his eye. His brother's forced smile and tightening grip on his shoulder sent a solid message, but he hadn't meant to back Austin into a corner. He'd just been honest. He did trust his brother. He did hope to work with him. But no doubt if he answered honestly now, he'd wreck every chance he had at rebuilding his relationship with Austin.

Nate cleared his throat. "I'm sorry, what was the question?"

Sydney laughed, but her narrowed eyes testified that she was about to give up on this story and the interview altogether. "You seem to have an idyllic brother relationship. Do you think that will carry into your working relationship?"

He couldn't lie. He was a pastor, for goodness' sake. Perhaps he could be intentionally vague. "We've had disagreements and will probably have a few about the square. But what brothers agree on everything?"

"What was the biggest thing you ever fought about?"

Really? Wasn't this supposed to be about landscaping? Maybe she was just trying to take the personal approach, but no way he was airing their dirty laundry out here in front of the town. Who knew what his brother would throw out, and that wouldn't help his image as the pastor either.

He'd go for something juvenile. "In eighth grade, he kissed my girlfriend."

"Sarah Fredericks was not your girlfriend." Austin shoved his arm and laughed. A forced laugh if Nate had ever heard one.

"Was too." He crossed his arms and tried to play the part of the teasing brother. Not that it was hard. This was how he wanted his relationship with his brother to be. This was how it had been.

"Let's hope Sarah Fredericks doesn't show up while you two are working together." Sydney focused on the camera and said a few more words before someone yelled it was a wrap. She looked back at them with her winning smile. "That went well. Thank you for your time. I'll be in touch, gentlemen."

Austin nodded toward his house and started walking that way without so much as a pause to see if Nate would follow. Which he did. But Nate didn't know if it was because he was simply following Austin's lead or because he had a few choice words for Austin as well—ones that couldn't be shared in public.

His brother may have thought that being on camera had made Nate nervous. But it was Austin who made him nervous. All he wanted to do was fix his relationship with his brother, but every attempt just seemed to make things worse.

Then there had been the fact that he'd been distracted by a five-foot-ten platinum blonde. Olivia hadn't so much as glanced in his direction as she stood between Derek Kensington and Ted Wilks.

Luke didn't care for the guys much, but Nate assumed it was old rivalries. After all, if anyone refused to judge a person by their past, it was Nate. But the way both guys had been looking at Olivia burned something inside him. Hadn't she bid on one of them during the bachelor auction last summer? She hadn't won, but the memory of her yelling out a bid had stamped itself in his memory.

Then again, he'd given up the right to have an opinion on who she dated.

He followed Austin into his rental and resisted the urge to slam his fist into the wall. His restraint was partly out of self-control and partly because he feared a well-placed punch might bring the place down. "You really think this place is better than sharing a roof with me?"

Austin didn't comment as he disappeared into

the kitchen, leaving Nate's mind to circle around to Olivia again.

It had been a stab when she crossed her name off the shelter list on Sunday. At least she hadn't left the kids' ministry. She came alive when she taught those kids. He'd miss that—er, the kids would miss that.

Nate dropped into the nearest chair as Shiro nuzzled her nose in his hands. What was he going to do now?

Austin reappeared with a Coke in each hand and held one out to Nate. "I bet you thought you were pretty funny with that 'My brother is a great man and I'll help him as much as he'll let me' comment. Well, that sure blew up in our faces, little brother."

Nate took the can and popped it open. "I wasn't trying to be funny. I do think you're a great man and—"

"So you were trying to manipulate me into hiring you as my assistant?" Austin leaned against the door frame, opened his can, and took a long gulp.

"I wasn't manipulating you. She asked me a question and I was honest. I was trying to help—"

"Help? Don't you see? They expect us to be pals now wherever we go. Work side by side—the symbol of family and small-town community." Austin straightened and flung his arms wide, nearly spilling the Coke. "If I want to walk away with any business whatsoever and you want to keep your congregation, then we're going to have to keep playing the part of best brothers. Do you see any other way?"

"We could get along. Forget the past." Nate mumbled the words as he sank back in the chair.

"You mean me forget the past." Austin spun the can in his hands a few times before he locked eyes again with Nate. "Yeah, well, I'm still living with the consequences of your actions. We can't all start a new life and a new career. Some of us have to stay behind and pick up the pieces."

Silence hung in the room. It wasn't like this was a new argument. Austin was right—Nate had left a wake of destruction. But how does one atone for sins like that?

"Have you been to see Dad lately?" Austin claimed the corner spot on the couch, leaned forward on his knees, and rubbed the back of his neck.

"I stopped by yesterday but he was napping. You?"

"I went up on Monday and this morning." Austin sat back and met Nate's gaze. "I settled the rest of his stuff."

Nate swallowed against his tightening throat. "Did he remember you?"

Austin shrugged. "One of the visits he did."

Man, it was hard watching their dad slip away like this. Such a harsh disease. "And the other?"

"He introduced me as Edward."

"Crazy Uncle Eddy?"

Their mom's brother had always been an odd one. Never married and had a beard that came to his chest. Although Nate would take that over being compared to Uncle Greg—the screwup. The one who had abandoned his family.

Nate leaned back and rubbed his chin with his thumb and forefinger. "You do sort of look like Uncle Eddy."

"Thanks a lot. Then you look like him too. People always say we look alike." Shiro laid her head on Austin's leg, and he scratched her neck as he stared off into space. "Do you remember when we tried to put spiders in his beard while he slept?"

"How could I forget? We got grounded for a month." Nate let out a laugh and Austin joined in.

Nate's breath died in his chest. How long since he'd made his brother laugh? This was what he wanted. A brother to laugh with at their childhood memories and struggle with through their dad's illness. "We had a lot of good times together."

Austin's face sobered. "That was a long time ago."

Just like that, the moment was gone. Nate pressed his lips together. If he could get Austin to let down that wall long enough, he just might remember the friendship they'd had and might have again.

"When are you going up next to see Dad? Maybe if we go together it'll be easier to place us." And maybe Austin would see Nate wasn't like his uncle in every way. He could be depended on when it came to family.

Austin didn't comment for a long time, then took another gulp of his Coke. "I'm going tomorrow at ten in the morning. Want to ride with me?"

Nate gave a mental scan of his calendar. Tomorrow wasn't ideal, but he'd make it work. "I have an appointment, but it should be done by then. I'll meet you there."

Austin lifted one eyebrow, his doubt evident.

"I'll be there. We're in this together. I promise." He shouldn't promise that. Too much in his life was out of his control between pastoring, coaching, and the fire department, but he couldn't let this opportunity with his brother pass.

Austin nodded once. "And the square? Are you in for pulling off the best brothers act?"

Nate's gut tightened as all the ways this could end badly trailed through his mind. The headline "Local Pastor Misleads Entire Congregation" being at the top. "I'll do it. But you have to let me help."

"Fine. You can help. But I'm hiring an assistant of my choosing. And don't expect this to change anything between us."

Nate stood but didn't comment. There was no agreement on that. After all, he was counting on it to change everything. That was the only reason he was willing to put his reputation and career on the line like this.

Libby hated waiting, and now she seemed to be waiting on everything: the library, news from Luke and Hannah, even moving into her own place. She pressed her hand against the twisting in her stomach. Being one part hungry and three parts stressed wasn't going well for her digestion. She couldn't do anything about the stress, but maybe it was time to eat.

Libby set her book aside and headed to the kitchen, letting her fuzzy socks slide across the wooden floor. Her phone rang and she claimed it from her purse as she walked by. "Hey, Mom."

"How is everything in Heritage?"

"Fine." Libby pulled out a bowl from the cupboard, then bent down to grab the cereal but came up empty. Right. She'd finished that yesterday.

"That wasn't convincing." Her mother's gentle voice carried over the line, stirring a well of homesickness in her chest. What she would give to be having this conversation curled up next to her mom, sipping a cup of warm milk as they binge-watched old episodes of *Downton Abbey*. Maybe she'd settle for a glass of milk.

She opened the fridge. No milk. "Maybe moving here was a mistake."

"Do you want to come home?"

"Yes. No. Maybe." Why did she carry all her stress in her stomach? A piece of toast might help. She opened the cupboard. No bread. Seriously? She'd managed to eat through all Hannah and Luke's food over the week.

"I know I gave you a hard time about moving there, and I'll admit that letting you go has been hard. But I think it's been good for you. This past week I've seen some of the old Libby reemerge, and . . . I'm proud of you."

"So, you think I should stay?" She slammed the cupboard shut, then swallowed and pressed her hand against her stomach as it rolled over. "I think I'm getting the flu."

"Calm down. Have you prayed about all this?"

Why did everyone want her to pray all the time? "I will." *Maybe.*

Darcy dropped his bowl at her feet. Right. She wasn't the only hungry one.

"You can trust an unknown future to a known God." Her mother's voice caught, and she cleared her throat before continuing. "I clung to that quote by Corrie ten Boom in the early days of Luke's disappearance, and the other day I tacked it up on my mirror again. Even when things feel confusing and dark, you can trust God."

"I need to go get some groceries." She hadn't meant to sound so harsh, but she just wasn't up to talking about God right now. "Love you, Mom."

"Love you too."

Libby dropped the phone in her pocket and reached for her keys. She eyed her bike as she slid into her car. Petunia always helped her think. But she couldn't manage the dog food on her bike. She pulled out of the driveway and headed north on Henderson.

Was staying in Heritage the right decision? Or going home? Then again, making the right decision didn't seem like something she was good at. She'd trusted the wrong guy in London, she'd trusted the wrong friend in college, she'd even trusted Luke's dad when he told her he was just taking Luke for ice cream. That had been her life's—and probably her mother's—biggest regret.

Maybe she needed to take people out of the equation and just look at the facts. She was a person of logic. Research. Maybe it was time for some logic on staying in Heritage or not. An old-fashioned pro/con list should do it.

Pro—living near Luke.

Con—he wasn't here.

Pro—he'd eventually return.

That left her in the positive, but the library was more than she bargained for, and that was a huge con. And if it went to the square, she'd have to work with Austin. After the look he'd given her during the interview, she could assume working with him would be a Godzilla-sized con.

Then again, she could create a library any way she wanted. The programs were in her full control—pro. Not to mention she had full control of the books ordered—pro. A year from now she'd still be the librarian and the Godzilla-sized con would have moved on. Pro. Pro. Pro.

But the only friend she had in town was moving away—con.

You want me to stay here, God? Here's a prayer for You. How about that someone I know would stay in town? Libby dismissed the thought. God didn't care about her or her problems, no matter what her mother said.

The local grocery store came into view. The storefront still held the look of an old general store, and Libby had a glimpse of what this town had been once upon a time. Living in a quaint small town—pro.

The printed sign on the door stating the credit card machines were down and they didn't accept out-of-state checks stopped her. Okay, not all small-town pieces were a pro. Maybe it was time to pay a visit to the local bank and open an account. That is, if she decided to stay. Until then, she'd have to make do with the twenty dollars she had. It should be enough.

Libby claimed the cart and priced dog food and milk first. After grabbing cereal and bread, she aimed for the eggs. Her heart did that little flip thing at the sale sign posted above. How sad was her life that a sale on eggs was the highlight of her day?

Her phone rang and she pulled it out as she checked the eggs for any cracks. "Hello?"

"Hey. This is Olivia. I haven't talked to you since the interview. How are you doing?"

"Fine." She set the eggs in the cart and did her best to steer it toward the checkout with one hand.

"I'll get right to the point. Grand Rapids has fallen through for now, so how do you feel about a roommate?"

Libby paused her cart. "A roommate?"

The prayer she'd flung at God came to mind. But God didn't do this. Olivia staying in town happened even before she'd prayed that. So that didn't count. Did it?

"If you don't like that idea—"

"No."

"No?"

"I mean no, that wasn't the hesitation. I love the idea."

"Perfect. I'll swing by Luke's in an hour and we can talk details."

An answered prayer might be stretching it. But a roommate was one more in the pro category. The pros were tipping the scales. And getting to move into her own space was a definite pro.

Olivia ended the call just as Libby's phone buzzed with an incoming text.

Mom

Never be afraid to trust an unknown future to a known God. —Corrie ten Boom

Libby read the message a few times, then slid her phone back in her purse. But what if she didn't feel like she knew God?

She made her way to the checkout, recalculating what she'd chosen. She should just make it. Thank goodness for no tax on groceries. It wasn't a fancy selection of food, but it would make do until she could get more cash.

Libby dug her twenty-dollar bill out of her wallet. Maybe she'd have enough left to buy a pack of gum. How pathetic.

A man stepped up behind her and started emptying his basket. Perhaps if she met more of the friendly people Olivia kept talking about, this place wouldn't seem so lonely. Libby turned with a smile. "Hi, I'm Li—"

Austin stood behind her, a look of annoyance on his face. "I believe we've met."

Looked like she was back to Mr. Mean Hot Neighbor. No, she had to stop thinking of him like that. But Austin seemed too normal—too nice. Mr. Williams. Yes, Mr. Williams was better.

Libby turned back to her groceries inching toward the checkout. The young girl working the register seemed new. Austin shifted behind her and checked the time. Poor girl, but couldn't she move it along?

Libby cast a side glance at his purchases: black licorice, peppermint sticks, and two cases of Ensure. Was the guy thirty or eighty?

The cashier said something to her, and Libby passed over her twenty.

"Um, the total is twenty-two dollars and forty-seven cents." The teenage clerk smiled at her again.

"How much?"

The girl's eyes widened. "$22.47?"

"What? I didn't even get my coffee. I thought the eggs were on sale." Libby hated the slight quiver in her voice.

"The Sweetfarm regular eggs are on sale. These are the farm fresh." The girl pointed to the words as if Libby needed help reading them.

Poor signage—con.

Libby cast a glance down the line at the three other people who were behind her. Great. She'd just leave the eggs and get them another day.

"Here." The rich baritone spoke from behind her as Austin leaned forward and handed the clerk a five.

"Wait, what?" But the clerk was already ringing it up.

This guy flipped hot and cold faster than the kitchen faucet. He couldn't play nice guy, then pull out Mr. Mean Hot Neighbor, and then expect her to accept his nice-guy routine at the drop of a hat.

"I'm not taking your money."

"You didn't. She did." His expression didn't change. Not even the hint of a smile. Maybe it was still Mr. Mean Hot Neighbor, just with money. Well, she didn't need his nice-guy act or his money.

"Your change, miss." The girl held out two dollars and several coins.

"It's not my change. It's his change." Why did she sound so hysterical?

"Just put it in her bag," Austin said.

The girl dropped the change in one of her bags and started ringing up his stuff. The man was infuriating. She dug into the bottom of her bag to locate the change. By the time she'd found the last penny, Austin was walking past her.

"Have a nice day." His tone remained dry.

This was so not over.

Austin pulled his keys from his pocket and shuffled them to find the right one as he exited through the automatic door of JJ's Food Mart. The warmth of the sun heated his back as he left the air-conditioning and aimed toward the company truck.

"I have money," Libby shouted from behind him. She struggled with her purse as she tried to control her grocery cart with one hand. "I am not destitute."

"Okay." He unlocked the passenger side of his truck and popped open the door.

"They don't take out-of-state checks, and that's what I have. See?" She stopped her cart next to him, yanked out a checkbook, and pointed to the address.

"I'm glad you have money." He dropped the bags on the passenger seat, shut the door, and tried to step around her toward the driver's side.

She blocked his path. "Here is your change." She dropped two wadded-up bills and some coins in his hands. "I'll write you a check for the rest. Two dollars and forty-seven cents?"

Austin shoved the change in his pocket. "Forget it. I don't need a check."

He tried to step past her again, but she didn't move. She just scrawled out $2.47 on the check.

"I don't want that."

"Too bad, I'm giving it to you." She ripped off the check and held it out.

"I won't cash it." He leaned against the truck.

Her eyes narrowed as her lips pressed together. "Mr. Williams—"

" 'Mr. Williams'? Isn't that a little formal considering you asked me to take off my shirt in our last conversation?"

"That was a medical issue." Her face deepened

to that same shade of red. "I just don't want to owe you anything."

This was all over two and a half dollars? Fine, if she wanted to square things up . . . "Let's see. I had to cancel my breeding appointment because of your dog. And now I have to redo my entire project because of you. Basically, until I met you, my life was going pretty smooth." Unless he counted Nate. "But by all means, let's fight over less than two and a half dollars." He slid past her cart, walked to the driver's side, and paused. "I thought you said you'd never had a conversation with my brother."

He'd promised himself he wouldn't bring it up, but he had to know. He'd been so sure she was different from Becky.

"I didn't. I don't know how he heard of my idea. I'm guessing my roommate Olivia told—"

"Roommate? You said you didn't have a roommate."

"I didn't, but I do now—"

"It doesn't matter. I have someplace I need to be. If you'll excuse me." He pulled open the door.

Her mouth snapped shut as she straightened her shoulders and backed her cart away from his truck. "I'll bring your money by later."

He paused with one foot in the truck. "I don't want the money. I didn't do it to make you feel indebted or to point out to you again how displeased I am with you and your dog. And it had nothing to do with all of your half-truths that you can't seem to keep straight—"

"I told you, I didn't—"

He held up his hand. "You needed a few bucks. I had it. End of story." He slid into his truck and backed out of the spot, but as he glanced in his rearview mirror on his way out of the lot, she still hadn't moved.

Austin turned north on the highway, flipped on the radio, and tried to prepare himself to see his dad and Nate. He hated putting his faith in Nate, but part of him believed his brother might keep his word and be there today. And if Nate arrived when he said, that would leave Austin about fifteen minutes to talk about the square and the business with his dad. But that would only work if it was his dad looking back at him and not someone who didn't know him.

Thirty minutes later, Austin offered two quick knocks before he pulled open the door to his dad's room. His father's eyes were fixed on the forty-eight-inch flat screen. Yankees versus the Tigers.

Austin dropped the bags on the counter in the kitchenette. "Who's winning?"

"The bad guys." His father muted the television as a commercial came on. He never had cared for the Yankees.

When his father looked up, Austin held his breath.

The older version of his own face crinkled into a smile. "Austin. Good to see you. What brings you by?"

Austin released his breath and started unloading the groceries into the cupboard. "I brought you some of your favorites. Can't just live on the cafeteria food."

"Thank goodness. Any licorice in there?"

Austin sat in the recliner next to his father's chair and tore off a piece of licorice before passing it over. "I wouldn't forget."

His dad smiled and looked back at the game.

"How are you doing, Dad?"

He held up his foot. "Got my cast off."

"That has to feel good. Starting to feel settled here?"

His dad shrugged, then winked at him. "Surviving another day. But I'm not sure if that's good or bad."

Austin's heart pinched. He knew his father didn't long for death, but the past ten years had been hard. Their mom's death, Nate's foolish choices, the struggling business, and now a rapid descent into early-onset Alzheimer's. Sixty-six was too young.

He knew heaven would mean healing for his dad, but Austin wasn't ready to let go yet. He needed his dad.

He swallowed the lump in his throat and patted his dad's shoulder. "You have to stick around a lot longer. You're the brains of this business."

His dad shook his head, bit off a piece of licorice, and reached for the remote. "It's your business now."

"Right." Austin leaned back. This was it. His father seemed lucid, and if ever he'd get him to agree to the ridiculousness of this job, now was the time. "Speaking of the business, there has been a new development with the Heritage job."

His father's hand stilled, but he didn't take his eyes off the TV.

"I know you'd hoped that this would be a big account for us. I even rented a house there, but I wonder if their expectations aren't a bit too high. It might be best to cut our losses now and try to get—"

"No." His father pinned him with a hard stare, his gray eyebrows forming a deep V. "I agreed to this. The company needs to abide by—"

"But they've decided they want to move a building there now. Not only does that mean a complete redesign of what I have, but it's also a longer time frame. I won't be able to take on any other accounts this season." Austin tried to keep the edge from his voice, but it didn't work.

"Why aren't you staying with Nate for this job? I know you think I was upset about moving in here. I don't love getting old, but I could see the need for it." He bit the nail of his thumb as a vague look crossed his face, but before Austin could ask about it, his dad stared him down again. "I was upset because you're renting a house. Your brother lives there."

That was the heart of the matter. It wasn't about the job at all. Everything was always about Nate. "Do you think the two of us living under the same roof would be a good idea?"

His father's hand came down on the table with a thud. "Yes. Why do you think I—"

"Agreed to the job? I've been wondering that very same thing." Austin clenched his jaw before drawing a calming breath. "If you think Nate and I are going to become the best of friends just because we share a roof or work on a project together, you're going to be disappointed."

Where was Nate? He should have been here by now. Austin checked his phone. Nothing.

His dad picked up the framed family photo and ran his gnarled fingers over the glass. "You two were best friends once."

"We were kids." He slid his phone back into his pocket.

His father's mouth turned down as he set the photo back on the table. "From where I sit, it wasn't that long ago."

"I don't think I can do this, Dad."

"It's your business. It's your life." His dad stared off for a minute before looking back at Austin, his eyes heavier. "Just don't leave opportunities on the table. Brothers aren't replaceable."

Austin had heard bits and pieces of the estrangement his father had with his own brother years before his uncle had abandoned his family.

His father's eyes closed for several minutes before he unmuted the game. When he looked up, he seemed genuinely surprised to see Austin.

Austin knew stress made his father's symptoms worse. "Hi, Dad."

"Austin, how are you? What brings you here?"

He swallowed down the lump that rose in his throat. His dad was slipping away now, and he couldn't stop him. Maybe he should be happy for the few lucid minutes he'd had, but he didn't want just a few minutes. He needed his dad. All of him. Not just a piece of him once in a while.

He cleared his throat as he tore off another piece of licorice and passed it to his father. "I just drove up from Heritage. Brought you some of your favorites."

His father reached for the candy. "I do love this stuff. Did you say you came up from Heritage? Nate lives there. Have you talked to him yet? You two need to talk."

"I saw him." He checked the time. Nate was fifteen minutes late now. Looked like another no-show.

"He's a good boy, that Nate. He's a pastor, you know."

Austin clenched his fist. "I know."

A woman in a set of pink scrubs poked her

head through the door. "How are you doing, Mr. Williams?"

"Great. This is my brother, Greg." He motioned to Austin. "We ran a landscaping business together when we were kids. Now my son owns it. He's a good boy. Both my sons are."

Austin offered a half smile to the nurse, and she nodded in understanding. "I bet you're getting tired, Mr. Williams. It's time for a nap, and you were up early this morning."

"I think you're right." He stood and looked around . . . lost.

Austin stood and hugged his dad. "I should get going anyway."

"Good to see you, Greg. Thank you for stopping by."

Austin didn't correct him. He just hugged him a little tighter. "Bye, Dad. See you Wednesday."

His dad wanted him to make peace with Nate. Nate who never showed up when it counted. Nate who left him to handle the family business and his dad's disease alone.

A weight pressed in on Austin's chest as he exited the room and made his way back to his car. He'd spent his life trying to make his father proud, but this time his dad might just be asking too much.

five

Why on earth would people voluntarily sign up for speed dating? Olivia searched the web again for an event listed within driving distance this week. Nothing.

The only one she'd found anywhere near here was more than three weeks away. There was no way she could get the article done in a timely manner. She'd emailed Mr. Lang about the problem this morning, then wavered between the fear of him telling her he didn't care and him telling her to write an article on something worse, like interview the local pastor.

Her computer chimed with an incoming email. Looked like it was time to find out.

To: Olivia Mathews

From: Frank Lang

Subject: RE: Speed-dating problem

Dating article pushed to a late September issue. See following schedule. Right now I'll give you a spot every other

Friday issue, assuming I like what you write. Don't disappoint me.

8/19—Late-summer Michigan flowers

9/2—Free-range chickens

9/16—End of the season at amusement parks

9/30—Modern dating

All articles are due by 5:00 p.m. on date listed.

The guy didn't waste words. And what a strange collection of topics. But what Mr. Lang wanted Mr. Lang got. She scanned the list again and blocked off some time to work on the articles. The one on Michigan flowers would be a snap. And she could almost write about free-range chickens in her sleep. Her parents had kept chickens since she could walk.

She pulled up the speed-dating signup page. Now she needed to find someone to drag along with her to speed dating. She shut her laptop and grabbed her purse as she headed out the door.

"Where are you going?" Her seven-year-old sister, Trinity, stood next to Olivia's car.

"She's probably going to go meet Naaaate," her

brother Caleb taunted from his bike as he stood next to the barn.

Trinity reached for the handle of the car. "I'm coming."

Olivia scooped her up. "Nice try. And no, I'm not going to see Nate. I'm going to see my friend Libby."

"Is she dating Nate?" Trinity hugged Olivia around the neck.

The idea jolted something inside Olivia. Not that she worried about Libby and Nate. But the truth was he'd eventually date someone else, and Olivia didn't know if she could handle watching that.

"No, she's my new roommate." She set Trinity down and slid into the car. She pulled out her day planner and penciled in some more time to work on the articles. She had to make these the best writing she'd ever done. There was no way she could stay in Heritage and watch Nate date and marry someone else.

Olivia waved to her sister as she pulled out of the driveway. Her mind spun with flower ideas until she turned down Henderson Street five minutes later. She edged through the four-way stop at Richard and Henderson and did a double take as she passed Luke's rental. Was that Nate in the bay window?

The buzz around the diner said he'd reported to a brush fire that morning. They had gotten it under control and saved all the nearby structures, but a part of Olivia had been holding her breath until she saw him again—whole, breathing, healthy.

Nate positioned a board above his head and then lifted a cordless drill. He was healthy all right. Even from here she couldn't help but appreciate how that action showed off his wide shoulders.

She hadn't talked to Nate since the day of her interview, and that was probably for the best. She couldn't seem to be around him without wanting to argue her point one more time or cast caution to the wind and kiss him. Especially on days he looked like this.

But it wasn't just his physical appeal that drew her in. He was wise and amazing with her family, and he had a calm confidence that seemed to anchor her. She loved serving alongside him and had actually envisioned building a family with him until he—

Police lights flashed in her rearview mirror, and Olivia glanced at her speed. Zero miles an hour. Had she really stopped in the middle of Henderson Road to check out Nate? She pulled into Luke's driveway and slid out of the car.

Officer Hammond pulled up next to her and rolled his window down. "Good afternoon, Miss Mathews."

"Afternoon, Officer Hammond."

"Always better to pull over before ogling the local pastor."

Olivia's face flamed. "Yes, sir."

"I'll say, my teenage daughters have stopped fighting me about going to church since he showed up. Although I'm not sure their motives are pure. Have a nice day." He chuckled as he rolled up his window and pulled from the curb.

Great, one more for the town gossip. She ran up Luke's porch and knocked.

Libby flung the door open, face red. "I should never have moved here."

Olivia opened her mouth to question her, but Libby disappeared back in the house. "I tried to make friends, be neighborly, but no."

Olivia stepped in and closed the door behind her. "Something happen?"

Libby upended a couch cushion. "First he accused me of being a liar, then he gave me money. Or maybe it was the other way around. Whatever. As if I would manipulate him out of the two dollars and forty-seven cents."

"He?"

She fixed the cushion and then upended another. "Found it." She stood, holding a quarter, then dropped it in a baggie of change. "Why would I want his money? See, I have money." She sealed the baggie and lifted it as if to display it. "I had to dig through junk drawers and seat cushions, but I can pay for my own eggs."

Olivia grabbed the cushion from the floor and

fitted it back in place. "Do you need to borrow some money?"

Libby lifted the bag higher.

"Right, you have money. Got it." Olivia walked into the kitchen and pulled two mugs and a tin of tea from the cupboard. "Let's start at the beginning."

Fifteen minutes later the teacups were empty, and Olivia had heard it all, from Libby's conversation with her mom to the two dollars and forty-seven cents.

"The man just drives me crazy." Libby rubbed her temple. "He really is Mr. Mean Hot Neighbor."

"Because mean people go around offering to pay for people's groceries?"

"Not the point." Libby stared at the baggie of change. "Okay, maybe it is, but he still drives me crazy."

Olivia set down her mug. "Crazy being the key word."

Libby dropped her head back on the chair and laughed. "I was like a possessed woman when you arrived, and over what? Two dollars and some change. What's wrong with me?"

"The Williams men seem to have that effect on women." Olivia gathered the teacups and carried them to the sink. "I still can't believe that Nate's brother moved to town and he never mentioned it to me."

"I just feel like nothing is going how I imagined. I thought I was finally moving forward, you know? But all I've done is move from my parents' house to Luke and Hannah's."

Olivia leaned against the counter. "Next step, roommates. When can we move in?"

"Luke said someone was supposed to give me the key after he fixed something there. But he didn't say who that is or when that'll be."

The image of Nate in the window flashed back to mind. "I've a pretty good idea." Olivia pulled her hair up in a messy bun and secured it with the band on her wrist, then propped her hands on her waist. "You coming or not?"

"Where are we going?"

"To our new place. Grab your baggie of change."

As they passed Austin's place, Olivia snatched the baggie from Libby's hand and ran up the steps. She slid the money into the mail slot and ran back. "Problem number one solved. On to problem number two."

When they arrived at Luke's rental, the door was open. Olivia took the porch steps two at a time and walked in. The key was confidence. She refused to let Nate know she was still hurting.

The place didn't look too bad overall. It needed a good cleaning, and no doubt Luke had plans to update the eighties motif, but for cheap rent, she could live with the dated flowered wallpaper. It was almost retro. Almost.

Olivia moved through the entryway toward the room where she'd seen Nate. He had his back to them and earbuds in his ears. He drove a screw into the hinge of the door frame.

Olivia straightened her back, drew in a slow breath, and plastered what she hoped looked like indifference on her face. "Yo, Nate!"

The drill stopped, and Nate turned around as he pulled out one of the earbuds. His gaze bounced between them before it settled on Libby. "Can I help you?"

Help Libby? Olivia was the one who'd called his name.

"Uh . . ." Libby's face reddened.

Olivia leaned against the wall. Indifference. Indifference. "This is Libby, Luke's sister. When can she move in?"

His face transformed into a genuine smile as he held out his hand. Of course Libby got a genuine smile. His eyes kept drifting to Olivia but never stayed more than a half second. "I think we met at Luke's wedding. But we both met a lot of people that day, so it's nice to meet you again. You're the one with the great idea for the library. Luke asked me to come finish a few things over here so it'd be livable for you."

"I'm not too fussy."

"But you may want stairs." He pointed to the

corner where the frame of the staircase still stood, but the steps were all absent. "It'll be about three weeks. Sorry."

Olivia pushed away from the wall. "But now you have a date and can make a plan."

"I'll drop the key by Luke's place when it's done." Nate set the drill aside, pulled a card from his wallet, and held it out to Libby. "Has my brother contacted you about the library? The town wants you two to work together to come up with a unified plan for the square. I can set up that meeting if you want."

Olivia poked Libby in the shoulder. "Tell him."

Libby's face reddened again as she took the card. "We've met. I'm not sure he wants to work with me."

"I'll talk to him."

"No—"

"He's not angry at you, trust me. This is about him and me, and I'll handle it." He looked at Olivia again and took a hesitant step toward her. "Olivia, can we talk?"

She stepped back and clenched her jaw to keep from saying something stupid—like "yes." She could no longer afford to let him see her heart—it hurt too much. "I think everything that needs to be said has been said."

"You're just throwing away our friendship?"

"Were we friends? Right now I don't even know." The words gutted her as they rolled off her tongue. Of course they had been friends, but if she'd read the relationship wrong, maybe she'd read everything wrong.

Nate winced, then he looked at Libby. "Nice to meet you again."

Olivia waited for Libby to exit, then slammed the door.

Libby stood on the sidewalk, mouth open. "And I thought I was bad at relationships."

"I'm not bad at relationships. He is." Olivia marched back to Luke's in silence. She claimed one of the recliners just before Spitz's nose landed in her lap. She kicked off her shoes, tucked her long legs up under her, and scratched the dog's ears. "What are you going to do with Spitz until Luke and Hannah get back?"

Libby reclined on the couch with Darcy nuzzled into her side. "There's a fence in the backyard at the rental, so I thought I'd take both of the dogs there if that's okay."

"Fine with me." More than fine. Something about petting the dog eased some of the tension inside her. As if Spitz didn't care about the past or the future. He just loved her in the now. In the now, there was no Nate to figure out, no job in Phoenix, and no list of articles to write for a demanding editor.

Some of the tension returned to her shoulders. "How do you feel about speed dating?"

"Excuse me?"

"Speed dating. It's when you meet twenty guys in one night in a round-robin style—"

"I know what it is. I just don't know of anyone who has done it. Is this for that article?"

Olivia dropped her head back and closed her eyes. "Yes. I already hate this assignment and I haven't even started. Will you go with me? It could be our first official monthly girls' night."

"We have a monthly girls' night?"

"We should. Doesn't that sound fun?" Olivia clapped her hands together and offered her best pleading expression. "Please."

"When is it?" Libby pulled out her phone.

"Three weeks." Surely her friend wouldn't have plans that far out.

"Fine, but you owe me. Big-time."

If speed dating was as bad as Olivia imagined it might be, that was an understatement.

She couldn't put this meeting off any longer. Libby pedaled down Henderson Street on Petunia, letting the brisk wind in her face fill her with courage. Many would say sixty degrees was too chilly for a ride, but she always found these days the most satisfying. As if the cold front put the steel in her veins that she needed to face Austin again.

She'd spent the previous weekend researching town squares, libraries, and even moving buildings. She'd not let Austin intimidate her again. They needed a unified plan, and he'd hear her out whether he liked it or not.

Libby pulled into Austin's driveway and stopped her bike behind his truck. Sliding off Petunia, she dropped the kickstand with her foot. But instead of popping into place, it dropped to the ground with a clang. Ugh.

"Petunia! You can't fall apart on me." She eyed the worn basket and chipped purple paint. Petunia had seen better days, but she'd been with Libby through so much. "I'll get that fixed, girl, but first, I must use this courage before I lose it."

She put the kickstand in the basket and laid the bike down, hurried up the porch, and gave three solid knocks. Nothing. He had to be here. His truck was here and she was ready for this conversation. She knocked again. Nothing.

A dog barked in the distance, and Libby followed the sound to the backyard. She peeked over the fence. A small, temporary greenhouse made out of PVC and stretched plastic took up a third of the yard. "Austin?"

Faint country music trailed out from the structure.

She tried again. "Austin."

Shiro's paws landed on the fence opposite Libby as the dog barked in her face. It wasn't an angry bark, but it was loud enough for Libby to jump back and land with a thud on her backside as the music turned off.

"What are you barking at, girl?" Austin's voice grew louder.

Awesome. Him finding her in this position wasn't quite the look of bold confidence she was going for. Maybe if she didn't move he wouldn't know she was here.

His head peeked over. "Libby?"

Or she could look ridiculous lying on the ground by his fence. She jumped to her feet and dusted off her backside. "We need to talk."

The midday sun highlighted his hair, and from here she could almost pretend he was the Mr. Knightley she'd first imagined him to be.

His expression darkened as he shook his head. "No."

But then his winning personality always showed up. Definitely not Mr. Knightley.

"What do you mean, 'no'? You have to talk to me. Nate said the town wants us to come up with a joint plan."

"Your part of the plan was adding the schoolhouse. The rest is my part." He walked toward his back door. "I have to be some-where."

He wasn't getting away that easily. Her courage wouldn't last long, and she needed to get these words out now. Unlatching the gate, she pushed through and followed him to his back door. "It'll only take a minute."

"I don't have a minute. Shiro." He snapped

twice, held the door for his dog, and disappeared into his house.

Ugh!

She followed him in and let the door slam behind her. "Please, Austin."

He stopped and looked back with one eyebrow raised.

Maybe she should have thought twice before following a strange guy into his house for the second time. Her hands began to shake and she shoved them into her pockets. "Why won't you talk to me?"

"You want to talk? Fine. You put me in a no-win situation." He strode through the kitchen, and she followed after him. Another cupboard had been removed since she'd been here.

She maneuvered between two five-gallon buckets of debris and stopped at a makeshift dining room table. Austin dug through some scattered piles of papers, sending a few drifting to the floor.

"The library move puts us so over budget that I'd never make a profit. They said that my profit would be the same, but I'm not sure what the committee was looking at. I don't see how to make this work. So I get to look like the bad guy when I say no. And I'm not lying when I say I have to be somewhere in ten minutes." He paused next to an open laptop, lifted a document, and held it out.

Libby took the paper and skimmed it over. Wow, that was a lot of red at the bottom. "It may have been my idea, but it was their decision—"

"It doesn't matter." Austin reached for his wallet and slid it in the back pocket of his dark jeans. "What does matter is that if we can't get that number to the black, it can't happen. And since your library put it in the red and you want to help so much, maybe you should fix it."

"Gracious of you."

"I aim to please." He grabbed his coat off the chair and picked up his phone.

"I'm pretty sure that isn't true." Libby looked over the numbers for a minute, but it was pointless. She didn't know what half this stuff was, let alone what was worth cutting. "Can I see the plans as they were?"

He sighed, then pointed to the wall behind her. "That's a rough sketch."

Libby examined the fine pencil drawings. This was better but still not helpful enough. Austin stepped up beside her and pointed to the drawing. The musky scent of his aftershave surrounded her. "Here is the square with the gazebo in the center."

Libby pointed to a few marks around the gazebo. "What are these?"

"The committee wants an open feel but a place for the community to gather as well. We already had something in three of the four corners of the square, so they think that adding your library is the answer to the fourth corner."

"But you disagree. Why don't you like the idea of the library?"

"I actually do like the idea. It's more original than anything this town had envisioned." He pulled another drawing from a shelf and unrolled it across the piles of paper. This one had the library incorporated into the square, only he'd placed it in the northwest corner instead of the northeast as she'd envisioned. It was perfect. "I think it's exactly what the square needs. But everyone is underestimating all that's involved."

He checked the time on his phone and picked up his keys. "It involves more than moving a building. We have to hire a contractor for the foundation, get it up to code, and modernize it. I can do some of the work, but we need someone who specializes in this type of work. That's money. Money not in the budget. Not to mention set up a library in it. It isn't me who disagrees, it's all that red that disagrees." He pointed again to the number on the paper in her hand.

Libby leaned over and studied the drawing closer. "What are the other three corners?"

He looked back at his drawing. "A playground in this corner. Then in this corner a fountain. That's the number there." He pointed to a large number in the budget.

"The fountain is the first thing that needs to

go." She held up the budget. "Is this your only copy?"

"No. I have it on my computer. I printed that out to show the committee."

Libby grabbed a pen and drew a black line through the number. "Not only are they a huge expense, but the maintenance is costly."

"That was a request by Mayor Jameson himself."

Libby waved away the concern. "I can take care of that."

"Just how are you going to do that?"

"He's a sentimental man, but he's also a logical man. When he sees the research I'll show him on town fountains, including maintenance cost and the percentage that fall into disrepair within twenty years, I believe he'll agree to cut it." She pulled a notebook from her bag and made a note. "What's in the last corner?"

"Clock tower." He spun his keys in his hand.

"I like that, but where is it on the budget?" She held out the paper and he pointed to the other hefty sum. Just what she was hoping. She drew another black line through that number. "Is this something that could be added later? Say, in a year or two?"

"I suppose so."

"I think if we pitch it right, they'll see the wisdom in waiting on that. If you cut those two, where does that put you on the budget?"

Austin took back the paper and made a few notes on it, then scratched out a few sums. "Close."

Libby looked over the numbers again and pointed to another line. "What's this cost?"

"An assistant for me. This is a big project, and with the building move it just got bigger."

"Nate said he'd do that job." Libby started to draw one more black line through that number.

"No way." Austin pulled the pen from her hand.

"He has experience and is willing to volunteer his time." She reached for the pen again, but he pulled it farther away.

"Of course he would. But he can't follow through with all the commitments he has. He volunteers as the basketball coach, with the fire department, on this committee, at the shelter. Am I missing anything else? He didn't even show up at our dad's yesterday like he promised."

Libby reached again and missed. "I understand you have differences, but you need to let those go for this. If you cut this position, will it balance?"

Austin looked at the paper again. "Yes. But that doesn't matter. The mayor will never agree to cancel both the clock tower and his fountain."

"Okay, here's the deal. I'll work out a foolproof proposal for you to present—"

"Why me?"

"I get nervous in front of people. You draw it up. Just like this one but without the fountain

131

or clock tower. Nate said the committee wanted us to work together to present a plan, and this is what we have. I'll be there, but you have to do the presenting. I'd freeze and that wouldn't help our case. If they agree, then you agree to use Nate."

"And if the committee rejects it?"

"Then the ball is in their court. They asked us to work together to come up with a plan we both agree on." She waved the budget in front of him. "Do we agree on this?"

"Fine, we agree." Austin checked his watch. "And now I'm late."

Libby followed him out his front door and down the steps as he marched to his truck. "I'll drop the proposal by tomorrow so you can look it over before you present it."

"Fine." He slid into the truck, started the engine, and rolled the window down, then checked his mirror. "I can tell you right now they aren't going to give up that fountain."

"Let me worry about that." Libby stepped back from the truck.

Maybe the meeting with Austin hadn't gone as smoothly as she'd hoped, but she'd accomplished her goal. And just in time. Her courage from riding Petunia was just about out.

"Petunia!"

The word was echoed by the sound of twisting and scraping of metal. Austin slammed on the brakes as Libby dashed to the back of his truck. The purple bike was wedged up under the bumper, the center of the frame bent in half.

"You killed Petunia!"

"You laid your bike behind my truck?"

"The kickstand was broken."

"A lot more is broken now."

Libby ran back to Luke's before she had a breakdown right here in front of him. Petunia was dead.

Austin grabbed the bag of gourmet coffee from the kitchen table along with his keys. He checked his reflection one more time in the cracked bathroom mirror. He ran his hand down his shirt and sighed. What was he doing? This wasn't a date. He was simply stopping by to congratulate Libby on a job well done—and get the forms.

He hadn't believed she could do it. But the mayor had given up the fountain and the clock tower without much of a fight. Libby had facts, figures, and testimonies backing up all her points. All he had to do was hand out her proposal and show his drawing, and they all agreed. The girl was a research queen.

He had a hard time balancing the calm, collected Libby who had bandaged his arm and convinced the council with the Libby who had lost her dog and chased him through the parking lot over a couple bucks.

Austin grabbed the baggie of change that he'd found in his mail slot, shoved it in his pocket, and locked the door. He walked across the driveway and up her steps. Barks echoed on the other side of the door as soon as he knocked. How many dogs did she have in there, anyway?

He shifted the coffee from one hand to the other as he eyed the crumpled bike that lay next to the porch. Could he have been more of a jerk? She'd made a dumb choice to lay her bike behind his truck, but he hadn't made it any easier on her. Coffee looked pretty lame next to the crushed bike.

The door opened, the air filling with Libby's laughter. "Olivia, you'll never—" The smile dropped from her face. "Sorry. I thought you were Olivia."

She held both dogs by their collar and wore a yellow checkered apron, a smudge of flour across her nose. Her hair was twisted into a knot on top of her head with two pencils sticking out of it.

She yanked the dogs back. "Darcy! Spitz! Sit."

Both dogs obeyed but stayed alert. Maybe she'd been working with them. Darcy's whole backside wiggled with his tail as if he was using all the self-restraint he possessed. Impressive obedience.

Austin lifted the bag of coffee higher. "I come bearing gifts. Can I come in?"

She snapped her fingers. "Darcy, Spitz, go lie down." With one last look at Austin, they both obeyed.

Libby paused only a moment before she stepped back from the door. Not the most welcoming invitation he'd ever gotten, but he'd take what he could get.

The sweet scent of cookies and the beep of a timer greeted him as he entered. Libby shut the door behind him. "Excuse me. I need to get that."

Austin followed her to a small, quaint kitchen with dark wooden floors and granite countertops. A bowl of batter and a tray lined with rows of cookie dough balls adorned one counter, while three stacks of books topped another. Was she baking or reading? "Did you get back to the store for more groceries?"

Libby pulled a pan of fresh cookies from the oven, causing his stomach to rumble. "No. I did get my account set up at the local bank today, and they said I could make a withdrawal tomorrow. Hannah had flour, sugar, oil, and chocolate chips on hand. Good thing you helped pay for the eggs." Without even a glance his direction, she added the uncooked tray to the oven and set the timer. "Want one?"

"If they're the same kind you gave me, I won't turn it down."

She added one to a plate and handed it to him. The soft cookie nearly crumbled in his hand, and the hot chocolate chips melted on his tongue. This was amazing. And gone all too soon.

His thoughts must have shown on his face, because she dropped another cookie on his plate.

"I didn't come to eat all your cookies."

She shrugged but didn't look at him. "I stress-bake. I prefer you eat them. Otherwise I'll stress-eat too."

"What are you stressed about? I thought you'd be thrilled that the plans passed." He picked up a copy of *Wuthering Heights* that was being held open by a wooden spoon.

"I was. I am. It's just I have a lot to plan when it comes to the library. The board just sent a whole file of forms they need me to complete by Friday. After two pages I started making cookies. Why are you here again?" Her voice held a slight edge.

He replaced the book and offered her his best smile. "Forgive me, where are my manners?"

"I've been wondering that since I met you."

He leaned back against the counter and grabbed another cookie. "I'm not *always* rude."

"You're right. You were quite charming when you were bleeding and needed my help."

She wasn't going to make this easy.

Austin held out his hand. "Let's start all over. Hello, I'm new in town. My name is Austin Williams. I'm the landscape architect for the square and will be working with you since the library is now a part of that plan."

The moment of truth. She hesitated, then after wiping her hands on a towel, she took his hand. "Libby Kingsley, librarian."

A smile touched the edge of her pink lips as her sapphire-blue eyes softened. She was beautiful; he'd give her that.

When she turned back to the stove, Austin rubbed his palms together, doing his best to erase the memory of her soft skin. He wasn't here to flirt. "I'm here because I was able to get a company scheduled to move the library in just two and a half weeks. I know that may sound like a lot of time, but when you're talking about moving a building, it's not. There is a lot of prep work that needs to be done. We hired a local contractor who was between jobs, so he's ready to start work tomorrow. That means I need those forms tonight." He pointed to the forms she'd abandoned to make the cookies.

"Two and a half weeks?" She picked up a cookie and took a bite. "Tonight?" She shoved the rest of the cookie in her mouth, reached for another, then paced toward the window.

"I've worked with them before. It will be fine." He moved the plate of cookies to the island. "They had a project fall through and think this is easy enough to put in its place. It's either that or they can't fit us in until late October if the weather holds. If not, then not until next season. But they're willing to rush this job for the publicity it'll bring."

"And now you need the forms tonight?" Libby walked back and reached for another cookie where the plate had been. "Did you move my cookies?"

"Yes. You said you don't want to stress-eat." He shrugged and held the plate out to her.

She shook her head. "No, you're right. I just thought I'd have more time. What do you need?"

"The contractor thinks we can tap into the water and sewer that used to lead to the Manor so we won't have to tear up the street." Austin flipped through the forms and then pulled out a page. "So this one should be easy."

Libby plopped back into the chair, flipped through the stack of triplicate forms, then dropped her head in her hands. "That only leaves twenty more."

He sat in a chair across from her. "What can I do to help?"

"Where do I begin?" She took the pile of forms and spread them out on the table, then slid one closer to him. "It wants to know the layout, where I want the outlets, the lights . . . How would I know where I want the lights? What if I choose to put the outlets along one wall now but then want them along a different wall after it's set up?"

Austin lifted the paper and began to read it through.

"I'm not good at this type of thing." Libby

grabbed a cookie and shoved it into her mouth, then lifted an eyebrow in his direction as if daring him to try to take her chocolate again.

He held up his hands in defense, then reached for the pencil and snagged another cookie for himself. "Let me help. Layout and design are kind of my thing. What do you have so far?"

She stood and pulled a binder off the desk, then set it in front of him. He flipped it open to a color-coded tab system. Talk about organization. This was the Libby who had convinced the board. This was the Libby he could work with.

For the next hour, they detailed everything from outlets to facilities. Libby was a machine once she set to work on something. She'd moved her chair closer and closer as she pored over each form with him.

"I think that about covers it." Austin slid the last form into the file and shut her binder. "You're so detail oriented, I should have you take over the financial records."

"Would those financial records be the ones covering your dining room table?"

Austin's cheeks warmed. "Maybe."

"I would love that." Libby clapped her hands as if he'd offered her a puppy. "I love spreadsheets. And those piles have given me nightmares."

"Are you serious?" Austin reached for the last cookie and popped it in his mouth.

"Absolutely." She looked over at him with a smile, then froze. It was as if she hadn't realized how close she'd moved.

He'd noticed.

He'd noticed the way her nose wrinkled every time she mulled over a problem in her mind. He'd noticed the way her blonde hair, which smelled like mango, refused to all stay up in that bun-twist thing. He'd even noticed that every time she loved an idea she'd bite her bottom lip. Like right now.

He'd noticed way too much. He broke eye contact and stood. "Why can't you talk in front of groups?"

Libby shrugged as she stood and put the binder on the desk. "I'm always afraid I'll say the wrong thing. I get tongue-tied around strangers."

"I'm a stranger. Or I was one." Austin slid his chair in and tucked the file under his arm. "You never seemed to hesitate sharing what was on your mind with me. You're one of the bravest people I know."

She leaned against the wall and looked down. "The first time I talked to you—"

"You mean the first time I yelled at you."

"Right. I didn't say much then. In fact, it took all my courage to bring the cookies back, and I think then my emergency response took over. How is your arm?"

"You tell me, Doctor." Austin pulled up the

sleeve of his T-shirt and turned his back to her. "It was sore for a few days, but it feels much better."

"You still have the butterfly strips on there?"

He shrugged. "The gauze didn't last beyond the first shower, but these have stuck pretty well."

"These need to come off." Her fingernails began picking at one of the edges of the bandage.

"Ouch. Stop that." He pulled his arm away.

"Don't be a baby. It's been a week." She grabbed his arm with her left hand and picked at one of the bandages with her right.

"I'm not being a baby." He couldn't keep the laughter from following his words as he surrendered to her hand. "Let me rip out your arm hair and see what you do."

Her touch was more gentle this time. That was worse, so much worse. He clenched his hands at his sides.

"You barely have any arm hair back here." She ripped the second one free. "All done. Just some residue."

She rubbed at it with her thumb and he grabbed her hand. When she stared at it, he dropped it. "Sorry. I'm a little ticklish."

Not really. But it was better than saying, "If you keep touching me like that, I'm bound to kiss you before I leave this house."

"I should go." Austin turned toward the door.

"I have a lot to do if we're going to be ready to move this building in under three weeks. We have a lot to accomplish before then."

As they approached the door, the dogs jumped up and Libby held them back.

He stepped out on the porch and pointed to Otis in the distance. "Is it just me or is it weird that the hippo moves around town?"

"Weird? Maybe. But likeable. And his name is Otis. Not *the hippo*."

He spun his keys on his finger. "I'll keep that in mind. Let me know if you need anything else."

"Nate's helping you, right?"

"Yup." He paused on the porch. "Now you've talked to my brother."

Libby squeezed out the door, leaving the dogs whimpering on the other side. "Briefly, but I haven't seen him walk on water yet. Then again, I barely know him after one conversation. Maybe walking on water will happen next time." She sent him a teasing grin but then sobered. "I did hear that he responded to a 911 call on Thursday morning. Isn't that when you said he bailed on you?"

He nodded as Libby offered a small smile and disappeared back inside. So, Nate did have a good excuse.

He pulled the baggie of change from his pocket and balanced it on the doorknob.

He had to be careful. The last thing he needed to do here was to lose his head or his heart. He had a job to do and a lot to get done in just seventeen days.

six

The library was set to be in place tomorrow, and Libby was way behind schedule. She opened the cover of the next book. It had been thirty years since this book had left these walls, and by the look of the cover, it wouldn't be a hot item once the library reopened. She ran the dusting rag over it and coughed.

She'd spent countless hours logging books, cleaning books, and boxing books, but it never seemed to end. Not to mention she'd squeezed in two trips to see Hannah and Luke and spent many hours researching the best antiques for the library. She had a small line item in the budget for the library's interior. Which meant she could afford one or two authentic pieces, but mostly she'd depend on secondhand finds.

She set the rag aside and scanned the book's cover with her phone. The phone beeped its recognition, and Libby compared the information to the book before adding it to the box. A few of the covers had been too old to be recognized, but overall the app had saved her a ton of data-entry time. She grabbed the next book on the shelf and paused. *The Hiding Place* by Corrie ten Boom. Why did that name sound familiar?

She pulled up the message from her mom.

Never be afraid to trust an unknown
future to a known God. — Corrie ten
Boom

Maybe she'd read this one before she shelved it.

"Knock knock." Olivia's face appeared around the door. A sneer replaced her bright smile. "You know, I never get used to how gross this room is. I always think, 'It's not *that* bad,' then I'm here and it's *that* bad . . . and worse. Anyway, I got all my stuff settled. You sure you don't need help hauling anything else over from Luke's to *our new place?* I don't get tired of saying that."

Libby wiped the dust off *The Hiding Place* and stood. "That's all I have until my parents arrive tonight."

"Right. I can't wait to meet them. We're still on for the speed dating Saturday, right?"

"I'm so behind on getting this boxed up, and the schoolhouse is being moved tomorrow." Libby grabbed her bag from the desk and slid the book inside. "There is a lot that needs to be done."

"Oh no. You aren't getting out of this." Olivia wiped off the top of a metal military surplus desk and sat on top. "You promised, and I already registered us."

"Fine. Fine. You win." Libby returned to the shelf and wiped down the next book. She scanned the cover and pressed her hand under her nose to keep a sneeze back. "But you owe me, and I look forward to claiming that. Like helping me move all these boxes to the library."

Olivia shrugged and leaned back on her hands. "My brother Gideon and his friends will do it."

"You have a brother?"

"Two, actually, and four sisters. I'm second behind Janie."

Libby paused her stacking. "There are seven of you?"

"Yup. The Mathews tribe." Olivia pushed off the desk and dusted off her backside. "And there are four of you?"

"Yes. Myself, Luke, and my twin brothers, Logan and Liam. They're both finishing up their last semester in college, so I don't talk to them much these days." Libby added the book in her hand to the box, then stood and brushed some of the dust from her pants. "When does Janie get back?"

"She got back two weeks ago. But they have been crazy busy trying to get everything going at the diner, and today she's visiting our grandmother up north. Anyway, I totally can get Gideon and his friends to help, but I thought you might want to ask Mr. Mean Hot Neighbor." Olivia wiggled her eyebrows. "Don't think I haven't noticed the flirting."

"What? I haven't said more than two words to him since he dropped off the financials at my place two weeks ago." She grabbed the next book in the lineup. Wait, had she scanned the last one? She scrolled through the data on the app. Yes, it was there. "We are coworkers. That's all."

Olivia picked up a book next to her and flipped through the pages. "Whatever. When he walked into the diner Friday, he searched the room for you. I could tell. And after he nodded hello across the room, you grinned for the next hour."

"I was enjoying my work." Had he really searched the diner for her?

"You were on your computer making that crazy spreadsheet. Even you aren't that big of a nerd. You like him. Admit it."

"Okay, here's the deal. I'll do this speed-dating thing, but you have to stop talking about—"

"Anyone here?" The deep voice followed by a knock echoed through the room just before Austin's face appeared around the door, his hands shoved deep in his pockets and his expression guarded.

She tried to think, to speak, but Olivia's words "You like him" kept looping through her mind. Like one of those annoying GIFs.

"And how are you, Austin?" Olivia stood and grabbed her purse.

Austin turned his attention to Olivia, and Libby closed her eyes to clear her head. But when she opened them, faded jeans and a snug navy T-shirt sent her pulse to rapid-fire once more. The guy looked ready for a photo shoot, and she probably looked like she'd spent the day in an attic.

"Catch you later, Libby." Olivia waved and offered a knowing smile just before she disappeared out the door.

Libby tucked a strand of her hair behind her ear but stopped herself before reaching for the mirror in her purse to make sure she didn't have a smudge of dust across her face. She refused to be one of those girls who fidgeted every time a cute guy came around.

Austin navigated the piles of books while he strolled around the room as if hanging out in this dungeon-library was something he did every day. "You weren't kidding when you said you needed a new location. This is . . . bad. Well, the schoolhouse is set to move tomorrow, and you should be able to get this stuff moved in there in a couple of weeks." He bent over and started scanning the titles of the books. "Can you let me into the heritage room that Hannah created? The mayor thought seeing some of the history would give me a better perspective on the town as I consider what plants to order."

"Of course." Libby reached for her keys. See? Coworkers. And since they were coworkers, maybe he could help her out too. "There are some antiques in Grand Haven that I'd like to pick up, but my car won't be big enough. Could you by chance go with me to get them? We could probably do it in an afternoon."

A smile tugged at the corner of his mouth. "Sure."

"Great." Libby sorted through her keys twice before she stopped on the one for the heritage room. She took a step toward the door, but he stood in the path—not that he had a lot of options for where to stand. She stopped in front of him and pointed to the door behind him. "Uh, I need to go there."

"Oh, sorry." He tried to step to the side, but there were piles of books everywhere.

She angled her body and squeezed past him. "No problem."

"Thanks for taking time to do this." His voice was much lower than it had been a minute before. The musky scent she remembered from the night they'd worked on the forms tickled her nose, and she found herself breathing a bit deeper.

"It's my job." Libby's voice wavered as she unlocked the door and darted through it. Why did she suddenly have to be so aware of him? It was all Olivia's fault. Her and her dumb suggestions.

Austin's gaze paused on her. "Libby, I was wondering if—"

Her phone pinged with a voicemail and she jumped. That was odd. She hadn't even heard it ring. "The cell service isn't great down here. Another reason the library needed to be moved."

A text popped up on the screen.

Luke
Hannah is having trouble. They're considering an emergency C-section. Nate is leaving in ten minutes. Be at my house if you want to ride with him. I'll call you when I know anything. Pray.

Emergency C-section? Libby's pulse sped up as she took in the time. That gave her seven minutes to get home or she'd miss the ride. She could drive herself, but she hated driving when she was stressed.

She shoved her phone back in her bag and ran for the door. "I've got to go."

"Is everything okay?"

She reached over, pulled an old journal of sorts from the shelf, and handed it to him. "Maybe this will have info on plants. I can get you back in later." She grabbed his arm and pulled him through the door before slamming it. Her fingers shook, and she couldn't even get the key in.

"Here. Let me." Austin took the keys and locked the door before handing them back. "What happened? Tell me how I can help."

"You can't. I'm fine. I just need to go." Libby took the stairs two at a time. This wasn't an attractive image to leave him with. But she couldn't think about that now. Luke needed her, and that was what moving here was all about.

Austin jolted upright with the chime of his phone. Had he slept through his alarm? He squinted at the clock—5:15 a.m. He hadn't slept through it. Who could that be at this hour?

He reached for his phone and hit Answer. "This is—" He shifted the receiver away from his mouth and cleared his throat, then tried again. "This is Austin."

"Mr. Williams, this is Charlene at Reflections Care Home."

He sat straight up. "Is my father all right?"

"He's stable, but there was a situation—"

"What kind of situation?" He stood and reached for a clean shirt.

"Please stay calm. He's in good hands. We deal with this type of thing all the time. He had an episode where he became confused and a little violent. But—"

"Violent?" Austin slipped the shirt over his head and grabbed the jeans he'd discarded on the floor yesterday. He'd never seen his father violent a day in his life. He'd even left the spanking to Austin's mom.

"This is not uncommon. The confusion can cause unusual behavior."

"But you said he's stable?" He wedged the

phone between his ear and his shoulder as he yanked on his pants and grabbed a clean pair of socks.

"Yes. The doctor on call prescribed a slight sedative, and he's currently sleeping."

"Okay." He dropped into a sitting position on the bed. Maybe he had time for a shower.

"He also reviewed your father's chart and, because of your father's age, wants to try more aggressive medication."

He stood and started finding cleaner clothes. "What does that mean?"

"The doctor would like to go over all this with you before he leaves. Would you be able to get here before seven a.m.?"

Austin checked the time again. He was supposed to be at the site by 7:30. But Nate had agreed to be at the site too, so maybe it was time to start putting some faith in his brother. After all, Nate had been at every meeting without fail.

"Mr. Williams?"

Austin checked the time on his phone again. "I'll be there in about forty minutes."

He ended the conversation and hit Nate's number. Voicemail. Hopefully that meant he was already up and in the shower. He left a quick rundown of events as he made his way to the kitchen, started the coffee maker, and let Shiro out the back door.

The journal Libby had given him yesterday still

sat on his table. He'd never seen her so flustered. He'd have asked her out if her phone hadn't interrupted them. He still hadn't figured out if the interruption had been a blessing or not. He had no business confusing their relationship, no matter how much she'd consumed his thoughts the past two weeks.

Ten minutes later he'd showered and returned to find a full pot of fresh coffee. He poured it into a travel mug and let the aroma awaken his senses. He took a scalding gulp and then checked his phone.

Missed call from Nate. He must have called back when Austin was in the shower.

He opened the door for Shiro and then dropped a scoop of food into her bowl. He knelt in front of her and scratched her ears. "I'll try to stop by for lunch."

He snagged his keys from the table and ran to the door, then paused halfway down the steps. The brass hippo was back, but this time it sat right in front of Libby's place—no, her brother's place. He shook his head and pushed Play on the voicemail as he dashed to his truck.

"Hey, Austin, this is Nate. It doesn't look like I'll be able to be there for the move. An emergency—"

Austin dropped the phone from his ear and hit Delete. Of course not. When push came to shove, Austin was left taking care of everything. Now he had only an hour to get to the care home and back if he wanted to be at the move on time.

As a pastor, he'd done this countless times, but it never got any easier. Nate slipped his coins in the coffee vending machine and jabbed at the buttons. The scent of the rich brew offered the promise of a good cup of coffee. It was a lie. This was his third cup, but he kept coming back. A glutton for punishment. He added more coins and watched another cup fill.

He picked up his phone and eyed the screen before shoving it back in his pocket and grabbing the other cup. Still no calls from Austin. Nate was supposed to help with the move today, and with the message Austin had left about their dad, he needed to be in Heritage. But with Hannah in emergency surgery, leaving wasn't an option either.

He'd called Austin and left a voicemail, but he had little doubt his brother wouldn't bother listening beyond "I can't make it today."

Just when he thought a crack was opening.

He wandered back into the waiting area of the third floor. Libby stood in front of a floor-to-ceiling window, looking out at the gray sky, her posture stiff as she hugged her body. Stepping up next to her, he offered one of the cups of coffee. "Any news?"

She accepted the coffee and shook her head.

Nate scanned the room. "Where's the rest of your family?"

"My brothers went to find food and my parents went to pray in the chapel." Her voice hitched on the word "pray."

"You didn't want to go with them?"

She shrugged. "I thought someone should be here in case Luke comes out with some news."

"I can wait if you want to go."

She spun the cup in her hands, took a sip, and then returned to spinning it. "I'll leave praying to them. God and I aren't on speaking terms." Her face flushed slightly, and when he didn't say anything, she cast him a glance. "What? No sermons about how I need to believe or have faith, or if I don't feel close to God then I'm the one who moved?"

Nate let out a chuckle. "We do like our catchphrases in the church, don't we?"

"But you aren't going to offer me one now?" She blew on the cup, then took another sip.

Nate shrugged and leaned against the window. A few of the trees in the distance were just showing the start of autumn. "Seems like you've heard most of them. And if I gave you another, would it make a difference?"

"No."

"Then I won't."

She studied him. "You're different from a lot of pastors I've met."

He rubbed the tattoo that peeked out his collar. "So I've heard."

She swallowed and shifted her gaze back out the window.

Nate took a long gulp of coffee. Often people wanted to say more. They just needed time and space to do so.

"Luke asked me to pray. My mom asked me to pray. Do you think this all happened because I didn't?"

Nate downed the last of his coffee, letting the bitterness roll over his tongue. He crushed the cup in his hand and pitched it toward the trash. "I know prayer works. But I also know God's answer isn't always what we want or expect."

"You think this would have happened whether I prayed or not?"

"In the words of Aslan, we will never know what could have been, only what still can be. Or something like that."

"*Prince Caspian.*"

"One of my favorites." Nate shoved his hands in his pockets. "I probably shouldn't misquote books around a librarian."

Libby laughed but kept her eyes fixed out the window. "It was close."

"I saw you reading *The Hiding Place.*"

"Have you read it?" Her face lit up for the first time.

"Years ago. Powerful story."

"That's what I hear." She pulled the book from her purse and ran her fingers over the cover. "I'm only a few chapters in, and although being the first woman to be a licensed watchmaker in Holland is impressive, she seems to live a pretty average life."

"You don't know the story?"

She held up her hand and slipped the book back into her purse. "No spoilers. I started reading it because my mother gave me a quote by her about fear, but so far in the story, she hasn't had too much to be afraid of."

"You'll have to tell me how you feel about that normal life after you finish the book."

"It's a boy!" Luke burst into the room still wearing blue scrubs made of paper. He pulled the cap off his head. "Hannah is through surgery and stable, but she lost a lot of blood, so she'll stay in recovery awhile. They had to do a full hysterectomy, but she's out of the woods and the baby is healthy."

A variety of emotions played across Luke's face as he delivered the words. Joy. Relief. Grief.

Luke had once told Nate that he longed for the big family he'd been deprived of as a kid. Funny how plans change in one second.

Libby's parents walked into the room, and everyone started talking at once.

Luke waved his hand and cut in. "He's just three pounds and two ounces."

His mother's hand covered her face. "So tiny."

"You can't go in to see him yet, but there is a window on the NICU, and they said they'd have him by the window for a few minutes." He pointed down the hall.

When everyone left to find the nursery, Luke gripped Nate's shoulder. "Thanks for coming, man. And thanks for bringing Libby. You're like a brother to me—it means a lot that you're here."

Nate's heart tripped at the word "brother." Maybe God's answer for a restored family wouldn't be through Austin. The idea tore at him. But the fact that Luke, who a year ago had no family to speak of and then was blessed with three siblings all at once, would share that title with him settled into the ache of his soul.

He swallowed back the rising emotion and offered Luke a quick hug. "No worries, man. Of course I'm here for you."

"I need you to watch out for Libby. She's new in town and doesn't know a lot of people. Just stop by every few days to make sure she's fine."

"Of course." That would be easy.

"Luke, there you are. How's Hannah?" Caroline said as she and Grant rushed into the waiting room.

Luke offered each a hug. "She's doing well, and so is our son."

"A boy." Caroline's hands flew to her face. "What's his name?"

"Joseph Chet." Luke slipped the cap back on. "I'm going to check on Hannah."

"Hey, Nate, is Austin here too?" Grant glanced around the waiting room.

"No."

"Right. I guess he doesn't know Hannah and Luke." Caroline brushed a strand of her long red hair behind her ear. "We know all of you so well, I have a hard time remembering that we aren't all one big happy family. How is Austin?"

"They're supposed to be moving the school-house today. And I was supposed to be there." He offered her a pointed look. "How do you think he is?"

She laid her hand on his arm. "He'll understand."

Nate shook his head. "If he lets me explain. Listening isn't always his strong suit."

Libby breezed into the room, face aglow. "That baby has stolen my heart." She scanned the group and paused on Grant. "You're the one who helped Austin move in."

Grant nodded. "That's me."

Caroline held out her hand. "I'm Caroline, Nate's cousin and longtime friend of Hannah, and this is my husband, Grant."

"It's nice to meet you." Libby shook her hand.

Nate checked his phone again. "Have you heard from Austin about the move today?"

Libby's face went slightly pink. "I haven't seen him since yesterday in the library."

"Oh, was he helping you move all those books?" Caroline asked.

"No, he just stopped to see the heritage room. And to ask me . . . I don't know, we got interrupted." Libby's eyes darted from person to person. "Not interrupted like that. I just meant he was about to ask me something—you know what, never mind. So, you're Nate's cousin."

Grant peered over Libby's head, behind him, then back at Nate. "Where did you get the coffee?"

"Around the corner." He motioned to the left.

Libby sighed as if thankful the focus was off her, but he could tell by Caroline's expression that her wheels were still turning.

Austin and Libby? Nate didn't see it. She was too nice for him. Caroline was way off on this one. Then again, she thought he should be with Olivia.

"Do you need to get back, Nate?" Libby looked at her watch.

He checked the time on his phone. "Unfortunately, I do."

Libby picked up her purse. "It was nice meeting you, Caroline."

"Nice to meet you. And I didn't mean to embarrass you. We just think Nate and Austin are the best and want to see them happy."

"I'm happy." His voice came out flat.

"Nate here refuses to date anyone."

"I went on a date." The one date with Olivia. But that was before his life had shifted. Now they were barely talking, not that he'd seen her much the past couple weeks. Probably out on her research dates. Why had she agreed to do that stupid assignment anyway?

Nate's hand clamped down on his keys, the metal biting into his palm.

He glanced back at everyone. They were all staring at him. Even Grant, who had returned with a steaming cup of coffee. He'd missed something. Shoot.

"Libby, your stuff." Her dad, Len, hurried into the room, his gray hair in disarray, testifying to his long, sleepless night.

All attention shifted to Len, and Nate let out a breath he hadn't realized he'd been holding.

"We were already on the road to your house when we got the call to come here. Your stuff is in our car. Your mom wants to stay here for a few days."

"We brought the church van; we can put it all in there." Nate spun the keys on his finger. "And I can help her unload it."

"Great. That would be a huge help." Len patted his pocket, then paused. "Ann has the keys. And she is still cooing over that baby. Let me run and grab them from her."

"We'll follow you back to get a glimpse of Joseph," Caroline said as she and Grant followed Len out.

Libby picked up her purse. "Olivia will be there to help us unpack."

"Olivia?" Nate choked on the word and then cleared his throat.

"She's my new roommate." Libby watched his reaction. No doubt the girls had talked. Awesome.

He forced a smile.

"She and I are going speed dating together tomorrow."

Speed dating? All the ways this could go wrong flipped through Nate's mind. She could meet a stalker, a psychopath, or even a Green Bay Packers fan. "Where is this speed dating happening?"

"I'm not sure. Olivia has all that information. But I can text you the details. If you want me to, that is. Who knows, maybe there's room for one more."

"I'd appreciate that." He hated the idea of speed dating, but he needed to talk to Olivia. And from what he understood of speed dating, he'd get a few minutes with her, even if it cost him an evening and his dignity.

seven

Other than the minor roof damage, the move had gone smoother than expected—even without Nate. And a new roof for a building that size was a small price to pay, considering all that could have gone wrong. Now Austin wanted to just put his feet up and watch football. But if he was going to continue getting cheap rent, he needed to keep up with his end of the bargain with the mayor. He placed his hand on his back and stretched against the pain. Besides, keeping busy would help him keep a certain blonde out of his head.

Who was he kidding? He'd buried himself in work for the past two weeks, and it hadn't done much good. He'd finally given in to the impulse to go see her yesterday, only to have her disappear without much of an explanation.

Her car had been in her driveway all day. He'd stopped by both houses, but she hadn't answered either door when he knocked.

Austin ran a box cutter across the length of the linoleum and then pulled at the exposed edge. A popping filled the air as the glue released. He rolled up the worn material, lifted it to his shoulder, and carried it out on the porch. A large dumpster had been dropped off yesterday. It took up half of his front yard and was quite the eyesore, but it made the demolition easier.

Nate's church van was backed up in Libby's driveway with the back doors open. Libby walked out of the house, and Austin stepped back into the shadows. No reason to look like he'd been waiting for her. Then again, if she did spot him here, he just looked like a creeper. Maybe he should see if she needed help.

Her blonde hair was in a loose knot at the back of her head. She had on the same fitted jeans she'd been wearing at the library yesterday, but now with an oversize sweatshirt that said "Canton Football." The muscle in Austin's jaw tightened. There was only one other person in this town who had been on his alma mater's football team.

Nate exited the house, pulled a box from the van, and handed it to Libby before shutting the van door. She disappeared inside and then returned and stood with Nate on the porch.

Austin's stomach churned. He couldn't hear what they said, but Libby reached up and offered a hug to Nate. Awesome.

He stepped out of the shadows. "It must have been some emergency." The words were out of his mouth before he could debate the wisdom of them.

Libby and Nate spun toward him. Libby's eyes widened when they landed on him. Hadn't she said she barely knew his brother? Didn't look that way to him.

Nate was off the porch first. "Austin, I just got back. I called, but—"

"It's handled. The building's all moved." He pointed to the new addition across the street. "And Dad's crisis is averted without you. Again. Besides, I can see you were busy. Don't let me interrupt." Austin dropped the linoleum in the dumpster with a bang and turned back toward the house.

"Hey." Nate stormed across the grass. "Nothing is going on here. I helped her move in. End of story. And we don't appreciate you insinuating otherwise."

Libby, her face crimson, caught up to Nate and placed her hand on his arm. She leaned toward him and again said something Austin couldn't hear. So, she *did* prefer his brother. Just like everyone else. Not a big surprise.

"—an apology." Nate's words broke into his thoughts.

He hadn't caught them all, but he could guess. Maybe what he said was harsh, but her and Nate? Really? Couldn't she be interested in someone else? Anyone else?

"Sorry." He locked eyes with Libby when he said it. He wasn't that sorry to Nate. "When you get back to doing that job of yours, I need to get back in that room. The agricultural journal from a farmer in 1894, although fascinating, didn't help."

He'd meant the last line in humor, but his tone fell flat. Guess this new little development was still too raw.

"Sure thing." Her words were tight, but they softened as she turned to Nate. "Thanks again for everything. I'll wash this and get it back to you."

As soon as she disappeared into her house, Nate rounded on him. "Leave her alone, Austin, or you'll have me to deal with."

"What if I don't want to leave her alone?"

Where had that come from? His whole plan had been to leave her alone. Leave everyone alone, do his job, and get out.

The scar above Nate's left eyebrow reddened. "No. She's off-limits. I'm serious."

"What?"

Nate crossed his arms and lifted his chin. "I told her brother I'd watch out for her until he got back, and this is me watching out for her."

A silver Toyota pulled into the driveway next to the van, and Libby's friend from the library got out. What was her name again? When she rounded the car and caught sight of Nate, the temperature cooled about ten degrees. "What are you doing here?"

The anger drained from Nate's face. "I was helping Libby move in."

"Of course you were." Hurt flashed in her face before she disappeared into the house.

Whoa. She seemed to be angrier at his brother than he was. He liked her better already.

"Olivia is off-limits too." Nate's words came out like a slap.

"Did you promise her brother too?" He crossed his arms, mimicking his brother's stance. "Who made you the guardian of this town? I'm pretty sure I remember a day that I had to warn girls away from you."

"Things are different." A muscle twitched in Nate's jaw.

"Yeah, well . . ." Austin nodded toward the girls' house. "It appears some things aren't. How many girls do you need following after you, Nate?"

Nate's face reddened as his hands clenched into fists.

Austin took a step toward him, spreading his arms out. "Go ahead, Pastor Nate. Punch me. Let the town see who you are."

Nate's eyes closed a minute before he let out a deep breath through his nose. "I'm not that guy anymore, Austin." With that, he stomped toward his van.

Austin's phone rang and he grabbed it up without bothering to look at the display. "Hello?"

"Don't you sound friendly." Grant's voice carried over the line.

Austin cast a final look toward Libby's house before returning to his. "It's been a day, that's for sure."

"Let me guess. It has something to do with Nate, a library move, and a cute blonde who lives next door."

Austin shut the door behind him and froze. Nate driving him crazy was an easy guess, but he hadn't told Grant about the library or anything about Libby.

When Grant's chuckle carried over the line, Austin dropped into his recliner, letting his head fall back. "Spill."

"We met her at the hospital today."

"Hospital?" Austin's heart sped up as the volume in his voice rose.

"Relax, dude. It was Luke and Hannah, Caroline's friends, your other neighbors. Anyway, they were having a baby and ended up in emergency C-section, but all is fine now."

That was why she'd sprinted out of the library yesterday. And why Nate was with her tonight.

Austin ran his fingers through his hair. He *was* a jerk.

It didn't matter. He'd seen the look on Libby's face—a look he'd seen on many people's faces. She'd succumbed to Nate's charms. Now in her eyes, Austin would always be the lesser brother.

"Caroline wants to know if you're going to ask her out."

"Ask out Libby?" She had to be kidding.

"Yes, Libby."

"Absolutely not." He'd be lucky if she'd still work with him. Besides, it was probably only a matter of days before she was dating his brother.

What she wouldn't give to be home curled up on the couch, watching Netflix. Olivia stirred her pop with her straw, scanned the Pine Top Lounge for potential dates, and sighed. Who was she kidding? She'd rather be getting a tooth pulled than be here speed dating.

But instead, she was here researching an article she didn't care about to get print time in a paper she didn't read. All with the slim hope they'd give her another shot at the job in Phoenix.

Could she really live that far away? Olivia shook her head and tried to realign her thoughts. Of course she could. In Phoenix, she'd have a job at a real paper and could write articles that might change the world. Maybe this article wouldn't change the world. But it'd open the door to one that would. And give her the needed space to get over Nate.

"Earth to Olivia." Libby nudged her shoulder. "You got me into this. No daydreaming in la-la land and leaving me to deal with Mr. Toupee and the creepy leer guy by myself."

"Sorry." Olivia shook Nate out of her mind and focused on the here and now. From what she could tell, the guys appeared put together. Nicely dressed—most of them. A few almost cute. Then again, the lights were pretty dim.

Shifting positions on the black bar stool, Olivia leaned toward Libby. "It looks like they do karaoke on Thursdays. We should come."

Libby's freckled nose twisted. "Absolutely not."

"What?" Olivia tapped the table. "I've heard you sing in the shower. You'd be great."

"One, I don't do the stage. Two, I don't sing in public. And three, I'll never do karaoke." Libby raised a finger with each point she made.

A man paused at their table and looked them up and down with dark, hooded eyes. He leaned on the table with his elbow, drawing attention to the chest hair that escaped his shirt where the top three buttons were undone. "Evening, ladies. Are you here for the speed dating?"

A shiver crawled up Olivia's spine. "Yes."

"I look forward to getting to know you and your hot selves in a few minutes." He offered a weird pointing gesture and then moved on to the next table.

Libby held up a fourth finger. "I'll never do speed dating again."

"Agreed. Sorry." Olivia finished the last of her Coke and searched for a waiter, but not one was around. She eyed her watch. They still had a few minutes.

Libby stabbed the remaining ice in her glass

with her straw. "Have you read *The Hiding Place* by Corrie ten Boom?"

"In high school. My youth group read it together." Olivia gave up on finding a waiter and pushed the empty glass aside. "Why?"

"I'm reading it. I'm not quite halfway through." Libby tapped at the empty glass with her nails. "So far it isn't what I expected."

"How's that?"

"Everyone talks about Corrie's great faith, but it seems to me it was her sister Betsie who had the great faith. Corrie seems so . . ."

"Normal?"

"Yes."

Olivia searched her memory for the details of the story. "I think when she—"

Libby held up her hand. "No spoilers. They just started hiding Jews. Don't get me wrong. That's brave, but it's her sister whose faith never seems to waver."

"Maybe that's why so many people are inspired by her story. More people can identify with a faith that isn't perfect." Her mind floated to Nate. How could he think she was looking for a perfect guy?

Before Olivia could say more, a lady approached a microphone and began directing people to their tables. Olivia found her table with a bold number fourteen on it and took her seat. Luckily, Libby was at table number fifteen, so at least they both had backup. She sent her friend an encouraging smile. She was here for research, but maybe they'd each find someone special tonight.

Her heart hammered as a man wearing a short-sleeved dress shirt with a blue tie took the seat opposite her. His dark hair was combed to the left, and his square glasses appeared too large for his face. "Hello, my name is Peter. I live in my parents' basement. My favorite thing to do is role-play Lord of the Rings with my friends."

Then again, maybe this was going to be a very long night.

After the first hour and a half, she'd met a gambler, an over-the-top Red Wings fan, and a guy who had her reaching for the hand sanitizer. There had been a few possibilities in the mix, but none measured up to Nate.

Ugh. She chastised herself for making the comparison.

She made a few notes for the article as the chair squeaked when the next guy took his seat. She fixed a practiced smile on her face and lifted her head. Nate.

"What are you doing here?" And how had she not seen him before now? That's what she got for being at the end. The rotation came from across the room. "You're speed dating now?"

His head dipped as he rubbed the back of his neck. "I just wanted to talk to you."

She motioned to the rows of couples. "This isn't a good time."

"It's never a good time for you. But I've got three minutes." He pointed to the digital countdown at the front.

Olivia crossed her arms. "My name is Olivia. I write for the *Grand Rapids Gazette*, and I recently had an article published on chickens."

Nate drummed his fingers on the tabletop. "I read that article. It was . . . interesting."

"Liar." Olivia took a drink of her water and tried to ignore the fact that Nate had taken the time to look up her article. It meant nothing.

"No, I'm even considering getting some free-range chickens of my own." Nate's eyes sparkled with a touch of laughter.

She released a humorless laugh. "In the parsonage's tiny backyard, or do you have a farm I don't know about?"

"Fine, I'm not getting chickens." Nate shook his head and picked at the table. "I miss how we were, Olivia. You're . . ."

"A great asset to the church?" She pointed at the time. "You told me. One minute left."

"Don't shut me out, Olivia. I know you want more, and I'm sorry I just . . . can't give you that. But I never thought you'd be one to pout—"

"You think I'm pouting?" A cold sensation ran over her.

"What else do you call this? You won't talk to me, you stopped going to the shelter, you—"

"Because it hurts too much." She finally locked

eyes with him. "Seeing you hurts. Watching the other single girls at church flirt with you hurts."

"They don't flirt with me."

The guy was clueless.

The silence stretched thin between them. She sighed. "Why do you care? You made it clear that I meant nothing more to you than anyone else at church."

"I lied." He mumbled the words as he leaned forward. "You *do* mean more to me. You've become my friend. My . . . best friend. I just . . . can't allow more."

"I don't know if I can do that."

Nate closed his eyes, and when he reopened them, red tinged the edges. He sent her a quick nod as the bell announced the end of that round.

His face brightened as he moved to the next table. Libby's table. With a real smile and everything.

"Hello."

Olivia turned her attention to the man across from her. He had piercing blue eyes and a strong jaw, and he gave her a smile that she didn't doubt had captured many hearts over the years.

He leaned forward on his elbows. "What does a pretty girl like you need a dating service like this for?"

"I could say the same about you." Her attempt at flirting came out flat, but the guy didn't seem to care. Instead, he launched into a long list of his finer qualities.

Somewhere between how much he could bench press and the number of countries he'd been to, Libby's laugh bubbled up from the next table. Nate was grinning and laughing himself. Why didn't he smile like that for her anymore?

"Excuse me, that guy already had his three minutes with you. This is my time." The guy tried to make it sound like a joke, but there was an edge to his words. Then again, he'd been following Nate in the rotation all night. She probably wasn't the first one whose eyes had wandered to Nate as this guy droned on.

"Hello?" At the guy's elevated voice, Nate peeked at Olivia, only to catch her staring at him. Awesome.

Olivia shot a glare at the guy across the table. "I think I've heard enough about you to make up my mind."

The guy's expression darkened, and they sat in silence for the remaining time. Olivia sipped her water while Mr. Bench Press glared into space. Oh yes, speed dating was wonderful.

Today she'd start feeling like a librarian, because today she had a library. Libby stood at the top of the steps and ran her hand over the rough wood of the front door. It still had the history that she'd seen that first day, but now it appeared less tired and more welcoming. She pulled the shiny brass key out of the envelope Nate had given her and ran her finger over the metal.

"Libby!" Austin's voice carried from across the street.

Her hand tightened on the key as he ran toward her. Deep breath. She'd been avoiding him since the encounter with Nate. But she wasn't sure if that was because she was mad at him or because when she'd told the story to Olivia, her roommate said Austin was jealous.

Austin jealous? Of what, that Nate got to carry her stuff?

Austin stopped at the bottom of the library steps. His white polo shirt fit tight at his shoulders and was tucked into tan cargo shorts that hung on his hips. His hair was still wet from a shower and his face was shaved clean. How dare he show up here looking all attractive when she still wanted to pelt him with books. Big books. "Hey, Libby, I'm . . . I, uh . . . What are you doing?"

"Trying out my new key." She lifted the key for display before inserting it click by click into the new lock.

"I've never seen someone take so long to open a door." Austin took the few steps up until he was standing next to her. "You've been in there a hundred times. Why is today so monumental?"

"Today I have my own key, and today I'm not here to give opinions on paint samples or light placement. Today I am the librarian." Libby turned the knob and pushed open the door, letting the squeak of the hinge settle into her soul.

"You're going to spend your day in an empty library?"

"It's not empty." Libby walked in, letting her eyes adjust to the dim light. The afternoon sun cast the room in a soft glow that highlighted the refinished dark wooden floor. They had been able to keep the original windows and trim, but three panes of glass had to be replaced. Austin had been so particular about the glass that there was no way Libby could guess which ones.

He flipped a light switch, flooding the space with fluorescent light. "Where did these boxes come from?"

"These are the books for the library. Olivia's brother and his friends moved them over yesterday for me."

"But why are they here? Now?" He stepped closer as he inspected the boxes, sending the scent of clean soap around her.

She inched farther away. "This is the new library. You said I could move them in after a couple weeks. It's been a couple weeks."

"That was before the roof got damaged in the move." His brows shot up as if she'd lost her mind. "We aren't ready for books."

"Nate said—"

"I don't care what Nate told you. I said it isn't

ready. We have plastic over the roof, but it's another few weeks before it gets replaced."

"Fine. Move them back if you want, but stop yelling at me." Libby eyed the piles of boxes and stopped. Odd. She was sure she'd taped all the boxes, but the one on the end was just folded shut.

Austin took a seat on one of the boxes. "I'm sorry. I shouldn't talk to you that way. I seem to lose my temper more often than not these days."

Libby sat on a box a few feet away. "You aren't always this charming?"

He leaned forward on his knees. "I've been trying to apologize to you for more than a week now. But you seem to be avoiding me."

"Possibly." She tried to ignore the wet lock of hair that fell across his forehead. It didn't work. "Can you blame me if this is what your apologies are like?"

"Right. I'm sorry for the other day . . . and for a minute ago."

"Did you apologize to Nate?"

"Yes." He rubbed his hands together but didn't look up. "Whatever is going on between you and my brother is none of my business."

"You're right, it's not." Libby leaned her head back against the rough wooden wall. "But nothing is going on."

His shoulders seemed to relax with that bit of information. *He's jealous.* Olivia's voice echoed through her mind. When Austin's eyes settled on her, she had to turn away from his intense gaze.

Libby lifted the edge of the box that was missing the tape. There was a one-inch gap between two books. Odd. Every space had been squished full with books. She read the titles of the books around it. Sure enough, one was missing. It was the first of a series, and she'd been careful to keep all series together.

"I should go. My dad is waiting at my place." He stood and shoved his hands in his pockets, then pulled them out again. "We're having a small picnic. You want to join us?"

"What?"

"It won't be anything fancy, but I can grill a fine burger. My dad would be thrilled if he got to spend the afternoon with a pretty girl rather than just me." He shifted from one foot to the other and then back again.

She should say no. Her emotions couldn't take another appearance of Mr. Hyde. Then again, he *was* trying, and the vulnerable expression that had filled his eyes when they'd spoken of his brother still tugged at her heart.

"Come on. It's just burgers." He held out his hand, and she let him pull her to her feet.

But with that look in his eyes and the way his touch made her insides flip around, it could never be just burgers with Austin. Still, she nodded, followed him out of the library, and pulled the door shut until it clicked.

Austin was a few steps ahead but slowed to let her catch up. "I'm not sure if I told you, but my dad has early-onset Alzheimer's. He has good days and bad days. He's on a new medicine. It does seem to be helping, but only time will tell."

"That must be hard."

"It is." He dropped his hands in his pockets again. "It has its challenges. If he says anything off the wall, it's usually easier to agree with him than try to correct him." He paused on the sidewalk, where Otis lay in their path. "That hippo is weird."

Libby bent over and rubbed Otis's shiny brass nose. "I think he's awesome. And you better start calling him Otis if you don't want to look like an outsider."

"I don't care. I am not calling it by name. They can run me out of town as soon as my job is done."

They made their way across the street to Austin's backyard, where his father was waiting with Shiro's head in his lap.

"Hey, Dad. This is Libby. Libby, this is my dad, Henry. The senior Williams of Williams and Son Landscaping."

"Son," not "Sons." He'd taken care to emphasize that.

Libby extended her hand. "It's nice to meet you. It's a fine Saturday, isn't it?"

"Sure is." The wrinkles around his eyes deepened as he seemed to be trying to place her.

Austin headed toward the door. "I'm going to finish readying the burgers."

Libby settled into a chair next to Henry. "Is this your first time in Heritage?"

His brow wrinkled. "I don't know." He chuckled as he tapped the side of his head. "Not what it used to be."

"No worries. We all forget things at times." Libby scanned the backyard. "Nate lives in town. Is he coming over too?"

"No. I think Austin said he had a church thing." He returned to petting the dog. The action seemed to ease some of the tension around his face. "Probably best. Those boys do fight sometimes."

Austin appeared in the doorway behind his dad as if ready to ask something.

"Don't tell Austin, but he has impossibly high standards sometimes." Henry held his finger to his lips.

Austin's jaw tensed at his dad's words, and he turned around, disappearing back into the house.

Henry ran his hands over Shiro for a few more minutes, then looked up at Libby and blinked. "I didn't know you were joining us, Becky. Did you bring some more of that peach pie?"

Becky? Austin's instructions floated back. *"If*

he says anything off the wall, it's usually easier to agree with him than try to correct him."

She reached out and patted his hand. "No peach pie. Not today."

Maybe Becky was a cousin.

When Henry went back to scratching the dog's ears, Libby stood and went to check on Austin. "Need any help?"

Austin pointed to a cutting board that had an onion and a knife resting on top. "Do you cut onions?"

"Sure." Libby turned on the hot water and started washing her hands. "Your dad is super sweet."

"He can be when he isn't bad-mouthing me." Austin shaped a hamburger patty, then slapped it on the plate with the others.

"He wasn't bad-mouthing you." She dried her hands and picked up the knife. "He was just . . . observing."

His head jerked up. "You think I have impossibly high standards as well?"

She shrugged as she cut off the end of the onion and started peeling back the outer layer. "Every time we fought, it was because I failed to meet your expectations. Either I'm lousy at living life or your standards might be a little high."

"There is nothing wrong with having standards." He reached for another ball of meat and started shaping it.

"No, but a life without grace for others' mistakes ends up being a pretty lonely life." When Austin didn't comment, she set to slicing the onion in wheels. "He called me Becky. Is that a family member?"

Austin's movements stilled before he dropped the patty on the plate. "No. Becky is just someone we used to know. You can throw the plant scraps in that bucket by the door. I'll compost them."

Libby added the onions to the plate and scraped the rest into the bucket. Her mind flashed to Olivia and what she'd say about this little lunch. Shoot. She was supposed to text her. She grabbed for her phone, but her pocket was empty. "I forgot my purse in the schoolhouse. I'll be right back."

She jogged back to the schoolhouse and stopped. The front door was open a crack. But she'd shut it—tight. Libby edged the door open with a loud creak. This time the noise felt less homey and more horror-flick-ish. *Please don't be a psycho killer.*

"Hello?" Libby's voice echoed around the empty room.

Nothing.

Maybe a thief?

She flipped the light switch and gave a quick scan of the room. No one. And her purse remained right where she had left it.

Weird.

She grabbed her purse but stopped. The flap on the open box was now bent the opposite way. She opened the other flaps. One book was still missing, but it had been the first book of the series before. Now book one was in its place, but book two had vanished.

It wasn't a thief or a serial killer.

Heritage had a serial reader on the loose.

eight

Why hadn't he just told Libby who Becky was? It wasn't like he had anything to hide.

Austin sat on the steps of the gazebo and slid his baseball cap back on. The midday sun was still a little warm for his tastes, but three weeks into September meant cool days were coming, and soon. He made a few notes on his clipboard, then set it aside. His heart just wasn't in it today.

A tightness squeezed his chest. His dad had called Libby "Becky" half the day at their picnic, and Libby never corrected him. She'd even stopped Austin once when he tried to correct his father. He'd nearly choked on his burger when his dad asked if they were still planning on a winter wedding.

Libby had dismissed it, but Austin had called it an early night for everyone. It had been a rough day for his dad, but Austin had never seen anyone so sweet and gentle with him.

She'd also managed to leave that baggie of change on his table at some point in the day without him noticing. A smile tugged at the corners of his mouth as his gaze traveled to the library door. Maybe he should go see what she was up to today.

Austin shook away the thought and stood. He needed to focus his time on saving the family business. Libby was becoming a distraction from that goal.

Austin made a note on the clipboard to mark the ground for the auger. That hippo better walk away again before the auger got here, or that could be quite problematic.

"Hey." Nate's voice came from behind him. "Looks like it's all coming together."

"Yup."

"I'm almost done in there." Nate stood on the steps of the gazebo and pointed at the one-room schoolhouse. "Have you been in to look?"

"Yes, looks good."

Nate leaned on one of the rails of the gazebo, wearing jeans and a white T-shirt. Must be a meeting-free day. "I thought you said you understood about the moving-day problem."

"I do." He added a note to call about the heirloom roses he'd ordered. "It's fine."

"If it's fine, then why do you still talk to me like we're barely more than strangers?"

"Isn't that what we are?"

"What do you mean by that?" Nate leaned back against the rail.

Austin slid the pencil behind his ear and tucked his clipboard under his arm. "I came to realize that a lot has changed over the years, and I don't really know you."

"Austin—"

"I'm serious. The town all talks about how you give the shirt off your back for everyone." He walked to the opposite side of the gazebo and leaned against one of the posts. "You're involved with so many committees, so many volunteer positions, so many visitations, that I wonder how you even have time to sleep. I can't believe what you've done with the inside of that library. It's like you have this compulsion to rescue everyone from everything, and yet when Dad needs you, when I need you, you aren't around—"

"No matter what I do, it isn't good enough for you, is it?" Nate turned away and leaned his elbows on the rail.

Good enough for him? His dad's voice from the other day rolled over in his mind. *He has impossibly high standards sometimes.* Maybe he did, but wasn't that better than having no standards? Some things should never take a back seat . . . like family.

"The Williams brothers. Just the two fellas we're looking for," Mr. Jameson yelled as he crossed Second Street, waving his arm. Two people trailed him. One was a man carrying an impressive news camera, and the other was that newswoman—Sydney St. James—in full makeup and a skirt. She seemed to struggle with her heels in the soft grass as they moved toward the gazebo, but her practiced smile never faded from her face.

"Channel 21 News is back." Mr. Jameson huffed as he stopped at the bottom of the steps. "They had come to interview me today about the progress and were thrilled to see that the building had already been moved to the site."

Sydney St. James surveyed the area, then pointed to the library. "Maybe on the steps of the library."

Austin looked down at his T-shirt and worn jeans. "I'm not dressed for an interview." Although more exposure was exactly the thing he needed for more business.

"You two look perfect. Trust me." Sydney eyed both men up and down.

Without waiting for input, she headed in that direction and motioned for them to follow.

Nate started walking toward the steps. Of course he did. The mayor wanted something and Nate jumped. No questions asked.

Austin tossed his hat to the side and followed. He ran his fingers through his hair, doing his best to erase the hat-hair look. For their first interview they had a makeup crew with nonstop touch-ups. Now they didn't seem to care if he'd even showered.

He stopped at the top step and waited while Sydney gave instructions to everyone. The guy with the camera counted down, then pointed to

Sydney. She lit up with that practiced smile once more. "At Channel 21, we pride ourselves on listening to our viewers. And after our feature on Heritage almost six weeks ago, you have asked what the Williams brothers are up to these days. Today I'm here to find out."

The Williams brothers? Wasn't this story about the town? He shot a look at Nate, but his brother just shrugged.

"As you can see behind me, the schoolhouse has been moved to its new location, and when I walked up, the brothers were discussing where to place the new sidewalks."

Not exactly, but small detail.

"Anyone who has been to Heritage in the past can appreciate all these two men are doing to transform the town. Tell me, Williams brothers, are you happy with the progress so far?" Sydney shoved the microphone toward him and Nate as if they were a package deal.

Austin leaned in. "We are. Moving the schoolhouse was challenging but worth it. And if all goes as planned, the library will be open by Halloween."

"What other plans do you have for the square?" She pointed the microphone toward Nate.

Nate? He didn't have plans. Williams and Son Landscaping had plans.

Austin spoke up before Nate could. "The adjacent corner will have a community playground. Various options have been discussed for the other two corners, but those won't be added until a future date."

"Great!" Sydney looked into the lens and smiled extra wide. "Now to a question we get asked most often by our viewers. Are you two single?"

Austin blinked at the camera. What kind of question was that? Was this a news show or a gossip show? He'd let Nate take this one.

Or not. His brother had gone three shades of red as he shifted from one foot to the other.

Austin leaned toward the microphone. "This project hasn't left much time for dating. We have both been putting in long days."

Sydney said a few more words, then the camera guy started packing away his equipment. That was it? No questions about the other landscaping they had planned? How would this help his business if all they asked him about was his dating life?

Then again, all publicity was good publicity, right?

The full moon made it a perfect night for her to catch the serial reader. Libby laid out a quilt on the grass next to Luke and Hannah's house. Their house shadowed her from the bright full moon so the serial reader would never see her. She dressed all in black, complete with a black stocking cap of Luke's she'd found. She was undercover.

She stretched out on her stomach and lifted the binoculars.

"What are you doing?"

Libby let out a little scream as she turned toward Austin's voice. "Shh. You're going to wreck my cover."

Austin stood about ten feet away next to his house, his hands in his pockets.

Libby pulled her black cap a little lower. *And please go inside so I don't die of embarrassment.*

Austin dropped down to sit on the blanket. "Seriously, what are you doing?"

"I'm watching for someone who has been sneaking into the library." Her voice was an exaggerated whisper.

"An intruder?" He grabbed his phone. "We should call the police."

She yanked his phone away. "No. A serial reader."

His right eyebrow lifted. "A what?"

She motioned him closer. She could watch while she explained, but whoever it was wouldn't come if he or she saw or heard them.

Austin stretched out on his stomach next to her. "Please explain."

"Shh." She put her finger to her lips, then lifted the binoculars again and peered around. "There was a book missing the other day. It was the first in a series, but then when I went back it was there, and the second in the series was missing."

191

He crossed his arms in front of him and laid his head down. "Are you sure you didn't just think you saw the wrong book?"

"That's what Olivia said, but then last night I went to show her, and the third in the series was missing." Libby scanned and rescanned the square. Nothing.

"Someone is breaking into the library to *read?*" Humor laced his tone.

Libby couldn't hold back a giggle. "Right? Whoever it is will be my new best friend."

"How do you even know they'll come tonight?" He rolled to his side and propped his head on his hand. He was just beyond the shadow of the house, and his dark hair glinted in the moonlight.

"It seems to take them one to two days to read the book, so it'll probably be tonight or tomorrow. But the farther you are into a series the faster you read, so I'm betting on tonight. I left the door unlocked."

"You're going to stay out here all night to see if this night reader will come or not?"

"Night reader. I like that."

Austin rolled onto his back and looked up. "You can see a lot more stars here than in Canton."

"Being away from the city helps. You should see the sky at Olivia's house. It's amazing." She peeked at him out of the corner of her eye. "Nice segment on Channel 21. I mean, I don't know

192

much about what you're up to here in Heritage, but at least everyone knows you're single."

"Don't remind me. That was about as embarrassing as it gets." Austin covered his face with his arm. "With any luck it'll be good publicity, and that's what I need."

She looked through the binoculars again. "Please tell me you don't own night-vision goggles."

"No." Libby handed them to him. "They're just regular binoculars."

"That's a relief." He pointed them at the night sky.

"Think I might be a stalker?" She pulled her black cap a little lower. "I could totally pull off being a spy."

He passed her back the binoculars. "You're too sweet to be a stalker or a spy."

She glanced over, and by the expression on his face, he was processing his choice of words as well. She rolled to her side so she could see him better. "Are we friends?"

He turned his head toward her. A hint of silver lined his face from the moonlight. "Why do you ask?"

"There are times we act like friends. And times—"

"When I act like a jerk." He looked back toward the sky.

"I wasn't going to say those exact words." She propped her head on her hand.

He rubbed his hands over his face. "I do want to be friends. I have issues with . . . my brother, and sometimes I let that anger get the best of me."

"I sort of picked that up." Libby picked at a seam in the quilt. "You're still mad he went to the hospital with me?"

"No." Austin sighed. "That was the right decision. And it was the right decision to meet with the concerned parents of the basketball team rather than be there helping us move our dad in. And it was right that he went on the 911 call the day he was supposed to meet me at our dad's. But do you see a pattern here?"

"Family always gets pushed aside."

"Exactly."

"Is your dad angry at him too?"

Austin tapped the ground a few times with his fist. "Nope. Nate can't do wrong in our dad's eyes. *Everyone* likes Nate more than me. Even my dad."

Nate may be easier to get along with than Austin, but Libby didn't like him more. Not that she'd mention that. "I doubt that's true."

"Feels true."

"But feeling true doesn't make it true. My bio-mom told me once that making bad decisions was in my blood." Libby rolled back to her stomach and plucked a few blades of grass at the top edge of the blanket. "She said that getting pregnant with me was her first bad decision, and choosing to have me was her second."

"How old were you when you were adopted?" Austin rolled to his stomach as well, his shoulder touching hers.

"Two. But my bio-mom is my mom's sister, so I still saw her on occasion until about fourteen. I think I was about seven when she told me that— it was just after Luke was kidnapped by his dad. She said that Luke had been kidnapped because I was destined to make bad decisions."

"Wait, what? That's a lot to take in. Your aunt adopted you and Luke—"

"No. My birth mom, Angel, abandoned me to her sister, Ann, when I was about a year old. Ann married a guy named Brian Taylor and they had Luke. They divorced and she married Len Kingsley, and they adopted me. Luke and I are cousins biologically but siblings through adoption."

"His dad kidnapped him?"

"Oh, right, you weren't here when all that went down last year. His dad disappeared with him when he was three, and we had no idea what happened to him until last year when he showed up on our doorstep."

"How did he find you?"

"Some investigator realized his birth certificate was a fake and put the pieces together." Libby plucked a few blades of grass and piled them on the quilt. "His dad had died in a car accident when Luke was five, and he grew up in the foster-care system under the name Luke Johnson."

Austin rubbed his eyes as if trying to piece everything together. "So, why would your mom—I mean, the woman who gave birth to you—blame you?"

"I was with him when his dad picked him up." Her voice cracked on the last word. She coughed to clear the growing lump. "I could have run and told our mom, but I didn't. His dad told me it was a surprise and I believed him."

"You have to know it wasn't your fault."

"I know. My parents—"

"Your adoptive parents?"

"Yes, my real parents. They've told me over and over that it wasn't my fault. They also have told me how thankful they are for me. That my birth wasn't a mistake." Libby picked a few more pieces of grass and let them sift through her fingers. "I know what my bio-mom said wasn't true, but there are times it feels true. But like I said, feeling true doesn't make it true."

"What do you do when it feels true?" Austin caught some of the grass she dropped, brushing her hand in the process.

Libby's heart sped up with the contact. She picked up another piece of grass and held it out on the palm of her hand. "I do the only thing I can when faced with a lie. I hold on to the truth.

I am not a mistake. I'm not bound to be like my mother."

Austin wrapped his fingers around the grass and her hand at the same time. "What's my truth?"

Libby willed her breath to an even rhythm. "Your truth is that Nate's a good guy, but he's not perfect, and . . . not everyone likes him more." Her voice was rougher than before.

"They don't?" His thumb moved back and forth on her palm.

She could barely think with him doing that. Austin had her so twisted around, she didn't know what to think anymore, and she needed to keep her head about her until she did know. She pushed to a sitting position. "You know what this means?"

"What?" Austin pulled back his hand and propped himself up on his elbows.

"We both shared secrets. You know what that makes us?" When he didn't answer, she nudged his side. "Friends."

He let out a small chuckle. "Yeah, okay."

"And you know what friends do?"

"What?"

"Give friends rides to Grand Haven in their truck so they can pick up an antique desk Friday."

"You need to go to Grand Haven Friday?"

"I do. Thank you for offering."

A distant squeak of the library door echoed through the night.

Libby whipped her head that direction. "They're here." She dropped back to her belly and snatched up the binoculars. "We missed them going in. Hopefully I'll be able to see them under that streetlight when they come out." She looked through the binoculars at the door, then dropped them. "It's too far." She jumped to her feet, dashed across the street, and ducked behind Otis's side.

Austin landed next to her with a thud. "How are you going to see like this?"

She pointed two fingers from her eyes to the front end of Otis, then from his eyes to the back end.

"Sure, give me the butt."

She stifled a giggle as she scowled and put her finger over her lips.

Creeping along on her belly, she peeked around Otis's nose just as a figure exited the schoolhouse and secured the door. The night reader wore a red hoodie and big jeans but couldn't be much over five feet. Maybe a junior higher? The hood fell back, and a long ponytail of dark brown hair fell out. This didn't help. She didn't know ninety percent of the people in town, and neither did Austin.

Libby stood up and sprinted forward before she could talk herself out of it. "Hi."

The girl's eyes widened as she tucked the book deeper in her bag.

Libby took a hesitant step toward her. "Did you get the next book?"

The girl ducked her head. "I'm sorry. I shouldn't have taken them."

"Library books are made to be checked out. But why all the sneaking around?"

"I . . . It's just . . . I'm sorry. I won't do it again." She turned to go.

Libby took another step forward. "Wait. Let's start over." She extended her hand. "Libby Kingsley. Librarian."

The girl's brown eyes narrowed on Libby a moment, then a soft smile soothed the harsh features of her face. She gave Libby's hand a solid shake. "Danielle Fair. Reader."

Her face looked young, but her solid grip and the way she held herself didn't say teenager.

"How about this, Danielle Fair, reader? I need some help with shelving books." Libby pointed at the schoolhouse. "You help me and you'll have all the access to the books you want and a place to read them. No questions asked. You can start tomorrow."

Danielle pushed her ponytail back over her shoulder. "I work a morning shift tomorrow, but I can be there after lunch."

"Sounds good." That narrowed her age to at least post high school.

Danielle nodded and then disappeared down the darkened sidewalk.

Libby ran back to where she'd left Austin hiding behind Otis. "Nice that you had my back."

"I thought one person chasing the poor girl in the dark was enough." He stood and brushed off his pants.

"True. Just so you know, I don't make a habit of chasing people in the dark." She made her way back to the blanket and bent down to gather her stuff. "Friday?"

Austin folded the blanket and held it out. "Sure thing, *friend*."

His phone rang. He pulled it from his pocket and fumbled it to the ground. Libby reached for it and handed it to him as the name *Becky* flashed across the screen. He declined the call and shoved it back in his pocket. When he looked at her, his smile didn't reach his eyes anymore. "See you Friday."

Interesting. Maybe Friday would open the door to the mysterious Becky. Even if not, she had a feeling it would be a day worth remembering.

Libby tucked the blanket under her arm. The baggie of change dropped from the folds to the ground. She bent over and picked it up. This was not over.

After this date she could wrap up her article and turn it in to Mr. Lang. Olivia eyed her watch, then checked her phone again. She'd driven an hour to the Woodland Mall in Grand Rapids to meet this guy—he'd better show. She'd picked a public place in the afternoon to make it as easy and as safe as possible. Though a blind internet date was anything but easy. And it wasn't completely blind. She'd seen his photo. But other than three photos and the bio on his profile, she didn't know anything about him.

"Olivia?" A guy slid into the seat across the café table. Chiseled jaw with a three-day scruff, messy blond hair, and intense green eyes. His online photo hadn't done him justice. Maybe internet dating did have its merits. "You're Olivia, right?"

"Yes, I'm sorry. And you're Tanner?"

He gave her a once-over before pulling out his phone and glancing at it. His smile tightened as his head bobbed. "That's me."

Maybe he was nervous. "Is this your first internet date?"

"Yeah. I signed up last week." He checked his phone again.

"What prompted you to sign up?" Did she sound too much like a questionnaire?

"I wanted to get back at my girlfriend— ex-girlfriend." His gruff tone emphasized *ex*.

Vengeful rebound boy. Awesome. "Did you two date long?"

"Three years." He scrolled through his phone and then tapped at the screen. "Want to go see a movie? There's a theater in this mall."

"That sounds . . . fun." A movie wasn't the best way to get to know someone, but it didn't matter. Tanner seemed interested only in getting back at his ex, and she hadn't come looking for a match made in heaven anyway. She just had to do the last bit of research for her story.

"How about *The Evil Dead Rise Again*?"

Then again, how long did she have to stay to consider it a date for the article? At least she'd had the good sense to drive herself. She reached for her cup of coffee. "I don't do horror."

"Really?" His voice dropped into an adolescent whine. "You're different than your profile."

"What?" Olivia coughed on the hot liquid. "I am not. Did you even *read* my profile?"

"No. But your picture was hot. Then you show up with a bun and glasses." He shook his head and scanned his phone again.

Okay, maybe the bun was too far, but the glasses were necessary. She'd torn her last contact that morning and her next box wasn't going to be delivered until Monday. She couldn't drive without contacts or glasses. "Sorry to disappoint."

He seemed to realize he'd been rude and tried to backpedal. "You're not *that* bad."

Ouch!

Maybe this was partly her fault. She hadn't spent much time on his profile either. She just needed a date so she could get the article done and turned in on time.

"There's a romantic comedy—will that do?" He rolled his eyes and rubbed the back of his neck, revealing a tattoo on the underside of his arm.

Her heart pinched as her mind floated to Nate. Wait, she wasn't going to think about him. Why couldn't she get that guy out of her head?

Her distress must have shown on her face. Tanner picked his phone back up. "So, no romance."

"I'm sorry. That sounds fine." She offered him a smile and stood as she pulled her purse over her shoulder.

Ten minutes later, Olivia stood in silence as the long line inched its way toward the ticket counter.

A curse flew from Tanner's mouth, and he ducked his head as they approached the window. He angled his face away from the line as he told the lady what movie he wanted and claimed his ticket.

"What are you doing, Tanner?" Olivia handed a twenty to the worker. "Same movie, please."

"It's my ex. The blonde in the back of the line with the big, uh . . . personality."

"Well, you wanted to make her jealous." Olivia shrugged as she took her ticket and change and headed toward the door.

"That's when I thought you looked like—never mind. Let's get our seats." Tanner marched past her.

Seriously? She'd leave now if she hadn't just shelled out cash for the ticket. At least she'd have a few interesting words for her article. She hurried to catch up with him as she tucked her change in her wallet.

Tanner yanked the door open. By the time she looked up, she couldn't stop or even get her hands out of her purse. *Smack!*

Pain spread across her face as she bounced back and landed with a thud on the ground, her glasses falling into two pieces.

She tried to focus on Tanner through her now blurry vision. He stared down at her with an expression that better be repentant. Not that he appeared as anything more than a fuzzy ball. "Sorry."

A warm sensation starting on her upper lip ran down her face as the metallic taste of blood filled her mouth. She looked down at her favorite white sweater as blood poured from her nose and she had nothing to stop it with.

A worker ran over with some paper towels. "Are you okay?"

Odd that the question came from a stranger rather than Tanner.

She held a towel to her nose, but the damage was done. "I'm fine." It sounded more like "bine" with the paper towel over her mouth and what felt like the beginning of a fat lip. "Danks."

"Are you sure?" The worker moved his head from side to side. Probably wishing he'd been on ticket duty today. "Maybe I should fill out an incident report."

"No. I'm bine." Olivia peered at Tanner through one lens of her glasses and closed the blurry eye. "I dink I just wan' to go home."

Tanner shifted his weight, crossing his arms. "But I just bought a ticket."

He couldn't be serious, but this wasn't the best timing for a joke.

"I'll tell you what. The movie is about to start. You get cleaned up and I'll save you a seat." He disappeared through the assailant door without even a glance back.

Tears pressed against the backs of her eyes, but crying would make her nose bleed harder. She felt her way over to a bench, then held up half her glasses so she could at least navigate her phone screen.

She tapped Gideon's name. Voicemail. Libby was picking up furniture with Austin in Grand Haven today. Caroline—too far. Janie had the diner. Her parents would come, but they had enough on their plates with her younger siblings' schedules. That left her with one option. She drew a slow breath and tapped the name.

He answered on the third ring. "Hello?"

"Nate? I need help." She tried to put strength in her voice, but just hearing his voice clogged her throat with unshed tears. "Can you come get be?"

"Yes." The jingle of keys echoed through the phone. "Where are you?"

nine

He wished she'd just tell him if he needed to go back and pummel some guy's face. Nate hadn't been in a fistfight since he'd turned his life around, but he'd won the last one and the way he felt right now, he could do it again. Olivia had sounded so angry and muffled on the phone that he'd pushed the speed limit the whole way. Finding her covered in blood hadn't been what he expected when he arrived.

Nate peered at her again out of the corner of his eye. All she'd said when he picked her up was, "I'm fine and don't ask." But with the bloodstains on her sweater and the way her lip was swelling, she certainly didn't look fine.

"Would you quit staring at be?" Her voice dripped with exhaustion and frustration. She opened the glove box and pulled out a roll of masking tape.

"Are you going to tell me what happened, or am I going to take a guess? The guy didn't—"

"Hit be? No." She started taping her glasses together at the bridge. "Did he take be on a lousy date, sback by bace with a door, tell be I wasn't bretty enup, and then go to the bovie without be? Yes, he did."

206

Her mumbled words tumbled out, but he got the point. It had been a bad date. Wait, had she said not pretty enough? Was she serious?

"He didn't hit be with the door on purpose. He was distracted by his girlbriend." She slid the glasses on and sighed.

"The guy had a girlfriend?" Nate's knuckles whitened on the steering wheel.

"Sorry. Ex-girlbriend. I think he knew she had a date there tonight, so he was trying to bake her jealous." She returned the tape to the glove box and slammed it shut.

"Wow, what a jerk." It took every ounce of strength not to turn the car around and get in that fight after all. The lowlife.

"At least it'll bake a good story bor the article." Her top lip looked as if it had fought with a bee and lost. Her glasses that were now held together by tape sat crooked on her nose. And her nose was bleeding again. She reached for the paper towel and dabbed it.

She was a mess. He'd never seen her look more terrible, and yet he'd never wanted more to pull her into his arms. He didn't realize that his thoughts had shown on his face until an empty Starbucks cup hit him in the side of the head.

"Don't laugh at be. This isn't bunny." She glared at him.

"I wasn't laughing. Honest." He schooled his features and tried to think of something else.

Although it might be best if she thought he was laughing at her.

They rode the hour back to Heritage in silence, and when he pulled up in front of her house, he didn't give her the option of just letting him drop her off. Getting out, he circled to open her door. Then, not trusting she could see the steps over her ballooned lip, he slipped her hand in his arm and led her to the door.

"I'm okay, you know." Olivia unlocked the door and walked in, tossing her keys on the side table.

"Get cleaned up and changed. I'll get you some ice for that lip." Nate headed to the kitchen and searched the drawers for a baggie. After locating one, he dropped a few ice cubes in it and wrapped it in a towel. He handed it to Olivia when she descended the steps a couple of minutes later.

She'd changed her shirt, washed her face, and ditched the harsh bun. Her lip still looked red and swollen but no longer like a walking crime scene. The ice had only grazed her lip when she pulled it away.

"Olivia, you have to leave it on there. You don't want the swelling to get worse." He took the ice from her hand. Capturing her chin with his hand, Nate placed the ice on her lip with his other hand. He tried to be gentle, but she winced and then took a slow breath. She closed her eyes, and he could see her willing the pain away.

Her white-blonde hair flowed freely around her face, and he could smell the fresh fragrance of the soap still clinging to her skin. Enjoying her closeness was a bad idea, but he couldn't stop himself.

When Olivia opened her pale blue eyes, begging him closer, Nate took a hasty step back and handed her the ice. "You need to keep it there for at least twenty minutes." He took a seat on the couch about ten feet away. "Are you going to tell me the whole story now?"

He wanted to hear everything and he'd wait all night if he had to—it just had to be at a safe distance. He hoped he wouldn't want to go pound someone afterward—pastors shouldn't do that.

"I told you. I ran into a door."

He swallowed a laugh and decided he needed better clarification. "A door?"

"Tanner was mad about . . . well, everything, and he opened the door. I wasn't paying attention, thus . . ." She motioned to her lip.

What a louse. "Did you say he said you weren't pretty?"

"Yes. No. Sort of. He asked why I wasn't as hot as my online profile picture." She shrugged. "He didn't care for the bun and glasses."

"Seriously? Even with a bun and glasses you're . . ." What was he saying?

Her brows lifted. "I'm . . ."

"Fine-looking." He stood and checked his

phone. An emergency call would be helpful right about now.

"Wow. I think I'd rather have Tanner's description of 'not that bad.' " Her voice dropped, mimicking Tanner's.

"Olivia—"

"Forget it." She dropped the ice on the table. "I'm not fishing for compliments."

The girl had no idea how beautiful she was, but she was right. It was best to let it drop. "Please tell me you're done with this research." Her going on another date might just kill him.

"My article isn't due until Wednesday, but I'll email it to my editor tomorrow. Oh, shoot." She winced and then flinched as the action must have caused her lip pain.

"What?"

"My car is still at the theater. I drove there, but when my glasses broke I knew I couldn't drive home. I can ask Libby to drive me, but I know she's stressed about the library. Janie is so busy at the diner these days that I never see her. I know she doesn't have the time." She paced the floor as she continued her external processing. "Derek works in Grand Rapids, right? Do you think he'd run me down—"

"I'll take you."

"What?" She stopped and looked at him, her brow wrinkled in disbelief.

Where had that come from? Another hour in

the car with Olivia wasn't going to help him keep his distance. But Derek wasn't a guy he wanted to see her spending her day with either. "I take Mondays off. I'll take you then."

She dismissed his offer with a wave. "Thank you, but I really need my car tomorrow. And it isn't safe to leave it there all weekend."

Tomorrow would eat into his prep time for Sunday, but if he stayed up late tonight, he could make it work. "Okay, I can take you tomorrow." He walked toward the door. He needed to leave before he said or did something really stupid.

"Nate . . ."

His phone chimed from his pocket, and he took another step toward the door. "I should take this. A pastor's job never ends. See you tomorrow."

"Running again, Nate?" Her words were quiet but made their mark. She had no idea how right she was.

Nate pulled his phone out and made a quick exit. He could have let it go to voicemail, but he couldn't have answered the questions in her eyes.

Now he just had to make it through tomorrow without letting his guard down any further.

Austin was trying to keep Libby out of his mind, so what did he do? Agree to spend the day with her.

He leaned against the side of the truck as Libby fawned over a pink bike with a white seat and wicker basket on the front. The midday sun highlighted her blonde hair as a light breeze blew a wisp that had escaped her braid across her face. She tucked the strand behind her ear, then bit her bottom lip. The tell that she really wanted something. And he was about ready to hand over his credit card to give it to her.

No. That was crazy. She wasn't his girlfriend. He'd been a fool to flirt with her the other night and give her hope. Seeing Becky's name flash across his screen had driven that truth home. He wasn't ready to date again—trust again. He had to be fair to her. He'd blocked Becky's number after that, but it had been enough. Enough to remember how toxic she'd been in his life. He'd wasted two years on her, and he wasn't ready to take the chance of that happening again. Not when he had a business to save.

He pulled out his phone and checked the time. They hadn't even made it into the antique store yet.

Austin picked up a leaf from the ground and spun it in his fingers. It was green with just a hint of yellow. The last strands of summer fading away. Fall had always been his favorite season. The cool weather, the bright colors, and watching the World Series with his dad. But this year it just marked the deadline for this project and served as a reminder that traditions with his dad were numbered.

He flicked the leaf back to the ground and

pushed away from the truck. He'd planned on arranging to have Nate or one of the crew bring Libby down in his truck. Then she had shown up at his house this morning in skinny jeans, a blousy white top that exposed her collarbone, and her hair pulled back in a fancy braid. Not taking her himself wasn't an option.

A young man exited the store with a smile that was about more than just a possible sale. He asked Libby a question, but Austin was too far away to hear. She stood and laughed, which only seemed to encourage the guy.

Austin walked over and stood a few feet behind her. Her back was still to him. He tried not to focus on the large freckle just under her right ear. He failed. Did she even know it was there?

When the guy made eye contact with him, Austin took another step toward Libby and held his gaze. "Are you going to get the bike, Libby?"

The guy swallowed hard and backed off. "Just let me know if you need any help." Then he disappeared inside.

"What a nice guy." Libby ran her hand over the bike again.

Maybe she did trust people too easily. "He was hitting on you."

"What? No. He was just telling me about the bike." Libby patted the seat. "But to answer your question, no, I'm not going to buy it. I need to research it first."

"Research it?"

"I don't want to make a bad decision." Libby pulled a notepad from her purse and started writing in it as she entered the antique store.

"It's a bike, not a car." He slid off his sunglasses and hung them on the front of his shirt.

She ignored his words and he let the matter drop as they entered the store. Libby stepped to the counter. "I believe you're holding a desk for me. The name is Libby Kingsley."

The woman started flipping through a stack of papers, then pointed to a cherry writing desk about ten feet away. "We moved it to the front for you."

Libby ran her hand over the deep red wood, then tested each of the drawers. "I'll take it. Can I look around before you ring it up?"

"Of course." The woman lifted a tag from the desk and replaced it with a Sold sign. "Just let me know when you're ready."

"Do you want me to load it in the truck?" Austin eyed the desk from different angles. It was big. Hopefully there was someone around to help him lift it.

"Austin, look at these." Libby stood in front of a case of antique books. Her fingers hovered over each of the titles as she read.

He stepped up behind her. "What are you looking for?"

"I collect early editions of Jane Austen novels."

She got to the end of the row and dropped her hand. "No Jane today. Aren't these old books unique? I thought about a bookshelf of old classics at the front of the room. Then again . . ." She approached a shelf that wasn't behind glass and lifted a book. "With my budget, I'll probably have to settle for unknowns. But they have the look I'm going for."

Austin picked up a book and flipped open the cover. A biography of John Black. First edition. He'd never heard of John Black. Maybe it was the only edition. He set it back on the shelf. "Do you own any first editions?"

"Of Jane Austen? I wish, but that would run over six figures. I just settle for antique versions." She picked up another book and flipped through it.

"Six figures? Wow. Have you ever seen one?" He eyed an old rocking chair next to him. Seemed sturdy.

"No. But I've seen a first edition of *Moby Dick*." Her voice grew a touch shaky.

The solid oak creaked as he eased into the chair. "In a museum?"

"No. I worked at a vintage bookstore in London." She kept her back to him, but her movements had stilled.

"Wow, London. That must have been amazing." He rocked back. This was a good chair. "Maybe I should buy this."

The bell over the front door rang, but Libby still didn't move.

Austin leaned forward. "Libby? Is every-thing—"

When she began to sway, Austin jumped up and caught her before she could fall. Then he scooped her up with one hand on her back and the other under her legs. Her face was ashen, her expression vacant.

He looked around the store. Where was one of her first-aid acronyms when he needed it? Maybe fresh air would help. He carried Libby outside to a bench along the sidewalk.

The woman from the counter appeared next to him with a bottle of water in her hand. "Do you need me to call an ambulance?"

Libby waved a shaky hand at her as the pink in her cheeks started returning. "No, I'll be fine."

Austin accepted the bottle from the woman and twisted it open before holding it out. "Drink." Maybe she was dehydrated.

Libby did as he said, then looked at him for the first time. Her cheeks flushed as she seemed to orient herself. "I'll be fine. I just need a minute."

"What happened?"

Libby took another drink of water. "I'm sorry. I haven't had an episode like that in over a year. It was my fault. I was running late and didn't eat breakfast. I'm fine." She pushed to a stand but began to sway.

"Whoa." Austin caught her as she tipped sideways. "Why don't we sit for a while? Maybe I can get you some food."

He scanned the area. A donut shop was across the street. He handed her the bottle and jogged over. He was back in record time with a white pastry bag and another bottle of water. He pulled a powdered donut and a chocolate-glazed one out of the bag. "Which one?"

Libby grabbed the chocolate one and took a bite.

"Want to tell me what that was about?" Austin settled on the bench next to her, slid on his sunglasses, and bit into the powdered donut.

"I worked in London at a little antique bookstore after college." She broke off a small piece of her donut and popped it into her mouth.

"You mentioned that." He opened his own bottle of water and took a long draw.

"One day I was held up at gunpoint for the cash in the drawer and the first edition of *Moby Dick*." Her face paled again, then she seemed to snap back to the present. "I guess talking about that book, combined with the bell—the London store had one just like it—all took me back to that day."

"They stole *Moby Dick*?"

"He stole several books, but the first edition of *Moby Dick* was the most valuable. It was in a locked case behind the counter and he forced me to unlock it." She took her time with her next bite, and he didn't push. "After I returned home, I had many panic attacks like that. They were quite debilitating. I moved back in with my parents and started seeing a counselor. Slowly, things got better, and they have been for a while. I'm so embarrassed."

"You have nothing to be embarrassed about." Austin angled his body toward her, pulling his knee up on the bench. "You're one of the strongest people I know. Not too many people stand up to me when I'm being stubborn, and you've given me a run for my money."

"Sorry about that too." She finished the donut and dusted off her hands.

"No. I'm sorry." His hand landed on her shoulder in a gentle gesture. "Can I get you another water?"

She shook her head and held up the half-full bottle. "No. I still have this one. I just need to sit a minute. Really. Let's talk about something else."

He popped the rest of the donut in his mouth and settled back into the bench. "Besides collecting Jane Austen books, what do you do for fun?"

She drew in a deep breath. A smile filled her face a moment before it faded. "I used to ride my bike."

Austin's gut clenched. And now she didn't because he'd run over it. "Sorry."

"It was more my fault than yours." She

shrugged, then paused as another smile tugged at her lips. "I do have another addiction, but I'm not sure you can handle it."

"Worse than antique books and bike riding?" He eyed her over the top of his sunglasses. "Ms. Kingsley, do tell."

"When I get a day to myself, I drive to a Carnegie library and get a photo of myself out front and a photo of me holding *Pride and Prejudice* inside." Her teeth tugged at her bottom lip. "I have a scrapbook of libraries I've been to. What can I say? I love books."

"How many Carnegie libraries are there?"

"Over fifteen hundred. Michigan had sixty-one, but only fifty-three are still standing. Not all of those are used as libraries now, but I would still love to see them." A small dimple appeared in her cheek as her face lit up.

Suddenly he wanted to find her a library, buy her a bike—anything to keep the horror from crossing her face again as it had done when she'd recounted the story.

Libby downed the last of her water and pitched it in the trash. "We need to get that desk and get back."

"You pay and I'll load it into the truck." Austin stood and offered her a hand up.

"Deal." Libby disappeared inside the antique store.

Austin lowered the gate on his truck. Ten

minutes later he had the desk loaded and strapped down. He'd had to swallow his pride and ask the bike shop guy for help. Fortunately, there were no customers there at the time and the guy was cool about it. He tested the strap. Seemed tight.

An antique key taped to the bottom of the desk caught his attention. He peeled it off and dropped it in his shirt pocket. Wouldn't want that to fly away. He raised the tailgate and rested against the side, but Libby was still nowhere in sight.

Austin reached for his phone and googled a few key words. The Carnegie library in Grand Haven had been demolished in 1967. He'd only missed that by more than fifty years. He slid the phone back in his pocket.

The pink bike still sat by the neighboring shop. Before he could talk himself out of it, Austin strode over, paid for the bike, and loaded it into the truck.

"You'll never guess what a deal I got. I'll definitely come back—" Libby's hand paused over her ear, where she had been brushing her hair back. "Did you buy that bike?"

"Yup."

"For me?" She ran her fingers along the soft pink paint.

"I would have to sacrifice my dignity to ride it, but I thought Nate might like it instead of that motorcycle he has." Austin reached for a cinch strap to secure the bike.

"Very funny. Why did you buy me a bike?"

"I did run over your last one."

"But it was my fault." She looked at him with her large sapphire-blue eyes. "I can't accept it."

Austin shrugged in response and worked the ratchet on the strap. "I can't return it, so you can buy it from me for $2.47. Don't pretend that you don't have that change somewhere on you to leave in my truck. I'm onto you."

The dimple appeared again as she tried to hold back a smile. She reached into her purse, pulled out the baggie of change, and held it out. "Deal." She patted the bike seat and glanced up at him again, now standing just a foot away. "Thank you."

Why had he bought the bike? There was only one answer that fit. It was the same answer as why he'd looked to see if there was a Carnegie library in Grand Haven. What was he going to do now?

Olivia slouched in her chair. Talk about bound up in knots. Not only had she yet to hear from the editor as to whether her dating article was acceptable or not, she was also counting down the minutes until Nate would show up at her door. Why had she accepted his offer to take her back to get her car? She should have waited until Libby was free. Or even her brother. Anyone but Nate.

She didn't know if she could handle being that

221

close to him again after last night. She closed her eyes against the memory. She was in worse shape than ever.

A ding filled the air and Olivia grabbed her phone. She pushed her glasses up her nose, trying to see clearer. These glasses were the worst with their heavy lenses. But with her others broken and still no contacts, she'd been reduced to her pair from her eighth grade year.

Olivia tapped the new email from Mr. Lang.

To: Olivia Mathews

From: Frank Lang

RE: Dating Article

I like it. It will run on the second page next Friday.

Next assignment: Fishing. Due 10/7.

Her stomach churned. On the positive side, this meant her articles were only a week apart instead of two weeks. And more print time meant one step closer to a real journalism job. But if there was anything that filled her with more dread than dating, it was fishing.

Maybe he'd be open to something else. She hit reply.

To: Frank Lang

From: Olivia Mathews

RE: Fishing Assignment

I have never been fishing.

The reply came almost immediately.

To: Olivia Mathews

From: Frank Lang

RE: Fishing Assignment

Perfect. Use that angle.

She reread the email. Angle? She hated lakes. Ponds. Pretty much any deep, dark water with lurking, slimy monsters. A shiver ran up her spine at the idea of a research trip—with fish. The fear of ending up in the water with those fish kept her to pools. Only pools. Well, that, and the fact that she could only dog-paddle. Not a save-yourself-from-the-center-of-the-lake type of stroke. But his email didn't leave much room for discussion.

A knock rattled the front door and Olivia shut her laptop, grabbed her purse, and pulled open the door. "Hi, Nate."

He wore a maroon sweater and dark jeans low on his hips. He shoved his hands in his pockets as he tilted his head, emphasizing his freshly shaven jaw. "What's wrong?"

She paused putting on her coat. "You can tell something is wrong with 'Hi, Nate'?"

He shrugged and walked toward the church van, leaving a hint of musky aftershave in his wake. "You're pretty easy to read."

Olivia pulled the door shut and hurried past him toward the passenger door. "I heard from my editor about the article."

"He didn't like it?" Nate opened his door and slid into the driver's seat.

"He loved it." She hopped in and slammed her door. "But the new assignment he wants me to do is on the great Michigan recreation of fishing, from the perspective of someone who has never been before."

"That should be easy." Nate set the engine to life and backed out of the driveway.

Easy? Was he kidding? Then again, he didn't know about her phobia. Because who was afraid of fish? And what grown adult in Michigan couldn't swim to save her life? Oh, right—that would be her. She leaned forward and pressed the third preset button, sending the oldies station blaring through the air. She adjusted the volume. "I've never been in a boat, let alone fished. Everly Brothers."

Nate conceded her answer, then leaned forward and switched to a country station. It was a game they'd started playing on their drive to the shelter. Crazy thing is, she hadn't even thought about it. She'd somehow dropped into their routine and so had he.

"Dustin Lynch." He tapped another button, this time classic rock, but an ad was running. "How could you have never been on a boat in Michigan? Water recreation is our great state's favorite pastime."

"Avoiding water recreation has always been my favorite pastime." She flipped it back to oldies. "The Monkees. How do you think I became good at basketball? Telling people you need to work on your jump shot gets you out of all sorts of things. How am I going to do this article? I don't even have a boat."

The next hour evolved from naming the band to music trivia to telling stories from their childhoods, like the time Nate left frogs in Austin's underwear drawer. By the time they reached Grand Rapids, Olivia was laughing so hard her sides hurt. She leaned against the door and took in the passing foliage that blurred into a mix of greens with the occasional red or orange patch. Fall was the best time of year. But a cold time of year to fish.

A shiver traveled over her. "Ted has a boat. Maybe I'll ask him if—"

"I can take you."

"What?"

His clean shave highlighted his tense jaw. "I have a fishing boat I bought last summer. I'll take you."

He flipped the radio back to the classic rock station, but she didn't know the song.

"You have a boat? Funny, you didn't mention that until I said Ted's name. Besides, I don't recall asking you."

"Well, you're not going out with Ted." The song changed to a commercial and he turned it to an oldies station. The Beatles sang about yesterday. A no-brainer, but neither jumped on it. "It'll have to be a week from Monday. Can you wait a week?"

Olivia's mouth had fallen open and she snapped it shut. First he'd jumped in at the mention of Derek's name. Now this? He couldn't have it both ways. They were either together or not. "I can go out with Ted if I want."

"Friends don't let friends date guys like Ted." He checked his mirrors and moved to the right lane.

"Who said date?"

"Trust me, Ted would find a way to make it a date. I've seen the way he looks at you." His words came out casual, but his concentration on the road seemed more than required to take the exit to I-96.

226

Olivia was done making it easy for him. "Maybe you should have told me that when I was doing the dating article. I could've gone out on a research date with him."

His ears reddened as he merged into the traffic. The silence stretched.

Finally, he spoke up. "Why do you want to be a journalist?"

"What?" Her hands flew into the air. "Where did that come from?"

Nate shrugged and changed lanes. "You don't have the cutthroat attitude of a journalist. How did you even decide on journalism anyway?"

"I wrote for my school newspaper and I was good at it. Why are we even talking about this? I don't have to justify my life goals to you."

"You're good at a lot of things. Is journalism your passion?"

"My passion?" Ugh. Where was another Starbucks cup when she needed one? Not only was he refusing to answer her question, but he was dropping into school counselor mode. He wasn't her counselor.

"When you do children's hour at church, you light up." He flipped on his turn signal and took the Leonard Street exit. "You don't seem to even enjoy these articles. Are you following your passion or just what you're good at?"

She pulled out her phone and typed a text to Ted.

> Hey Ted, I need to go fishing to research an article. Any chance you can take me out this week?

She hit Send and drew a deep breath. No matter how much she'd rather go with Nate, she had to separate herself before she went crazy.

She glared at him across the van. "You aren't one to offer advice on following your heart."

"What are you talking about? God called me to be a pastor. I am a pastor. I'm following the passion God gave me."

"What about in relationships?" She leaned a little closer. "Are you following those *passions?*"

His Adam's apple bobbed before he leaned toward the door. "Olivia, I know—"

"No, you don't know, and that's the thing." The chime of her phone stole her attention.

> **Ted**
> If you want a date with me, babe, all you have to do is ask.

Exhibit A of why Nate didn't care for him. The guy was all ego and all talk. But she'd known him since they were kids, and aside from the tiresome pickup lines, he was harmless.

> Haha. I need to research for an article on fishing.

Fine, I'm up for "fishing." Thursday? I
have that day off.

Oh brother. She'd ignore that one. She pulled
up the app with her diner schedule. Thursday was
empty.

Great—pick me up at 10 a.m.

See you then.

It was done and his final reply wasn't
suggestive. Progress.

Nate turned into the mall parking lot. "Is your
car where I picked you up at the theater?"

"No, it's by the food court."

Nate pulled the van to a stop two spots from
her car.

She yanked open the door and slid out before
he could speak. "Thanks for the ride. And don't
worry about fishing. Ted's available and we
already set a date and time."

Nate's lips thinned into a line, but she slammed
the door before he could reply. She wasn't trying
to make him mad. But if he didn't want her, it
was time to set some of her own boundaries.

ten

Why did people have such a hard time being honest? Libby peeled the tape off another box of books and set it aside. She couldn't wait until the roof was done so she could start shelving these. She would ask Austin when that might be, but he wasn't answering her calls. She'd even stopped him a few times in the square, but he only gave her one-word answers to every question. He'd bought her a bike, and now the guy didn't seem to know how to act around her. Maybe he regretted it. But it was a bicycle, not a ring. She had no expectations.

"Why are men so difficult?" Libby shot the question at Danielle, who reclined against one wall, reading.

She put her finger in the book to hold her place and stretched. "I have no idea, but if you find out please let me know."

"Is there a man in your life making it difficult?" Libby dropped into a folding chair and reached for her water bottle.

Danielle laid her book aside and pulled her knees up to her chest. "I have about ten men in my life that make it difficult."

"Ten?" Libby let out a loud laugh.

"Not romantically. That would be zero. But

that's probably because of the ten. A dad who doesn't think a girl is as capable of running a business as his strapping, clueless boys. Four brothers who readily forget that I'm not another brother. And the five guys at the shop who see me as just one of the boys." Danielle pulled her ponytail holder out of her hair and combed it through with her fingers.

"You work at a shop?" Libby downed the rest of the water.

"My dad owns Dan's Garage." With her hair down around her face, it softened her features and made her brown eyes look huge.

"Do you like working in the shop?"

"Love it." Danielle stretched out her long legs and crossed them at her ankles. "There's something about rebuilding an engine and listening to it rev up for the first time."

"I could see how that would be satisfying."

"I want to take over the business, but my dad is still holding out for one of my thickheaded brothers to step up. Them being boys and all." She picked at the weathered floorboard beside her. "I love my dad, but he's stuck in about 1950. He didn't even want me working in the shop, but when he realized I could rebuild a carburetor in seventh grade, he gave in."

Libby stood and grabbed the broom. "So how do the guys you work with make your life difficult?"

Danielle held up the book. "If any of them caught me reading this, they'd never let me live it down. Not to mention they'd start doubting my abilities in the shop. It's better when they forget I'm a girl."

Libby set to sweeping the dust and debris left behind by the electrician and drywall guy. "Is that why you dress in a way that hides your shape?"

Danielle looked down at her shapeless jeans and baggy T-shirt. "I guess. That and a lack of knowledge. My mom died when I was about five, and I learned the easiest way to get along in my house was to blend in with the boys."

"And now?"

"And now the only guy I have any interest in doesn't even realize I'm a girl." Danielle shrugged and leaned back against the wall.

"We could do a makeover." Libby paused her sweeping. "Olivia would love it."

Danielle held up her hands like a shield as a look of horror crossed her face. "No thanks."

A knock at the door filled the room just before a guy with dark hair that curled out from underneath a red baseball cap poked his head in. He looked about Danielle's age. If Libby remembered right, he was one of Olivia's brothers.

Danielle shoved the book behind a box and jumped to her feet, then grabbed her ponytail holder and secured her hair back. "Gideon. What are you doing here?"

"There you are, Dan." He stepped in the rest of the way. His red-and-blue flannel shirt untucked from his jeans and a worn backpack slung over his shoulder added to his country-boy look. All he needed was a guitar and an old pickup truck. "A bunch of the guys were going to grab pizza after work. Thought you might want to join us. Someone said they saw you walk in here, but I didn't believe them. What are you doing?"

Danielle grabbed her bag. "Just helping Libby, but I can go."

Gideon nodded at Danielle. His pale blue eyes warmed as he extended his hand and offered Libby a boy-next-door, chocolate-melting smile. "Hi. I'm Gideon Mathews."

"Libby. I'm your sister's roommate." She shook his hand and then glanced at Danielle.

Danielle grabbed the book from behind the box, tucked it deep into her bag, then smoothed back her ponytail.

"Right. You're the librarian that we moved the books for. Nice to finally meet you."

"Yes. And thank you for that, by the way." If Libby was a betting woman, she'd put money on Gideon being the one Danielle didn't want seeing her as one of the guys.

He took a step closer to Danielle. "Did you need more help? I can help Danielle."

Danielle's eyes widened.

"No, she's got it. We work well together. It's a *girl* thing."

He raised one eyebrow at Danielle, then shrugged. "Okay. Let me know if you do need any more help." He offered a wave before heading out the door with Danielle not far behind.

Libby's stomach growled just as a text pinged her phone. She dug in her bag and pulled it out.

Olivia
Donny's for dinner in 10?

Yes. Starving.

Libby pocketed her phone and locked the door behind her. She walked through the grass and crossed at the corner. Austin exited the bank just as she passed. She paused to keep from running into him. "Oh. Hi."

He stepped back and shoved his hands in his pockets. "Hi." He opened his mouth to say something more, then shut it and pointed toward the square. "I've got to get back to work. I'll see you around."

She'd never understand that man.

The dinnertime rush was in full swing at Donny's. Libby wedged her way through a few people waiting for a booth and claimed the first empty bar stool she came to. She dropped her purse on the next stool to save it for Olivia.

"Libby. How are you?" Janie appeared in front of her, her brown-black hair tied back in a bun and a towel slung over her shoulder. "The library is looking good."

She'd met Janie a few days ago when she stopped to visit with Olivia. She couldn't get over how different they looked. But evidently Janie took after their mother's Italian heritage and Olivia had all the Scandinavian side of the family.

"The library is a lot of work, but it's coming along. I'll take a coffee and wait to order until Olivia gets here. She should be here soon." Libby pulled two packets of sugar and a packet of creamer from the basket nearby. "I just met your brother."

"Gideon or Caleb?" Janie pulled a mug down and filled it with black goodness.

"Gideon." Libby tore the top off one sugar packet and dumped it in. "Does he date a lot?"

"Not much. But he's adorable, isn't he? I think half the girls in town would date him if he gave them a chance."

"Do you know what type of girl he likes?" Libby added another sugar and opened the creamer. On her third circle with her spoon, she lifted her head and found Janie staring at her. "Oh, no. Not for me. I mean, he has to be almost ten years younger than me."

Janie offered a little laugh. "Who are you thinking?"

Libby tapped her spoon on the side of the cup, then set it on the napkin. "I really can't say."

Janie leaned forward. "I've always thought he should date Danielle Fair."

Libby paused with the mug halfway to her mouth. "Right?"

"Olivia and I have been saying that for the last year. They're best friends, you know. But Gideon assures us that he just doesn't see *Dan* that way, and he says she has no interest in him."

"I can almost guarantee one of those is wrong." Libby lifted her eyebrows as she took a sip of coffee.

"What do you know?" Janie's eyes widened as she leaned closer.

"I don't *know* anything, but I think Danielle has a big crush on him. Only she doesn't know how to get him to wake up and see her not as one of the guys."

The bell rang, announcing someone was ready to pay their bill. Janie glanced over her shoulder as she headed that way. "*That* we can work with."

The bar stool next to Libby shifted. "You're late." She grabbed a napkin and wiped at a ring that had formed under her mug.

"Glad to know you were waiting for me," an unfamiliar deep voice rumbled next to her.

Libby turned to find a set of shocking green eyes. The guy's curly red hair conveyed a boy-next-door look, but the smirk on his face erased any question as to whether he knew how cute he was. She'd dealt with this type before—no thanks. "Sorry, I thought you were someone else."

"Too bad. I wouldn't mind a cute thing like you waiting for me. My name is Ted." He offered his hand and she ignored it, but it didn't seem to faze him. "You new around here?"

Ted. Where had she heard that name? Right. "You're the one taking Olivia fishing." When his eyebrow lifted, she added, "She's my roommate."

"Great, then you can help me out. Can you tell her we need to reschedule? It beats trying to track her down. I came in hoping she was working today, but no luck."

"And you can't text her because . . . ?"

"Let's just say I went fishing yesterday and didn't catch anything, but the fish caught my phone. I can't get one until tomorrow and I'm lost without it."

"Sure, I'll tell her. But she'll be here any minute."

"My ride is waiting for me. You're the best." Ted winked at her just before he hurried out the door.

"That guy is a piece of work. Don't go falling for him."

Libby whipped around at Nate's voice and found him sitting one seat beyond where Ted had just been, coffee already in hand. How had she missed him coming up?

"Don't worry. He's not my type."

Nate hesitated for a moment. "Will you do me a favor?"

"That depends on what it is." Libby pulled out her phone and sent a text to Olivia.

> Where are you?

She started typing another.

> Just met Ted. Interesting guy. He has to
> can—

"Don't tell Olivia that Ted had to cancel."

Her thumbs paused on the keyboard. "What? Why not? She needs to arrange something else for the article."

"I'll take her."

"That's crazy." She hadn't finished the text, but she hadn't deleted it either. "Why not just tell her that you're taking her instead?"

"She'll just wait and reschedule with him." He gripped his mug tighter, pleading in his eyes. "Please. I've been going insane since she told me she was going to be spending time with that guy. You can't honestly say that you want to see her with him?"

"No. I want to see her with you." She sent him a pointed look.

"It isn't that simple." His face reddened as his

eyes dropped to his coffee. "One more thing. Will you . . . find out when he was supposed to pick her up?"

"Relationships don't have to be this hard, you know." Libby's fingers hovered over the half-finished text.

The bell chimed over the door again, and Olivia hurried in with her purse in hand. She dropped it in the space next to Libby. "I need to check something on the schedule, then I'll be out."

Nate gave Libby one more pleading look before he headed for the door.

Libby had just finished deleting the text when Olivia walked up. "What were you and Nate talking about?"

"Not much." Libby swallowed. "When are you going fishing?"

"Thursday at ten. Why?" Olivia picked up a menu and started looking it over.

Libby's heart thumped in her chest. "Thought maybe we should plan fish for dinner."

"Absolutely not." Olivia offered a half laugh, but her eyes were still questioning. Great. Olivia could tell she was hiding something, which meant now she thought Libby and Nate had secrets. But if she tried to clarify, Olivia would pull the whole truth out of her.

Libby hated keeping secrets, and here she was keeping one from one of the few friends she had in town. But it was for Olivia's own good.

Because Nate was right. She didn't want Olivia spending the day with that Ted guy. Olivia might think she was too smart to fall for his charms, but Libby had thought that about Colin too, and, well . . . she wanted more for Olivia.

This couldn't be happening. Libby sprinted through the front door of the schoolhouse and did her best to tug a box of books away from the steady stream of drips. The muscles in her shoulders burned as the moist cardboard scraped against the wet floor. She gave another tug just before the soggy box gave way and sent a pile of books across the floor.

Libby landed with a thud on her backside. Maybe she needed to get help, but Olivia was working tonight, and Austin had been the one who had told her the roof wasn't ready. Ugh—she hated it when he was right. But it wasn't even supposed to rain until the end of the week. Leave it to Michigan's weather to turn on a dime.

There was no way around it. She'd made another wrong decision, and she didn't need an I-told-you-so lecture right now.

Libby picked up one of the spilled books and thumbed through the soggy pages. They were already beginning to pucker. If too many got damaged, she wouldn't have enough to make a full library.

The beating of the rain against the window

stole any hope it would end soon. Maybe she could make sure every box was in a dry spot. She glanced around the room as a drop of water splattered on her cheek. Ahh! Was there no safe spot in this building? She eyed the ceiling as water snaked across the rafters, finding new avenues to the floor.

She shoved to a stand, pulled up her hood, and tightened her coat. Rain prickled her cheeks as she rushed out the front door. Dusk had come early with the thick clouds blocking out the sun.

Libby circled the building until she located the offending corner and squinted beyond the rain. The wind had pulled free the plastic that had been nailed down in this corner. It seemed like an easy fix. The ladder still rested against the roof, and someone had left a few tools in the corner of the schoolhouse. She raced back inside, dodging a puddle that was forming at the bottom of the stairs.

The old Libby would never have considered climbing a ladder in the rain, but she was a new, improved Libby. She could do this.

When she got to the corner of the schoolhouse armed with a hammer and a few nails, the ladder seemed to have grown. This was possibly a very bad idea, but how hard could it be to grab that plastic, pull it down over the corner, and secure it?

Libby slid the nails into her coat pocket and

looked at the hammer. How did people carry a hammer up a ladder? Holding it in her left hand, she used it like a claw as she climbed up.

One step. Two. Three. Four.

Maybe she should stop counting. Rung by rung she made her way to the top. She shivered against the howling wind and reached for the plastic. It was well out of reach, and unless she wanted to channel her inner Spider-Man and walk on the wet roof, there was no way she'd get to it.

"What are you doing?" Austin's voice boomed over the rain.

Libby jumped and clung to the ladder. "Why would you scare me like that? I'm on a ladder."

"Why are you climbing my ladder? In the rain? Get down."

Libby made her way back down until they were eye to eye. "I need to fix the roof. My books are getting wet."

Austin lifted her from the ladder and set her back on the ground.

"Stop that. What are you doing?"

"What am I doing? I'm trying to keep you from killing yourself."

He claimed the hammer and nails, climbed to the top of the ladder, and in record time accomplished what she'd been trying to do. Blast him and his long-arm reach.

When he dropped back to the ground, he eyed her for a moment, then lifted the ladder away from the building and laid it on its side just before the wind and rain picked up.

Libby ran for the door of the schoolhouse, but he just followed her in.

"Are you done trying to kill yourself, or do I need to stay?" He shook some of the wetness from his hair. "I swear, until I met you, I didn't know someone could cause my life so much chaos."

"I wasn't trying to kill myself. I was fine. I could have—"

Her words died as his head tilted to the side with a disbelieving expression on his face.

"Okay, maybe I couldn't have. But I wasn't trying to kill myself."

"Just to be safe, I'll take this back home." He waved the hammer in the air.

"Fine. I was done with it anyway. Now I need to see if I can save any of these books."

Austin stepped over to the spilled box and picked up a book. "This one is a lost cause, but I can't say"—he examined the cover—"*Love's Tender Fury* is a great loss."

"I don't know. Any Jennifer Wilde novel was quite popular in the seventies and eighties. That book had forty-one printings in the first five years."

"Wow. Does she still write?"

"He. Jennifer Wilde was Thomas E. Huff along with about five or six other pseudonyms. And no, he's not still writing. He died in 1990."

"How do you know all that? Is he your favorite author?" He grabbed a few other spilled books and set them out to dry.

"No. I just love research and I remember most of what I read. Most kids watch superhero shows and wish to be the hero or the one who falls in love with the hero. Me? I always wanted to be the researcher who found out the key that solved the mystery. Like Alfred to Batman—"

"Or Fitz and Simmons from *Agents of S.H.I.E.L.D.*?"

"Yes! Or Felicity to Green Arrow." She grabbed the edge of another box and yanked it farther away from a puddle, then dropped a towel on the puddle.

"You have a Felicity vibe going on there. All you need is glasses to disguise how beautiful you are. Maybe you're more Pepper Potts to Iron Man."

"What?" Her foot slipped on the wet floor, setting her off balance and onto her backside. Ugh.

A smile tugged at his lips as he held out his hand. "Easy there."

She accepted his hand and pulled herself to her feet. "I'm no Gwyneth Paltrow or Emily Bett Rickards. I'm more Alfred. I'm not great at relationships."

"Why do you say that?"

She finished mopping up one puddle and moved to another. "Remember that guy I told you about who robbed my bookstore?"

"Yes."

Libby wrung out the rag in the bucket and went back to wiping the nearly dry spot. "He was my boyfriend. Or I should say, I thought he was my boyfriend. I do think he liked me at first, but not enough to keep him from holding a gun to my head for the right price."

When Austin didn't comment she glanced up. The muscle in his jaw twitched as his hand crushed the book he was holding.

"Easy, killer." She reached out and took the book. "It was three years ago, and he was carted to the Tower of London by a bobby."

"They still use that?"

"No. It was a joke to lighten the mood. But he did go to jail, and I'm fine now."

His hand landed on her arm as she walked past, pulling her to a stop. His thumb traced a small circle on her arm. "Are you? Fine now?"

The warmth of his hand seeped through the thin material of her shirt. Her gaze followed his arm up to his shoulder and then to his silver eyes less than twelve inches away. Was she fine after what Colin had done? Most days. Was she fine right now with Austin this close? Exhilarated, elated, even giddy maybe. But fine? Not so much.

"How did he even know about the books?" His voice was lower now and laced with a rough edge.

"I fed him all the information he needed. How much they were worth. Where those books were generally bought and sold. My gift of research helped him bring down a little bookstore, and I . . . felt like an idiot."

"It wasn't your fault." He grabbed a few of the soggy books and fanned them out.

"I know, but I honestly thought he asked a lot of questions because he was trying to learn about something I was passionate about." She fanned out another book and laid it out on a rough table made of scrap wood and sawhorses that Nate had thrown together last week.

Austin added a book to the sawhorse table, then locked eyes with her. "I'm sorry you had to go through that."

When she didn't answer, he brushed a piece of wet hair that still clung to her face behind her ear. Slow. Lingering. "What happened Friday?"

Libby blinked a few times but couldn't seem to make herself look away. "As I told you, I had panic attacks for a while after the holdup. I think Grand Haven was just the perfect storm of me not caring for myself, the books, and the bell. If you hadn't been there—"

"But I *was* there." His gaze traced her face before he leaned a fraction of an inch closer.

What was going on? Did she want this? She couldn't trust the wrong person again.

She trusted him not to hold her at gunpoint,

but did she trust him not to break her heart? Not to mention he'd ignored her for the past three days.

His breath mingled with hers as he tucked a lock of hair behind her other ear, then traced her chin with his finger as his eyes started to close.

"Is Shiro pregnant?" Libby's words came out louder than she intended. Much too loud, since he was only about two inches away.

He pulled back and dropped his hand. "What?"

That was a good question. Of all the things she could have said, she had to ask if his dog was pregnant.

"I was just curious if you knew yet—"

"No, she's not." He took a step back as all emotion disappeared from his face.

"No puppies. Great. Well, I mean, everyone loves puppies. It's just a lot of work, and you have a lot of other work right now."

Oh my word, Libby, stop talking.

Austin stared at her before he backed up another step, nodded once, and turned toward the door. "I should go."

No. "Sure. Okay."

She didn't want to push him away; she just wanted him to pick a lane.

He grabbed his coat and disappeared out the door. He'd even left his hammer.

She didn't want him to leave. She just needed to be sure. But could she ever be sure? It didn't matter. The way he looked when he headed out that door, he wasn't coming back anytime soon.

If she were more Pepper Potts, she would have interrogated him until she knew he could be trusted. Then again, if she were Pepper Potts, she might have kissed him senseless first and then started the interrogation. But no, she was Alfred all the way.

Libby walked over to the window. The sky seemed to open up as the rain pelted down harder and faster. But what if she didn't want to be Alfred? She'd set out this summer determined to redefine herself to move forward. This wasn't moving forward.

Maybe it was time to choose to be less Alfred and more Pepper.

Before she could question the sanity of this plan, Libby scooped up the hammer and ran through the pouring rain toward Austin's.

How could he have left that ladder up against the schoolhouse?

Austin stacked an empty pot on a shelf and dusted the dirt off his worktable as the rain pelting the plastic roof of his greenhouse grew louder. His heart had nearly stopped when he'd spotted Libby at the very top. Talk about a rookie construction mistake. Some kid could have killed himself. Libby could have killed herself. He'd been way too distracted lately, and he couldn't afford a mistake like that again.

A few feet away, the plastic door was pushed aside as Libby charged in. Wet curls clung to the sides of her face as she wrapped one arm across her body and held up his hammer in the other. "I have your hammer."

His hammer? Of all the things he thought she might say, that wasn't it.

Her knees began to shake, and she hugged herself a bit closer.

"Libby, you're freezing." He took the hammer from her hand. "I could have gotten it later. Go home and get warm."

"N-no. I have something to s-say."

"Fine, but you're soaking wet." Austin grabbed a sweatshirt he'd tossed aside the other day and threw it at her. "Put this on, then yell at me."

Libby eyed him, shed her wet coat, and hung it on a planter hook by the door. By the time the sweatshirt descended on her shoulders, the fight seemed to have left her. "Why do we have such a hard time being friends?"

Friends? The problem was that somewhere between their fights and disasters, his feelings for Libby had moved out of the friend zone into unfamiliar waters. And when he'd tried to act on those feelings a few minutes ago, she'd backpedaled about twenty feet.

But he couldn't say all that. Instead, he offered

a shrug and pulled one of his roses that he needed to repot to the table. "Nate and I can't seem to get along either. Maybe I'm not very good at friendships."

Of course, his issues with Nate weren't at all the same.

"Maybe you just need someone to teach you how to be a friend." A half smile tugged at her lips, and he looked away.

Friend. Think friend.

"What are these plants? They're beautiful but look almost wild." She leaned over the heirloom roses he'd potted and smelled one of the blossoms. She lifted her eyebrows and held up a finger. "Friendship lesson number one. This is where you explain the plant, why you're growing it, and why you spend so much time here in your greenhouse."

He couldn't stop the slight chuckle that rumbled in his chest. "Is that so?"

"Yes." Libby didn't hold his gaze but instead bit her lip as she returned to examining the plant. Maybe she wasn't as confident as she wanted him to think.

He stepped around the table to where she was standing. "That's a Rebecca Louise, an heirloom rose."

"Heirloom rose?"

"Heirloom roses refer to roses that existed before 1867. That was when they first started creating hybrids. The roses you see in stores are all hybrids grown for color, stem strength and straightness, and smell. I guess in a way, you're right, it's more wild than those."

"Where did you get the plants?"

"You can order them online. I thought these might look perfect around the schoolhouse. More authentic. Although I'll order the ones I'll use for the square. I can't grow that many in here in time."

"I love it." She meandered around the small space, studying each rose. "This place is magical. You should put white lights in here."

"White lights? How would that help the plants?"

"It probably wouldn't, but it'd be pretty."

"I'll keep that in mind."

Libby ran her fingers over the petals of a light pink rose. "Did you have a greenhouse at your last place?"

"In Canton? Yes. I keep a greenhouse going if I can wherever I am. It's my place to hide away and de-stress." Austin plucked the dead leaves from the pot in front of him. "Do you want to help me repot this rose?"

"I don't want to kill it."

"It's a plant. A fairly hardy one at that."

She seemed to weigh her options a moment, then lifted her chin. "What do I do?"

Austin grabbed a larger pot from the shelf and

set it on the table. He picked up the potting soil. "First you need to add a bit of soil to the bottom."

Libby pulled out a large scoop with both hands and dropped it in the pot. "Like that?"

"Probably not quite that much. You still have to fit everything that's in this pot in there." Austin dumped some soil back in the bag and made a small divot in the bottom. "Now lift the pot with one hand and wrap your hand around the base of the plant with the other. Careful of the thorns. Wait, you may want gloves." He grabbed a pair off the table and handed them to her.

The gloves were too big for her, but she slipped them on and gripped the plant as he'd said.

"Now turn the plant upside down and let everything fall out of the pot. It should stay in a clump for the most part."

Libby's hands gripped the plant tighter. "What if I drop it?"

"Then we'll pick it up."

"But it'll damage the plant."

"It'll be fine, Libby. Trust yourself."

She swallowed and turned the pot over slower than he could have thought possible. "Now what? Help! I'm going to drop it."

"You're doing great. Now lift off the pot." He put his hands on the sides and helped her lift.

She inspected the ball of dirt and roots. "I did it."

"You did." He set the empty pot aside and

pointed to the one they'd readied. "Now put that in the new pot."

Libby placed it in the larger pot with more precision and care than he'd ever given a plant in his life.

"Now put in more soil to fill the edges."

"How long have you been growing plants?"

"I wanted to be a botanist. That was my major at U of M. But that didn't work out. Maybe a little of that passion remains."

"Why didn't it work out?" She scratched her forehead, leaving a smudge of dirt behind.

"My brother drove the company van into a storefront while he was drunk. He wasn't on the company insurance, and unless my parents were willing to take him to court for it, they were liable along with our business. Budgets were cut, the money for U of M was gone, and I was needed to keep the family business alive. Sacrifices had to be made." Austin walked the empty pot to the shelf. "So I dropped out of U of M. I finished my landscape architecture degree through night classes at a local college, but it was never my passion. I did it because my dad needed help."

She peeled off the gloves. "So, Nate's bad choice derailed your life."

"Yup."

"Is that why you hate him?"

"I don't *hate* him. I'm angry that he caused so

253

much chaos in so many lives and doesn't seem to have to account for it."

"So much chaos? Was there more?"

Austin sat on the edge of the table. "The business was nearly ruined. Not only did I rearrange my life because of it, it also added stress to my parents. They even had to take out an extra loan against the house. But Nate? He went on to make bad decisions for the next year. By the time he got his life together, we had almost dug ourselves out of the hole and were surviving again. Our dad told Nate he wanted him to have a fresh start."

"Wow."

"Then Nate got the call of God to become a pastor, and now everyone loves perfect Pastor Nate. When he graduated from seminary, my father said he'd never been prouder." He gripped the edge of the table as the memory burned inside him.

She placed a hand on his arm but didn't say anything.

" 'Never' is a pretty big word." He pushed away from the table and moved the spade back to the shelf, the tool clanging in the silence. "It didn't matter that I'd done everything he'd ever asked of me. It didn't matter that I'd thrown away my plans to keep the family business going. He was proud of Nate because he'd become a *pastor*."

Libby brushed a hand across his shoulder. "I'm sorry, Austin."

He turned to tell her it didn't matter, but the look in her eyes stopped him. She wasn't offering pity. She *was* sorry. Sorry that his dream had been ripped from him. Sorry for his dad's words. And sorry that his relationship with his brother was still not right.

Her hand slid down his shoulder to his forearm. "Why don't you pursue this botany dream now?"

He shrugged, then stared at her hand, which was now toying with a scar on his forearm. "I'm not sure I want that degree anymore. I'd love to open a greenhouse, but if I don't save the business, who will? And it's important to my dad. It's all he has left."

"That's why you need good publicity for the business now."

"Yes. So I can't have beautiful women falling to their death from the roof of the library. Talk about bad publicity."

Her cheeks turned pink. "You think I'm beautiful?"

She had to know she was beautiful. But the shocked expression on her face said otherwise.

"You're one of the most beautiful women I know. At least when you don't have dirt smudged across your face." Austin rubbed at the smudge with his thumb.

Her eyes closed with the touch of his hand, and her teeth captured her bottom lip.

"Libby, you made it pretty clear at the

schoolhouse that you didn't want me to kiss you. I respect that. Unless you've changed your mind, we need to stop this." He took a half step back.

Libby's eyes popped open. "You think I don't want to kiss you?" She spun and paced the two feet to the table and back. "What I want is to stop dealing with Dr. Jekyll and Mr. Hyde. Every time I think we're getting close, you push me away again. I wasn't willing to have you kiss me only to act like I don't exist tomorrow."

The barb hit its mark. She was right. In his desperation to figure out his own mind, he'd been completely unfair to her.

"I came here not to give you back that dumb hammer. I came to find out if this"—she pointed between them—"is something. And when I say 'something,' I don't mean hot one day and cold the next." She placed her hands on his forearms, her thumb finding the scar from last summer again. "I came to find out what you want."

"I want . . ." What did he want? He didn't want to be trapped in a relationship with a person he couldn't trust. But that wasn't Libby. That was Becky, and it was time to get that straight in his mind. Libby wasn't Becky. He took a half step forward, leaving only inches between them. "I want you." He ran his hands up her arms and stopped at her collarbone.

"And I want you." Her voice came out a bit

rougher this time. "But I may have stopped the kiss because I was a little . . . scared."

"Of me." He loosened his hold.

"No." She tightened her grip. "Scared to care for someone again. Scared to try."

He brushed a piece of wet hair from her forehead. "Sometimes all you need is twenty seconds of insane courage."

"I've heard that before." Her head tilted as if she was searching her memory. "Mark Twain?"

"No. *We Bought a Zoo.*"

She laughed and swatted his arm.

His thumbs traced the edge of her jaw. "Are you ready for some insane courage?"

"Yes."

His thumb traveled along her bottom lip. "Can I kiss you now?"

"Yes."

He leaned closer, brushing his lips along her jaw until he found that freckle just below her right ear that had been driving him crazy the other day. "You're very agreeable tonight."

Her breathing slowed as he moved his lips back toward her mouth. "Would you just kiss me al—"

Austin silenced her protest with his mouth. Her lips were soft and warm and tasted a bit like summer rain. She moved her hands up behind his shoulders and back down his arms. He let go of the need to be right, to be perfect. Here he could just be in the now. He drew in a slow breath as every nerve in his body ached for more. More of Libby, more of her touch, and more of the escape from the stress of life that he found here in her arms.

Libby responded to him, matching his pressure and gripping his shoulders, pulling him closer. He could lose himself in her without one regret.

When he released her, she took a step back, her lips red and a bit puffy. She offered a hesitant smile and moved toward the door. She pushed it open but turned back at the last second. "Thanks for teaching me about plants. Good night." Then she disappeared into the rain.

He'd put Libby through so much, their first date had to be epic. But when? His schedule with the square had his calendar filled. Except for next Friday. He winced. That was when he'd scheduled the rose delivery. The heirloom greenhouse was booked up, and getting that date had taken him weeks. If he canceled, who knew when they could come again.

But all he needed was someone to sign for the delivery. Nate wanted a chance to prove himself. It looked like next Friday he was going to have a chance.

eleven

She should be mad—furious, actually. Olivia tightened her grip on Nate's waist and buried her face in his back to hide from the wind. The last thing she needed was bugs in her teeth. Maybe they should've taken her car. But when he'd shown up that morning to take her fishing instead of Ted, she didn't know if she should be thrilled that this was what Libby had been hiding from her or frustrated that Nate seemed to want it both ways. He didn't want to be with her but didn't want her with anyone else.

She climbed off the bike and eyed Nate as he slid off his helmet. Even with helmet hair, he was distracting. A grin filled his face as he reached up and tugged a leaf from her hair. Right. Because after a ride through the country, he was ready for a model shoot and she needed defoliating.

Nate dropped the leaf and started down a narrow path that cut between the trees. "This is Chet Anderson's land. Luke and I leave our boats over here."

Olivia's fingers combed the rest of her hair in search of any more leaves as she walked. She'd have to tie it back for the ride home.

It was only about thirty feet before the path

opened into a clearing that dipped to the edge of a good-sized lake. One large oak stretched out over the water, but most of the trees stopped about fifteen feet back from the shore. Tall grass lined the shore and dipped into the lake, with just a handful of pale yellow wildflowers left over from the summer.

"What lake is this?"

"It's a little finger off of Stony Lake. It has a couple small rivers that flow through it, but the current isn't too bad right here. Nothing we can't handle coming back. The boat is just over here." Nate stepped over a log about knee-high, then offered her his hand.

She slid hers into it, trying not to think about the warmth, the rough callouses against her palm, or what it would feel like to be held by those hands. Okay, maybe she wasn't trying very hard.

After she hopped the log, he dropped her hand and moved ahead. "We just need to push off. I brought all the fishing stuff down this morning when I still had access to the van."

Olivia paused at the water's edge, and her pulse began to speed up. Somehow in the events of the morning, she'd been so caught up with everything that was happening with Nate that she'd forgotten the real problem.

Fishing. In a lake. With fish. She might be sick. She sat on a log and drew in a huge breath.

Then there was the little detail she didn't like to confess to anyone. "Do you have a life jacket?"

"Yeah, we always keep them in the boat." Nate pulled something from his pocket and then leaned down into the boat.

"Can I wear it?" Olivia stepped closer. "Why is there a hole in the boat?"

"It's for the plug." He held up a cap-looking thing. "With all the rain yesterday, I had to make sure it was fully drained."

Something in her face must have given her away, because he hurried to her side. "What's wrong?"

"It's nothing." A cool sensation washed over her, and she shoved her hands in her pockets to keep from shaking.

He stood in front of her. "Olivia, it isn't nothing. Talk to me."

She eyed the dark water, then looked back at him. "I don't like fish."

A smile tugged at the corner of Nate's mouth. "Is that all? We don't have to eat them. Just a quick catch and release."

"No, it isn't the eating. It's the touching."

He offered a shrug. "I'll take them off the hook."

"And the seeing."

"Seeing?" One eyebrow lifted as he rested his hands on his hips. "How are you going to fish without seeing fish?"

"I haven't figured that out. I think I'll be okay

if they don't surprise me. I just hate the fact you can't see where they are in the dark water." A shiver traveled the length of her body.

Nate grabbed a life jacket from the boat and handed it to her. "I've never had one jump in my boat before."

"I'm serious." She dropped the life jacket around her neck. Of course, it would have to be a ridiculous orange one with the tie at the chin. "I don't think them being on a line will be as bad. It's mostly seeing them in the water doing that slithery-jerky thing they do."

"You mean swimming." He let out a laugh this time.

"This isn't funny." She made an attempt at a bow with the straps but failed. "Didn't you say once in a sermon that you had an irrational phobia of snakes?"

"Yes."

She dropped the straps and pointed at the stick next to his foot. "What if I told you there was one by your foot?"

Nate let out an unmanly squeal as he jumped from one foot to the other. "Where?"

"There is no snake." Olivia giggled, then worked at tying the straps once more. "It was an example. That's how I feel about fish."

"First of all, not funny." He pointed a finger at her, but there was still laughter in his eyes. "But fish?"

Her second attempt at a bow didn't go any better. "I can handle spiders, snakes, and mice, okay? It's a phobia. By definition it's irrational."

He pulled the straps from her hands and tied a bow. "You don't have to do this."

"Yes, I do." Why was her voice thick all of a sudden?

He grabbed the waist strap and stretched around her to secure the final buckle. "Why?"

"The *Phoenix Tribune* said that—"

"I didn't realize you were still hoping to get that job." Nate's lips thinned a bit as he popped the buckle into place.

She tried to force a look of indifference. "It's not like I have anything holding me here."

Nate winced. "Right. Well, let's do this so you can write that article. And I'll do my best not to surprise you with any fish. I promise they won't jump in the boat. And this is a flat-bottom rowboat. Pretty stable."

"I'm not a good swimmer."

Nate squeezed her hand. "I promise not to let you drown." He dropped her hand and pointed to the boat. "In you go."

She put one foot in the boat and it swayed under her. She screamed and grabbed the side. "I thought you said it was a stable boat."

"It is, but it's still a boat. You can't stand in it." Nate grabbed her hand again and helped her sit. Then in one swift movement, he pushed off and

263

jumped in the boat. It offered only a small teeter as he did. Show-off.

It was a warm day for the first of October, but there was no doubt that the cold nights had chilled the water. She shaded her eyes against the late morning sun reflecting off the water as Nate pulled against the oars. The motion defined the muscles in his wide shoulders, and Olivia found herself thankful for fishing for the first time in her life. Ten minutes later, they'd made it about a hundred yards down the shore and about fifty feet out.

"This is my favorite fishing spot." He pointed to the edge of the woods. "You see that little shed-looking thing right through those trees? That's Chet's ice-fishing hut. He let Luke and me use it last winter. That reminds me, I need to check to see if I left a few things in there when we're done here."

"Fishing through the ice? I'm not sure if that would be better or worse. I think I'd be afraid the ice would crack."

"We make sure the ice is plenty thick first." Nate picked up a pole and started doing something with the end of the line. "Are you ready to give fishing a go?"

She peeked over the edge of the boat, then back at Nate. "The way I see it, people fish all the time and fail. I don't have to catch anything to make the story believable, but I do have to at least make an effort."

Nate popped open a box of small slimy orange spheres and stabbed one with the hook. "I bought these last year and never had any luck with them. This way you can say that you used bait, but the chances of you catching anything go way down. I already added the bobber and weights earlier. You're all set."

"Perfect." Olivia reached for the pole, then held it over the side, letting the hook dip just below the surface.

Nate tried to cover his laugh with a cough, but it didn't work.

She glared at him. "What?"

"You need to cast it."

"Cast?"

"Let me show you." He readied another pole, tilted it back, and then gave a quick flick of his wrist. The hook sailed about thirty feet away before sinking below the surface.

She tried the same, but hers splashed down about three feet from the boat.

Nate pointed to part of her pole. "You have to press that button as you cast it forward."

She tried again and it went about fifteen feet. Good enough.

"Having fun?" Nate leaned back and crossed his legs.

"I just choose to believe that we're simply in two feet of water and there are no fish in the lake." Her bobber moved. Olivia screamed but held on. "You said this wouldn't catch anything."

Nate sat forward. "Fish are fickle creatures."

"Not helpful. What do I do now?" The line darted under the surface of the water.

"We have to pull it in and get the hook out of its mouth." He held out his hand. "I'll take care of it. Hand me the pole."

"No, I can do this. I have to do this." She drew a slow breath and gripped the pole with two hands. "Tell me what to do."

He pointed to the crank by her hand. "Wind the reel."

She did and prayed for calmness with each turn of the handle. It wasn't tugging too much, so the fish couldn't be very big. She could handle a small fish. When it surfaced, the thing couldn't have been more than six inches long. She held it up by the line. "I caught a fish. I shall call him Nemo."

He released a small chuckle, then reached for the glorified minnow and undid the hook. "Maybe you'll be a fisherman after all."

He tossed the little guy back in just before his rod began to move. Maybe fishing could be fun. Nate grabbed his pole and began to reel it in. He made it seem effortless, but his pole seemed to bend a lot more than hers.

She eyed the water and watched for Nemo's brother to appear. Instead of a cute little fish, a wide mouth with tentacles on its lips appeared. As the rest of the body surfaced, Olivia's heart rate doubled. It had to be over a foot long and the ugliest fish she'd seen in her life.

Her breaths were coming faster. Why wasn't there enough oxygen in the great outdoors? "Wh-what is that thing?"

"Catfish." Nate eyed her, the fish still tugging against the line. "Sorry. I won't pull him into the boat, but I need to get the hook out." He grabbed it by the mouth, tipping the boat to one side.

Olivia screamed and gripped the sides.

Deep breath. She could do this.

Nate worked again to free the hook. "Almost done."

The fish thrashed in the water, splashing water over the side of the boat.

The next thirty seconds were a blur. Olivia scrambled back, which set Nate off balance. She may have stood up. Who stands up in a boat? Maybe a person who can think of nothing but getting away from that fish. Nate yelled her name just before cold water stole every thought.

Cold took on a whole new meaning when it was shooting knives at every inch of his skin. Nate surfaced and scanned the water. The boat floated a few feet away. His favorite pole was a complete loss. With any luck, the catfish got free first. Olivia floated about ten feet away, kicking her feet wildly as her hands splashed in every direction.

He swam toward her. "What are you doing?"

"Scaring the fish away." Her voice was winded. The girl was going to wear herself out.

"You don't have to do that. They'll simply be afraid of you in the water."

"But what if—"

"I promise. They won't get you. But I can't get close with you kicking like that. Stop and I'll help you get to the shore before we freeze to death."

Her kicking slowed, but when she spoke a tremble filled her voice. "I can't do this."

He swam a bit closer. "You already are. Just remember, two feet of water—no fish."

She tried to move in his direction but seemed to be fighting the life vest. "If it were two feet we wouldn't have to swim."

He swam next to her and slid his hand around her middle. "Fine. Six feet of water—no fish."

Her muscles softened at his touch and she gripped his shoulders. Keeping one arm around her, he used his free arm to swim them toward shore.

They crossed the path of one of the oars and he reached out for it. "Can you hold on to this?"

Her knuckles whitened as she gripped it with two hands. "Where's th-the oth-ther one?"

"Drifting toward those overhanging trees with

the boat. With any luck, the trees will stop them from going too far."

"Do you n-need to g-go af-fter them?" Her chin shook as shivers raked her body.

"Let me get you to shore first. Try to relax. You're safe. I promise."

The warmth of her body next to his warmed his veins up a bit. He'd tried to rationalize over the past months that his attraction to Olivia was just a natural physical response. He was a man and she was beautiful. There was nothing unique or special about it.

But after having her arms wrapped around him on the bike and now this—even with the ridiculously large life vest—Nate didn't think he could keep lying to himself. After all, Libby was beautiful and it didn't bother him to think of her spending time with Austin. But just the idea of Olivia with Ted had choked his thoughts all week. He'd gotten nothing done at work in days. His sermon on Sunday would show it too.

Nate's foot hit the ground and he turned to grab Olivia under the legs.

Her eyes widened. "What are you doing?"

"I can stand, but it's about six inches of muck before anything solid. I thought you'd prefer not to walk in it."

She buried her face in his shoulder, a citrus scent still lacing her hair despite the lake water. "Yuck—don't tell me."

He chuckled. "You asked." He stepped out of the water and found a flattened spot of grass before setting her down.

"I lost my shoes." She stood shivering as she hugged her life jacket.

He untied the straps of the vest and helped her lift it off. "Let me go get the boat and pull it up on shore so it doesn't float away." He walked down to where the boat had caught in the trees and waded in.

It would be easiest to hop into the boat and paddle it back to where they had gotten in, but one look at Olivia shivering in a ball and he knew he couldn't do that to her. He'd get her someplace warm and then come back for the boat.

He tugged the boat back up on shore, tossed the life jacket and oars inside, and jogged back to Olivia. He picked her up again, her soft curves fitting perfectly against him.

"Wh-what are you doing?"

"You have no shoes. You can't walk through the underbrush without shoes. I'll carry you over to the ice-fishing hut. I think I left some clothes in there."

"I'm too heavy to carry that far."

He laughed but Olivia just scowled. She really thought she was too heavy? "I think I can handle it. Now relax."

Olivia buried her face in his chest, which had more to do with keeping warm than with intentionally driving him crazy—but she was doing that just fine without even trying.

Nate did all he could to keep his mind on the task at hand and not on the woman in his arms. It wasn't working. He set her down on her feet next to the small structure and walked in. It wasn't a fancy ice shanty, but it had the basics.

The heater and most of the supplies had been cleaned out, but on a sunny day in February, he'd shoved some extra layers in one of the cabinets built along the wall. And if Luke hadn't bothered . . . Nate popped open one cupboard and then the next. Bingo. He pulled out a thermal shirt, a sweatshirt, and a pair of sweatpants.

Olivia stepped in behind him. "Wow. It's so cute."

Cute? He'd never thought of a fishing hut as cute. He was pretty sure Chet had made it with scrap lumber.

He held out the clothes. "You'll freeze on the back of the bike like that. Get changed. Then we can head back to town and I'll drop you off at your place, or . . ."

Why had he said "or"? "Or" wasn't a good idea. The longer he spent with Olivia, the more his resolve weakened. But he wasn't quite ready to say goodbye yet.

He looked up. She was hanging on his words, waiting for the "or." Maybe she wasn't quite ready to end the day either.

"Or I can start a fire while you change." His voice came out rough, and he cleared his throat. "Then we can warm up a bit before we ride back."

Her eyes lit up. Oh, he was on dangerous ground here. "A fire sounds nice. It'd be good for you to warm up too."

Warming up didn't seem to be his problem.

Nate exited the hut, shutting the door behind him. He gathered some wood and brush, ignoring the little voice in his head calling him all kinds of fool. Then again, he was already in over his head when it came to Olivia. He might as well enjoy a bit of the drowning.

The fire sparked to life with little encouragement. He'd just added another log when the door to the ice hut creaked open.

His sweatshirt and sweatpants were much too big and hid any trace of her figure, but Nate struggled to keep his mind from wandering where it shouldn't. Maybe it was seeing her in his clothes that felt intimate, natural, right. Or maybe it was the way her teeth worried her lip. Whatever it was, it took every ounce of strength Nate had to keep from closing the space and kissing her the way he'd wanted to since their first date over a year and a half ago.

"I thought you might want to wear this." She held up the thermal shirt.

"Thanks." He turned his back to her as he

ungracefully peeled off the wet shirt. He tossed it aside with a slop and reached back for the thermal shirt, but she was no longer holding it out. "Can I have the shirt now?"

"I want to see your tattoos."

"What?" He angled more toward her but still kept his left shoulder facing away.

"I want to see your tattoos."

"No you don't." He held out his hand again.

She shook her head and held the shirt closer to her chest. "Yes I do. I've seen most of them anyway."

Maybe she was right. She had this elevated view of him. Maybe it'd be best to show her his feet of clay right up front.

Nate faced her, giving her a full look at all his markings. Warmth crawled up his skin as she moved closer, studying each mark.

"I know 'master of my fate' was the first, but what was the second?"

This was it. The moment she'd get a real look at who he was. He pointed his left shoulder toward her. Four simple capital letters. JESS.

She nodded as if it didn't matter. But it did. If she cared for him even a fraction of what he felt for her, seeing someone else's name on him like a claim of ownership had to sting.

Her fingers reached out and traced the letters. "That must have hurt."

"No more than any of the others." He kept his

eyes on the woods, willing himself not to look at her. Not to enjoy her touch.

"I don't mean the tattoo." Her pale blue eyes looked into him. "You don't take relationships or tattoos lightly, so I'm guessing when things with Jess ended, it hurt."

He offered a slight shrug. "She woke up and realized she deserved better than me. She was right. She's now married and has three kids: Chase, Aaron, and Lincoln." His heart suffered a familiar pinch.

She dropped her hand and locked eyes with him. "She didn't deserve better. You just had a lot of growing up to do."

Growing up? That was an understatement. He'd been nothing but selfish—turned out, even worse than his uncle. He reached for the thermal shirt, but she didn't yield. "She was right to end things."

"What was your third one?"

"This tribal tattoo that covers my shoulder." He angled his right shoulder toward her.

"Is that what that is? What's the meaning?" She leaned closer, studying it. Her warm breath drifted across his skin.

He shoved his hands in his pockets. "It means I was very drunk after Jess and I broke up and I wanted a large tattoo to cover her name."

Her brow pinched. "But her name is on—"

"Like I said, I was very drunk." He crossed his

arms as Olivia tried to hide her smile and failed. "You sure you want to hear all of this?"

She mimicked his gesture. "Yes. Does the tribal tattoo have meaning?"

"Not that I've been able to find. Some do. But from what I can tell, this is more just art that they were featuring at the place I got it."

"Did you ever consider getting another one to cover 'JESS'?" She inspected the letters again.

"No. At the time I thought it was a sign we'd get back together. And now . . . I just haven't."

She waited for more of an answer. But he wasn't ready to talk about why he still had it.

When he didn't offer any other information, she examined his tattoos again. "What came next?"

He turned his back to her so she could see the one between his shoulder blades. "It's called a triquetra. I got it just after my mom died. She was Irish and loved all things Irish. I wanted something to remember her by but refused to get the Celtic cross since I was still doing all I could to run from God at that point. But God has a sense of humor, because later I found out that this is also referred to as the Trinity Knot. It was used by the Irish for generations to represent the Holy Trinity."

"Even when you were running from God, He never stopped pursuing you." Her fingers traced the lines of the knot, and he fought to keep still.

"You could say that." He drew a slow breath

and faced her. He pointed to the Greek letters over his heart. "This is the last."

"What does it say?" She reached out but stopped before touching him.

"It's *grace* in Greek. It's pronounced *charis*."

"Because you've been saved by grace."

"Yes."

"And now you're a new man."

"Yes."

"And you believe that God has forgiven your past and you're new in Him. That your past in no way stands between you and God anymore."

What was she getting at? "Yes."

Her eyes narrowed on him as her arms crossed. "Then why does it have to stand between us? You preach grace. Why can you not accept it for yourself?"

Ahh. That.

Nate claimed the shirt and slipped it over his head. "You can't tell me that after hearing all that, I'm still the prince you were dreaming of since you were a little girl."

"I don't want a prince. I want you." She inched closer and ran her finger along the points of the tribal tattoo that peeked out of his collar.

Nate closed his eyes, willing himself not to feel—not to react. Was she trying to kill him?

"Your past is not who you are—it's who you were. And these tattoos are not who you are. They're just the surface. Who you are is in here."

She placed her hand over his heart. "And I like that man."

"So the tattoos don't bother you?"

"Bother me?" She tilted her head back with a laugh. "My point was that I like you for who you are as a person. But trust me when I say that I have a lot of appreciation for the surface as well." She ran her fingers over his shirt that now hid each of the tattoos. "I like you . . . all of you."

Nate leaned closer with every touch, his pulse drumming through his ears. "Olivia . . ."

"Stop pushing me away." Her whispered words brushed across his lips as her hands skimmed slowly along his arms up to his shoulders and then back down to his fingers. On their second trip, she tugged at his elbows until his hands reached her waist. "I want you, Nathan. Your past, your future, all of you."

They were so close in height that her wide blue eyes were just inches away. Her lips brushed across his in a featherlight touch, then along his jaw.

Every desire Nate had been pushing down over the past year and a half rose to the surface. His hands gripped her waist and pulled her close against him, bringing her lips back to his. Her mouth was cool and soft as he'd always imagined it might be. And when she released the tiniest of moans as her lips moved against his, it was as if every cell and every nerve of his being reached out for her, wanting more—needing more.

He'd had his share of kisses in his life, but they had been purely physical. Escapes. This? It was as if Olivia had reached into his very soul—into his darkest parts—and accepted him, wanted him. This wasn't an escape. He'd never felt more present. Every inch of him wanted every inch of her closer.

If only . . .

Nate stilled at the reality of what he wanted to do right now—where he wanted to take the kiss.

He pulled back. Olivia's lips were red and puffy, but her eyes were bright. They held a touch of laughter as if she'd just gotten off a roller coaster and wanted to go again. Every inch of him ached to pull her close once more, and maybe that would be the right choice. Just maybe, Olivia was right and he had been a fool to push her away before.

Then again, maybe that was his hormones speaking, and with the taste of her still on his lips, he might not be able to judge between the two. He needed to clear his head. He couldn't afford to make the wrong choice again.

Nate dropped his hands and stepped back. "You stay by the fire. I'll row the boat back, then bring the motorcycle here to pick you up and take you home."

"Nate?" A quiver in her voice laced the word.

He didn't turn back. She was asking a question he couldn't answer right now.

twelve

There were some quirky things about this town, but that hippo had to be number one. Austin stood in the southwest corner of the square and eyed the flags he'd laid out. The auger was set to arrive Monday to drill the anchor posts for the playground, and the brass beast couldn't be more in the way.

Austin peered through the optical level and checked the readings against what was written on his clipboard. He'd written it down wrong. What was his problem today? He erased the wrong number on the clipboard as his gaze flicked to the library. *Stop it.* She wasn't going to just appear and be looking for him. Besides, he had a job to do. He stared at his clipboard. Where was he again?

The dirty pink eraser rubbings still sat where the wrong number had been. He brushed at the paper and wrote the new number in its place.

He walked over to a flag and moved it by six inches. He checked his numbers again. This was ridiculous. Someone had to know how to move that brass beast.

Austin glanced at the library again. Maybe Libby would have an idea. He slid the clipboard under his arm and strode to the library. He knocked twice, then pushed the door open. "Hello?"

The mess from the rain had been cleaned up, and the boxes of books were covered with plastic. He'd gotten the roofers to move their date up a week, but that still put them a week out from a new roof.

"Can I help you?"

Austin spun toward the feminine voice and paused. The gray coveralls and ball cap didn't seem to match the voice. But the feminine features were definitely there in her eyes.

"I was looking for Libby."

She tucked whatever she was reading behind a box. "She went to see Luke and Hannah at the hospital today. She'll be back tonight. Are you Austin?"

There was something familiar about her. "You're the night reader."

"The what?" She stood up a little straighter.

"The one we saw sneaking in to read books."

"Yes. But I go by Danielle." Her face reddened as she shoved her hands in her pockets. "Libby was looking for a key to the desk. She thought you might have it."

Right. The key. He'd put it in his shirt pocket and then . . . who knows what. Maybe it was still there. But he'd done laundry, so it could be anywhere. "Tell her I'll look for it."

"Okay." Danielle picked up her bag and took a few steps toward the door. "Do you want to lock it or—"

"I'm leaving." Austin left and pulled out his phone to check the time. He was supposed to meet Nate at the diner for lunch in fifteen minutes. Maybe he'd head over now. It wasn't like he was getting a lot done here. It was just past noon, so there should be a fair number of people who might just know how to move the hippo.

He jogged across Second Street to Donny's, the bell chiming over the door as he pulled it open. He surveyed the room as he walked in and then cleared his throat.

"Excuse me." His loud voice echoed through the room, and the conversation slowed to a stop. "Sorry to disturb your lunch. But the hippo needs to move. An auger will be arriving Monday to drill the anchor points for the playground, and the hippo is in the way."

Everyone stared at him like he wasn't speaking English.

He offered his best smile. "I just need to know who to talk to about moving it."

Again, nothing.

He had no desire to bust up a town ritual, but he also didn't want the hippo to get damaged. That would really put a damper on their tradition. He kept his smile in place, but now it felt a bit forced. "The alternative is that I move it with—"

281

"Trying to move Otis is a five-thousand-million-dollar ticket." A little girl who looked about seven spoke up. She propped her hands on her hips as her blonde pigtail swung back and forth. "And my brother will punch you."

"A five-thousand-dollar fine, Trinity." Nate walked up and stood next to Austin. "And no punching. I don't think Gideon would appreciate you offering to get him into any fights."

"Nate!" She jumped up to give him a high five. "You're here. This guy has your face. But I knowed it wasn't you because he doesn't have the drawings on his arms. And you'd never try and move Otis." She sent another scowl toward Austin. "And he called him *the hippo*—he didn't even know his name."

Another Nate fan, of course. But Austin knew how to talk to kids. He squatted down to look her in the eye. "I just don't want it to get hurt by the big machine coming, Trinity. Do you know how it moves?"

She crossed her arms and rolled her eyes. "*He* walks when people aren't looking, duh."

"Cabbage." A woman's voice carried from a nearby booth.

He stood and moved to a booth packed with four gray-haired women. One he'd met a few times when he came into the diner. Lucy, was it? She took a sip of her coffee, but her eyes stayed on him. "If you want Otis to move, you feed him cabbage."

She'd always seemed lucid when he encountered her, but maybe not. "I can't feed him anything. He's a statue."

She looked at the little girl and back at him. "Lay the cabbage by his mouth. He'll move when he's ready."

"Or you could take me out on a date, sugar, and I'll tell you how he moves." The oldest woman of the group spoke up. She patted her gray hair pulled back in a bun as she sent him a wink.

"Oh, Margret." Another of the women swatted her arm. "You don't know how he moves any more than anyone else."

Margret scowled at the woman. "He doesn't know that. And he's cute."

He had no response for that. "How will putting a cabbage next to it"—he glanced at the little girl—"next to him—help?"

"It'll give him the energy to move." Trinity patted Nate on the arm and then whispered loudly, "Your brother isn't very smart."

"Trinity. Come finish your pie." Janie spoke from behind the counter.

As soon as the girl wandered off, Austin lifted one eyebrow at Lucy. "You know how the statue moves?"

"No. Honest. But I remember different times when it really needed to be moved, people would put a cabbage by its mouth. It's been years. But I have lived here a good while."

The woman with short hair and bright red lipstick tapped her finger on the table. "I do remember my father doing that very thing once."

There had to be almost three hundred accumulated years in Heritage between the four of them. "You're saying that not one of you has any idea who moves it or how it moves."

They all shook their heads. Either this town was full of better actors than Hollywood or no one really knew.

Nate tugged on his arm. "I got us a booth."

Austin slid into the spot opposite Nate and shook his head. "Let me guess. You don't know how the hippo moves either."

"Nope. And I've yet to meet someone who claimed to have a guess." Nate set the menu aside without looking at it. "And Trin is right. All the locals call him Otis."

"I'm not a local." Austin grabbed the other menu and looked it over. "Did you see a key when you were at my house feeding Shiro the other day? An antique key. Maybe lying on a table somewhere."

"No. Is that what you wanted to ask? I'm all for having lunch, but you could have asked me that on the phone."

Right. To the point. Why was this so hard? "I need a . . . favor."

"From me?"

"Yes." Austin shifted in his seat. If he wanted

to take Libby on the date he'd planned, then he needed to let go of a little of his pride.

"I'm listening."

"I need you to sign for a delivery."

"That's all? The way you're acting, I thought you were going to ask for a kidney."

Austin huffed. "My kidneys are probably in better shape than yours."

"Liver, maybe. But I think my kidneys are valuable. I had a guy offer me a lot of money for one once." Nate patted his side. "But I didn't sell it. I never knew if you'd need one."

Austin shook his head and reached for his wallet. He pulled out a card and slid it across the table. "It's a special delivery of heirloom roses that I'm going to plant around the schoolhouse. There's a long waiting list, so I can't reschedule. You have to sign for it—they won't leave them."

Nate picked up the card and read it over. "No problem. What do you have going on?"

"I'm taking Libby on a date."

Nate's movements paused, and he looked up without commenting.

"I know what you said before." He ran his hand across the dark gray surface of the table. "But I really . . . like her."

"And Becky?"

Austin sat back and drew a deep breath. "Honestly, being away from her is like a breath of fresh air. I hadn't even thought about her since

I moved here—that is, until two weeks ago. And I only thought about her then because Dad kept calling Libby 'Becky.' "

"That must have been awkward."

A waitress set two waters and two straws in front of them.

Nate smiled at her. "We need a minute."

Austin dropped a straw into his drink and wadded the wrapper into a tight ball in his fingers. "She just dismissed it as a part of his Alzheimer's."

"Did you explain later?"

"I will. I'm not quite ready to throw all my dirty laundry at her." Austin set the wrapper aside and leaned forward. "Have you explained to Olivia about your past?"

"Most of it."

"But not all of it."

"No." Nate stirred his drink with his straw and looked back at Austin. "But maybe it's time." He reached for his phone, then stopped. "Some things need to happen in person. I'll go tonight."

"I'm not trying to call you out. I'm just saying that certain conversations need to come at the right time, and Libby and I aren't there yet."

"No, I get it. But I think it's come for Olivia and me." Nate slid the card with the delivery information into his shirt pocket. "I'll sign for the order. And I hope things work out for you and Libby. I mean that."

"I'm not trying to be a jerk." Austin rubbed the back of his neck, then leaned forward on the table with his elbows. "But I need to know I can trust you on this. This can't be something you flake on."

The muscle in Nate's jaw twitched. "I'll be there. I'll tell the station I can't be on call that day, and I'll work from your house. You can trust me."

"I hope so." Austin picked up the menu again. One item taken care of. Now it looked like he was going to do something he'd have sworn he'd never do—buy a cabbage for a statue.

Another stellar review from Mr. Lang and another few bucks in her pocket. Olivia reread the email from him and made note of when her fishing article would run in the paper. If things kept up, she might have enough of a print portfolio to show Phoenix before Christmas.

The idea of moving 1,600 miles away didn't have the same appeal as it had before—especially after Thursday. But part of her still longed to be a journalist, and if she didn't keep working toward that, what was she working toward? She didn't want to be a part-time waitress the rest of her life.

So until she had a solid reason to stay in Heritage, she had to keep moving forward. And right now, moving forward meant turning in another article that impressed Mr. Lang.

The question was, what should she write next? She'd submitted a list of ideas to him last week, but he'd yet to get back to her. As long as it wasn't something crazy like bungee jumping.

She could write an article on tattoos. The image of Nate standing shirtless in the woods returned once again to the front of her mind. Not that her brain had yet to wander too far from that memory. No, it ran more like a broken record in her head. That and their kiss.

She'd never kissed anyone before, so she had nothing to compare it to, but . . . wow.

He'd started the kiss gentle and tender, but it was as if he was holding back. And after all this time—all the waiting—the gentleness wasn't enough for Olivia. She wanted more. She'd been so embarrassed when her desire and frustration escaped in the form of a slight moan, but for whatever reason it shifted Nate into a new gear. He was no longer tender and careful. He wasn't rough, but a hunger in him came to the surface. And the way his hands gripped her back, she had never felt more desired in her life.

She'd pretty much lost all thought by the time Nate pulled away. Her skin still hummed with the mere thought of it. She'd actually believed for a fraction of a second that the kiss meant something. Meant that he'd come to his senses. Meant that they could be together. But one look at his face had shattered that idea like a glass bowl hitting the tile.

Still, if he thought of that kiss even half as much as it was running through her mind, he might come around. He still seemed to be avoiding her, but it was different now. A couple of times he looked as if he were about to approach her but then changed his mind.

She'd often heard talk about a physical spark between two people, and Olivia had always dismissed the idea. But kissing Nate? Yup, she'd call that a spark. He might have been the one to stop it, but she had a feeling he'd been as affected by it as she had.

A knock at the door interrupted her thoughts.

Olivia opened the door. Jackson Mackers? He'd been one of her closest friends in high school, but she hadn't seen him in years. "I can't believe you're here. How long has it been?"

"Too long." He wrapped her in a giant bear hug, lifting her off her feet. Which was no small task with her five-ten height. He smelled of expensive cologne, and his shirt was not off the rack from Penney's. Did selling an app for a million dollars make someone a millionaire, or did that take at least two million?

He set her down and stepped back. Same ol' Jackson, but his blond hair from high school had been trimmed into a professional business cut. "Good to see you too."

"Come in." Olivia opened the door wider. "Want me to make you some coffee?"

"You always did know my weakness." Jackson followed her to the kitchen and took a seat at the secondhand oak table.

"My roommate just made fresh cookies." Olivia poured water into the coffee maker, added the grounds, and pressed the button. "I can't believe you surprised me like this. Why didn't you tell me you were going to be in town? How long are you here for? How did you know where I live?"

"Whoa. Let me catch up. My mom told me where you live now. I'll be in town a while. You look good." Jackson took a cookie from the plate and peered out the window that faced the square. "I almost didn't recognize the town. My mom said there had been a lot of changes, but I never expected this."

"No kidding." Olivia pulled two mugs from the cupboard, avoiding the one with the large chip. "You remember Hannah Thornton? It's Hannah Taylor now—"

"Wait. I thought I heard she married Luke Johnson." He ran his hand over a worn spot in the table. No doubt he was used to five-star living.

"She did, but it turns out his name wasn't really Luke Johnson. It's Luke Taylor. His dad—"

The front door burst open.

"Look who I found on the front porch." Libby's voice echoed through the house. "I told him he had to come try my new cookie recipe. Plus I needed his help."

Libby walked in with a bag of groceries in her arms, followed by Nate holding a second bag. His eyes connected with Olivia's. A bit of that longing she'd seen before the kiss saturated his gaze. She took a half step toward him. Then his gaze shifted to Jackson.

Oh. Shoot.

Nate looked back at her, his brows lifted.

"This is my old friend Jackson," Olivia said. She'd tried to emphasize the word "friend" without it sounding like she was trying to. "Jackson, this is my roommate, Libby, and . . ."

She glanced out of the corner of her eye toward Nate. *What? My friend? The guy I kissed? The guy who refuses to be my boyfriend?*

She looked back at Jackson. "Pastor Nate."

Nate dropped the bag on the table with a thud. Hope there wasn't anything breakable in there. He extended his hand to Jackson. "That's me. Her *pastor.*"

Jackson stood and took the offered hand. "Olivia and I go way back."

Wide-eyed, Libby started putting away produce in the fridge. Well, this wasn't awkward.

"I was just pouring coffee." Olivia pulled two more mugs from the cupboard as the gurgling sound of the coffee maker announced it was ready. "Nate, how do you take yours?"

"Black."

She filled two mugs, then added a spoonful of sugar to one of them, stirred it, and held that one out to Jackson and the other out to Nate.

Jackson accepted his coffee with a slight smirk and took a sip. "You know just the way I like it, even after all these years."

Nate's knuckles whitened as they tightened on the mug in his hand. "Actually, I need to go. There's something I need to talk with Austin about. Thanks for the cookie."

He set the mug on the table, lifted a cookie from the plate, and turned back to the door.

No.

"Mr. Lang said the fishing article was perfect. Thank you," Olivia blurted.

Nate paused but didn't turn. He gave one nod and then he was gone.

Libby's gaze bounced from Olivia to Jackson to where Nate had just disappeared.

Jackson finished his coffee in a few large gulps and stood. "I hate to run off too, but my mom is expecting me home for dinner. Maybe we could find a night next week to grab some dinner and catch up. I'd love to hear how you're doing."

"Of course." Olivia forced a smile to her lips. No fair to ignore Jackson because Nate couldn't seem to make up his mind. "Do you still have my cell?"

"Yes. I'll text you." With those parting words, he was gone.

Libby cringed as the front door shut. "Sorry."

"It's not your fault." Olivia dropped into a chair at the table.

Libby shut the fridge and folded up the grocery bag. "Where are the dogs?"

"Took them over to Luke's for a bit while I was vacuuming. They were going nuts." She snatched a cookie from the plate and took a bite.

"Darcy hates vacuums." Libby slid the bag in the drawer and stepped back to where Nate had dropped the other one. "So, Jackson. He's cute."

"Yeah, I guess." Olivia closed her eyes and rubbed her temple. This was all going to give her a headache. "We're just friends."

"Does he know that?"

Olivia's eyes popped open. "What do you mean? We've always been friends."

Libby shrugged as she unloaded cans and pasta. "He wasn't looking at you like a friend. That's all I'm saying. And Nate?"

"What about him?"

"You can't tell me that whole exchange wasn't awkward." Libby carried the cans to the cupboard.

"Nate . . ." Olivia smacked the table. "Nate needs to figure out what he wants." She crossed her arms on the table and rested her head on them. "He kissed me."

"What? When?"

"On the fishing trip."

"Like, a little kiss, or . . ."

Olivia lifted her head and looked at her friend, who stood with a can of green beans paused halfway to the shelf. "Or a feel-it-to-your-toes-and-leaves-you-thinking-of-nothing-else-for-days kiss? Yup, that one."

Libby raised her eyebrows and finished her task. "And now?"

"Now I don't know what he's thinking." Olivia pushed to a stand and marched Jackson's mug to the sink. "He's been avoiding me. Until today, that is, when he decided to show up right when Jackson was here."

"Are you going to call him?"

"In a minute. Let him stew a bit." Olivia rinsed the mug, then smacked it down in the sink with more force than she intended. The handle snapped off. "Why do the Williams boys have to be so complicated?"

"Tell me about it."

Olivia dropped the broken handle and mug in the trash, then pulled her phone from her pocket. She tapped Nate's number, but it went straight to voicemail. Of course. Olivia set her phone aside. She brushed the crumbs from the table into her hand and carried them to the sink.

"What are you going to do about Nate and Jackson?" Libby claimed a cookie from the plate.

"Jackson and I are only friends. And Nate won't take my call. But I *am* going to find a way to get him to talk to me, even if I have to kidnap him."

Olivia's phone pinged with an incoming email. She snatched it up and tapped the screen.

To: Olivia Mathews

From: Frank Lang

Subject: New Assignment

The Williams brothers are making quite the story lately. You live right there and I want the inside scoop. Not the same one everyone's telling. Find a new angle and make it good.

Olivia sighed and dropped her head in her hands. She rubbed her neck. Why couldn't it have been bungee jumping?

She refused to finish this book. Libby slammed *The Hiding Place* down on the edge of the couch and stormed out the front door, letting it slam behind her. She plopped down on the top step and wrapped her arms around herself. The clear night sky had stolen any warmth the sun had left that day, and the streetlights washed away all but the brightest stars.

Betsie had died. Libby pressed the palms of her hands to her eyes to keep from crying.

She had dealt with book death before, but this was different. Betsie had been real, and God really hadn't saved her. Corrie had fought the whole book to keep her sister alive, and in the end she'd died anyway. How could a loving God allow that?

If she'd been Corrie, she'd have given up. Actually, that was exactly what she had done. After Colin. Even after Luke's disappearance, she'd never looked at God the same.

But the book wasn't over, which meant Corrie's story didn't end when Betsie's did. When Corrie faced her biggest fear, she kept going. When God hadn't answered her prayers the way she wanted, she kept on believing. Why?

"Libby?" Austin stood on the sidewalk, a bag in his hand. "Is everything okay?"

She hadn't seen him besides a quick hello since their kiss, and the last thing she wanted to do was unload on him. She forced a smile and leaned against the railing. "Yup."

He set the bag at the bottom of the steps and took a seat next to her. "Why don't I believe you?"

She sat back up and wrapped her arms around herself again as her body released a shiver. "Why does God allow bad things to happen?"

He let out a low whistle as he shed his coat and

dropped it on her shoulders. His musky smell and warmth covered her. "That is a big subject for a late-night porch sit."

"I'm reading a book about a woman who goes through so much, and when God didn't answer her prayer, she just kept on believing in Him. That's crazy."

Austin leaned back on his hands and stretched his legs out. "We could talk for days about this and never come to an easy answer, but I will tell you something my grandmother told me. She made these amazing quilts. One day I saw the one she was working on, and it looked . . . well, terrible. There were strings everywhere, and the edges didn't seem to line up. I asked her why she was making an ugly quilt."

"It was the back side of the quilt, wasn't it?"

"Yes. But as a child I couldn't see that. All I saw was a mess of threads. She laughed and turned it over for me. Then she pulled me up into her lap and said, 'Austin, things in life may not always look perfect from your angle. But never forget there is a Master at work, and He has a whole different perspective than you do.' I guess even then she could see my 'impossibly high standards.' "

"Do you really believe that there is a Master at work?"

"I do. I'm not always the best at living it out, but I do believe it."

"Do you think that what happened between you and Nate is part of the messy side of your quilt?"

"No. Maybe. Probably." He leaned forward on his knees and rubbed at the back of his head. "I will never be one to claim I have it all figured out. But I do know when I push God away, He doesn't force Himself on me. And when I look for Him, He tends to find me."

"Look for God? How?"

He shrugged. "Go to church. Read the Bible. Read books like the one you were talking about. God isn't hiding from you. He wants to be found." After a long pause, he glanced over at her. "Not to change the subject, but—"

"You think the kiss was a mistake."

"What? No. Do you?"

"No, but we haven't talked since then, so I thought . . ."

He turned toward her and took her face in his hands. "I'm sorry. I've been crazy busy with the square. But no, I don't think it was a mistake."

As if to prove his point, he leaned in and angled his mouth over hers. He tasted of grape ChapStick and smelled of brisk autumn nights. There was something about touching him that filled her with energy and the need to be even closer. As if her very skin called out for him. He ended the kiss and wrapped his arms around her, pulling her closer and tucking her under his chin.

He was so gentle with her. It had been two

months since she bandaged his arm that day, and the memory of the muscles in his arms hadn't done him justice. But his strength didn't frighten her as she might have guessed. If anything, she felt safer, protected. He was her own Austen hero—actually, Austin hero, but Jane still would've approved.

Austin brushed a stray hair from her face and tucked it behind her ear. "I'd like to take you out Friday. All day."

"What are we doing?"

"It's a surprise." He dropped another quick kiss on her lips, then leaned back. "There is one more thing. Do you remember when my dad—"

A car door shut, and they both jumped. Olivia stood by her hatchback a few feet away in the driveway. How had they not seen her? She must have pulled up while they were kissing. Libby's face warmed at the thought.

Austin smirked as he stood and picked up his bag. "We'll finish talking on Friday."

"Till Friday." She started to take off his coat, but he shook his head.

"I'll get it later."

"What's in the bag?"

"Cabbage for the hippo." He reached into the bag and held up the green leafy ball as he faded into the darkness.

Olivia walked up and dropped into Austin's spot. "Let's talk about what is going on with you and Austin. I do believe I saw two kisses since I arrived."

"We have a date Friday."

"That's all I get?" Olivia gripped Libby's arm. "I need details."

Libby's heart rate sped up. She was definitely not as practiced at being so candid like Olivia. "Maybe we should first talk about what you're going to do about Jackson and Nate."

Olivia leaned back against the opposite railing and closed her eyes. "Jackson. It's perfect on paper, I just don't feel that way about him. He texted me and wants to take me to dinner next Saturday, but I don't really see that changing anything."

"Because of Nate?"

She covered her face with her hands. "How dumb am I? I thought Nate might actually come around after our kiss on Thursday."

"Not dumb. Optimistic. I know I'm still praying he comes around." Libby paused as her own words echoed in her mind. *Praying?* Why had she said that? Was there a Master working on her life? Corrie ten Boom had been convinced there was one working in her life.

Libby didn't know if she could ever trust God again, but maybe today she just needed to turn the page—in *The Hiding Place* and in her life. "Do you still need help in the nursery at church?"

"Always. Why?"

"I'm not ready to start attending, but maybe the kids' area is a good place to start."

Olivia's face brightened into a smile. "I couldn't agree more. And so do about half a dozen six-year-olds."

Libby shook her head. "I said nursery."

"Who better to tell those terrors—uh, I mean, sweet cherubs—stories than the librarian?"

The idea of children gathered around her was familiar and comfortable. She had to start somewhere. Maybe the beginning was the right place to start.

thirteen

Libby glanced from the passing foliage to Austin in the driver's seat of the truck, his left arm in the window while his right arm held the top of the wheel. He had insisted on picking her up at eight o'clock this morning, and since then they'd been driving down a road she'd never been on. From the way he kept glancing at his GPS, he hadn't spent too much time here either. Which brought her back to the question circling her mind. "Where are we headed?"

He brushed his dark hair away from his forehead. "You don't seem to understand the concept of the word 'surprise.'"

She understood surprises. She even liked them—sort of. But she also liked to know, research, be well informed.

He'd worn a buffalo-plaid shirt and jeans. So they weren't headed to a fine restaurant, but his clean-shaven jaw and hint of aftershave said that he'd taken time with his appearance. As the morning sun warmed the cab, he'd pushed up his sleeves a bit, exposing his muscular forearms.

She'd seen him briefly each night this week. But he'd been so exhausted from helping with the new library roof that he'd barely been able to keep his eyes open. The day he'd been running between the roof and the auger, he'd actually fallen asleep mid-conversation with her. Mumbling in his sleep about cabbage.

But Otis had moved in time for the auger, and the roof was done. With any luck, today would be a restful day for him.

She watched the side of the road for a town name. "And we're going to be gone all day?"

He reached across the seat, grabbed her hand, and ran his thumb across her knuckles. "I wanted you to have a memorable first date. I had fun planning this, and I think you'll like it too."

Nothing like a bit of pressure. "I'm sure I will." Or she'd lie.

"Who's the guy I saw you talking to on your porch yesterday?"

"Jackson. He stopped by to talk to Olivia."

"Are they a thing? I thought something was happening between her and Nate." He let go of her hand and checked the GPS again.

"There should be." She leaned forward and turned down the radio. "But Nate needs to let go of the past."

"Nate?" He lifted one eyebrow at her, then fixed his eyes back on the road. "He's the king of letting go of the past."

"I know he hurt you, Austin. But if you look at his life, you could see he's not. He beats himself up over what happened. He doesn't think he deserves Olivia, so he pushes her away. He volunteers with the fire department, high school basketball team, and at some shelter. He wants to help with the family business, so he went to bat at the town council to get you the contract. He knows money is tight, so he's been working off some of your dad's bill at the care home on Saturdays. Is there anything I'm missing?"

"Wait, what? Say that again?" Austin quickly braked to avoid hitting the car in front of him.

Libby's seat belt jerked her back in place.

"Sorry."

She adjusted the strap and searched for words. Did Austin not know? "Which part?"

"The part where he went to the town council to get me the contract and that he's working off my dad's bill. Both of those are news to me." He flipped on his blinker and turned right, then crossed a bridge over the Muskegon River.

"I'm sorry. I probably wasn't supposed to say anything. I thought you knew."

"No." He shook his head again. "Why doesn't he think he's good enough for Olivia?"

Libby shrugged. "Life choices. Mistakes. Something about an uncle."

"Uncle Greg? He abandoned his wife and kids. That's not Nate." He ran his hands over the steering wheel a few times. "Besides, don't pastors preach grace and forgiveness?"

"He does. But I think he forgets to preach

it to himself. Then again, forgiveness isn't an easy thing, whether you're forgiving yourself or others. If it was, you would have forgiven Nate by now." She smoothed down a tear in the upholstery.

"I'm . . . trying. I left him in charge of a very important delivery today."

"Really?" She reached over and squeezed his arm. "That's great."

"He better not mess it up."

She shoved his shoulder. "Austin!"

"I'm kidding." He tapped at the steering wheel as he checked his map again. "But if he misses this delivery, the nursery can't come back for another few weeks and will charge an additional fee. They were pretty adamant about both those points."

"Nate can handle it." She let her hand linger on his shoulder as she rested her head back. She could get used to drives in the country with Austin. "Now, where are we headed?"

"You're terrible." He slowed the car as they entered a small town.

"Can you at least tell me what town this is?"

He pointed to an approaching sign. "Newaygo."

Libby sat up straighter and studied a storefront to her right. This Old House Antiques. "I bet I could find some great stuff in there. Are we going antiquing?"

"Nope." Austin turned left onto Wood Street

and then right into a parking lot. He slid out of the truck and jogged around the front to open her door. "This way." He led her down the sidewalk in the direction of the antique store but pulled her to the left before they reached the street and paused in front of a small gazebo. There was something almost familiar about it, but how could that be possible?

Libby ran her hand along the smooth wood as she eyed the simple design of the railing and frets. What really stood out on the eight-sided structure was the pagoda roof and cupola on top. She only knew those terms because she'd looked them up after seeing . . . "This looks like Heritage's gazebo."

"Good eye." He checked his watch, then eyed the structure. "I believe it was the inspiration for the one in Heritage that Luke designed. He just created it on a larger scale. But this isn't what we're here to see."

"It's not?"

"Nope." He took her hand and led her through the gazebo to the front of a building. It was a beautiful building with a stately veranda over the front steps, held up by two concrete pillars. Two old-fashioned light posts with globe lights on top stood like guards on each side of the door. The front of the veranda boasted the word "LIBRARY" in large capital letters over the entrance.

"You brought me to a library?" She spun toward Austin and gripped his arm.

"Not just any library." He pulled a paper from his pocket and unfolded it. "The Newaygo Library was funded in December of 1913 by the Carnegie Foundation. It was the fifty-first of the sixty-one libraries funded in Michigan and is still in operation today."

"You brought me to a Carnegie library?" Her hand flew to her face. She might just swoon. This was the most romantic thing anyone had ever done for her. She reached up and wrapped her arms around his neck, squeezing him in a giant bear hug. "Thank you."

Austin leaned down and brushed his lips across her forehead. "Now let's get you that picture."

"Right." Libby rushed to the bottom step, spread out her arms, and smiled.

Austin held up her phone and snapped a few photos.

"Now I have to go find *Pride and Prejudice* and get a photo with that. Do you think it's open?"

Austin looked at his watch. "It will be in about one minute." The lock clicked in the door. "Good, they're early. We have to be back on the road in less than fifteen minutes."

"Fifteen minutes?" She spun to face him. "What could be more important than a Carnegie library?"

"More Carnegie libraries. I've scheduled as

many as I can today. We can't get to all sixty-one today, but I think we can hit eight."

Libby blinked back tears. "You planned all this for me?" No one had ever planned a whole day for her, especially a day of traveling a couple hundred miles just because of her silly affection for libraries.

As if reading her mind, Austin wrapped her in a hug and pressed his lips to her temple. "And I'll plan trips to the other fifty-three if you'll let me. Now, where's that *Pride and Prejudice*?"

He'd show Austin that he could depend on him, even if it meant sitting here for two hours waiting for a truck to arrive. Nate scratched the back of Shiro's ears as she lay lounging on the couch next to him. The girl didn't have a care in the world. Must be nice.

A text came in and he pulled his phone from his pocket.

Olivia
We need to talk.

He sighed and dropped his phone on the couch. Maybe she was right, but until he knew how to respond to the questions he'd seen in her eyes, what was the point?

Their kiss had haunted him night and day, and it had taken all his strength not to drive to her place and kiss her again. Maybe he would have if Jackson hadn't been there when he showed up the other night. But Jackson's presence had been like a spotlight on the truth. God had someone better for Olivia, and he needed to stay out of the way.

He pushed to his feet and paced to the kitchen and back. Just a simple text from her had sent his mind back to their kiss. The fire, the softness of her lips, the feel of her hands as she pulled him close.

Ugh. He kicked at a roll of carpet. He needed something to distract him or he'd find himself waiting for the truck at her place.

He grabbed a tennis ball from the table and bounced it a few times. Shiro came alert. This would do. He tossed the ball toward the kitchen, and the dog scrambled after it. She returned it to his hand and sat waiting for another chase.

He tossed it again. This time his aim was off. It bounced off the doorway to the kitchen, shot back at him, then rolled under the couch. Perfect.

He picked up his phone, flipped on the flashlight, and knelt down to peer under the couch. A piece of metal between the floorboards glinted in the light. He picked at it with his fingernail. "What could this be?"

After a couple tries, a miniature antique key popped free. Could this be the key to the desk Austin had been looking for? Then again, it could have been here in this house for years and no one would have noticed.

With a groan from Shiro, Nate snatched the ball and tossed it her way. He climbed back to his feet and spun the key in his hands a few times. Maybe he should see if it fit the desk. It wasn't like the schoolhouse was that far away. He'd hear the truck and could run back across the street before anyone was the wiser.

He grabbed his phone as another text came in.

Olivia
Nate, please call me.

His fingers itched to call her back. No. He set the phone on the table and dug his fingers into Shiro's thick white fur. "I'll be right back."

Nate grabbed his coat and jogged across the street toward the schoolhouse. At least the rain had stopped. For now. He opened the door and scanned the large space for the desk. That's right, they'd moved it to the back room while they were painting.

He moved to the mudroom along the back wall. The desk was the only thing in there. The space itself wasn't that exciting. A miniature square window provided just enough light. A storage space once upon a time, maybe. He eyed the way the walls joined. Probably a later addition to the structure of the schoolhouse.

He bent over the desk and opened and closed the top drawer. Then he slid the key into the hole, turned it, and tugged again. Locked. That answered that. He unlocked the drawer and set the key on top of the desk. Now he'd have taken care of two problems for his brother.

He peeked out the miniature window that faced Austin's house and then turned back to the door. Olivia stood silhouetted in the doorway.

"Yaah!" He jumped back, pressing his hands to his chest. "What are you doing?"

"I came to talk to you."

"You came to scare me." Nate offered a forced laugh as he moved to step past her.

She blocked his way. "We need to talk."

"Okay. But later." He tried to exit on her other side.

She blocked him again.

Seriously?

"You've been ignoring me ever since we went fishing." Her hand waved around in the air. "Except for the other night when you stopped by for all of ten seconds."

He leaned against the wall. "You and Jackson seemed fine without me."

"Why did you stop by that day?" Her voice was softer now.

He propped one foot up on the wall behind him. "I don't have time for this right now." He pushed off the wall and tried to move past her once more.

"Neither of us is leaving until we talk." Olivia grabbed the door and slammed it shut. The wood rattled with the force, followed by a solid clunk.

The doorknob had fallen off.

This couldn't be happening. He rushed over to the door and crouched down. He ran his fingers over the ancient wood, looking for any sign of weakness—other than the knob. Nope. He wasn't getting this door open without tools, and there was nothing in this room but a desk and a key.

He reached for his phone but came up empty. He'd left it on the table. "Okay, we need to talk, but right now I need to be somewhere. Call someone to let us out."

Olivia had lost that confident look. "I don't have my phone. Where's yours?"

"Mine is at Austin's, where I was waiting for an important delivery. Where's yours?"

"Charging. I saw you come over here and just grabbed my coat. I didn't think I'd need to call for help."

The rain picked up again, echoing on the roof above them. Perfect. They couldn't even yell for help. No one would hear them.

The roar of a diesel engine grew louder, followed by the squeal of air brakes.

Nate dashed to the miniature window. A delivery truck sat in front of Austin's, and a man stood on his porch, clipboard in hand. As if sensing his desperation, Olivia hammered at the broken door with the metal knob.

Nate banged on the window, shouting at the top of his lungs, but it was useless. No one would hear him over the engine and rain. The man checked his watch, knocked again, and waited only a minute before he hopped back in his truck and drove away.

Nate sank down against the wall as his head dropped into his hands. Austin was going to kill him.

The day had gone better than he'd dared to hope. Austin leaned back on the stiff lobby chair and took another gulp of his coffee. Thank goodness he'd thought to stop at Starbucks before they'd come here. That coffee machine didn't look appealing.

Austin picked up the *Newsweek* and thumbed through it, then glanced at his watch. They needed to leave in thirty minutes if they wanted to make their final stop, but if the way Libby's face had lit up when he mentioned stopping by the hospital to see her nephew was any indication, this time was more important than another library.

They had already made it to seven Carnegie libraries: Newaygo, Sparta, Portland, Albion, Jackson, Hudson, and Adrian. Adrian was no longer used as a library, but the amazing architecture with the turret had definitely been worth the stop and photo. She'd seemed to love every one. And Austin found the whole adventure more exciting than he'd expected.

He'd started to drop the *Newsweek* back on the end table when the words *Reader's Weekly* with a tiny photo of him and Nate in the corner stopped him. He exchanged one magazine for the next and thumbed through it until he found the article on Heritage.

He scanned the article. The lady had made Nate and Austin out to be the next Property Brothers duo. If only that were true. Nate didn't want anything to do with the business beyond this Heritage assignment, and the photo they'd snapped definitely didn't capture the tension Austin had felt that day. Had Nate really begged the board to give them the contract? He tossed the magazine back on the table.

"You must be Austin." A man entered the waiting area in a gray T-shirt and jeans. He didn't look like Libby with his dark coloring, but she'd said that they were only cousins biologically.

Austin stood and offered his hand. "Austin Williams. And you're Luke?"

"Yes. Libby's brother and your neighbor. I recognized you from the article." Luke pointed at the table.

Austin glanced back at the magazine. "Yeah, that was . . . interesting."

"Thanks for bringing Libby. It can get lonely here, and the visit is good."

"Is Libby enjoying her time?"

Luke motioned to the door. "You can see them from the window if you'd like."

He led the way to a wide window that overlooked a nursery full of recliners. Libby sat in one, holding an infant tinier than Austin had ever seen. A few wires led from the baby over Libby's shoulder and attached to machines.

"He's so small."

Luke laughed. "Here I was thinking how big he was getting. You should have seen him a month ago. I could hold him in one hand. His diaper folded up was barely bigger than a Post-it Note."

"Are you enjoying being a father?"

"More than you could know. It's also a mix of emotions. Knowing how much I already love him gives me a better understanding of what motivated my dad. But I also have a better understanding of the kind of pain he caused my mother. Kind of a crazy thing to balance in my mind."

"Libby told me a little bit about your past. She's amazed how you've been able to forgive your dad."

"I'm not sure I've completely forgiven him. I'm working on it. But there are times I'm faced with a deeper understanding of what he took from me." Luke rubbed the back of his neck. "And I find myself choosing to forgive him all over again."

Libby waved from the other side of the window, and Austin waved back. "Why would you forgive him? He doesn't deserve it."

Luke's eyes drifted back to his family. "Forgiveness is never deserved. It's a gift. If you earn a gift, it's not a gift anymore—it's a wage. The way I see it, if people deserved forgiveness, then there is really nothing to be forgiven. But more than that, I'm not forgiving him for his sake. He's not even alive to know one way or the other."

"Then why?"

"Unforgiveness breeds anger and bitterness. I don't want that for me." Luke tapped his finger gently on the glass. "And I don't want that for them. Because that kind of bitterness spills all over those close to you."

If someone else had said that, Austin would assume it was a backhanded comment about Nate. But Luke didn't really know him.

Austin had trusted Nate today, but he didn't know if fully forgiving him would ever be an option. Even if Libby was right and Nate was still beating himself up. He'd cost Austin too much.

On the other side of the glass, Libby tenderly cradled the baby, a gentle smile on her face.

Had his bitterness and anger spilled on her? His mind flashed to many of their fights since he'd met her. How many of them had sparked to life because he was blinded by his anger toward Nate?

Luke shook his hand again. "Anyway, I just wanted to introduce myself. Both as your neighbor and as your date's brother."

His grip tightened. It seemed all in fun, but Austin definitely got the message. *Libby is my sister, and I'm watching out for her.*

"I need to get back in there." Luke slapped Austin on the shoulder. "Hannah said I had to give her a chance to meet you too."

Luke disappeared down a hall and a moment later entered the nursery. He pointed to Austin on the other side of the glass and said something Austin couldn't hear. They all laughed, and Hannah stood and walked to the door. Whatever he'd said, Libby still smiled. That had to be a good sign, right?

When Hannah appeared in the same hall Luke had disappeared down, she stared at Austin a full five seconds with piercing brown eyes before extending her hand. "Hannah."

He shook her hand. "Austin."

Luke might have made it clear he was watching out for Libby. But Hannah, with her hair up in a loose bun and one eyebrow raised, definitely gave off the lawyer-for-the-

317

prosecution vibe. "How long do you plan on staying in Heritage?"

"I'm not sure."

"Are you serious about Libby, or is she just a distraction while you're here?" The smile never dropped from her face during the question. No doubt for Libby's benefit as she watched them from the other side of the glass. "Libby is special. She's been hurt before. Be careful."

Austin shifted his weight from one foot to the other. Maybe he needed his own counsel. "I know. She's not just a distraction. But I don't know what the future will hold."

"Caroline, Grant, and Nate all seem to think highly of you. I'll give you the benefit of the doubt." She turned so her back was to the glass, the smile vanishing from her face. "Don't prove them wrong."

He didn't know if he should laugh or say, "Yes, ma'am." Instead, he just nodded. No wonder she got along so well with Caroline.

When the silence stretched, they both faced the glass and Austin finally spoke. "Did you say Nate spoke highly of me? I have a hard time believing that."

"Then maybe you don't know your brother as well as you think."

That did seem to be the theme of the day.

"Nice to meet you. Be good to her." She patted his shoulder and left as his phone pinged with a text.

Heirloom Gardens
Delivery unsuccessful. No one present
at delivery site to sign. Call office to
reschedule.

He gripped his phone tighter, then willed his
hand to relax before he cracked the screen. He
didn't know his brother? Maybe he was the only
one who did.

fourteen

Maybe trying to force him to talk hadn't been her best plan ever. Olivia stared at Nate sitting against the wall with his head in his hands. Neither of them had spoken since the truck drove away about fifteen minutes ago. She'd opened her mouth several times but then snapped it shut. The way his jaw repeatedly clenched and unclenched, she'd decided to give him a minute. Or fifteen.

Sliding down the wall, Olivia dropped into the spot next to Nate on the floor. "I *am* sorry. I didn't know this would happen."

He stretched out his legs in front of him and picked at the weathered boards. "I know."

"I'll tell Austin—"

"It won't matter." He pulled one knee back up and rested his elbow on it. "He sees what he wants to see. Always has."

"What's up with you two?"

Nate straightened his arm across his knee with his forearm facing up. His fingers traced the tattoo before offering her a forced smile. "Bad decisions. Some mine. Some his."

"What bad decision did you make?"

"I drove the Williams and Son delivery van into a storefront while drunk."

Olivia pulled her knees up under her. "Ahh. Not the best decision. But didn't insurance cover it?"

"Nope. I wasn't on the insurance because I had chosen not to be a part of the company." He rubbed the back of his neck but kept his eyes on the door. "My dad had to either pay the damage or press charges against me. My dad paid it. It almost put the company under."

"Did you pay him back?"

"At first I didn't appreciate it. I was still too messed up." He stretched out his legs in front of him again and leaned his head back. "Then once I got my life straightened out, I tried to pay my dad back. I didn't make enough to put much of a dent in it, but even what little I did have he wouldn't accept. He said I needed a new start. No baggage. It definitely gave me a lesson in grace."

"Does your brother know you tried to pay him back?"

"It doesn't matter. He feels I took that money from the business, his business. And now he feels I've trapped him in this job when he doesn't realize that it was the only hope Williams and Son Landscaping had left."

"What do you mean?"

Nate pushed up and went to inspect the broken doorknob again. As if he hadn't already done that ten times. "Over the past few years, Austin moved into a more hands-on position and left the books to my dad. Dad told me about a year ago that they were barely running in the black. The symptoms of early-onset Alzheimer's were showing up long before he told us."

Olivia grabbed the broken knob from where it had rolled and held it out. "That must have been hard."

"It was." Nate took the knob from her hand and worked the metal this way and that, as if trying to fit it back together. "Bills weren't paid. Customers weren't called back. And by the time he recognized he needed help, he'd nearly run the business into the ground. When he got the official diagnosis, he was going to have to liquidate the business to pay for the care facility. I made sure Williams and Son's bid for the square was the lowest. Even a smaller profit margin meant some profit. I had even planned for Austin to live with me to save money, but he didn't go for that."

Olivia stood and sat on top of the desk. "Does Austin know any of this?"

"No. My dad made me promise not to tell him. That's between the two of them." Nate dropped the doorknob and stood.

"And the delivery?"

He walked over to the small window again. "Something I promised to take care of while he was on his date with Libby."

"I'm so sorry, Nate."

"No. I'm sorry. I should've come and talked to

you and not been a coward." He shoved his hands in his pockets and turned his back on the window.

"Were you coming to talk to me that day when you stopped by?"

He finally made eye contact with her. "You mean when *Jackson* was there?"

Was it her, or did he say that name a bit weird? "What were you going to say?"

"I don't know."

"Liar." Olivia slid off the desk and took a step toward him.

He stepped back until he hit the wall. "Did Jackson ask you out?"

"As friends."

"He didn't mean it as friends." He rested against the wall and leaned his head back.

"Jackson and I are just—"

"You may have said yes as friends. But trust me. There was a whole lot of man-speak going on that day, and Jackson didn't ask you out as just friends."

"You guys barely said two words to each other."

"We didn't have to."

"Man-speak doesn't use words?" She slid her hands into her back pockets and took another step toward him. "Do you just grunt at each other, or is it telepathy?"

A smile tugged on the side of his mouth. "I can't tell you. Guy code and all."

"Is that so?" She took another step.

Nate broke eye contact and turned back to the window. "Jackson seems to be Mr. Prince Charming himself, the kind of guy you've been waiting for."

Ugh. She spun and paced back toward the door. "You got that he's perfect for me from man-speak too?"

He turned and leaned against the wall. "I may have asked Thomas about him."

She closed the distance and poked him in the chest. "You check up on my dates, kiss me in a way that curls my toes and has me thinking of little else night and day, and you still want to stand there and say there is nothing going on between us?"

"You think about that kiss night and day?" His voice had dropped to a husky tone.

"I just mean . . ."

His gaze dropped to her mouth.

She licked the edge of her lip and swallowed. "Do you?"

He reached up and ran a thumb down her cheek. "You have no idea."

His hand slid along her jaw to the back of her head. He offered the gentlest tug before bringing his mouth down on hers. Last time he'd been gentle and testing in the beginning. This time it was as if they picked up where the last kiss had ended. As if he too had replayed that kiss over and over in his mind and this time intended to finish it.

When his hands slid down her sides, she nearly melted into him. Her back arched as she pushed up on her tiptoes, pressing into him. Warmth poured through her that was both strange and new from her inexperience and yet also familiar in the rightness it left in its wake. It was like snapping the last piece into a puzzle and finally seeing the picture come together, a picture of a future so beautiful and perfect she'd have surrendered her heart right then and there if he didn't already possess it.

He pulled back only enough to catch a breath. His forehead rested against hers, and he ran his thumb gently along her bottom lip. "Don't go out with Jackson."

"What?" Jackson who? Oh, wait. Was he really trying to have a conversation when he'd just turned her brain to mush?

His fingers found the skin just above her waistband. "The idea of you going on a date with him drives me crazy. Please say no."

She kissed the rough stubble on his chin, soaking in the musky scent she'd come to identify with him. "If this is happening, then that's a given."

Nate's hands stilled.

The warm sensation cooled in an instant. Olivia leaned back and looked him in the eye. "This *is* finally happening, right?"

He remained silent as his shoulders tensed.

The beautiful picture of hope washed away like a chalk drawing in a downpour. She stepped out of his arms. "You want me to say no to Jackson, but you don't want to give me someone to say yes to?"

The door burst open behind them with Austin filling the frame. "This is why you missed the delivery?"

One look at Nate's hair and the pink stain around his lips and there was no hiding their kiss.

Austin's eyes blazed, but he didn't hang around for more conversation.

Nate rushed after him. "Austin, wait."

In their wake Libby stood in the doorway, eyes wide. "Sorry."

"It wasn't Nate's fault." Olivia shook her head. "I accidentally locked us in."

"I guess you were serious about kidnapping him." Libby laughed and followed Austin. "I'm going to go try to calm him down."

Nate had stopped by the front door. He glanced at Olivia and then back at the storage space. "I should get going."

Olivia lifted her chin and pushed past him. "Me too. I have a phone call to return."

His brother had dropped the ball, and he was left picking up the pieces. Again. Austin adjusted the heat and then checked his GPS. Three hundred miles round trip—perfect. Just how he wanted to spend a Saturday. Especially after he'd already paid for delivery.

His phone rang and he answered it through the radio. "This is Austin."

"Hey, where are you?" Libby's voice filled the car.

"I'm driving to Linden. I have to go pick up the flowers that Nate blew off."

"He didn't blow them off. It was an accident. Olivia said—"

"You know, it'd be nice if at least my girlfriend took *my* side sometimes." He checked his mirrors and moved to pass a semitruck.

"Girlfriend?" Libby's voice squeaked.

Where had that come from? He was so frustrated about Nate that he hadn't really been thinking through his words.

"Yeah, a friend who's a girl." Great, now he sounded like he was in junior high.

"I *am* on your side. I just think you should listen to your brother's side." When he didn't comment, she went on. "I'd have gone with you."

"I wanted some time alone. To think."

"Oh."

Shoot. Not like that. He just hadn't wanted to listen to someone defend Nate the whole time. Man, he was really hitting them out of the park today. His call waiting beeped and his dad's name flashed on the display.

"I have to take this call."

"Bye." Then she was gone.

Ugh. That wasn't what he'd meant. Phone calls weren't his strong suit.

He sighed and accepted the call. "Hey, Dad."

His dad's voice replaced Libby's. "I thought you were stopping by today."

Austin winced. With everything that had been going on in Heritage, he'd missed the last two visits. "Sorry. I have to drive over to Linden today. I'll come by tomorrow though."

"Your brother just stopped by." There were a lot of words unsaid in his dad's tone.

"Then I guess you know why I have to drive to Linden." Austin rubbed his hands roughly over the edge of the steering wheel.

"He mentioned it. Accidents happen." Was his dad referring to the missed delivery or the accident that had derailed their lives?

"They happen a lot with Nate."

"Are you ever going to forgive your brother?"

Austin checked his mirrors and moved into the passing lane again. "Every time I think about it, he goes and does something to show me he doesn't deserve it."

"Deserve it? Who deserves forgiveness?"

Luke's words from the day before replayed in his mind. *Forgiveness is never deserved. It's a gift. If you earn a gift, it's not a gift anymore—it's a wage.*

Austin paused with his mug halfway to his mouth. "Baby?"

Caroline's eyes popped wide and her hands flew to her face.

Grant shook his head. "She didn't want to tell people yet. We just found out yesterday."

Austin stood and embraced her. "Congratulations."

When he pulled back, there were tears in her eyes, and she dabbed at the corners of them with a towel.

Austin searched his mind for what he'd done wrong. "Don't worry, I won't tell. Your secret is safe with me."

"It's not that. She tears up at everything these days." Grant snaked his arm around her waist and pulled her onto his lap. "She's cute when she cries. I'll keep her."

Caroline snuggled into her husband's side. "Back to these feelings. I hear it was quite a date."

"From who?" Austin turned his mug in circles on the table.

"Hannah. She was totally impressed, by the way."

Austin stopped his turning and looked up. "She kind of scared me."

"She's intense, but you'll love her."

"I'll take your word on that." He took a long drink. "The date was great, but I may have messed everything up already."

"In less than twenty-four hours? Austin James Williams, what did you do?"

"Libby called me on the way here and I was still frustrated. She was defending Nate. I don't know. I'm not good at talking on the phone."

Bitterness spills all over those close to you. He'd spilled, all right. And once again it was Libby he'd spilled on.

Caroline stood and pulled some cookies from the cupboard. "If she likes you as much as I think she does, a bad phone call isn't going to end that."

"Really?"

She opened the cookies and set them on the table. "You have impossibly high standards for others—"

"So I hear." He grabbed a cookie and shoved it in his mouth. The hint of lemon seemed to fit his mood.

"And impossibly high standards for yourself. Give yourself a little grace and call the girl. Oh, wait. You really are bad at communicating on the phone. Go see her when you get back tonight."

"And open up." Grant grabbed two cookies of his own. "Seriously, show her what's going on inside. It's like crack to these women."

Caroline shrugged, then wrapped her arms around her husband's neck. "It's true."

Austin took another gulp of coffee as ideas flipped through his mind. "Do you own any white Christmas lights, by chance?"

• • •

Why did relationships have to be so complicated? Libby shoved her phone into her pocket and dropped onto Olivia's bed.

Olivia stood in front of a full-length mirror holding one shirt in front of her, then another. The closet stood open and an antique chair next to it was covered in clothes.

"Wear the aqua one." Libby picked up a small decorative pillow from the bed and spun it in her hands. "It makes your eyes pop."

"I know." Olivia held the shirt in front of her again as she eyed her reflection. "I just bought it for . . . something else."

Libby stretched out on her stomach, using the pillow to prop herself up. "You mean someone else."

"Maybe." Olivia's nose wrinkled before she stood up straighter. "But you're right. It looks better, and I'm moving on."

"Are you sure?" Libby checked her phone. Still no word from Austin.

"I'm sure that I'm done waiting. I can't do this seesaw of emotions anymore." Olivia tossed the brown shirt to the pile, then pulled the aqua one over her head.

Libby pushed up on her elbow. "You two looked pretty cozy when Austin and I found you."

"He wants to be with me. Just not enough to get past the lies in his head. And I can't fight that battle for him." Olivia started digging through a pile of shoes on the floor of her closet. "Enough about me. How was *your* date?"

"Great until Austin got the text about the failed delivery."

Olivia waved a shoe in the air. "My fault. Sorry."

Libby rolled onto her back again, letting her head hang off the edge of the bed. "I tried calling him this morning."

"And?"

"He called me his girlfriend, then backpedaled to 'a girl that's a friend' faster than the weather changes around here."

"Ouch." Olivia reappeared with two shoes in hand and sat on the bed.

Libby sat up and leaned against the headboard. "Right? The date was really good, but I don't know."

The doorbell chimed, and Olivia shrugged as she walked out the door. "Ready or not, here I go."

Libby picked up her phone. "Ring. Ring."

A chime filled the room as the phone vibrated in her hand.

Libby almost dropped it. That had never worked before. She checked the text.

Austin
Come to the greenhouse?

The greenhouse?

Libby slipped on a clean sweatshirt and ran a comb through her hair. She hadn't planned on seeing him tonight or she wouldn't have washed off her makeup. Oh well, time to be real.

She hurried down the steps, across the lawn, and through his side gate. The greenhouse was lit up with tiny lights shining through the plastic. Had he done this for her?

She pushed the plastic door aside and gasped. Every surface, every space on the floor, and every shelf was covered with rose petals. "Wow."

Austin's chest brushed against her back as he reached around, holding a single cut rose in front of her face. He leaned down and placed a kiss under her right ear. "I'm sorry about this morning's conversation."

She took the rose from his hand and turned to face him. "Which part?"

His hair wasn't in its normal well-groomed state, his chin had a full day's growth, and the 350 miles he'd driven weighed on him. The shined-up image for the date had been nice, but this was life. This was the Austin she could fall in love with.

"I'm sorry I was grumpy. I'm sorry I didn't listen to you. And mostly I'm sorry I called you my girlfriend and took it back."

Libby ran her fingers over the rose in her hands to keep from reaching for him. "Are you sorry you called me that, or are you sorry you took it back?"

"Both." He brushed a piece of hair from her face and tucked it behind her ear, lingering as he went. "I'm sorry I called you that because it was being a bit presumptuous. I planned to ask you first."

"Really?"

"Despite this sounding a bit junior high . . ." Austin took the rose from her hand and set it aside, then slid his hands to the small of her back. "Libby, will you be my girlfriend?"

She lifted on her toes to brush a kiss across his lips. He pulled her closer. It wasn't the hurried kiss like last time but was full of tenderness. His fingers trailed up and down her sides, then wrapped around her back. She let her body mold to his as she wound her arms around his neck. She'd kissed other guys before—Colin had kissed her plenty. But it had never felt like this.

In all of Jane Austen's novels, she never described one kiss between her characters. Many speculated that it was because it wasn't proper for the time. But as Austin moved his lips against hers, Libby knew the real reason Jane left them out was that no words could adequately express this feeling . . . this connection. In Austin's arms, every worry that clouded her mind went silent. It was as if nothing existed outside this kiss. Not the future. Not the past. And if she never left this moment, she'd be okay with that.

After a few minutes he leaned back, pressing his head against hers. He took a few deep breaths as if trying to regain his control. "Have you had dinner?"

He was really thinking of food at a time like this? Then again, a distraction was probably best for both of them. "I have not had dinner yet."

"Good." He dropped a quick kiss below her right ear, then tugged at her hand, pulling her deeper into the greenhouse.

"Why do you always kiss me there?"

"I just love your freckle there. Does that bother you?" He led her down the path of petals to a red gingham blanket with an old-fashioned picnic basket in the center.

"I love it, actually." She reached up and rubbed under her ear. "But I didn't even know I had a freckle there."

"You didn't? Then I discovered it and claim it as my spot." He gave her another quick kiss there and motioned for her to sit.

Candles held down the edges of the blanket as Michael Bublé sang softly from a speaker.

"I'm impressed." Libby took a seat on the blanket and stretched her legs out.

"I got the lights and basket from Caroline—oh, and the music. I didn't know who this guy was. But the petals were all me."

Libby picked up a handful of the petals and let them fall through her fingers. Every color of rose was present, creating a mosaic of soft velvet. "Where did all these come from?"

"I had hoped to fill the greenhouse with the order. But I forgot they'd be dormant—necessary for fall planting—and don't look like much besides a bunch of sticks. But the nursery had these. They remove the blossoms when they get too large." He settled down on the blanket next to her.

She picked up another handful and drew them to her nose, savoring the sweet scent. "Why don't you get a larger greenhouse and grow roses?"

Austin opened the basket, pulled out a box of fried chicken, and held it out to her. She took it and then pulled out a bowl of grapes and some carrots. "I don't have time for this and the business."

"But you get more excited when you talk about these flowers than I've ever seen you when you talk about the landscaping company." Libby peeked in the basket. Chocolate cake? Oh, he was good.

He stared at her with a thoughtful expression before he shook his head. "If I don't run the landscaping business, who will? I have to make it work. For my dad and his dad before him."

Libby reached for a grape and popped it into her mouth. She wanted to suggest he talk to

Nate about it, but she had a feeling that wouldn't go over too well at this point. If she'd learned anything from today, it was not to get between the brothers.

fifteen

Why was he letting this get to him? Nate checked his watch. Fifteen minutes until the service started and he couldn't even tie his tie. He tugged the knot to the left as he inspected his reflection. Why was he even wearing a tie? He never wore one. He'd hoped that it would distract from the dark circles testifying to his sleepless night. Nope. It just made him look stiff, uncomfortable.

He pulled the tie loose once again and tossed it onto his desk. He slammed the cabinet hiding the miniature mirror and sank into his office chair.

Why couldn't he get the image of Olivia and Jackson at Donny's last night out of his head? Jackson was a solid guy. He was exactly what Nate had said he wanted for Olivia. Then why did he want to punch the guy in his perfect white teeth? That would cause quite the scene in the Sunday greeting line.

A knock echoed through the small office space just before Luke's head popped around the door. "Have time for a long-lost friend?"

Nate jumped to his feet. "Dude! What are you doing here? Is the baby with you?"

"No. But the doctor is thinking maybe in a couple more weeks. My parents came to the hospital for the weekend, so I was able to convince Hannah to drive here for the day. Libby has been doing a great job taking care of the place, but there are still a few things we need to do."

"It's good to see you, man." Nate moved around the desk and hugged Luke.

"You too." Luke settled into the chair opposite the desk. "Actually, you look terrible. What's going on?"

Another quick knock filled the room just before Libby opened the door. She looked straight at her brother. "I thought I saw you come in. What are you doing here?"

"Hannah is here too." Luke stood and hugged Libby. "We thought we might go to lunch with you and Austin, assuming things are . . ."

"Very good. Yes and yes. I have to teach in the kids' area, but tell her to come find me."

"I will." Luke dropped back into the chair.

"And would you talk some sense into this guy?" Libby pointed at Nate as she moved back to the door.

Luke looked at Nate and then back at Libby. "Nate?"

"I'm fine." Nate sank into his chair again.

Libby crossed her arms. "Your shirt is buttoned crooked."

Maybe that was why the tie had looked so off.

Luke looked between them again. "What's going on?"

When Nate didn't comment, Libby shook her head. "Two words. Olivia and Jackson."

Luke's brow wrinkled. "The guy she dated in high school?"

She had dated him before? Nate thought he might be sick. Wait, she said she'd never dated anyone.

Libby shook her head. "They were only friends. And they *are* only friends. But it might not stay that way if this guy"—she pointed at Nate again—"can't get his act together." She checked her watch and then waved. "I gotta go. See you after."

Luke looked back at him, eyebrows raised.

"It's nothing." Nate adjusted the buttons on his shirt.

"Obviously." Luke settled back and propped his foot on the opposite knee.

"I'm serious." Nate stood to check his reflection again. "I just didn't sleep well last night."

"Because of Olivia and Jackson?"

"I don't know." He finger-combed his hair. That was better. Sort of.

"Then why do you look like you want to punch something every time Jackson's name is mentioned?"

Nate leaned his head back as he clenched his fists at his sides. "I don't know. She deserves a guy like him. I need to be happy for her."

"Wait. Happy for her? I thought you liked

her, and I thought she liked you too. I think that means you should fight for her."

Nate didn't comment as he checked the time. He had only ten minutes before he was supposed to go up front. He reached for his Bible.

"Do you know why I held Hannah at a distance for so long? I thought she deserved someone richer than me. Smarter than me. Well . . . better than me." Luke stood and leaned on the desk. "You don't think you deserve Olivia. And you're right."

Nate grabbed his stack of notes. "What?"

"You don't deserve someone as great as Olivia, and I don't deserve someone as great as Hannah, and Hannah would tell you she doesn't deserve me. But that, my friend, is grace. And grace is a gift."

Nate stared at his notes now crumpled in his hand. His sermon topic today: grace. God sure had a sense of humor sometimes.

"I'll talk to you later." Luke checked his phone. "Hannah is looking for me."

Nate smoothed out his notes and slipped them into his Bible. Why did he find it easier to accept grace in the form of forgiveness but not grace in the form of a gift like Olivia?

His alarm on his phone chimed. Time to greet people. He headed to the lobby and plastered on a smile. The sun shone through the front window, lighting the people as they filed in the front door. At least the predicted storm hadn't arrived yet.

A large group gathered around the coffee station as young Jimmy grabbed a donut from the table—not his first, judging by the chocolate on his cheek. The praise music that floated from the sanctuary grew in volume, announcing it was almost time.

A guy wearing an argyle sweater and lime-green pants approached. Nate knew most locals, and this guy looked more New York City than small-town Heritage.

He extended his hand. "Welcome. Is this your first time? I'm Pastor Nate."

The guy's brows lifted as he stared at the tribal tattoo peeking out of Nate's collar. "Randy. I'm just visiting."

Movement at the main door snagged his attention. Olivia and Mr. Perfect himself, Jackson. Her blonde hair fell in curls around her face, and her dress hung from her shoulders down below her knees, showing off her athletic curves. She was gorgeous. Her eyes landed on him for a minute and then flicked away. He didn't deserve her, but could he accept her love as a gift?

Nate turned back to Randy, but the guy was already moving to his seat while jotting notes in a blue notebook. Okay, then. He'd botched that welcome. He made his way to the front of the church.

Olivia sat next to Jackson in the third row. He leaned over and said something in her ear, and she laughed. She leaned over and wrote something on his paper, her hair falling over his arm. Jackson smiled as if he'd won the lottery. Could the morning get any more difficult?

The worship band took the stage and Nate closed his eyes, trying to shut everything else out. Halfway through the first song, a calm settled over him. God had been with him every Sunday. He would be with him today. Even if he had to face Olivia and Jackson together.

He lifted his head just as the back doors opened once more and Austin walked in. He slid into the last pew and locked eyes with Nate.

Nate had wanted this. Prayed for this. But by the look on his brother's face, he was here waiting to roast him alive. The peace Nate had found evaporated again.

Grace. This topic was looking less and less attractive by the minute.

Nate was a better speaker than Austin had given him credit for. His brother knew his Bible. And he had a way of making it understandable. Austin might consider attending a church like this if . . . well, if Nate wasn't Nate.

He'd hoped to sit with Libby, but she was volunteering with the kids. Nate had paled when their eyes met, and Austin had softened his features after that. He wasn't here to heckle his brother, just understand him.

The building had been pretty close to what Austin expected. A touch of history with its stained-glass windows in front and along the side walls, and modern thrown in with two projection screens up front. The pews were well-worn, smooth wood. The kind he and Nate had loved to slide across as kids.

Austin lounged back in the pew as the rest of the congregation filed out—many stopping to shake his brother's hand. People loved Nate. That had always been true. And he seemed to be making a difference here in the town.

Why did their dad care if Austin forgave Nate or not? Why couldn't the two brothers just go their own ways? People lived estranged all the time. He didn't need to forgive him.

Unforgiveness breeds anger and bitterness that spill all over those close to you.

But he'd been angry at Nate for so long, he wasn't sure he could let it go if he wanted to.

Olivia stood a few rows up with Jackson as the guy shook hand after hand. People seemed to love him almost as much as they loved Nate. Olivia's eyes had darted to Nate repeatedly as she waited, but he hadn't given her more than a glance. Austin would never understand his brother.

Jackson placed his hand on Olivia's back and guided her toward the door. Olivia hesitated only a moment before following him out.

A guy who'd been scribbling notes in a blue notepad since the end of the sermon stood and smirked all the way up the aisle. Austin blinked at his pants. Lime green. That was a bold fashion statement for this town. But the guy seemed to wear them with confidence.

Austin's phone vibrated and he lifted it to read Libby's text.

> Rough day in the kids' area. Going home to change clothes. Luke and Hannah want to take us to lunch. Meet at my house.

He tapped out that he'd be there and dropped the phone back in his pocket as Nate slid into the pew next to him. "What did you think?"

Austin took in the old stained glass above the pulpit depicting an empty tomb. "Pastoring suits you."

"Thanks. What made you decide to come today?"

"Dad." He leaned his elbows on the pew in front of him. "He told me it was time to forgive you."

"But you disagree."

Austin maneuvered to the aisle. The sanctuary was empty now. "I don't think you deserve it. But you don't think you deserve it either, so I'm not sure why we're at an impasse here. Do you want me to forgive you to make Dad feel better? I don't think it'll stop you from living a life of penance."

"What are you talking about?" Nate stood and followed him down the aisle. The back door had been shut, but he still kept his voice low.

Austin shoved his hands in his pockets. "Why did you become a pastor?"

"What?"

"Are you trying to make up for your past?"

"I can't make up for my past." Nate's response was quick and automatic. "Besides, my past is forgiven."

"Do you believe that? Because you're as hung up on your past mistakes as I am. Only I can't decide who you're trying to earn forgiveness from. Me? Dad? God?"

"You don't know what you're talking about." Nate's hand gripped his Bible.

"No? Then why did you go to the board and beg them to give our family the contract? You knew we were inches from bankruptcy, and it'd take a Hail Mary pass like this job for any hope of pulling us out of the red. Well, guess what? It still might not be enough."

Nate spun back and took two big steps toward Austin. "I didn't beg."

"No, you just promised them conditions that no sensible company would have agreed to. I didn't even have the budget for a full crew."

"I tried to help more." Nate poked at his own chest.

Austin stalked toward the door but paced back. "I used to think you flaked on helping with the family because you were lazy. Now I find out that you did it because you're working yourself into the ground. You're working full-time here, part-time with me at the square, and part-time at Dad's facility to help cover his bill. We haven't even touched on the volunteering you do at the shelter, sports teams, and fire department."

"How did you find out about—"

"Dad's facility?" Austin shook his head. "Does it matter?" When Nate didn't comment, Austin took another step toward him. "Someone reminded me recently that forgiveness isn't deserved. It's a gift. Grace. I came here today to see if I could forgive you."

"And?" Nate met his eyes.

"For someone who preaches grace and forgiveness up there"—Austin motioned to the pulpit—"you seem to be more of a faith-by-works kind of guy with a savior complex thrown on top."

"Whatever." Nate made a face and started to turn away.

"You don't believe me? Save the business, save Dad, and let's not forget that you want to save Olivia."

Nate marched toward the front. "You don't know what you're talking about."

"You weren't the only one raised in the church, little brother." Austin raised his voice across the distance. "Just because I don't have some dark, sinful past doesn't make me less saved than you. And just because I don't have a seminary degree doesn't mean I can't read the Bible."

Nate pointed at Austin. "I've never said that."

Austin took a cooling breath as he rubbed his forehead. This conversation wasn't getting them anywhere. He dropped his hand and raised his head. "I guess I always felt that if I forgave you, then no one would hold you accountable for the mess you left. But it seems I was wrong. It turns out that you seem bent on beating yourself up for both of us. So, consider yourself forgiven. Not that it will keep you from punishing yourself." He waved his hand toward his brother and headed toward the back door. "Now you can tell Dad I've forgiven you and check that off your list of things to fix."

"That's it?" Nate's angry voice chased him down the aisle.

Austin shrugged. "Not all brothers are close."

He pushed out of the sanctuary, ignoring Nate's voice calling him back. The door rattled to his left, and he caught a blur of lime-green pants as they disappeared down the sidewalk. He'd assumed the church was long empty or he'd not

350

have raised his voice quite so much. He shook off the conversation and hurried toward the car. Time for a relaxing afternoon with Libby.

Two showers in three hours. Libby ran a comb through her wet hair and prayed again that she wouldn't catch the stomach bug that had landed in her lap. Literally. The poor kid had been playing in Sunday school one second and emptying his stomach the next.

Libby gathered her clothes, took them to the laundry room, and dropped them in the washer. She added a fair amount of soap to be sure and then turned the water to hot. She walked to the kitchen sink and washed her hands one more time. The lemony scent filled the room and erased a bit of the foul odor that seemed to cling to her.

She lifted the vase that held the single rose Austin had given her last night. She held it to her nose, letting the sweet scent surround her, then added a little more fresh water and returned it to the windowsill. She pushed aside the lace curtains, but there was still no sign of Austin. A red Mustang was parked at the curb in front of Austin's house. Who was that?

Her phone chimed and she grabbed it.

Austin
I'll be there in five.

Before she could even reply, the doorbell echoed through the house. Libby reached for the dogs on instinct but stopped. Hannah had taken them to her yard just after church.

Libby pulled open the door to a man in bright green pants and an argyle sweater. Must be the Mustang owner. She paused with one hand on the door. "Can I help you?"

"Hello, I'm Randy Kruger. I'm doing a follow-up story on the square and wanted to ask you a few questions." He pulled out a blue notebook and pen from his bag. "Do you have a moment?" He waved his notepad at her.

"Oh, of course." Libby motioned to the wicker chairs on the porch.

"Thank you." The man flipped to a clean page and settled into the chair. "You were hired to be the librarian, is that correct?"

"Yes." Libby pushed her damp hair behind her shoulders. She really should have taken time to reapply her makeup and straighten her hair. At least the guy didn't have a camera.

He made a note, then pushed his glasses up on his nose. "Originally the library wasn't a part of the plans for the square. Whose idea was it to add it?"

"Mine. I saw the one-room schoolhouse at the edge of town and knew it was a perfect fit."

His brows lifted a bit as his pen scribbled words across the page. "So, you designed the square."

"No. Austin is the architect for the square. I just had the idea to add the library." Libby shoved her hands under her legs to keep from fidgeting.

"But that is the main change to the square." He tapped his pen against the paper and looked at her. "Didn't Williams and Son Landscaping have a plan finalized when they bid the contract?"

"There was a plan, but the town wanted changes. They had wanted a fountain, and I helped convince them that wasn't a wise use of money."

"So, you did decide the layout of most of the square?"

"No. I just offered ideas. Austin made it happen. You should interview him." She grabbed her phone and checked the time. Where was he?

"Are you aware that Williams and Son Landscaping is almost bankrupt?"

"What?" Libby snapped her attention back to the man. She knew that Williams and Son was struggling, but bankrupt?

He charged on as if her answer didn't matter. "Do you feel that other landscape companies should have been considered?"

Was this an interview or was she on trial? "Austin is doing a great job."

"With your help. Wouldn't a landscape company with more expertise in building relocation, not to mention located closer to Heritage, have been a better choice?"

"I'm done talking." Libby stood, but that didn't deter him.

"Do you feel that maybe Nate Williams abused his privileges with the board to funnel the grant money to try saving his family's business?"

Libby hurried down the steps. "This interview is over. I have lunch plans, and you need to leave."

The man offered an evil grin if she'd ever seen one, then winked and walked down the steps, past the Mustang. He slid into an old hatchback across the street and pulled away.

What a jerk!

Libby glanced down at her phone again. Her hands were shaking. Maybe she'd wait at Austin's. She sent him a quick text as she crossed the grass to his porch.

She didn't bother knocking, she just let herself in and dropped onto the couch.

"Austin, is that you, love?" A woman's voice floated in from the other room. "If you want me to think of this place as home, then we have to have a talk about this kitchen."

A chill ran through Libby as she tried to piece together this alternate reality she'd stepped into.

When she didn't respond, a tall, shapely woman with long black hair appeared in the doorway to the kitchen. She wore designer jeans that fit snug to her legs, a white blouse that had to have cost more than three of Libby's shirts, and the apron that Austin had worn the day he made burgers. "Oh, hello. Can I help you?"

Help her? What was this woman doing in her boyfriend's house?

Shiro trotted in from the kitchen and licked Libby's hand.

"Oh, baby, leave this nice lady alone. Come to Mama."

Shiro quickly obeyed and walked back toward the kitchen, stopping to let the woman's long red nails scratch her head.

That shook Libby out of her daze. "Excuse me, *who* are you?"

"Strange question for someone who just barged into my house, but I hear small towns can be strange." She held out her left hand so that a large diamond could be seen glittering from the third finger. "I'm Austin's fiancée."

Fiancée? The air rushed from Libby's lungs. "I have to go." She stood and fled out the door. She had just reached the bottom of the steps when Austin walked up.

"I'll be ready to go in five." He leaned forward to plant a kiss on Libby's cheek, but she jerked back. "Libby?"

The door to the house creaked open as the woman stepped out. "Surprise, Austin."

Austin's face paled, then reddened to the point that Libby feared he might not be breathing. "What are you doing here?"

"You said that if I loved you, I'd come. Here I am." She struck a little pose, seeming oblivious to the tension around her. "Does your friend Lizzy want to stay for lunch? I put spaghetti on. I know it's your favorite. Then some of my special peach pie for dessert."

Libby had heard enough. She turned away, but Austin grabbed her shoulder. "Let me explain. She's my *ex*-fiancée. I have no idea what she's doing here."

She studied him for the truth but couldn't make sense of anything. The woman still stood at the door, the large diamond sparkling from her hand. "She has a ring, Austin."

"Because she wouldn't give it back."

She turned away again, but he blocked her path. His hands gently landed on her arms, and it took all her willpower not to step toward the warmth they offered.

"I need you to believe me. I love *you*."

Everything spun around her. Colin had said he loved her once too. But Austin wasn't Colin, and he'd proven his love time and again lately. She reached up and ran her hand along his clean-shaven jaw. "Do you really love me?"

"Austin, I'm going to pretend you didn't just say that." The woman's words were laced with anger.

Austin's jaw twitched as his head whipped back to the porch. "Becky, if you don't—"

"Becky?" It hit Libby like a smack in the face. She dropped her hand and backed up.

Austin's eyes locked with hers again, but now they were filled with fear—or maybe that was guilt.

"Your dad called me Becky. Your phone call the night of spying was from Becky. You said it was *nothing*." The last word came out with extra bite. She pushed past him, but he followed her all the way to her car.

"It *is* nothing. And I'd have told you about her at the right time. I was going to tell you at the end of our date, but I got sidetracked with Nate dropping the ball. You *know* me. Do you really think I would stand here and lie to you?"

Would Austin lie? Everything in her wanted to scream no. But Colin had lied. Luke's dad had lied. And hadn't Austin lied to the reporter about Nate's and his relationship? Maybe that wasn't the same thing, but she couldn't ignore it as she was trying to determine truth from fiction.

"I don't know." Libby slipped into her car and started the engine.

"How can you not know?" Austin's words carried over the sound of the engine. "Don't go."

She ignored him as she backed out. Becky still stood at the top of the steps, smiling and waving. Libby needed to figure things out, and she wasn't going to do it while his ex-fiancée kept chiming in—if she really was an ex.

Libby didn't know where she was going, she just drove. About a mile out of town, she found herself at the plot where the schoolhouse had once stood. She pulled into the little drive and shut off the engine.

So much had happened since she stumbled across that building on her bike ride with Olivia.

She rested her forehead on the steering wheel as tears poured down her cheeks. Maybe Becky really was an ex. But why hadn't Austin told Libby about her before? There had been so many opportunities when she'd shared about Colin and everything that happened in London.

The rumble of an engine grew louder and Libby checked her mirror. Nate pulled his motorcycle next to her car and cut the engine. He slid off his helmet and peered at her. He looked like he was about to ask if everything was okay but stopped. No doubt her puffy red eyes answered that.

Nate climbed off his bike, sat on the hood of her car, and patted the spot next to him. So like Nate. Always there ready to help solve someone's problems.

Libby climbed out and sat next to him, pulling her knees up to her chest.

Nate didn't say anything. He just waited.

"Becky just showed up."

He let out a low whistle. "That girl has the worst timing ever."

"You know her?"

"I know of her. Caroline and Grant never had a kind word for her."

"Are they still engaged?" She studied his eyes for some glimmer of hope.

He leaned back on his hands but kept his gaze fixed in the distance. "My understanding is that they broke things off before Austin moved here. Then again, Austin and I don't share much these days."

"She seems to think they're still engaged." A little hiccup escaped with the last word.

"From what I've heard of her, she's the worst. Manipulative. Selfish. And just plain mean. But I guess you'll have to decide if you believe Austin or her."

"Is this where you give me a story from the Bible and tell me it's my grace point?"

"Am I that predictable?" Nate dropped his head in his hands. "When I came here fresh out of seminary, I was sure I had all the answers. Right now I can't even find my own answers."

Libby stared out at the field of brown grass. "But if you don't have the answers, then who does?"

The rumble of Austin's truck grew louder just before it pulled off the road. Austin rushed around the front of the truck but paused when he caught sight of Nate sitting next to Libby.

Libby slid off the hood, shoved her hands in her back pockets, and drew a deep breath. "Hi."

He didn't say anything. He just looked from her to Nate.

She took another step toward him. "Nate explained about Becky and—"

He took a step back. "And you had no problem believing him."

"What?" Libby looked back at Nate and then at Austin. "No, he just told me about—"

"About what I already told you. You didn't believe me, but I guess I'm not as trustworthy as *Pastor* Nate. Right?"

She stepped toward him again, but he held up his hand. Maybe it had been a mistake not to hear him out, but she hadn't run to Nate. How was she the bad guy here?

Libby crossed her arms. "You could have told me about her before. But you didn't."

"You probably would have checked the facts with Nate anyway." Austin rubbed his hands over his face, then walked back toward the truck. "I thought I had at least one person in my corner. I guess I come in second to Nate with everyone."

"Austin!" Libby yelled after him, but he was already in his truck. He revved the engine and pulled away without a backward glance.

Of course he didn't look back. Austin didn't offer second chances.

sixteen

What was the phrase? When it rains, it pours. Nate had never seen the truth in that statement until today. He jogged toward the double doors of the church, doing his best to stay dry. There had been a steady mist for an hour, but now it was beginning to fall in heavy drops.

Nate pushed through the front door and paused. Mayor Jameson sat in the waiting area outside his office. His round belly stretched the buttons of his suit coat, his ever-present smile absent.

"Afternoon, Mayor." Nate extended his hand. "What can I do for you?"

The mayor stood and shook it. "Sorry to drop in without an appointment."

"I always have time for you." Nate opened the door to his office. "Why don't we sit down?" He stepped around his desk and motioned to a chair for the mayor.

The mayor sat, then laid his briefcase on his lap and clicked it open. "I assume you saw the article by *West Shore Entertainment* online this morning."

The mayor pulled out a printed copy of the article and laid it on the desk, but Nate didn't pick it up. He'd read it after a heads-up from a mysterious text first thing that morning, and he didn't care to read that garbage again. But even from this distance, the words *misappropriation of funds, nepotism,* and *unqualified* jumped off the page.

The mayor shut his briefcase and set it aside. "Those are some pretty serious allegations."

"You were there." Nate leaned forward on the desk with his elbows. "You know that wasn't how it went down."

"Right you are." Mayor Jameson's head bobbed a few times. "However, I've been contacted by *Reader's Weekly.* They're freezing the funds until they look into the matter."

Freezing the funds? That meant no check for Austin.

The mayor took out a handkerchief and dabbed at his forehead. "I'm hoping to have it all cleared up in a week or two, but these types of things can take time. It could take months."

Great. Time was one thing Austin didn't have.

Nate steepled his fingers. "Is there anything I can do?"

"No, you hold tight. We'll get it worked out." The mayor shoved the hankie back in his pocket and stood. When Nate came around the desk, the mayor dropped his arm around his shoulders. "The truth will set you free. Isn't that right?"

"That's what they say." Nate walked the mayor to the door.

Dale Kensington sat waiting in the lobby, his silver head bent over his phone. He stood up at their approach, pulling his briefcase under his arm. Whatever Dale was here about, Nate doubted it would end with a side hug.

The mayor smiled at Dale and shook his hand, but Nate would have sworn that neither of the men truly meant it. The mayor paused as if to say something more but instead just nodded and grabbed the umbrella he'd left by the door.

Dale's eyes settled on Nate before he motioned to his office. "We need to talk."

Nate held the door open wider and led Dale to the chair the mayor had just vacated. He couldn't ignore the contrast of the two men. Dale had the other guy beat in hair and the cost of their suits. But Dale was half the mayor in girth and—in this case—character too. Nate had only seen that look in Dale's beady little eyes once before, and that was when he was trying to buy Luke's house from under him last year. This wasn't going to go well.

Dale set his briefcase on the floor next to him and pulled out a file. "I'll get straight to it. I never thought my brother should have hired you, and it seems I was right."

That was getting straight to it, all right.

"People are always going on about how people change. But what's the old saying—'you can't change a leopard's spots'?" Dale opened the file and pulled a copy of the article out. He waved it in the air, then dropped it on the desk. Great, now he was gathering a collection.

Nate gripped the arms of the chair until his fingers ached. "The article is misleading."

"Maybe. But it's what people will remember. It's what they'll believe. Not to mention it shed a lot of light on you and your brother's relationship, which seems to be different than you shared in that interview." Dale slapped the article on Nate's desk. "If you had any respect for this town, you'd resign from your position on the council and as pastor of this church."

"The mayor doesn't agree." Nate drew in a slow breath through his nose. Losing his cool at this point wouldn't help his case any. "I didn't do anything wrong."

"I disagree. You've done a lot of things wrong in your life." Dale refocused on the contents of the folder in his hand. "What about getting kicked off the football team in high school for drinking?" He pulled out the article that had run in Nate's high school paper and dropped it on the desk.

"Two charges of drug possession." Two copies of his mug shot hit the desk. "And then the DUI that totaled your father's company van." He added the article that had run in the paper along with the issued ticket. "That nearly took down the family business, didn't it? The same family business that you arranged to get the contract to settle your guilt."

Dale pulled out a larger stack of papers. "Then there are the parties. The internet never goes away, does it?"

Page after page of photos printed from Facebook landed in front of Nate. In most he had his arm around a girl and a beer in hand. The one of him kissing a girl turned his stomach. He didn't even remember her name. He'd deleted as many as he could and untagged himself, but Dale was right, the internet never fully went away. How many hours had the man spent gathering all this?

Dale smacked the rest of the file down on his desk. "I can't say that spells out pastor material."

"I've done all I can to make restitution for those, and God has forgiven me."

"Does that make you an example to the church? I can't help wondering if my brother knew about all of this when he convinced the board to hire you."

"He knew. The whole board knew about my past." Nate clenched his fists. He hadn't passed around a photo album, but he'd been candid. "I'm forgiven—"

"Forgiven by God, yes. But the town of Heritage deserves someone who can lead by example. The last church board may not have believed that, but I'm on the board now." Dale pointed to the stack of papers. "You're not the pastor for us. I'll expect your resignation by the end of the day." He slapped his briefcase shut, stood, and strode out.

Nate winced as the door slammed on his office and on his calling. He stared at his sins laid out in front of him, all in neat black-and-white copies.

The truth will set you free? Sometimes.

Other times the truth stood as an irrefutable testimony against you.

Part of him wanted to fight, but if he fought Kensington, he could expect it to get ugly. And when it got ugly in the church, no one won. It would be better to disappear and not taint all the good he had done here. Besides, not every part of him disagreed with the man.

Nate powered up his computer, opened a Word document, and began typing out a letter of resignation.

No matter how many times she read it, she couldn't believe what she was seeing. Olivia sat at the dining room table, scrolling over the article on her tablet. She moved back to the top and started reading it again. The same bold headline kept flashing back at her. "Local Pastor Misappropriates Town Grant Money to Save His Family Business."

Talk about misrepresenting the truth. But how many readers would believe it because it was on the internet?

The article went on to claim that Austin wasn't

qualified for such a large project. And quoted Libby saying that she'd been the one to design the square when Austin couldn't come up with a design that the town would accept. He was going to love that.

Olivia checked the time. She needed to leave if she was going to make her meeting with her editor. Her phone rang. *Frank Lang* flashed across her caller ID.

"Hello?"

"Do you know what I'm reading right now?" The bite in his words couldn't be missed.

"No, sir." But she could sure guess.

"A front-page article about the town where you live. A front-page article gracing the cover of our competitor." His volume rose with each sentence. "A front-page article covering the topic I asked you to cover and you said there was no story there."

She almost printed it off just so she could rip it up. "The article isn't telling the whole story."

"But you knew there was a story, didn't you?"

Her hesitation was enough.

"Don't bother coming in for the meeting. And don't bother turning in any more articles. I don't think you have what it takes to be a reporter."

The line went dead and Olivia dropped her phone on the table. That was it. Any hope of getting a good recommendation from Mr. Lang was gone.

Libby pushed through the front door with Darcy and Spitz on their leashes. She detached the dogs and filled their waters.

Olivia waved her tablet in Libby's direction. "What did you say to that reporter?"

"What do you mean?"

"You haven't seen it?" Olivia held the tablet out.

Libby took it, and her eyes widened and filled with tears as she scanned the material. "He misquoted me. I didn't mean—"

"Reporters don't care what you mean. They care what you say. What did you say?" Olivia grabbed her tennis shoes by the door, slipped the right shoe on, and bent to tie it.

"I said more than that. I—"

"I was supposed to write this story, but I didn't. I couldn't do that to Nate." She shoved her left shoe on. "But with a few words, it's all gone. I lost my job, and who knows how this will affect Nate, not to mention Austin."

"Why did you lose your job?"

"I told my editor there was no story." She stood and pointed at the tablet again. "Misleading or not, there is a story there. And I didn't write it because *I* don't do that to *friends*. I'm going for a run."

Libby followed her out the door. "Olivia, wait."

"I can't." Olivia spun to face Libby again. "We can talk later, but right now I need to calm down and check on Nate."

Another tear ran down Libby's cheek, and she wiped it away as she backed up. Olivia pushed out the front door and picked up her pace until she was at a steady jog, ignoring the rain.

Five minutes later, she walked through the front door of the church and into Nate's office. He sat expressionless in his chair as he leaned back, staring at his computer. His shirt was rumpled and his hair lifted as if he'd run his hands through it a few too many times already.

Olivia brushed her wet hair away from her face and took a step closer. "Nate?"

He blinked a few times and looked up. "Olivia. Hi. What are you—"

"I'm so sorry. It wasn't me." Olivia circled the desk and pulled him up into a hug.

"I know." His warmth surrounded her as his musky scent wrapped her up. His breath grazed her neck as he seemed to lean into her for support.

She leaned back until she could look him in the eye. "We'll get this figured out."

He stepped out of her embrace, and she missed his warmth and touch immediately. She'd left a wet spot on his shirt, but he didn't seem to notice. "I'm still done."

She gripped his arm. "What? No."

He pointed to a pile of photocopied pages. "A gift from Dale Kensington. Hand-delivered with a bow and a threat." He dropped into the chair and rested his head back. "I think he's been waiting for the right day to use that information. He never did like me."

Olivia circled the desk and picked up a mug shot of a younger, much angrier-looking Nate. Under that, there was an article with a photo of a crushed van and a destroyed flower shop. "This is your past. It doesn't mean—" Her words failed her as a photo of Nate passionately kissing a girl in a small bikini caught her eye. Her hand shook as she picked it up. "Is this Jess?"

"No." He pressed his fingers into his eyes. "I don't know her name."

A chilling numbness started in her fingers and spread up her arms toward her chest. He didn't even know her name. In the next photo, he had a beer in each hand and his arms around two girls. By the look in their eyes, they were all plastered. She flipped to the next photo and the next. Each turn of the page revealed a photo more incriminating than the last. She swallowed against her rough throat and dropped the pile.

The room tipped a little, and Olivia reached for a chair as her stomach rolled over. She looked up and found him waiting.

"That's not even the worst of it, Olivia."

There was more?

He opened a side drawer in his desk, pulled out a photo, and slid it across the table.

Olivia picked it up. It was a picture of a boy about five years old. A clone of Nate if she'd ever seen one. The dark hair, the silver eyes, even the cowlick on the left side of his forehead. She'd guess it was Nate from years back, but his clothes looked like anything you'd find in a Gap Kids today.

"His name is Chase." Nate leaned his elbows on the table as if the weight of the world pressed down on him.

"You have a son." When he didn't deny it, she looked up at him. "Have you told anyone?"

"Luke. I told him last year when I was going through some stuff."

Olivia's fingers shook as she set the photo back on the desk right next to the stack of photocopied pictures.

Nate watched her. Waiting for her to say that all of this was a part of his past. That it didn't matter. That she still wanted him.

She'd said it before. So why wouldn't the words come now? Her mind was a muddle of thoughts. Every time she closed her eyes, all she could see was *her* Nate, who refused to let her close, wrapped around women he didn't even remember.

Then there was Chase. What did that even mean?

Her breaths shortened as everything in her ripped apart. Every picture she'd created in her mind of their future shattered on the floor. She needed more air. She needed to think.

She pushed to her feet. "I gotta go."

Nate's eyes shut a moment. Then he stood and nodded at her, his eyes red with emotion. "I know."

"I'll talk to you later." She stumbled toward the door. It was raining harder now, but that didn't even slow her down. She needed a long run.

She pulled the door shut behind her but didn't miss Nate's quiet words that followed her out. "Goodbye, Olivia."

What had she been thinking? Libby's front door rattled as Austin pounded his fist against it. He flipped through the pages he'd printed off as thunder echoed in the distance and dark clouds covered the sun. The wind whipped stray leaves through the porch, one smacking him on the side of the face. He peeked through the window on the door and banged again.

Libby pulled the door open as she held an excited Darcy back. When she looked up at him, her eyes were puffy and red. "Austin, I'm so sorry."

"For which part? For telling this Randy Kruger that I wasn't qualified?" He waved the article in the air. "Or for the part where you claimed to design the square because I couldn't come up with a good idea?"

Libby winced and shrank back down. "I didn't say that."

"It's in black and white." He lifted his voice to be heard above the thunder.

A low growl rumbled from Darcy's chest, and Austin took a few breaths to calm down.

Libby pushed the dog behind her, walked out on the porch, and shut the door. She wrapped her sweater tighter around her. "He twisted my words. That's not what I said."

Austin paced to the edge of the porch. Drops speckled the sidewalk and the road. He paused and drew a few breaths. "Why were you even talking to him?"

"I was trying to help." She wiped a tear away with the back of her hand. "Give you better press."

"Better press?" The pages wrinkled in his tightening grip. "I couldn't get much worse press than this. I'll be lucky if anyone will hire Williams and Son after this. But that doesn't matter because they've frozen all the money until *Reader's Weekly* can look into the claims that Nate misused the funds."

"That's the crazy thing." Her hair whipped around her face in the wind. She pulled a band from her wrist and tied it back. "The reporter never asked me about the money. I don't know where he would have come up with that idea."

The sky opened up, sending rain angling down in sheets. His house was half obscured through the rain. "He had to get it from somewhere, and it seems like you were his only source in town."

"I promise it wasn't me." She put her hand on his arm, but he flinched away.

"I have to go." Austin charged down the steps into the rain and across the driveway. The cool rain soothed the fire that burned inside.

"Austin, wait." Libby's muffled voice carried through the rain, but he didn't stop. He yanked open his front door, walked in, and stood dripping in his entryway.

Libby burst through the door behind him, her hair plastered to the side of her face.

She wanted to talk? Fine. He grabbed the notice he'd gotten from the bank on Friday and held it out to her. "Do you know what this is?"

"No." She took it and scanned it over.

"A notice saying that if I don't make a large payment by this coming Friday, they are going to repossess my truck." He sank down into the recliner and buried his head in his hands as the reality of his situation threatened to choke him. After a moment he looked up at her. "Guess when I was supposed to get paid."

"F-Friday?" Her chin quivered as her hands shook.

"But now the money is frozen and I have no way to pay this. Without the truck, the company is bankrupt." He stood and grabbed his U of M sweatshirt, then stopped in front of her. "I didn't think anything could be worse than watching you run to my brother."

He closed his eyes against the memory that still burned through him. He'd never known an ache like that. He didn't know if he wanted to hurl or punch a wall.

He handed her the sweatshirt and turned away. "But that article has destroyed me."

"But if we explain—"

"No." He spun back to face her. She had the sweatshirt on now, and his mind flashed back to the night in the greenhouse. It had been raining then too.

As if reading his face, she took a hesitant step toward him, her teeth biting her lip.

He stepped back. "This isn't one of those situations you can just talk your way out of. There isn't research that'll make enough money appear to pay my bills. It's over."

She shivered and hugged the sweatshirt closer. "What's over?"

"Everything. My business. My time in Heritage."

"Us?"

He shoved his hands in his pockets to keep from reaching for her. "We were done the minute you believed Nate over me."

"Austin—"

He took another step back, his dad's words echoing in his head. *He has impossibly high standards sometimes.* Maybe he was being unreasonable, but he couldn't get the image out of his head of her sitting on her car with Nate— listening to Nate . . . believing Nate.

"I was a fool enough to believe you might actually choose me." His voice was strained, and he cleared his throat. "But I was wrong. He won you over, and I'll always be second-best in your eyes."

She took another step toward him. "Austin—"

"You should leave."

Tears ran down her face, but she didn't argue. She walked out the door and out of his life. He couldn't be with someone he didn't trust, and he'd never be with someone who didn't trust him fully.

He had to remember that as the bile rose in his throat. He tugged his soaked shirt over his head and whipped it at the laundry room, then clenched his fist to keep from punching a wall. Then again, a broken hand might feel better than this. Not that he could afford the hospital bills.

Shiro peeked out of the bedroom and ambled over to lick his hand. He dropped onto the edge of the couch and buried his hands in her scruff. "Where have you been, girl?"

At another crack of thunder, the dog whimpered and jumped up next to him on the couch. She'd probably been hiding under his bed.

An alarm sounded on his phone. He eyed the screen and tossed it aside. It was a reminder to call a guy in Canton back about a contract for next summer. He'd have to call and tell him it wasn't going to happen. Williams and Son Landscaping was officially out of business.

seventeen

How could this have happened? Libby opened her suitcase, dropped it on the bed, and wiped away her tears with the back of her hand. She'd messed up everything. Austin, Olivia, Nate—they all hated her.

Her phone rang and Libby snatched it up. "Hello?"

"Libby?" Her mom's voice reached through the phone, tugging at her heart.

"Mom." A cry escaped as she said the word. She dropped to her bed and pressed her hand to her mouth to hold back the sob, then swallowed back the rock in her throat. "I'm coming home. I'm packing now."

"Libby, honey. Deep breath." Her mother spoke slowly with controlled words. "I talked to Luke, and it isn't as bad as you think."

Right, Luke. He'd stayed in Heritage Sunday night when she was so upset after her fight with Austin. He'd probably heard the whole saga when he stopped at Donny's for breakfast on his way out of town. Or at least some of it. But he didn't know she was at the center of it all.

"If Luke said it wasn't that bad, then he doesn't know everything." Libby grabbed her wireless earbuds, stuck them in her ears, and connected the call through them. She started pulling her shirts out of her dresser and tossing them toward the suitcase. "Austin's company has to file bankruptcy, Nate is leaving the church, and Olivia got fired. All because I trusted the wrong person again."

She gave her mom the rundown as she tossed the shirts toward the suitcase, two-thirds of them unfolding as they went.

Her mother cut her off. "You made a mistake, yes. But you didn't make all the mistakes that put Williams and Son Landscaping that close to bankruptcy. You didn't cause Pastor Nate to make his choices, and you didn't tell Olivia not to write the story she knew was there. They made their own choices, honey."

She scooped up her socks next. "I know, but—"

"Mistakes happen. The question is, what are you going to do now?"

"There is nothing I can do." Libby dumped the armful of socks in the suitcase. "That's why I'm coming home."

"Libby, I loved the three years you were home. We had so much fun, and selfishly, I wanted you to stay. But over the past month, I've seen the Libby we used to know reemerge."

Libby dropped onto the bed and lay back to listen to her mom.

"The Libby who was fearless. The Libby

who wanted to move to England and work in a bookstore. The Libby who was always determined to find a solution to every problem."

Libby rolled to her side as Austin's scent surrounded her. She jerked her head up. Austin? His sweatshirt lay next to her pillow. She fingered the edge of the soft cotton. "I can't be that person. After Colin—"

"What Colin did was wrong, and I struggle with my anger toward him often. But you get to choose if it defines you now. He stole three years from your life." Her mother's voice softened as if she fought with her own emotion. "Don't let him steal any more."

Was that what she was doing? Had she really allowed Colin to steal her life? She closed her eyes and pictured him with the gun barrel pointed at her. Only this time, the sting wasn't so sharp. This time it was overlaid with the image of Corrie ten Boom with a gun pointed at her head. Only the police hadn't come to rescue Corrie, and Corrie hadn't been able to run home. At least not for a long time and not until after many more horrors.

Libby pulled Austin's sweatshirt to her face again, then tossed it toward her desk. She couldn't hold on to the hope he'd change his mind. Austin didn't give second chances. "I read *The Hiding Place*. I finished it two days ago."

Her mom cleared her throat as if to find her voice again. "I didn't know you were reading it. It's a powerful story."

Libby stood and picked up the book from her nightstand. "I wondered why she spent so much time in the beginning of the book on everyday life that had nothing to do with the war. Then it hit me partway through. Corrie ten Boom wasn't an exceptional person."

"Many may disagree with that."

She set the book aside and dropped onto her stomach on the bed, pulling a pillow under her. "But if the war hadn't happened, we'd never have heard about her."

She rolled onto her back and stared at the water-stained ceiling. What had Olivia said? Maybe that was why people could identify with her—because her faith wasn't perfect.

Libby sat up, picked up the book again, and ran her hand over the cover. "Her life was difficult and messy from her perspective. But she always held to the truth that there was a Master at work. And as the war and hard times came, instead of running she simply sought God and did what she could with what she had that day. And day after day of doing what she could for God evolved into an exceptional life."

Corrie didn't allow the Nazis to steal her life, and maybe it was time for Libby to take hers back as well. Her life wasn't exceptional, but maybe day after day of doing what she could with what she had was enough.

"I think I need to stay, Mom. I don't have all the answers, but maybe that's okay. Maybe today I just need to work with the answers I do have."

"That's my girl. Call me later."

Libby ended the call and pulled out her earbuds. She wiped away the smudge of mascara under each eye and walked across the hall. Her hand hesitated over Olivia's door before she gave it three solid knocks.

"Come in."

Libby opened the door. Olivia lay on her back on her bed, her eyes red from crying. Her hair had been pulled up in a messy bun, but it was wet. Her shorts and shirt looked soaked as well, but Olivia didn't seem to notice as she tossed a basketball straight up and caught it. "Yes?"

"I have an idea."

Olivia tossed the basketball and caught it again. "No thanks."

"I know you're mad at me—everyone is mad at me. I deserve it." Libby pushed the door open all the way and sat on the edge of the bed.

"I'm not mad at you. I know the guy twisted your words." Olivia sat up so her back was to Libby and spun the ball on her finger.

"Then why are you shutting me out?"

"I'm just . . . mad." She caught the ball and smacked the side of it. "I'm mad that people like that have a job as a reporter when I can't even get my foot in the door. I'm mad that Nate's walking away from the church." She flopped back on her bed and covered her face with a blanket. "And I'm mostly mad at myself because after everything I said to Nate about his past not mattering, when I was faced with it head-on, I crumbled under the weight. I couldn't think of one thing to say. I just . . . left."

Libby tugged the blanket until it slid off Olivia's face. "Have you tried to talk to him?"

"He won't answer my calls. And when I go to the house, he's either not there or not coming to the door. Outside of breaking in the window and waiting until he shows up, I'm not sure how I can talk to him."

"I affirm your choice in not committing a felony." Libby crossed her legs on the bed. "He'll come around."

"You didn't see his face." Olivia's eyes filled with more tears. "Besides, after that article and Dale, I don't think I could say anything to change his mind at this point."

Libby pushed to a stand and tapped Olivia's foot. "Then we'll have to make them all come around."

"All?"

"Yes. Nate, Austin, the church, Dale Kensington—okay, maybe not Dale Kensington, but the rest of the town, *Reader's Weekly*—all of them."

"How?" Olivia sat up straighter.

"By telling the real story." Libby grabbed Olivia's computer from her desk and handed it to her. "You and I both know that the only thing that sells in journalism better than a scoop is a tell-all piece. And I think it's time for us to tell all about Heritage. I was keeping all the financial records of the project. I had to turn them over to the mayor, but I have my own copy. And he's on our side. We could find out if they have minutes from the meetings when the committee voted on the landscaping company."

"What will I do?"

"You will be the amazing reporter you are and find the real story."

Olivia took the computer and set it aside. "But who'll publish it?"

"Maybe no one, but we can make sure the town reads it. And the people of *Reader's Weekly*. It may be too late to save Williams and Son Landscaping, but it isn't too late to save Austin's and Nate's reputations. I can do the research, but I can't do it alone. Are you with me?"

"This may not work." Olivia picked up her laptop and opened it.

"I know. But then we can walk away knowing we did all we could with what we had today. I'm done with what-ifs and if-onlys in my life."

Olivia sat up a bit straighter. "I'm in."

• • •

He'd had a lot of tough conversations with his dad over the years, but none had been this hard. Austin shifted in his spot on the couch. He'd arrived at the care home thirty minutes ago, and he'd yet to bring up why he'd come.

"Nuts! What do you think this is, spring training? This is the playoffs, get some glasses." His dad yelled at the umpire on the TV, then looked at Austin. "Did you see that?"

Austin blinked at him and then the TV. "Sorry, I missed it."

His dad stared at him for a full five seconds before he clicked off the TV. "Okay, spill."

"You didn't have to do that." Austin reached for the remote, but his dad stopped him.

"You're more important. And the good guys were losing anyway."

Austin drew a deep breath and leaned forward on his knees. "The thing is, Dad . . ."

Here it was. But how did he tell his dad that everything he'd worked for his whole life was gone?

"Go on."

"Williams and Son is bankrupt." The words tumbled out in rapid succession.

His dad sighed and sank back into his spot on the couch. "Is that all? The way you were acting, I thought you were dying. Nate was here earlier to tell me he was leaving the church.

I thought maybe it was my day for bad news."

"It *is* bad news." He faced his dad squarely. "The business is *done*."

"Yeah." His dad walked over to the kitchen, holding the counter for balance.

Why wasn't he reacting?

Austin tried again. "Like, over. Kaput. Nada. No more. Finished."

His dad poured himself a glass of orange juice and returned to the couch. "I understand what bankrupt means. That medicine has been helping, you know." He tapped at his head.

"I know." Austin leaned back in his spot and took in the white wall next to the TV. They had never gotten up any decorations for that one. Was it strange that he kind of liked it that way?

When his dad still didn't react, he looked over at him. "I guess I thought you'd be more upset."

His dad took a large gulp of juice and set it on the end table. "It's hard to say goodbye to anything. But life keeps moving on."

"I wanted to make it work for you, but—"

"For me? You mean for you." His dad's brow wrinkled.

Austin shrugged. "Sure. I just didn't—"

"No. Not *sure*. Yes or no." When Austin didn't answer, he pressed on. "Why did you want this business to succeed?"

"What do you mean? It's our business."

His dad held up a hand. "No. Now it's your

business. Don't think about it. Gut reaction. Why did you want Williams and Son Landscaping to survive?"

"To make you proud."

His dad sighed and rubbed his gnarled hands together, then looked Austin straight in the eye. "Austin, I *am* proud of you."

"But the business—"

"Failed. I'm sorry I didn't leave it to you in better shape." He took another drink of juice. "But I've always been proud of you. Why would you think otherwise?"

"You never say it." Austin stood and walked over to the empty wall. "You always questioned whether I was up to the task of running the business. And all I hear about over and over is how proud you are of Nate."

"I am proud of Nate. I'm proud of both of you. I never . . ." His dad's voice grew rough. "I never questioned if you *could* handle the business. I was trying to find out if you *wanted* to handle the business."

Austin turned around and leaned against the wall.

"Don't get me wrong. You're a fine landscape architect. But I never really got the impression that it was your . . . passion. And to be honest, it wasn't my passion either."

"What?" Not his father's passion? It had been their life.

"It was your grandfather's passion. I did it because . . ." He shrugged. "Well, because it needed to be done."

A rock landed in Austin's gut. Hadn't that been basically what he'd said to Libby?

"Maybe I celebrated Nate more because that boy always followed his heart, whether good or bad." He leaned back on the couch and stretched out his arms across the back. "I've always been a little jealous of that. I played it safe. But I never wanted you to think I wasn't proud of you. You're one of the hardest-working people I know. But do you want landscaping to be your whole life? Is it your passion?"

Passion? No. "To be honest, I'm not sure when I stopped enjoying it, but it's been a long time since I was excited about Williams and Son."

"Then this isn't a failure. This is a new start. An empty canvas."

An empty wall. The unmarked white surface held endless opportunity.

The weight that he'd been carrying since he took over the business lifted as his father's words sank in. He was free for the first time to do whatever he wanted. But what did he want?

Libby's words echoed in his mind. *Why don't you get a larger greenhouse and grow roses?* Could he do that? Yes. He could do anything he wanted now. Success wasn't guaranteed, but maybe failure wasn't the worst thing either. Maybe the worst thing was failing to try.

He looked up to find his dad studying him. His dad. Not a man who looked like his father but whose mind had betrayed him. It was his dad. Present. Aware.

He'd begged, prayed for months for one more clear talk with his dad. Maybe it was the medicine and maybe it was a miracle. Either way, it was a gift that he'd treasure as long as he lived. For Nate's sake, he hoped his brother would be granted a few of these moments as well.

"Wait, did you say that Nate is leaving the church?" He'd been so consumed with his own train wreck that he hadn't even considered what the article would mean for Nate. He'd guessed that his brother would get some backlash from it, but to fire him?

"It was more than the article. A board member created a whole file on his past and threw it in his face."

"Can they do that?"

His dad sent a pointed look at Austin. "You do it all the time."

The truth landed like a smack to the back of the head. It wasn't the same. Was it?

"I have got to get going, Dad." Austin pulled his keys from his pocket. "I have a lot to think about."

"What are you going to do next?"

Austin stared at the blank wall. "Start fresh."

His dad stood and nodded his approval. "I like that."

Austin wrapped his arms around his dad, holding on a touch longer than usual. He couldn't hold on forever, but he thanked God for today. "It was good talking to you, Dad."

Tomorrow would be his last official day. Nate lifted his diploma off the wall and ran his hand over it to remove the dust. Somehow he'd thought that a degree would make a difference. Turned out that Xerox copies carried more weight than credit hours. He didn't blame them. He'd been waiting for this since he took the pulpit his first Sunday.

A knock at the door echoed in the nearly empty room.

Nate added the frame to the box. "Come in."

Chet Anderson opened the door. He was dressed in his Sunday best circa 1975. He tugged at his collar, then walked in and extended a gnarled hand.

Nate shook it. It seemed frailer than the last time he'd seen him. He'd recovered from the stroke, but it had aged him.

Chet yanked off his flat cap as if just remembering he was wearing one and twisted it between his hands. "Can I talk to you, Pastor?"

"Sure thing." Nate moved the boxes from a chair and then claimed the other one. "You can just call me Nate."

Chet nodded as he sat down. "The thing is, Pastor, did you know that I'm a cousin to the Kensingtons?"

"No. I didn't know that." Nate sat back, unsure where this was going.

"Our moms were cousins. Dale and I never really got along, but George and I, we were pretty close on account of—" He paused and shook his head. "Anyway, we were close."

"He was a great man." A slight ache filled his chest for the man who'd been his mentor for such a short time. George Kensington had been the backbone of this community, and his absence was still keen a year and a half after his death. Not just for Nate but for everyone.

"Yes, sir. Many in the town didn't even know because we hung out at . . . odd times. Anyway, one night when we were . . . working on a project, he started talking about you." Chet pulled a folded-up envelope out of his pocket and smoothed it against his leg. "He was all excited because the board had agreed to offer you the job." His smile doubled the wrinkles on his face.

"That was just over two years ago."

"Yup. Then a strange look crossed his face, and he told me that if there was ever a day that you decided to let your past interfere with your present, I was to tell you to stop it. I told him to tell you himself, and he just shrugged like he knew something I didn't."

"I appreciate you coming here." Nate shifted his position. "But you don't understand the situation."

"I told him you wouldn't listen to me." Chet wagged one of his gnarled fingers. "Only I told him a little more colorfully." His face reddened with the admission. "The next time we . . . worked on our project, he gave me this. Told me to hold on to it if this day ever came." He handed Nate the folded envelope. Nate's name was scrawled across the front.

Just seeing George's familiar writing twisted something inside him.

"I've done my job." Chet pushed to a stand and walked to the door. He paused and turned back. "I may not understand the details, but I do know you're the first pastor we ever had that I listen to. You aren't boring and you make it simple."

"Thank you." Nate tapped the envelope in his hand as Chet disappeared out the door. He slid his finger under the seal, pulled out the stationery, and unfolded it.

From the desk of George Kensington.

Dear Nate,
If you're reading this, then I'm sorry. I'm sorry that you're doubting yourself right now, and I'm sorry I'm not there in person to remind you of the truth.
You have made mistakes. You were

up-front with the board, and everyone was aware of your past when we voted unanimously to hire you.

You have been forgiven. End of story.

Don't let what God has forgiven stand between you and what He's called you to do.

George

He smoothed out the letter. Why had God let George be taken from him? If George were still here, none of this would be happening. But he wasn't here, and he didn't know back then what Nate would be facing today.

Another knock echoed through the room. He'd never had this many visitors when he was on the payroll. "Come in."

Luke pushed the door open and dropped into the chair.

Nate added the letter to the box. "I thought you went back to the hospital."

"I did. But I made another trip back because I heard my pastor resigned." Luke leaned forward and plucked a metal globe off Nate's desk.

"Yup." He tapped the side of the box. "I turned in my resignation, and I told them I'd be out by tomorrow."

"Want to talk about it?" Luke tossed the globe from one hand to the other.

Nate picked up the file and handed it to Luke. "This pretty much says it all."

Luke set the globe back in its holder and took the folder. He scanned the file, his brows lifting at several points. Then he shut the file and stood. "Follow me." He grabbed the metal trash can by the door and walked out.

Nate pushed out of his chair. By the time he caught up with Luke, his friend stood in the church parking lot with the trash can in front of him and a lighter in his hand.

He glanced at Nate, sparked the lighter to life, and held it under the file until the flames licked along the papers. When the flames began to reach his hand, he dropped the file in the trash can and let it burn. "That, my friend, is what forgiveness looks like."

"Those are only copies." Nate shook his head. "Dale has more."

"I know. But I'm not talking about Kensington's forgiveness or the church's." Luke shoved his hands in his pockets and met Nate's gaze. "I'm not even talking about forgiveness from God, because I'm pretty sure you get that. I'm talking about you forgiving yourself. Let it go, man."

Nate tapped the side of the trash can with his foot. "Easier said when your accusers aren't dropping files off."

"From what I heard, you didn't need Dale to drop them off. You've been living in your grave clothes for a while."

"My grave clothes?"

"Wasn't it you who preached about how when Jesus raised Lazarus from the dead, the first thing he said to Lazarus's friends was to unbind him and let him go?"

"Yeah." Nate shrugged. It was a touch surreal being preached to by someone he'd mentored.

"You also said we can't cling to the grave God called us out of. That file was your past. Not your present." Luke pointed to the final embers consuming the papers. "Those are your grave clothes. It's time to let them go."

"Austin thinks I volunteer out of guilt. He may be right." Nate rocked back and forth on his heels. "You think I should give up all the volunteering?"

"No." Luke shoved the lighter back in his pocket. "Serving the community is good. Just make sure you do it out of love and not guilt. And you may not want to overcommit yourself."

The last few embers faded from orange to black in the bottom of the trash can. "How did you get so smart?"

Luke folded his arms and smirked. "I have a great pastor."

"I don't know about that. Lately, I don't have answers for anyone."

"Correct me if I'm wrong, but I'm pretty sure you weren't called to have the answers. You were called to point to the one who has the answers."

Nate shoved his hands in his pockets. "I know that, but—"

"You've helped me through some tough times. Now let me do the same for you." He pointed to the pile of ash. "This is just a metaphor. This isn't the answer. I'm not the answer. And you're not the answer to this church or anyone in it. You're just the guy who points to the answer."

A tendril of smoke from the ashes curled up into the air. "How do I do that?"

"Like you did with me. Tell the story and tell it well." Luke pointed skyward. "He'll do the rest."

Tell the story. He could do that.

"And while you're at it, stop slapping God's hand away. He's giving you a gift. Accept it."

"A gift?"

"O-liv-i-a." Luke shook his head. "Was I this dense when it came to Hannah?"

"Yes." Nate let out a laugh. Then it died as the memory haunted his mind. "You didn't see Olivia's face after she read the file."

"What file? All I see is a pile of ash." Luke's hand landed on Nate's shoulder. "Consider this the official ripping off of your grave clothes."

"What about Chase? That isn't a file I can burn. And I don't want to."

"True. But it isn't a file you can do anything about right now either. That's one you have to leave in God's hands and see what He'll do with it."

Luke walked back toward the church, leaving Nate with the burned remains of his past.

eighteen

This had seemed like a better idea when she didn't have the eyes of the town staring at her. Libby stood on the steps of the library and scanned the crowd. She and Olivia had been posting flyers, making phone calls, and sending emails for the past two days, and it seemed as though their work had paid off. Three news crews had shown up, and at least two papers. This was either the best thing she'd ever done or her worst mistake yet. More than half the town had shown up, but she still didn't see Nate, and this wouldn't work unless he came.

Libby shifted from one foot to the other and checked the time on her phone. Where was Olivia? Libby had done the research and Olivia was supposed to deliver the speech. That was the deal. She didn't do speeches.

Her phone buzzed with a text from Olivia.

I'll be there by the end. So sorry. Explain later.

This couldn't be happening. Libby scanned the mob of people. Maybe she could wait Olivia out. But if they didn't start soon, then people would leave and this would have all been for nothing.

Libby's thumbs flew across the keyboard.

What about the speech?

You'll have to give it.

No.

YES! You can do this!!

But she couldn't do this. She wasn't a public speaker. She was a librarian . . .

And Corrie ten Boom had been a watchmaker.

She didn't have to be Winston Churchill. She just had to do what she could with what God gave her today.

With shaking legs, Libby climbed the steps and faced the crowd. She picked up the mic from the karaoke machine Olivia had set up and lifted it to her mouth. "Th-thank you all for coming today."

Her voice cracked on the final word. She cleared her throat and tried again.

"As many of you know, Heritage was featured in a recent article. They quoted me—misquoted me—on many things. I can't tell you the exact words I used, but I can tell you that the landscape architect who was hired wasn't hired because he was Nate's brother but because Nate knew his brother was the best man for the job."

A murmur traveled over the crowd, but Libby pressed on. "The town took six bids before they decided, and Williams and Son Landscaping underbid every one of the very companies that *West Shore Entertainment* said were overlooked."

The crowd quieted.

She skimmed over the notes she'd prepared for Olivia until she found her spot. "N-Nate did his research, and his family came up with the lowest bid. I don't think that's a misuse of funds but the wisest use of funds." She paused and held up a clipboard. "I have a detailed list of expenses as well as other bids that Heritage explored. Williams and Son Landscaping was the best choice for this project. Olivia and I have already submitted this same information to *Reader's Weekly*, and I expect they'll agree that there has been no misuse of funds."

The people glanced around the square but remained quiet.

Here was the big one—the one where the people would either rally behind her or run her out of town. "I know this isn't a church meeting. But since half of you out there go to the church, I want to use this opportunity to say that I believe not only should Nate be allowed to stay, but you should be begging him to stay."

That stopped everyone.

"What about the fact he lied to that news anchor?" Ted Wilks spoke up from the front.

"I think if you look back, you'll find that Nate never said anything untrue." She'd requested the transcript from Channel 21 and pored over every word said. "However, you're right that he didn't fully divulge the situation."

"Isn't that the same as lying?" Ted again.

"I've only lived in Heritage a couple months, and I've learned a few things. First, I've learned it's a town full of generous and kind people. It's also a place of mystery and secrets . . . like Otis the hippo."

The crowd chuckled a little. Maybe she could do this.

"But most of all, Heritage is a place where we're all one family. A family that forgives. A family that helps each other up. Austin and Nate may not have the ideal relationship that the media portrayed a couple months back. But who hasn't had a time when you fought with a sibling?" That got quite a few nods. "Did you have to explain your disagreement to the whole town?"

"And what about the photos I uncovered from his wild youth?" Dale Kensington moved closer, staring her down. "You want that type of person leading the church?"

Olivia ran up from the side, panting, and reached for the mic. "I would like to answer that."

Libby handed over the mic and leaned back against the library door. *Thank you, Olivia.* She'd reached the end of her courage.

Olivia scanned the crowd before her gaze seemed to settle on someone in the back. "I've served in many of the ministries with Pastor Nate over the past two years. I've seen him speak with kindness and respect to a woman in the shelter. I've seen him hold the hand of a man in his last days at the care home. I've seen him speak truth to the youth in such a way that their faces light up. Yet when I was faced with the ugliness of his past, I'll admit that I ran."

A murmur traveled through the crowd.

"But don't you see? Nate is an example of God's grace. He is a gift to us. We all have sin. If we can't believe that God can transform a person like Nate, why should I believe He can transform a person like me? I bet each of you can think of times when Nate spoke truth to you, and your life is different because he moved to town. Do you really want to let him leave?"

An uncomfortable silence settled over the crowd. When Libby didn't think she could handle it anymore, Chet Anderson walked to the front and took the mic. "My name is Chet, and I know Nate has made a difference in my life. I think he should stay."

Over the next hour a nonstop stream of people came up to the mic, some from the church and some just from the community. A few were kids Nate had coached, others were guys he served with as a volunteer firefighter. People told of how Nate had touched their lives with a word, with a listening ear, or just by being there when they needed someone.

Libby sat on the top step and leaned back against the library door. Her legs still shook with adrenaline. Public speaking seemed to have taken everything out of her. Only time would tell if Nate would get his job back or if this would be enough to save Williams and Son Landscaping, but she'd given it all. She'd done all she could with what God had given her today. The rest was out of her hands.

He'd managed to stay hidden at the back of the crowd for most of the meeting, but the way people started sending looks his way, maybe he hadn't been as hidden as he thought. Nate pulled the hood of his sweatshirt back and shoved away from the tree.

If they expected him to get up and talk, they'd be disappointed. He wasn't sure he'd ever speak again with this lump in his throat. It had lodged there after about the third person took the mic.

He'd never have guessed he'd made a difference in this many people's lives. He hadn't thought of it as helping them. He had just been himself.

Bo Mackers, the chairman of the board at the church, walked up, pulled a letter out of his pocket, and held it out to him. His furry eyebrows lifted as he waited. "I didn't know if you wanted to take that back."

Nate took the envelope and broke the seal to his resignation letter. "Testimonies or not, Dale Kensington isn't going to like this."

Bo shrugged and smiled wide enough to reveal a missing tooth on one side. He leaned closer and spoke for Nate's ears alone. "Irritating Dale Kensington seems to be a specialty of mine lately."

Nate tapped the paper against his hand, then realized that they'd gathered the attention of the square. The mic had gone silent as everyone waited to hear Nate's decision.

"I think I can help with this." Thomas, Hannah's brother, stood a few feet away. Releasing Janie's hand, he reached in his pocket and pulled out the lighter Luke had used before. "Luke said you might need this."

Nate took the lighter from his friend. Burning this letter wouldn't make his problems with Kensington go away. There would always be people who brought up his past. But maybe it was time for him to stop being one of them.

He took in the crowd. Some were still against him. But more were for him. Olivia stood on the library steps, watching him. He might not deserve her in his life. But a relationship with her was a blessing he was finally ready to accept.

With his eyes still fixed on Olivia, he flicked the lighter to life. He held it under the paper and let the flame lick at the edge. When the fire crawled up the side, Nate dropped the paper on the sidewalk.

As the letter burned away, the rest of his grave clothes loosened and fell off. Freedom. What an amazing gift. Peace washed over him, and he didn't know if he wanted to scream in joy or collapse in relief.

Members of his congregation began to clap as they stood with him. Some smiled, others nodded encouragement, and Lucy wiped away tears with the back of her hand.

He might face this battle again, but if that day came, he'd look back at this memory and remember. He was forgiven. A new man. He was free.

Olivia waited at the top of the steps with a soft smile. Nate took a step in that direction.

Bo reached out and shook his hand. "Welcome back, Pastor."

"Thank you. Now there is someone else I need to speak to." Nate took another few steps but didn't get far. Every few feet another well-meaning person would stop and hug him, thank him, and want to tell him what it meant to them that he was staying.

By the time he made it over to where Olivia

had been standing, she'd disappeared. He paused at the top of the steps and searched the crowd. When he found Libby, she pointed to the door behind him. He nodded his thanks and slipped inside the library.

The room was dark, and he waited for his eyes to adjust. As the room took shape, he scanned the aisles of shelves that now housed books but still came up empty.

The door to the room where they'd been trapped stood open, and he strode to it and peeked in. Olivia sat on the desk with her back to him, her head down, eyes closed. She wore a long, flowing white skirt and a green top. With the way the light from the window lit up her pale blonde hair, she appeared almost angelic. His gift from above.

As he stepped toward her, a board creaked under his feet. Her head shot up. A smile filled her face as her teeth tugged at the edge of her lip.

He stopped in front of her and leaned down until they were eye to eye, resting a hand on either side of her on the desk. "Nice speech."

She placed her hands on the sides of his face and looked into him. "I'm so sorry, Nathan—"

He closed the distance to her lips. They'd talk, but that could wait. Right now he needed to cherish her, love her, and accept the gift of her love.

Her lips were soft and laced with a touch of salt. Their other kisses had been out of passion and desire. This kiss was his tender promise of his whole heart given to her—holding nothing back. He took his time getting to know her and letting her know him.

She still ignited him, but it was more than physical. His heart burned for Olivia. Not with the kind of fire that destroyed but the kind that refined and transformed so that he'd never truly fit with anyone but her.

He pulled away a fraction of an inch but kept his forehead against hers. "Last time we were right here, you said you wanted someone to say yes to." He ran a finger down the side of her face, capturing a lingering tear along the way. "Say yes to me. I'm not perfect. I have scars, but I love you. Fully. Without condition."

She gasped at his words and leaned back just far enough to look him in the eyes.

He ran his fingers along her jaw, then followed the path with a row of soft kisses. "I know I don't deserve you, but if you'll let me, I'll do all I can to love you with all I am for the rest of my life. Choose me."

Olivia lifted his chin until he was looking at her again. "I'll always choose you."

His lips found hers again, and he pulled her tight against him as he deepened the kiss. He slid his fingers into her hair as she trailed her hands up and down his back.

Finally Nate pulled away, struggling for breath.

"Please tell me you aren't one for long engagements."

"Long engagements?" Olivia's head dropped back with a laugh. "We just started dating thirty seconds ago."

Nate kissed her neck. "I knew I wanted to marry you two years ago on our first date, and everything I've learned about you since then has only confirmed that."

Her head snapped up and she lifted one eyebrow. "For knowing it on our first date, it took you long enough."

Nate leaned back as he took her hands in his. He stared out the window and searched for the right words. He looked back at Olivia, her expression open.

"The week after our first date, I ran into Jess at a mall in Grand Rapids of all places. She had her husband and three kids with her. One look at her oldest, and I didn't have to even ask if he was mine. You saw the photo."

"Did you know she was pregnant when you broke up?"

"Yes. But she told me she got rid of it, and I was so messed up back then I never gave it much thought." He struggled against the emotion clogging his throat.

"What did she say when she saw you? When you saw Chase?"

He squeezed her hands. "She told me that my

name wasn't on any records and I'd have to take her to court to get a paternity test." He let go of one of her hands and rubbed the back of his neck. "I hadn't even said a word. I was just staring at her in shock. No doubt the kid believes that the dad he's always known is his father, and I'm sure she was afraid I'd step in and destroy that. Selfishly, I wanted to. But as we talked, the dad had taken the three boys to look at a toy store. And the way Chase hung on the guy's arm and chatted away a mile a minute to him, I could see that he was happy. They're all happy. What right do I have to come in and tear that apart?"

"That has to be so hard. You have no contact?"

He pulled her to a stand and tugged her toward the front door, walking slowly. "I asked if I could give child support and she said no. I gave her my email and told her to let me know if they ever needed anything. After a month, she started sending me photos once in a while. But that's it."

Olivia squeezed his hand and leaned into his shoulder. "Jess might change her mind as he gets older. He might need medical information someday."

"I've thought about that. I started a bank account for him and a box of letters. I know the chances are slim." He paused in front of the main doors. "But that's the secret not even the town knows because it isn't my story to tell."

"Thank you for trusting me with it." She pulled

him close and pressed her lips against his. This time it wasn't full of passion but rather a promise of acceptance and confidence. She leaned back. "It's a mystery of human chemistry and I don't understand it. Some people, as far as their senses are concerned, just feel like home."

Nate gripped her arms and pressed his forehead to hers. "Did you just quote *High Fidelity* to me? Now I know I love you."

Olivia laughed and traced his jaw with her finger. "And I know if you ever leave me, it will be for John Cusack."

"Not a chance. But I may require you to watch all eighty-eight of his movies." He pulled back as she opened the door.

"There you two are." Libby stood at the bottom of the schoolhouse steps. "What happened earlier? You better have a good reason for leaving the stage to me."

"Oh. I forgot." Olivia gripped his arm. "The *Chicago Free Press* approached me about writing for them."

"What? That's awesome." Libby looked from Olivia to Nate and back to Olivia.

Chicago? Nate calculated the miles. That'd be some commute. "Would you live in Chicago?"

"No. It's freelance. I can work from a home office. They'll fly me from Grand Rapids to Chicago every few months, but I could stay in Heritage."

Libby nudged her side. "I thought you were ready to get out of this town."

"I seem to have a strong reason to stay." Olivia tugged Nate closer, then looked back at Libby. "But it didn't look like you needed me up there. You were amazing. Next stop, karaoke."

"I'm on such a high right now, I might just agree to that."

"Are you serious? Tomorrow night is my family's fall bash. We always do karaoke. You and me, babe. We're taking the stage." Olivia went off on a tangent about all the different songs they could sing for karaoke.

Nate eyed his brother's house. The truck was there, but the windows were all dark. Nate had hoped he might come tonight. Then again, other than a paycheck, Austin wasn't all that attached to the future of Heritage.

Even with everything that had been said, he didn't see *Reader's Weekly* issuing the funds in time to save Williams and Son. No doubt Austin would be out of here within the week. Looked like reconciling with his brother had been a pipe dream after all.

This was what it felt like to have nothing left. Austin sat on his front step as a tall man with a mustache and coveralls winched his truck up on the flatbed. The banging metal sounded like the slam of an iron gate on his company. Williams and

Son Landscaping—a three-generation business—was no more.

Austin rubbed his hands over his face but couldn't look away. It would have been less humiliating to at least let him drive the truck somewhere and drop it off. Nope. The bank wanted to make a show of it.

He'd heard the meeting had gone well yesterday and Nate would be staying. It looked like everything had turned out all right, except for Williams and Son Landscaping. But other than the humiliation of it, letting it go was a huge weight off his chest. He just had to figure out what he'd do next.

There was no movement at Libby's house. He hadn't seen her since their last fight. He'd been too harsh, but he'd still been dealing with the raw rejection of when she'd chosen to believe Nate.

The rumble of a motorcycle grew louder as Nate came into view. He pulled off the road and around the flatbed and parked in Austin's yard. "Hey." He pulled off his helmet and dropped the kickstand.

"Come to gloat?" Austin pushed on a raised nail on the steps. It didn't budge. He'd need to remember to nail that down later. He shook his head. There wouldn't be a later. Without a job, he couldn't even afford reduced rent. "Or maybe to say, 'If you'd lived with me like we planned, you might have had enough money and you could have—' "

"I just came to say I'm sorry." Nate dropped next to him on the step.

"You're sorry?"

"I'm sorry you're going through this." Nate set his helmet aside and unzipped his leather jacket. "I'm sorry I cost the company so much money a few years ago. And I'm sorry you had to drop out of U of M because of me."

"Who told you?"

"Libby."

Of course. "She seems to talk a lot lately."

"The article wasn't her. Well, the interview was, but most of that information he had on the business, our relationship, my involvement in pushing for you guys to get the job . . ." Nate looked at the truck, then back at Austin. "That came from us."

"What are you talking about?"

"I was looking at one of our security cameras because we were trying to find where a raccoon keeps getting in. Anyway, the reporter was standing in the foyer during our whole argument at church."

Austin searched his memory. "The guy in the lime-green pants."

"The very one."

Austin propped his elbows on his knees and dropped his head in his hands as the truth sank in. "I sure wrecked that."

Nate rested back on his elbows. "Go apologize."

He picked up a pebble and threw it at a knot in a nearby tree but missed. "She still didn't believe me when it mattered."

"Did you believe her when she said she didn't give the reporter information about the business?"

Austin had picked up another stone but paused mid-throw. "But that's—"

"Different? Not really." Nate grabbed a small rock and tossed it at the knot. Miss. "Why didn't you ever tell her about Becky?"

"I don't know. I guess I hated the fact it took me so long to see who Becky was. I feel like a fool when I talk about her. I . . . didn't want Libby to see me like that."

"But you've changed."

"Have I?" Austin picked up another pebble and rolled it over in his fingers.

"Did you let Becky manipulate you into taking her back?"

"No. I asked her for the ring back."

"And?"

"And when she realized she couldn't control me anymore, she took off." He lobbed the smooth pebble toward the knot but was way off. "But she left the ring. I can sell that at least."

"See, you are not the same Austin. Now stop feeling sorry for yourself and go apologize to Libby."

"Why would she forgive me?" Another toss. Another miss.

"Because she loves you. And when you love someone, you have to decide if that relationship is worth more than the self-righteous feeling of holding something over their head." Nate tossed another pebble and hit the knot.

Austin rubbed the back of his neck. "Are you talking about Libby or me?"

"I'm sorry. I wasn't going to go there. I just . . ." Nate stood and paced a few feet away, then turned back. "I'm going to say my piece, then I'll never bring it up again."

"Okay."

"God has put several solid friendships in my life. Grant, Luke, and Thomas have been there for me over and over. These guys have become like brothers to me. But they're not my brother." His voice hitched. "You are." He kicked the ground and locked eyes with Austin. "But I'm letting go of my mistakes. I love you, but I can't surround myself with people who are only reminding me of who I was."

"What are you saying?"

"You're my brother. You were my first best friend, and I still want to have that type of relationship with you. I love you. I think both of us know that little speech you gave in the church wasn't forgiveness. And if you can't forgive me, I can't do this"—Nate pointed between them—"anymore."

Austin had lost Libby, his business, and now his brother. He was batting a thousand today. At

413

this rate he'd be left alone. Did he really want to be that person?

He rested his elbows on his knees and dropped his head in his hands. "Even if I want to forgive you, I don't think I can. It's like it's become part of who I am."

"Sin has a way of doing that."

The word settled like a punch to his sternum. Sin?

Nate shoved his hands in his pockets and shrugged. "The Bible is pretty clear about forgiving one another."

He'd never really thought about it that way. In his mind, it was between him and Nate alone. But maybe the unforgiveness had seeped into every part of who he'd become. It stood between him and his dad, between him and Libby. Even between him and God.

"I've been angry at you for so long, I'm not sure how to stop."

Nate sat next to him on the step again. "You forgive me today. And when you wake up tomorrow you may have to forgive me all over again. And the next day, and the next. Until one day you'll realize that it's just gone."

"How do you know so much about this?" Austin picked up another pebble and tumbled it between his hands.

"Because for years I've been trying to forgive myself."

Austin dropped the rock and picked up another. He ran his thumb over the smooth surface. "And now?"

"Today was the first day I didn't have to do that." Nate's voice held a lighter tone than usual.

"What happened?"

"I finally ditched the grave clothes."

"What?"

Nate patted him on the back. "I'll explain that later. What I need to know now is where do we stand? When I get on my motorcycle, is it going to be 'see you later' or 'goodbye'? Your choice."

What did he want? Part of him still wanted to be right, but more than that, he wanted his brother back. He wanted to let go of all this anger he'd held for so long. "I can't promise we won't ever fight again."

Nate grinned as he leaned forward on his elbows. "I'm not sure I'd believe you if you did."

Austin whipped the pebble at the knot and hit it solid. "But I choose today to forgive you."

And like a snap, the words freed something in him. The weight of self-righteousness that had been so heavy for so long was gone.

His brother's eyes, red with emotion, were fixed on the ground as his fists tapped the step beside him. "Thank you."

They had a long way back, but they were both on the road. And from here the road didn't look as long as it once did.

"What are you going to do about Libby?" Nate wiped away a single tear with his thumb and looked up at him.

"What can I do?" Austin stretched his legs out in front of him as he leaned back.

Nate stood and zipped his leather jacket. "You can go to her and apologize. Beg her forgiveness."

Beg? Austin had never begged in his life. The idea sent a chill through him. But the idea of a life without Libby left him cold to the bones. "What if she doesn't forgive me?"

"Trap her in a small town until she does." Nate lifted his helmet from the step. "That's how I got you to forgive me."

"Funny."

Nate walked to his motorcycle, flipped his helmet over, and pulled out the straps. "She may forgive you and she may not, but you won't know unless you ask."

Austin pushed off the steps and eyed Libby's house. "I don't even know where she is. She hasn't been home—"

"She's at the Mathews farm."

"Where?"

"Olivia's parents. They're having a fall party." Nate fastened his helmet and straddled the motorcycle. "I was headed there when I saw you sitting here."

Austin shoved his hands in his pockets but

came up empty. He didn't have keys. He didn't have a truck. "I don't have a way to get there."

"I only have my motorcycle, and I'm not riding double with you. I love you, man, but no." Nate secured the strap and started the engine.

Austin searched his mind but came up empty. He needed wheels. Libby's pink bike with the flower basket and bell leaned against the side of her house. He pulled out his phone and opened a map. "I have a way. What's the address?"

nineteen

Why had she agreed to do this? Libby sat on the back bumper of her car and drew in a slow breath. In through the nose, out through the mouth. In. Out. She leaned back. The sky was streaked with orange and pink from the setting sun. She pulled her coat a bit tighter as the evening shadows stole what little warmth there had been. Then again, she'd been chilled standing next to the four-foot bonfire five minutes ago, so maybe this chill had less to do with the weather and more to do with the idea of taking the stage again.

Karaoke had sounded a lot better when she was still riding the adrenaline rush of convincing Nate to stay. Now that it was two songs away . . .

Her phone buzzed and she scanned the text.

Olivia
We're up soon. Where did you go?

Not helping.

Purple spots floated across her vision. *Please, Lord, I can't pass out.* She picked up one of the paper bags lining the driveway that had a jack-o'-lantern face drawn on it and a candle inside.

She blew out the candle, dumped the rock on the ground, and held the bag up to her mouth.

In. Out. In. Out.

She returned again to her spot on the bumper and breathed into the bag a few more times. The faint ringing in her ears competed with the music from the party.

Libby closed her eyes and breathed into the bag again. In. Out.

When she opened them, Austin was riding toward her on her pink bike.

First the spots in her vision, then the ringing in her ears, and now she'd tipped over into hallucinations. Her subconscious had chosen the two places she found safe and merged them into a ridiculous picture to deal with this stress. She should lie down. Or maybe she'd already passed out.

Austin stopped the bike right in front of her and jumped off. "Libby, are you okay? You don't look so good."

She blinked at the man in front of her. He didn't disappear, but he looked at her with such intense emotion she had to be dreaming. When his hand gently brushed her shoulder, she jumped. "You're real?"

"Yes, I'm real." Austin dropped the kickstand and climbed off the bike. His eyes traveled over her as he seemed to be evaluating her health. "Are you okay?"

"You rode my bike." She was breathing a bit better now.

"I'd have bought a bigger one if I'd known we'd have to share it." He took the bag from her hand, then brushed her hair back from her face. "Do you want me to go get you some water?"

"You said you'd have to sacrifice your dignity to ride it." She stood up straight. If she'd realized it wasn't a hallucination, she might have taken a photo.

"I'm pretty sure I did, if all the honks and waves I got on the way here were any indication." He pressed his palm to her forehead. "Are you sure you're okay?"

His touch didn't do anything to slow her pulse. Her breathing sped up again. She drew in a slow breath through her nose as she took a step back. She couldn't open her heart up to him like that again. "Why are you here?"

He shifted from one foot to the other and back. "I came to see you."

Maybe she was hallucinating after all. Austin had made it pretty clear that he didn't want anything to do with her ever again.

"First to beg your forgiveness." He took another step toward her and lifted her hand in his, his hold gentle but firm. Warmth traveled up her arm as his thumb ran back and forth across her knuckles. "I was way out of line when I yelled at you. All of the information the reporter got about the business wasn't your fault. It was mine. And even if it had been your doing, I had no business treating someone I loved that way."

Her knees weakened and she leaned back against the car.

"You love me?" She might need that paper bag again.

"Until I met you, I didn't think I could ever love again—trust again. Then you taught me what real love looks like." He tucked a piece of hair behind her ear. "But if it's too soon or if you feel that you can't forgive me—"

Libby gripped him by the back of the neck and pulled him to her lips, pouring all of the emotion and passion that had been building over the past few days into the kiss. Then Austin took control, sliding both hands to the back of her neck and slowing the kiss down as if he wanted to capture and remember everything about this moment. His thumbs traced both sides of her jaw as he took his time.

Each tender placement of his lips was an apology for the past and a promise for the future. There was a lightness and freedom in him she hadn't detected before. She'd have to ask him about that . . . later. Now she was just going to soak in each tender touch of his hands and the way his soft lips made her skin hum with desire.

"Libby?" Olivia's footsteps crunched on the gravel driveway. "Oh, hi, Austin."

Austin pulled back and offered a small wave. "Hey."

Libby buried her face in the front of his shirt, trying to pull herself back to earth. His musky scent surrounded her as his chest shook with a small laugh.

He entwined his fingers with hers. "I think Olivia has seen people kiss before."

"Done it a few times myself, actually." Olivia held up two cowboy hats. "We're up next. Do you still want to do this?"

Austin glanced between them. "Do what?"

Right—karaoke.

The crumpled jack-o'-lantern paper bag mocked her as the unsettling desire to hide flooded her again. She drank in Austin's smile, his words from before coming back. "Like you said, sometimes all you need is twenty seconds of insane courage or embarrassing bravery for something great to happen. It's time to channel my inner Pepper Potts."

"I'm pretty sure the guy from *We Bought a Zoo* said it, but I'll take it."

She stepped away from Austin without dropping his hand, picked up the bag from the ground, and shoved it in the basket of the bike. "I'm ready." She squeezed Austin's hand and dragged him behind her. He tugged her back just long enough to drop a kiss below her right ear. His spot. Yes, she was ready for this.

She dropped his hand as they wound their way through the small crowd toward the stage where seven-year-old Trinity belted out the words to "The Gambler." Most of the guests sat on bales of hay under the lights and Japanese lanterns that crisscrossed from the stage to the barn.

She passed Danielle, who was sitting next to Gideon. On his other side, a pretty little blonde with a little too much makeup for Libby's taste kept leaning over, whispering in Gideon's ear. Libby offered Danielle a half smile and mouthed, "Hang in there."

The song ended just before Olivia yanked Libby's hand and pulled her up on stage. Great, not only did she have to face her fear, but she had to follow the most adorable act of the night. Olivia shoved a mic in her hand and dropped the cowboy hat on her head. Twenty seconds of insane courage or embarrassing bravery. This was definitely the latter. Sure, she'd sung in the shower many times, and she sang at church when everyone else did, but she'd never sung in front of an audience.

The music started, but it was the wrong song. She didn't even know this song. Her head whipped around to Olivia, but the girl didn't even seem rattled. She just held up her finger and ran off the stage toward the DJ.

Libby looked out at the crowd and tried to swallow against her dry throat. The muscles in her knees quivered as fifty pairs of eyes stared back. Slowly they began to talk among themselves and she drew a slow breath.

Ted, who was sitting down front, sauntered to the stage. "How about that date later?"

Before she could even think of a response, Austin dropped a hand on his shoulder. "She's with me."

Ted glanced between them, then took a step back.

Austin motioned her closer, and she leaned down to hear him.

He placed a kiss on her lips and winked. "Knock them dead, Pepper Potts."

Her legs stopped shaking and suddenly she was ready. To sing. To be on stage. To face whatever came at her.

Today was it. Libby lifted a large pair of scissors and, with the help of the mayor, cut the red ribbon that stretched across the library steps. As the pieces drifted down, applause filled the square and children scampered up the steps. Libby bit her lip to hold back the tears.

The library was open, and it couldn't be a better day for it. The maple trees across Second Street and Richard Street were all at peak color. And the temperature was just cool enough to enjoy the cider and donuts she'd prepared, but not so cold she'd need to keep the door shut.

Libby made her way down the steps to where Austin and his dad waited next to Otis.

"What do you think, Dad?" Austin patted his father gently on the back.

"I think this is a strange place to put a statue of a hippo." He eyed the brass statue and scanned the area. "Seems in the way here."

"I didn't put him here. Otis . . ." Austin glanced at Libby, but she just shrugged. "Moves on his own."

His dad lifted an eyebrow. "The room next to mine opened up if you ever want to join me at the care home."

"Very funny. What do you think of the square?"

"Amazing. Those flowers are just beautiful." He pointed to the pots filling the steps of the gazebo.

"They're from Austin's own greenhouse." Libby touched Austin's arm. "The freshly planted ones won't bloom until spring, so we thought the gazebo needed some extra color today. Did he tell you he's opening an heirloom greenhouse right here in Heritage?"

"Yes, he did." His dad stood and patted Austin on the back. "Now I need to go check out the inside of the library. I hear both my boys worked hard on that."

"We'll catch up with you in a minute, Dad." Austin pulled Libby closer and pointed east of the square. "Did I tell you I'm looking at buying the land this library was on to set up a nursery?"

"I think that sounds just like what Heritage needs," Hannah said as she walked up.

Luke trailed a few feet behind with Joseph in his arms. The baby was still tiny but alert. Luke held him over Otis, his small booties skimming the brass back. "His first slide down Otis. A Heritage rite of passage. What do you say, little man—are you ready for a back flip off his nose?"

"I think he's a little young for acrobatics." Hannah rolled her eyes and shifted the diaper bag to her other shoulder. "Maybe wait until he can hold his head up properly."

Luke slid Joseph down the nose and back into his arms, then leaned toward his ear. "Don't worry, dude, she can't always be watching."

Libby lifted him from Luke's arms. "When can I babysit again?"

"How's tonight?" Luke checked his watch. "In an hour?"

Hannah laughed and hit her husband's arm. "Sorry, someone is ready for a night out."

"If she can't, I can." Olivia walked up hand in hand with Nate and wiggled Joseph's foot. "Yes, I can. Yes, sir."

Luke leaned closer to Nate. "Good luck with the 'let's wait to have kids' conversation."

Olivia made a face at Luke and turned to Libby. "Sorry we're late. It took longer than expected."

"It?" Libby looked from Olivia to Nate.

Nate held out his arm, which had a two-inch

gauze bandage on it. He peeled back the tape to reveal a new tattoo with the words "Christ is" wrapped around the first *M* in "master of my fate."

"Nice." Luke gripped his shoulder.

Libby scanned Olivia's arms. "Did you get one too?"

"No. I told him I might get a matching triquetra on my back, but not until after the wedding."

"And I told her I like her just the way she is." Nate pulled Olivia close and offered her a kiss on her nose. "But it's up to her."

Libby slid her hand into Austin's and pulled him close. Just three months ago she'd been almost too afraid to get out of her car. She'd had no idea what was ahead of her. Unknown job, unknown friends, unknown place.

The quote her mother had sent her came floating back. "Never be afraid to trust an unknown future to a known God." Those were words to live by.

Acknowledgments

I never thought there would be anything harder than writing that first book. Until I had to write my second book. But my faithful God always seemed to put the right people in my path to help the dream come true. And like always, there are so many I want to thank.

My Lord and Savior—Thank You for the gift of writing, for leading me on this grand adventure, and most of all, for opening my eyes to this dream of writing in a slow, gentle way and keeping me on the path when I was ready to give up.

Dave and Joyce Thompson—Thank you again for all you do to support my writing. You guys are such a gift. I wouldn't be the mother, wife, or author I am without your support and lending hand.

Scott Faris—Not only are you my champion, my love, and my hero, but you even read my stories and offer so much insight to make them stronger. You give up so much to make this dream possible. You're my biggest blessing.

Zachary, Danielle, and Joshua—Thank you for meal help, housecleaning, and even reminding me to drink water. You are such blessings to my life. I couldn't do this without you.

Dave and Jan Faris—I couldn't ask for better in-laws. I appreciate your support and how you took in my family when I needed a quiet house to finish this book. Love having you so close.

Andrea Nell—You are the best craft partner ever, one of my dearest friends, and a gift from God. Thanks for taking the time to read and help make the scenes sing.

Mandy Boerma—You, my friend, rock! Thank you for reading and rereading to help make the story stronger.

My Book Therapy—I am a published writer because of My Book Therapy, and that is not an exaggeration. The teaching, the books, the retreats—they built my career. I thank you.

Susan May Warren, Beth Vogt, Rachel Hauck, Lisa Jordan, Alena Tauriainen, and Melissa Tagg—Thank you for your encouragement, talking me off ledges as "second-novel syndrome" set in, and basically praying me through this book. You are all a gift in my life.

My agent, Wendy Lawton—Thank you for believing in me and my story. And thank you to the entire Books & Such team. It is a privilege to be a Bookie!

My editor, Vicki Crumpton—Thank you for taking a chance on me and my stories. Thank you for your wisdom, guidance, and patience as I worked through second-novel syndrome. I am so grateful!

The Revell team—Being a part of this house is a dream come true. You are all so amazing, and knowing you and working with you is such a gift. I am so excited to be a part of the family.

Libby, Hannah, Leah, Danielle, and Ellie—Thanks, girls, for lending your names to the series. It has been fun.

Lloyd and Judy Ganton—Thank you for opening your lovely home so I could hide away and get this book done on time.

Sandra Richter—Thank you for teaching me to "tell the story and tell it well."

My WiWee girls—Andrea Nell, Alena Tauriainen, Lisa Jordan, Kariss Lynch, Jeanne Takenaka, Tracy Joy Jones, Michele Aleckson, and Mandy Boerma. Thank you for all the support and encouragement—you girls rock!

My AZ Tuesday night writing group and my MBT huddle—I always appreciate your encouragement and support.

Tari Faris has been writing fiction for more than thirteen years, and it has been an exciting journey for the math-loving dyslexic girl. She had read less than a handful of novels by the time she graduated from college, and she thought she would end up in the field of science or math. But God had other plans, and she wouldn't trade this journey for anything. As someone told her once, God's plans may not be easy and they may not always make sense, but they are never boring.

Tari has been married to her husband for eighteen wonderful years, and they have three sweet children. In her free time, she loves drinking coffee with friends, rock hounding with her husband and kids, and distracting herself from housework. Visit her at tarifaris.com to learn more about her upcoming books.

Books are produced in the United States using U.S.-based materials

Books are printed using a revolutionary new process called THINKtech™ that lowers energy usage by 70% and increases overall quality

Books are durable and flexible because of Smyth-sewing

Paper is sourced using environmentally responsible foresting methods and the paper is acid-free

Center Point Large Print
600 Brooks Road / PO Box 1
Thorndike, ME 04986-0001 USA

(207) 568-3717

US & Canada:
1 800 929-9108
www.centerpointlargeprint.com